HARD FEELINGS

K.M. Galvin

Hard Feelings

Copyright © 2023 by Kelsie Galvin

All rights reserved.

Cover Design by Okay Creations

https://www.okaycreations.com/

Editing and Formatting by Jovana Shirley at Unforeseen Editing

https://www.unforeseenediting.com/

No part of this book may be reproduced or transmitted in any form or by any means, electronic or mechanical, including photocopying, recording, or by any information storage and retrieval system without the written permission of the author, except for the use of brief quotations in a book review.

Events in work are fictitious. Any similarities to any persons, living or dead, are purely coincidental and not intentional by the author.

ISBN-13: 979-8-218-13491-4

OTHER TITLES BY K.M. GALVIN

Twenty-Something Duet
Going Forward
Coming Home
Beauty and the Book Boyfriend
Adrift

"You drown not by falling into a river, but by staying submerged in it."

—*Paulo Coelho*

One

I sigh as the last bell of the day rings; the weight around my shoulders lessens as the tension I typically carry around all day disappears. I made it through the first month of senior year without any major incidents.

It's Labor Day weekend, and the town will be buzzing with vacationers from the city, looking to relax at our lake.

And more importantly, I, Glory Purcell, will get three whole days away from this place.

You know that scene from *Heathers* where Veronica is walking down the hallway and runs into Heather Duke, covered in soot, looking like shit, talking about how she just got back from hell?

That's how I feel every time I leave this place, like I've been through hell.

I can feel in my bones that this year will be different. Thanks to my soccer career here, I already have early acceptance to the University of California in Los Angeles. All I have to do is maintain my GPA, and I'll be far away from this shit town.

Galway, Georgia, seemed like a small slice of heaven when my family moved here from Atlanta when I was five. Even then, I recognized how special and beautiful this place was.

The green forests, glassy lake, and winding roads at the bottom of the Blue Ridge Mountains conjured all kinds of daydreams.

But the best thing—and the worst—was meeting the King family. Sebastian, Elizabeth, and their son, Killian, became the beginning and end of my family here in Galway.

As for Killian and me, it was like discovering a piece of myself I had been missing my whole life. Soul mates didn't have to be romantic, which certainly wasn't the case when my gray eyes locked on his bright hazel eyes.

"Fire and ice," our mothers used to joke.

Killian was all passionate emotion, whereas I was cold calculation. I took my time on things, weighing all options. Killian used to call me Glory the Sloth while he ran full tilt into everything.

Of course, all this changed. I soon became an open wound that this town poured salt in over and over. I wore anger as embittered armor, lashing out at everyone. Especially those who loved me and always, always at Killian.

Killian, who became everything to me—my brother, my best friend, my champion, and my protector. No one believed in me more, and no one loved me better.

He was the best thing to ever happen to me—until he became the worst.

My mother and his father's affair shook the foundation of Galway. In a town this small, something like that is about as destructive as a bomb going off. People choose sides, and no one chose the Purcell's, not when the King family essentially employed over half the town.

That, and women always bear the consequences of men's choices.

Everything changed when they both left, leaving two families destroyed in their wake and a sleepy town drunk with scandal. At thirteen, it seemed like my world was ending.

My father lost his job at the King Family Farms; apparently, he now had a conflict of interest and couldn't be trusted to do their books. He had to turn to freelance as a CPA, essentially only getting hired during tax season. It always baffled me that people would spit in front of us on the streets but come knocking on our doors when they needed something.

Hatred is a fickle thing.

It meant, as soon as I could, I would have to get a job to help make ends meet. Babysitting was out of the option, as mothers would look down their noses at the thought of leaving their kids around a home-wrecker's daughter.

Or more likely, their husbands, as if the problem were the teenage girl, not the idea that your grown husband would try something with a minor.

My mother had done more than destroy our family. She'd tacked a scarlet letter onto the daughter she left behind.

Elizabeth King, the one person in the world who should have hated the sight of me, was the only one who gave me a job. I helped her out at home with the cleaning, cooking, and other errands while she took on the entire operation of the farm herself.

She refused to let it go under even if that meant accepting help from the daughter of the woman who had stolen her husband.

Elizabeth is a complicated woman, but she's a fair one in the end.

King Family Farms actually comes from Elizabeth's side of the family. As in Sebastian took *her* name when they married. That was the OG scandal in Galway before Sebastian and my mom decided to unleash their selfishness on the entire town.

HARD FEELINGS

Her parents were old money, as in *old*, old.

Growing up here, you can't escape the King family history. Their influence is stamped on the names of shops, streets, and even the elementary school. Luckily, they've used their influence for good, which is why it was so newsworthy for this esteemed family to get taken down a peg.

There is little the public loves more than cracks in the foundation of an esteemed house.

Killian used to complain about the pressure he felt, having to live up to his family name. He would buck up against his family's reputation, causing trouble but still toeing the line.

As much as he hates having the road mapped for him, however many detours he might try to make, Killian will always end up with his family.

On the other hand, I have no idea what I want to do besides play soccer, but for the next eight months, I just have to focus on graduating and socking away any extra money I have. I'll always be thankful to Elizabeth for not holding a grudge against me because my dad and I truly need the money.

Housecleaning for Elizabeth has put food in our fridge and a burden on my shoulders. Between being the varsity girls' soccer team captain and the emotional float my father uses to stay above drowning, I am beyond ready to run. Run so far away that this place will be a distant nightmare.

California seems far enough.

Out of reach.

Beyond *his* grasp.

Because the day his father left became the day Killian King's love turned to hate. I look exactly like my mother. I have the same fine-boned features with gray eyes, a small nose, and a soft, wide mouth belying a sharp tongue. I'm a mini Caroline Purcell.

Around the same time my mother left, I went through puberty, which in itself was traumatic. I had to ask my father for pads and tampons, crying as I hugged a hot water bottle to me from the pain of my cramps and, Lord … the migraines.

I get vestibular migraines, meaning I get intense vertigo and dizziness along with the debilitating pain. It's part of the reason I rarely drive. Our health insurance barely covers the shots I take when I'm having an episode, but I do a good job of avoiding my triggers.

Which, unfortunately, are wide and varied. Menstruation, dehydration, stress, dairy, alcohol, and even the freaking weather can set me off. Luckily, they don't come often enough to qualify me for a disability, but when they do come, I'm completely debilitated.

It's one of the first major things in my life that Killian doesn't know about. I don't know why I get so hung up on that, but I do. Sometimes, when I'm trying hard not to cry from the pain because that will only make it worse, my will crumbles, and I end up wanting to call him and tell him to come over.

I hate feeling so vulnerable without my best friend to protect me. In the end, I suffer alone, and when the pain passes, bitterness comes. A bitterness because I'm unable to make that call and have Killian comfort me.

My dad does what he can, essentially changing how we eat and helping to create a whole routine for me when I'm having an episode. Cassidy, my other best friend, supports me the best way she can in those moments by just being there and ensuring I've always got water or a sports drink handy if I start to feel something coming on.

She even carries an extra shot for me when we go to away games or tournaments, just in case I go down fast. Even still, in those moments, surrounded by people who love me, I want Killian.

But losing your best friend is a special kind of agony that we're seemingly always unprepared for.

I think, growing up, we know romantic partners come and go. There are movies, books, and songs dedicated to describing that feeling and showing the ways we can process that loss, but for some reason, there's very little discussed about the loss of friendship. It's always worse to lose someone you chose as family, who loves you without obligation but simply because you are yourself.

And it decimated me.

I'm forever changed by his and my mother's abandonment, and as much as I wish I didn't still care, I do. Love is not a faucet you just turn off, no matter how much I wish I could.

"What's up, Glory Hole?" Sean Courtland sneers as he bumps me from behind, nearly knocking me to the ground.

"Back the hell off, knuckle dragger," Cassidy snarls as she comes up beside me, shoving Sean in the process.

Cassidy is the only reason I haven't run away already. She's my confidant, and the best striker this school has ever seen. Cassidy is infamous at this school and nearly untouchable, thanks to her twin brother, Tanner who was beyond overprotective.

Both have riotous red hair. Cassidy's falls nearly to her hips, making her look like an exotic mermaid with bright green eyes, a curvy body, and a sultry face. Anyone would easily drown for her and do it happily.

If only she didn't hate every single person at this school.

Her brother, Tanner, is her masculine counterpart, his hair several shades deeper than her copper. They are both tall for their age—Cassidy topping five-ten, Tanner taller at six-one and still growing. They are like two pillars of flames and the only people who care about me at this school.

It is a major point of contention between Killian and the twins, considering Tanner is *his* best friend.

Unlike Killian and the rest of this fucked up town, they didn't blame me for having the misfortune of being my mother's daughter.

HARD FEELINGS

"I hate that they call you that," Cassidy growls under her breath, looping her arm through mine, and begins walking toward our lockers.

"You can blame Killian for that one," I mutter, all earlier optimism dashed completely.

I have the unfortunate luck of being named Glory, which, of course, reminds teenage boys far and wide of the term *glory hole*. Something thirteen-year-old Killian thought would be hilarious to call out at the homecoming game while I carried drinks for Cassidy and me up to our spot in the bleachers.

We were freshmen, so while boys were disgusting and obsessed with sex, everything about it grossed me out, and I loathed anything remotely referring to sex and me because of what had happened with my mother.

The immediate laughter from the entire football team made me rush up the stairs to get away, miss a step, and trip, spilling both drinks on Mr. Cadle, the principal.

Just thinking about it gives me secondhand embarrassment for my younger self.

My mother said she named me Glory because I was her crowning glory when I was born. Naturally, it spawned all kinds of hellish nicknames. My first acne breakout? Gore-y. The one and only time I went on a date? Whore-y. And there was Glory Hole—we can't forget that one.

At least they were original.

After everything went down, the worst thing I could imagine was being the center of attention, and in the years that followed, Killian, intentionally or not, went out of his way to make sure I was the very center of his in the worst way.

Glory Hole. It doesn't even faze me anymore.

I open my locker and throw my bag inside before slamming the door shut, the sound echoing off the nearly empty halls.

"Jeez, Glo, who pissed you off this fine day?" Tanner chuckles as he comes up behind me.

Cassidy and Tanner have lockers next to me, thanks to their last name being Putnam.

"Tanner, can you speak to your troll of a best friend and tell him to lay off? It's senior year. He'll never have to see me again soon enough." I bat my eyelashes at him playfully.

Tanner groans. "Please, I do not want to get in the middle of your war, Glory. Besides, you are a topic completely off the table for him."

"Weird since he can't seem to keep my name out of his mouth," I grumble, giving his side a squeeze in understanding.

"And what a mouth it is," Cassidy sighs.

5

I grumble loudly because, despite all the boiling rage lingering under my skin at the mere mention of Killian, I have to agree that he's … incredible to look at.

Dammit.

It seems fate wants to punish me—sins of the mother and all that since Purcell women can't seem to help being attracted to King men.

Killian looks like no seventeen-year-old I've ever seen unless they're popping steroids like Tic Tacs. He's topping six foot five and likely still growing—his incredible height a gift from his father.

I remember Elizabeth massaging his legs to help with the pain because of how fast he grew. When we were eight, there was a brief moment when I was taller than him.

That lasted all of a minute.

I'm still bitter about my average height when all my friends—and enemy—are giants. The last thing I want is for him to look down on me, literally and figuratively.

His wavy, thick black hair is styled in an undercut that makes girls go nuts, especially when some of it falls into his eyes.

Not me, mind you. I would jump at the chance to shave him bald.

Add that to a body that spends most of its time in the gym and bright hazel eyes that burn through you, and Killian King is almost otherworldly.

I fucking hate it.

Give him a humpback or a giant wart, something!

Cassidy and I wave her brother off as we head into the girls' locker room. Shoving my backpack into my gym locker, I grab my practice uniform and get dressed quickly. Standing in front of a mirror, I wrap my long hair into a tight ponytail and give it a good glare.

There have been so many times I've been tempted to cut it all off or dye it. Anything to ruin what Killian used to love, but I just can't.

Maybe, one day, he'll do something so terrible that he kills off everything I have left for him, but until then, I hold on to the memory of me whispering my dreams while he played with my hair.

I'm a masochistic idiot.

"Come on, Glo. We know you're hot. Let's get a move on." Cassidy slaps my ass as she heads out with the rest of our team. "And don't forget your sunscreen!"

Rolling my eyes, I spray myself down with SPF 30. She's such a mom. With Killian and my mom gone, Cassidy has appointed herself my keeper, becoming hypervigilant about my health.

I love her to death, but I wish she'd chill.

Running out onto the field, I breathe in the cool air. Summer is just beginning to end, but already, it feels cooler. Fall arrives earlier in the mountains.

HARD FEELINGS

It's my favorite time to play.

The air chills my skin, so every hit from the ball stings. It's weird to love the burn, but it makes me feel alive.

It also means football is in full swing, so Killian is kept busy. Idle hands are the devil's tools, and a bored Killian makes for a creative tormentor.

"Girls, four laps around the field and maintain an easy pace because you're going straight into wind sprints." Coach Yi blows her whistle, and we all start our lope around the field.

I watch the sun start to dip behind the mountains as we run. It's beautiful here, especially in this season. It's probably the only reason I'm going to miss this place. Well, besides my dad.

But I'm out of here right after graduation, and Killian knows it. UCLA's soccer camp starts in the beginning of June, so it will be a *fuck you later* to everyone, but my dad, Cassidy, and Tanner.

The next half hour goes quickly as we run through drills and warm our muscles. Then, Coach blows her whistle and points to the weight room.

Groaning, I grab my water and catch up with Cassidy.

"I don't know how she expects us to do weights after that freaking run she had us do over the weekend. My quads are shredded," I murmur, hiking my knees up high to stretch them a little.

"You'd better be careful before you tear something. You're already doing two-a-days like some female Terminator." Cassidy glances at me, concerned.

"Spot me?" I ask as we enter the huge weight room, ignoring her completely.

"Glory, I'm serious. You do not want an injury with your scholarship hanging in the balance." Cassidy grips my arm, but I shake her off.

"I'm fine. Trust me, I will not screw up the opportunity to put an entire country between Killian and me."

"An entire country, Glo? Seems excessive," a low voice murmurs from behind me.

I don't need to turn to see who it is; his voice is as familiar to me as my own.

"Killian, death wouldn't be far enough away from you," I growl before staring pointedly at my best friend while making my way over to the bench press.

He chuckles as he walks away, and I refocus as I lie down on the bench.

Ignoring all the hard bodies around me, I count my reps out loud while Cassidy stands above me, hands at the ready should my muscles quit.

This is the only part of my practice that I can't stand. The ten-minute overlap where the girls' soccer team and the football team share the weight room before they head out for the rest of their practice.

During our seasons, it's really the only time I see Killian, and he's usually too focused on his workout to pull any of his shit.

1

I get off the bench, using the bottom of my shirt to wipe the sweat off my face, and switch places with Cassidy.

The sounds of weights clanging, laughter from the guys as they finish up, and the pumping of the radio fade as I get lost in the repetitive motion of Cassidy lifting and lowering the weight bar.

It's why, when I hear cursing, followed by the loud sound of glass breaking, I jolt so hard that I nearly cause Cassidy to drop the bar on herself.

"Fuck! I'm sorry, Cassidy." I wince, but she waves me off, eyes on the commotion.

Killian has Morris Felts by the throat, slammed against the wall, and the look on Killian's face as he leans close, whispering something in Morris's ear, has my heart pounding.

"Glory—" Cassidy whispers from behind me, and I shake my head, grabbing her arm to keep her quiet.

Tanner jumps over a weight bench and latches on to Killian's arm. "Let him go, bro. You want to fuck up your last season because some mouthy sophomore pissed you off?"

Killian's response is to only squeeze tighter. Morris lets out a choked gasp, and when his face turns an alarming shade of red, I step forward.

The second I move, Killian's eyes flick to me, and I see that his pupils are completely blown. He looks scary and psychotic, and what the fuck am I doing?

"Kills," I call softly, purposely using my childhood nickname for him, "let him go."

He doesn't move, so I eye Tanner, nodding slightly to the door, and Tanner jumps into action, getting everyone out of the room with a sharp warning that he'll get anyone who talks kicked off the team.

"Cassidy, leave," I tell her firmly as I move closer to the bomb that's seconds from going off.

"Absolutely not. Do you expect me to leave you with Hulk Smash over there? Hell to the no," Cassidy scoffs.

"Cassidy!" Tanner barks from the door and stares his twin down until she sighs loudly and moves toward her brother, stopping briefly next to Killian. "You harm a hair on her head, and I'll cut your dick off."

My lips twitch with barely contained laughter, and Killian's gaze tracks the movement, his eyes finally showing a little life behind them.

"Is this who you are now? Violent? Scary?"

I move closer to him, noticing his grip loosen enough for Morris to slip away. And he does instantly, leaving me with the loose cannon.

"You don't know what he said," Killian says quietly, rage coloring his words.

I laugh, crossing my arms. "And what could he have said that would warrant your reaction?"

HARD FEELINGS

Killian's brow lowers as his lips curl in disgust. "He said, despite you being a diseased slut, like your mother, at least he could go raw in your ass without fear of his dick falling off."

If this were a few years ago—hell, if this were a couple months ago—I'd have gotten upset, but the comment rolls right off me. "Well, it seems someone missed Health class because you can still get STIs from anal sex."

Killian crosses his arms over his massive chest, causing his biceps to bulge. "That's all you have to say?"

I roll my eyes and grab my water bottle. "I don't understand, Killian. Isn't that what you want? I mean, if we're comparing the things that have been said to me or about me, my father, or my mother, today has been a walk in the park."

"What?" he barks, body going rigid.

I laugh coldly, eyeing him skeptically. "You can't treat me like the town pariah, practically labeling me trash, and not expect everyone else to fall in line. You're Killian King, prince of Galway, and I'm just the daughter of the home-wrecker who broke up your family."

I ram my shoulder into him as I pass on my way out. "Don't be so shocked, *Kills*," I say mockingly. "I'm paying every fucking day for our parents' mistake while you ruin my entire high school experience, but don't worry; you won't have to deal with my filth for much longer. Graduation will be the best day of my life because I'll never have to see you or this backwoods town again."

I slam the door closed behind me and find Cassidy and Tanner standing there, waiting.

"Go get your boy," I sigh.

Tanner shoves the door open and disappears inside.

"You okay?" Cassidy asks, chewing her lip as she studies me worriedly.

"Fine." I roll my shoulders and step beside her as we head back to the locker room. "He's just mad that other people are playing with his food."

"And you're the food?"

I shrug. "Morris is new and doesn't know how this place works."

"It's really fucking weird that Killian thinks he's the only one who can treat you like shit."

"People are afraid of him"—I point behind me toward the weight room—"with apparent good reason, but just because they don't say shit in front of him doesn't mean they don't run their mouths behind his back."

"Well, he knows now." Cassidy grimaces.

"I don't see why he would care. He literally created this entire environment."

Cassidy loops her arm through mine. "Girl, he lives in another dimension, where he is the only injured party, and with his dad not here and his mom an emotional wreck, he has no one else to take his pain out on."

"He's a bully—simple. I'm done taking his shit. Go to fucking therapy or talk to Tanner. Stop being a selfish asshole. My life changed that day too."

"I know. I'm sorry." She hugs me to her side, and I suck in a hard breath, annoyed at the burn behind my eyes.

I haven't cried over Killian King in years, and I won't now.

"It is what it is—at least for now. In a couple of months, I'll never have to see him again."

I don't know if I will ever stop being angry with him and my mother. The thought that I'll have to live with this pain and anger frustrates me more than anything they've ever done to me. At least with my mother, we knew why she was leaving. But Killian …

Cutting me off without a word, refusing to talk to me, even look at me unless it was to spew vitriol my way … it hurt more than I can put into words.

I had gone almost my entire life telling him everything, sharing all of me with him, to nothing overnight. Killian was such an intrinsic part of me that, even to this day, if something happens, I'm reaching for my phone to tell him before I know what I'm doing.

There are days I've found myself running up his drive without even thinking. Cooking larger dinners to account for how much his bottomless stomach could consume. Setting the DVR to record his shows. So many things I did instinctually that I have to rewire now.

And the fucking *shame.* Not only for being related to someone who helped blow up our families—his father is just as much to blame—but the shame I feel every time I allow myself to miss him when he's terrible to me.

It's wedged so deep in me that I don't know if I'll ever share that much of myself with another person. Even Cassidy. I'm constantly muting myself or avoiding arguments, afraid that if I say or do the wrong thing, Cassidy will leave too.

I walk around on eggshells constantly.

I know it's not going to happen. I argue with myself about it all the time. Cassidy sees it, and she gives me a lot of grace, but I know it can get annoying to reassure me we're okay.

The fear of abandonment is so much more paralyzing because you find you're a puppet to the fear. Doing anything to appease it or just giving in and pushing people away before they get the chance to leave.

Cassidy tugs on my hair to get my attention.

Shaking it off, I turn to her and give her what I hope is a convincing smile. Judging by the concern in her eyes, I've failed.

"I'm okay, Cassidy," I say softly, turning away so she doesn't know it's a lie.

"Eight more months, Glo. You got this." Giving my hair one last tug, she swings her arm around my shoulders, and we head back to the locker room.

TWO

The second we walk through the front door, Cassidy collapses on the couch and kicks her feet up onto my coffee table, sighing loudly.

"Another long day at the office, Cassidy?" My dad laughs as he brings us giant water bottles. "Here, drink up. You need to start hydrating before your scrimmage tomorrow."

Grimacing at how tight my hamstrings feel, I take the water and start guzzling before settling down next to Cassidy, groaning loudly. "Thanks, Dad."

"Glory, please tell me you're not also doing morning workouts still." My dad frowns before leaning down and grabbing the dirty practice gear from my gym bag.

"She totally is," Cassidy chirps before crushing her empty water bottle.

"Glory—"

"Dad, it's fine." I wave him off, glaring at Cassidy. "I'm going to stop now that the season has officially started."

He relaxes before making a show of gagging at my clothes. "Holy hell, kiddo."

Giggling, I lean my head back on the couch as he walks into the laundry room and throws them in the washer. "I get my smelliness from you, Dad!"

"Hey, listen, I know you're a middle-aged woman who goes to sleep at nine at night, but you have to come to the game tonight." Cassidy stretches as she gets up off the couch.

"Cassidy, no. We have to be up early tomorrow—"

"Please, Glory. Please? Please! Please. Please, please, please!" she chants.

"Oh my God, fine! Just shut up!" I interrupt, rolling my eyes at her antics.

"You won't regret it." Cassidy beams and grabs her keys off the coffee table.

"I absolutely will. No good can come from me going to a football game. Especially after today," I mumble, picking at my cuticle.

"It'll be fine. I'll be back in two hours to get you. Dress cute!" she calls out as she runs out the door.

"Why bother?" I grimace.

"What happened today?" Dad asks as he comes back into the kitchen.

Heaving myself off the couch, I come up behind him as he pulls two fillets of cod and assorted veggies out of the fridge, and I give him a big hug.

"Nothing. Don't worry about it." I squeeze him before running upstairs while he sets up our dinner.

"Is it nothing? Or something I don't have to worry about?" he yells up.

"Both!" I slam my bedroom door shut and head to my bathroom for a shower before I eat.

I can't believe I agreed to go to a football game.

Ugh, idiot.

Football in the South is a religion, even at the high school level. It is a pageantry of the male persuasion, though I'm sure they would all scoff at that description.

But it totally is.

Our team, specifically Killian, acts like they're going off to battle. Their faces are pictures of ferocity and focus. It's the exact opposite of the screaming girls cheering them on and yelling from the stands.

Hair curled to perfection, faces made up so well that a Kardashian would be jealous, with just enough skin showing to be tantalizing, but not giving away all their secrets.

Forget pageantry; it's a hormone-driven mating ritual.

Like that dancing bird, flashing its colorful feathers to attract a mate, on this documentary I saw on Netflix last night.

As the girls in front of me all scream as one of our running backs runs the ball in for a touchdown, the bird comparison seems even more accurate.

Smirking at myself, I tug my oversize cardigan around my shoulders, tucking my hands under my armpits for more warmth. It practically reaches my denim-clad knees, but the chill of oncoming fall still manages to seep through.

Wiggling my toes inside my Vans, I try to generate heat. I'm sitting at the top-right corner of the home team bleachers, which only makes it worse.

HARD FEELINGS

Originally, I wanted to sit on the hood of Cassidy's Jeep on the hill overlooking the field, but compromise is the key to a successful relationship. Also, she would have stolen all the laces from my cleats.

"You know, when I said to dress cute, I didn't mean the exact opposite. You look like you escaped the home, Granny," Cassidy tells me as she climbs the stairs, handing me my corn dog and fries before sitting next to me. "It's a little annoying that you wouldn't even go to the concession stand, Glo."

I take a huge bite. "And have them spit in my food?"

Cassidy scoffs and takes a sip of the sweet tea we're sharing. "You really paint yourself as this pariah, but no one is going to spit in your food."

Glaring at Killian as he takes the field, I take another bite from my corn dog. "You never know."

Killian turns and stares right at me, as if he could hear me. He didn't even scan the crowd, just knew exactly where to find me, as if his evil Spidey-Sense were tuned into me.

Squinting menacingly behind my wire-framed glasses, giving peak Granny vibes, I flip him the bird.

Cassidy laughs before tugging my hand down. "I get it, but maybe don't flip our star player the bird on the home team's side." She tilts her head toward a group of girls who are glaring at me.

I point my corn dog stick at them. "It's not like I want his attention! Please distract him until graduation," I tell them.

They huff in outrage before turning around.

"God, you can be such a savage sometimes," Cassidy murmurs lightly before scooting closer for warmth.

"Cold?" I smirk before opening my giant sweater and wrapping a side around her.

"There are sacrifices we make for fashion," she tells me primly while snuggling even closer.

Cassidy is dressed to impress. She pulled her hair into a high pony and is wearing cutoff jeans—so short that I see why some people call them coochie-cutters—and our team hoodie but modified to slide off the shoulder. She looks effortlessly pretty.

I refused the outfit she'd brought me but did allow her to braid my hair into a crown.

Sighing heavily, I passively watch Killian beat the shit out of people on the field.

"How long do I have to stay here?" I whine as Killian sacks the other team's QB, and the crowd goes wild.

Killian looks toward us again, and I give him a slow clap.

Yes, yes, Killian, we all see you playing whack-a-mole with the other team. Very impressive.

Meathead.

"You gotta stop," Cassidy says, leaning into my shoulder.

"Hmm, no, I don't think I will." I grin a little crazily at her, the adrenaline from pissing him off racing through my veins.

"What's gotten into you? You've made it your job to fly under his radar for the last three years."

I shrug because I don't know where this came from; I only know that seeing the big asshole almost remove someone's head for saying something about me triggered the little demon on my shoulder.

"He's gotten under my skin for years. He's been a petulant child, and now, he wants to act surprised that people followed his lead? I think it's time to show Killian just how big of an asshole he really is."

"Okay, I'm not sure if you're aware that you're whispering like Liam Neeson from *Taken*, but you're freaking me out, Glory."

I stand up. "I'm leaving. Sarah Kate"—I point to our co-captain sitting with a bunch of our teammates—"has been trying to get your attention for the last ten minutes. You'll be okay without me here."

"Dude! What the hell is going on with you?" Cassidy yells as I run down the bleacher stairs.

Killian's on the sidelines now, watching me, along with everyone else, as I make a spectacle of myself.

"Pay attention to the game, roid rage!" I yell as I pass him and head toward Marcus Tyler, captain of the boys' soccer team and one of the few guys at this school who treats me with respect. "Marcus! Can you give me a ride?"

He hops up from his seat with the rest of the boys' team and slings an arm around my shoulders. "Shaking things up, Glory?"

"About time, don't you think?" I grin at him, giving his waist a squeeze in thanks for the help.

As much as I'd love to say there was something between Marcus and me, it honestly couldn't be more platonic. He's been pining after Cassidy since they were in diapers, and I suspect he took up soccer just to be close to her.

I climb into his truck and slam the door shut. "Thanks again, Marcus. I hope you don't get any shit for giving me a ride."

He rolls his eyes as he climbs in beside me and starts the car. "Glory, I couldn't give a shit what anyone thinks about you and me being friends. I know you've got one foot out of this town already; I ain't too far behind."

I raise a brow in question.

He flashes me a grin. "You're not the only one heading out west."

I whack his arm. "You'd better not be pulling my leg, Marcus Tyler!"

He laughs. "Nah, I'm serious. You're gonna have a buddy out at UCLA."

"Hell yeah!" I whack him again in excitement. "That's amazing, Marcus! I'm so happy for you." I shoot him a grin. "And me. It won't be so scary

HARD FEELINGS

now, moving clear across the country, if I know I've got at least someone in my corner."

"Yeah, same ..." He trails off, and I recognize the look on his face. It's his *thinking of Cassidy* face.

"Listen, Marcus, I know—"

"Ah, let's not, okay, Glory? I know you mean well, but I don't want to get into it about Cassidy." He runs his hand through his hair in agitation, and I sigh heavily.

I could kick Cassidy's ass, truly. Marcus Tyler is subtly hot, if you like tall, dark-skinned nerd gods who could bench-press you while waxing poetic about the advances in solar energy.

He's *the* perfect guy, and if Killian wasn't a King, Marcus would be running this entire school. The Tyler family is no slouch in terms of the upper crust of Galway, given his mother is the freaking mayor and all.

"Why are you staring at me so hard? Are you pretending you can shoot lasers out of your eyes again?"

My Grinch smirk grows as a plan formulates in my head. "I've got an idea."

"Ah shit ..."

ThRee

The adrenaline from last night's bravado made it difficult to sleep, so I'm up before the sun to go for a run before our scrimmage this afternoon.

Listen, I know it's stupid to do workouts outside the ones scheduled with the team or the conditioning assignments our coach gives us, but the only time I ever feel in control is when my feet pound the pavement.

James Purcell is a deep sleeper, so the chances of a lecture this morning are slim, but just in case, I program the coffeemaker to have a fresh pot ready an hour from now. It should give me plenty of time to get back before the dad beast awakens.

Stepping out onto our deck, I sit on the stairs and tie my sneakers, glaring across the lake. I hate that I can see Killian's house from mine. I hate that it sits up on that hill, looking down at me, sneering probably, if a house had the ability to show expression.

Rolling my eyes at my ridiculous thoughts, I roughly rub my legs, warming them up before getting up and setting off.

It's a familiar route, one I've taken for a decade. It used to be the path I'd take to Killian's for sleepovers, movie nights, and birthday parties. When my parents fought. When the silence said more than the screaming.

When I just needed to see him.

Now, I take it purposely to remind myself that I don't care how he treats me, that his loss of friendship doesn't haunt me, and in the hopes that if he sees me running by, Killian will see how unaffected I am.

My feet barely make any sound as I race over the soft ground. I could run this route with my eyes closed and never hit a tree. I know every inch of this forest, so when a large black blur sprints by in my periphery, I pick up my pace and tear through Killian's backyard, nearing the road.

My breath escapes me in terrified gasps as thoughts of wild animals chasing me down run through my mind. I should yell for Killian, anyone, but some insane part of me thinks that if I can reach the road, I'll be fine.

My heart pounds as the dense woods start to thin, and I glance behind me when I slam into something, landing hard and choking as the wind is knocked out of me.

"What the fuck?!" A growl vibrates underneath me, and it's only then I realize I'm sprawled on top of Killian.

Rolling off him, I cough and blink at the sky, trying to catch my breath. "Glo—"

"Stop calling me that," I wheeze, wincing as I sit up and take stock of my body, rolling my ankles and bending my knees. I feel okay—thank God.

Killian hops to his feet with way more agility than a guy his size should have and offers me a hand.

Snorting in disbelief, I push myself to my feet, brushing pine needles and dirt from my bare legs.

"What the hell are you doing out here?" he pants, staring down at me.

Tightening my ponytail, I notice he's also in running gear … if you can count loose black basketball shorts and sneakers running gear.

His wide chest shines with sweat, glinting off tight pecs and abs as he inhales and exhales, slowly getting his breath back.

"What does it look like, genius?" I shoot back.

"It looks like you're trying to be a wolf's next meal," he says with a smile—or I guess it's more baring his teeth than a smile.

When he looks down at me like this, black hair falling into his eyes, it's more likely he'll take a bite out of me than a wolf.

"Speaking of … I think there was some kind of animal following me." I bite my lip, looking around warily.

Killian considers me with hooded eyes. "Animal, huh? Sure it's not just your imagination?"

My eyes narrow at the thinly veiled humor in his voice. "You're right. The only animal out here is you."

He rolls his eyes at me. "What are you doing, running in my woods, Glory?"

"Your woods? You own the whole forest, Killian?" I lean over to retie my shoes, stretching my knees to my chest as I try to look more casual than I feel. "Listen, just pretend you didn't see me. Should be easy. I haven't existed to you in years."

I mentally slap myself the second the bitterness leaves my lips.

So much for proving I don't care about him.

Not waiting for a reply, I take off and try to forget his face when I said it, but the look of anger and regret stays in my mind for the rest of my run.

HARD FEELINGS

I arrive at our practice field thirty minutes before kickoff. It's a friendly scrimmage with the neighboring school's girls' team, but the rules are tighter during these games. No slide tackling and absolutely zero tolerance for any illegal blocking. The last thing either coach wants is for a player to get injured.

Spotting Cassidy's Jeep, I walk my bike over and dump it in the back, knowing she'll give me a ride back to my house. Turning, I face the park containing four fields, and it's then I notice the football team.

"Shit," I curse under my breath.

Before our parents decided to implode our lives and leave me to deal with the aftermath, Killian used to be in the stands at every game, cheering me on. He was always the loudest, louder than even my own family.

It was the same for me.

Nothing in the world could separate us, nothing stronger than the support we gave each other.

I try not to notice his absence or my mom's, but the sound of my father's voice, now the only one in the stands, is like seeing lightning without the thunder.

Hitching my bag higher onto my shoulder. I cross the field, refusing to acknowledge the football team as I catch up to where Cassidy is already waiting for me.

She meets me halfway and grabs my hand. All bravado from last night is gone. I need my best friend, and she clearly recognizes that. I don't ever have to say a thing; she always knows.

"Don't let this get in your head, Glory," Cassidy says quietly as I set my bag down and drop to the ground to slip off my Nike slides and put on my turf shoes.

"It's a practice game, Cassidy," I say quietly, yanking my laces tight.

"Just making sure you remember that," Cassidy jokes as she yanks me back up beside her once I'm set. "Besides, the twat is in attendance."

Throwing her arm around my shoulders, Cassidy nods her head to the annoyingly perky blonde ponytail bouncing across the field as she throws herself into Killian's arms.

Curling my lip, I zip up my bag and stow it under the bleachers. "Like I give a shit."

"It's not you I'm worried about, Glo; it's the fucking target Killian painted on your back for his fan club."

Britney Watts goes to a private school about thirty minutes away. Unfortunately, the school, Covington Prep, has a long-standing agreement to scrimmage us on Labor Day weekend every year.

Our teams don't play each other in the regular season, and our coaches decided more exposure could only improve the teams. While Britney doesn't go here, money attracts money, so she and Killian run in the same circles.

Unsurprisingly, as a result, she hates my guts by osmosis and makes it a freaking point to come at me every year.

Having Killian here is only going to amp shit up.

"You should ask Coach to switch your position, so you can get practice elsewhere and avoid Backwoods Barbie over there."

Yanking my socks over my shin pads, I tell Cassidy blandly, "I'm not running away from her."

Her giggles travel across the field, and I find myself glancing their way against my better judgment.

Killian's doing that *hot football player* thing, where he doesn't wear a shirt so it's miles of tanned muscles in stark contrast to the white of his pads while his black football pants hang on his hips. He looks indecent, like he should be on the cover of every romance book.

Asshole.

As if he heard me across the field, his eyes flick to mine, and the mothereffer smirks.

Narrowing my eyes, I mouth, *Fuck off,* which makes him laugh.

Britney's green eyes track where Killian's attention went and attempt to eviscerate me from across the field.

"If she pulls one illegal move today, I'm taking her out," Cassidy mutters as we join the rest of the team for a brief warm-up.

I slap my hand against Cassidy's in agreement.

"She can pull whatever she wants; I'm not feeding into it. Not with UCLA hanging in the balance."

Nothing—not some imaginary grudge this girl thinks she has with me, not my father, not Killian, *nothing*—is going to stop me from getting the hell out of this town.

I want to be somewhere that isn't a constant reminder of Killian and my mother everywhere I turn. I crave anonymity, a fresh start.

Coach blows her whistle, startling me, and waves us over.

Stretching my arms behind my back, I walk over to huddle up with the rest of the team.

Coach grabs her clipboard and starts calling out positions. I tune her out until I hear, "Purcell, center midfield, but I won't hesitate to pull you if I see even an ounce of overexertion. Don't think I don't know what you do in the mornings and on the weekends. I'm not about to lose my captain to an injury before the season starts."

Groaning, I keep my eyes on the ground. I would bet my life my dad called Coach. "You don't need to worry about that anymore," I promise her.

HARD FEELINGS

"Hmm." She looks at me skeptically, and I can't really blame her, but I mean it. I can already feel my shins aching; I know it's time to back off.

"You know the rules; keep it clean, and remember, this is a scrimmage. I'd better not see any slide tackling or roughing anyone up. Any of that, and you will immediately sit out the first two games. The same goes for Covington."

Coach blows her whistle again, asking us to get into position, and I smack Cassidy's butt as I run onto the field behind her. Normally, we do a coin toss to determine initial possession of the ball, but Coach always lets Covington go first.

I don't really care who goes first; it's not going to make the ball go in our net. Their center forward moves fast, opting to try and go down the side of the field as their midfielders sprint past.

Midfielders are typically the fastest and do the most running. We have possession of the ball the most, so we have to be. Cassidy says I'm so good because I have such a low center of gravity since I'm so short.

She's hilarious.

I hang back, knowing my defense is about two seconds from stealing that back and booting it far down the field. They've got cannons for legs, and they can easily send a ball flying the entire length of the field.

My chest warms as the fun of the game and pride in my teammates fill me. Fine, maybe I'll miss *some* things when I leave.

"Glory!" Stacey, our center defender, calls out, grabbing my attention as she rockets a pass my way.

I hold on to it easily, Cassidy keeping pace in front of me, providing cover, but even still, I'm nearly knocked off my feet when a bony-ass elbow digs into my stomach.

Fucking Britney.

Shoving my weight to my left, I knock her back far enough to give the ball some air toward Cassidy, who is in position and does a header right into the net. The satisfying whoosh of the ball meeting net greets my ears and puts a smile on my face as I turn around to get back in position, passing Britney with a wiggling wave of my fingers.

"Watts! Keep your elbows in, or you're out!" Covington's coach yells as we pass her, and I keep my smirk to myself.

"Let's go, Glory!" I hear someone yell out and grin when I see Marcus sitting in the bleachers with some of the boys' team.

Smiling, I wave and feel eyes drilling a hole into my back. I don't need to turn around to know it's Killian. The feel of his attention is as familiar to me as a soccer ball against my feet.

"Why the hell is Marcus here, cheering you on?" Cassidy halts next to me, practically hissing as she eyes him.

"We're going out tonight." I try not to laugh as she gasps.

"Glory, what?!" she yells, but before I can respond, a chorus of whistles and yells erupts from the field next to us, drawing our attention.

Killian is helmet to helmet with another player, muscles swelling with aggression, and I can practically feel the rage in the air.

The football coaches rush to the players and back them up away from each other. What Killian's coach says has him looking right over to me, and that hot glare connecting with mine has chills racing down my back.

I know there's a phrase about someone walking on your grave, and I never understood it until now. Killian looks like he wants to put me six feet under.

"Why can't you leave him alone, trash?" Britney snarls at me, redirecting my attention.

"I'm not doing anything." I roll my eyes, genuinely confused about how she thinks any of that has to do with me.

The football team is a bunch of raging testosterone and privilege—that combo makes those idiots do all kinds of stupid shit.

"Back off, Watts." Cassidy takes her position, blocking Britney from my view, and I glance back over at Killian, who's now sitting on our bench instead of his team's, mile-long legs spread out before him, arms crossed over his massive chest, looking not unlike some lazy-ass king.

Ha! King Joffrey Baratheon maybe.

"Head in the game, Purcell!" my coach yells, and no sooner is she done with that sentence than something slams into me, knocking me clear off my feet.

If the blinding pain in my side is any indication, I landed wrong.

I gasp in short spurts, trying not to panic when I find it difficult to draw breath easily. I can hear Cassidy yelling something as I squint up at the sky. It's too bright. I can't see anything. I can't feel anything.

God, please don't let anything be broken.

My hands grasp at the grass, tugging, pulling it out, anything to try and ground myself so I can take a deep breath.

Killian's head appears above mine, worry marring his brow as he places his giant hand on my chest. The pressure of his hand and his sudden appearance momentarily shock me out of my panic, and I'm able to breathe deeply, albeit painfully.

Cassidy is there the next instant, shoving him away from me. "Do you see now, you fucking asshole? Get away from her."

"Cassidy …" I whisper, half admonishing and half in pure terror that I've hurt myself.

Coach is there next, ordering everyone to back off as she runs through an injury check. I wince when she gets to my ribs and watch nervously as her brow furrows.

HARD FEELINGS

"That hurt?" she asks, and I nod slightly, wincing again as she probes my left side. "Okay, it doesn't feel broken, but we need to get you to urgent care to make sure. You'll probably have to get them X-rayed."

I'm already shaking my head before she finishes. "I have shitty insurance, and there's no way we can pay for that. If you don't think they're broken, I'll just ice, wrap them up, and be careful."

"Sorry, kiddo, school policy."

"I'll take her." Killian's growl cuts through everything, and I look to find him pacing back and forth a few feet away from me.

"No way," I protest immediately.

"I can take you, Glo," Marcus says from his place next to Cassidy, earning himself a death glare from the Grim Reaper pacing behind him.

"How about you all get a grip? She's my best friend, so I'll be taking her," Cassidy says pointedly to Killian. "Come on, Glory. Hold your breath and think of UCLA," she cajoles, and Coach helps me carefully to my feet.

I'm gasping and sweating by the time I've got two feet firmly on the ground. "Fine. I'll go with Cassidy," I concede, purposefully ignoring Killian.

"I'll text you later, Glory. Want me to grab your bike out of Cassidy's car and bring it home?" Marcus offers.

I nod gratefully, trying to suppress a snicker when he presses a chaste kiss to my forehead. He's laying it on thick, and I love it.

Killian looks like he's ready to rip Marcus's head off, and I can't help but laugh a little, bringing that death glare my way. The whole plan was for Marcus to pretend to be interested in me as more than just friends to piss off Killian. Not that I think Killian would be jealous, but it's more Marcus and me thumbing our noses at me being labeled persona non grata at this school.

If Cassidy happens to take a second look at Marcus in the process, then all the better, but I told Marcus if she asked me what was up, I'd tell the truth. I don't lie to my best friend or manipulate her feelings. I also refuse to put her in a position where she'd feel like she was betraying me because I know Cassidy likes Marcus. She just refuses to do anything about it.

Cassidy is so determined not to become her mother—married with kids before twenty—that she's sworn off any relationships until after college. I get not wanting to follow in your mother's footsteps, but I also don't think having a relationship is a one-way street to marriage and children. Not that I'll say that to her. Cassidy is great at calling me out on my own bullshit, and I'm uninterested in getting my own logic thrown back in my face.

I take a step, but when I start listing to the side, Killian lifts me as if I weighed nothing.

"Lift from your legs, Kills!" I laugh, the pain making me a bit delirious.

"All right, giggles, I texted your dad. He's going to meet us there." Cassidy passes us, our bags looped over her shoulders as she heads toward her car.

"I'm gonna catch up with her and grab your bike," Marcus mutters as he abandons me with the grumpy behemoth.

I close my eyes and do my best to pretend I'm anywhere else right now. Oh, I'll decorate my dorm room! White bedspread and sheets, easy to bleach in case they get dirty—something my family figured out early on when I would pass out, exhausted after a game or practice, and leave grass stains on my bedding. Thor poster above my desk, for obvious reasons. If I'm going to be distracted while doing schoolwork, it might as well be by those biceps.

"I can feel how hard you're thinking, Glo," Killian says quietly.

"Stop calling me that, Killian. Nicknames imply friendship—something you torpedoed with your inability to process trauma."

"Fucking hell, Glory." He laughs at my bluntness.

"Ah, yes, your other nemesis. Truth!" I lift my fist to the sky like a dummy, only to cry out in pain immediately. Okay, so no raising fist victoriously.

Killian tightens his hold, bringing me higher up on his chest until my head is level with his. Being this close to him while he is holding me protectively … it's a lot.

"Don't pretend like the last few years didn't happen, Killian," I whisper brokenly.

"I'm not." He sighs and rests his head against mine momentarily. "That doesn't mean I can't wake the fuck up and realize what a dick I've been."

"I don't care if you've finally realized this. The damage is done, Killian. I don't want to talk about this, and honestly, it's really not cool to be pushing this conversation when I'm in pain."

While I'm weak.

Killian doesn't say anything else, and I stay silent for the two-minute walk across the parking lot.

Cassidy has her Jeep running and the passenger seat reclined all the way back so I can relax without putting pressure on my ribs.

"Hey, girl, you look a little green." Cassidy opens the door and watches as Killian sets me down gently, grabbing the seat belt and buckling me in before I get the chance. "Also, don't worry; Covington's coach totally saw Britney illegally check you. She's done. Good-bye to your season, you lunatic."

"I'm going to handle her," Killian grunts, running those bright eyes, greener than amber in this light, over my face one last time before closing the passenger door.

"Oh, yeah, protect your little stalker girlfriend," Cassidy scoffs, shoving Killian away from her car as she moves around to the driver's side.

Killian glares at Cassidy. "She is not my girlfriend." He turns back to me. "She'll pay for this. Every cent. Get me that bill, Glory. I'll be following up with your dad to make sure."

HARD FEELINGS

"Leave my dad alone, douchebag," I warn halfheartedly, closing my eyes to fight off nausea.

I feel his hand grip mine tightly for a moment before he tells Cassidy to take care of me.

"Yeah, no shit, twerp. She can always count on *me*."

I laugh lightly at her ferocity when it comes to protecting me. "I love you so much, Cassidy Ann Putnam."

"Right back at ya, cupcake."

FOUR

The rest of the day is mind-numbingly boring. From the two-hour-long wait at urgent care just to get in to see a doctor to another hour of waiting for the X-ray results. Bruised ribs for the win.

Dad is furious, pacing back and forth, on the phone with my coach, demanding how this could have happened under her watch. It's truly the angriest I've ever seen him. But I'm okay, all things considered.

I hope Britney's head explodes, knowing she didn't take out my entire season.

I will have to sit out for two weeks while my ribs heal, icing them as much as possible and keeping them wrapped tight. I'm already planning what conditioning I can do without hurting myself more, but Dad and Cassidy have warned that if they catch even a light sheen of sweat on my brow, there will be hell to pay.

Translation: I've now got *two* helicopter parents.

Dad's got me surrounded by pillows on the couch with my favorite blanket and a giant jug of water to "stay hydrated because hydration helps you heal, Glory Jane," and he's making my favorite dinner of cauliflower in vegan mac and cheese with ketchup drizzled all over it. Dairy is a huge trigger for me. I miss you, cheese and ice cream! Thankfully, alternative diets are hugely popular now, and there are lots of options for me.

Cassidy went home after I got settled in, promising to fill in Coach on my behalf. That was hours ago. The sun has long since set as I turn on my dad's and my favorite show, *Veep*.

"Here you go, kiddo." He holds the plate of food out to me while circling the couch to join me with a plate of his own. Dad opted for a salad and not the processed monstrosity that I'm having.

He sighs heavily as he sinks into the couch, and when ten minutes pass without him touching his food, I prod him into telling me what's clearly on his mind.

"Dad, what's up? I'm okay," I ask over a mouthful.

"I know; I know. I just—" He clears his throat and faces me warily. Now, I'm worried. "I had to tell your mom."

Wrinkling my nose, I focus on my plate of food. "Why?"

"Well, she's your mother, for one."

"Does she know that?" I take a big bite, irritated with my tone. I hate that I even care.

"Glory ..." He sighs heavily again, and I roll my eyes.

"What does she want?" Because he wouldn't be bringing this up if there wasn't more than him just informing my birth giver.

"She wants to come see you; she's worried."

"No, absolutely not. You know how it has been for us here since she took off; her coming back will just make everything worse."

Dad leans forward, resting his elbows on his knees, and rubs his face roughly. "I know. That's what I told her."

"Dad, seriously, if I had the ability to jump up and go to my room, that's what I'd be doing, so let's pretend that just happened and end this conversation."

"I know things have been hard—"

"I am literally here with bruised ribs because she set a ball into motion—"

"Glory Jane!" my dad interrupts. "I understand it's easy to blame your mother because she left, but it takes two people to have an affair. I'm not even blameless in all of this. I had my eyes and ears closed so tightly in my marriage that I didn't see what was happening right in front of me, and I dropped the ball with you when she left. I hate myself for it."

"Daddy," I whisper as tears flood my eyes.

Rubbing a hand over his dark hair, he faces me. "All I'm saying is that this is more complicated than what you've reduced it down to. And I get it, kid—I do—but she didn't leave you; she left *me*. Things are not that black and white. We're your parents, but we're also human, and we fuck things up sometimes."

I shake my head and focus on my food, absolutely not touching that sentiment with a ten-foot pole. "I just don't know how you can forgive her."

"I've been talking to someone, you know, and I think you should too. I'm trying to find my way to forgiveness because it's important to me that you don't get lost in the middle of this. I won't let my resentment taint your life, Glory."

Too late.

HARD FEELINGS

It's what I want to say, but I don't. I've become remarkably adept at keeping my thoughts and feelings to myself.

Dad grumbles at my lack of response and turns the volume up on the TV.

When I say my mother is selfish, I don't just mean her having an affair.

My mother is an only child, and she was doted on and given everything she could wish for by her parents. They had been trying to have a child for years, and my grandmother was in her mid-forties before she conceived my mother. A miracle baby.

I sometimes think part of the reason they gave her whatever she wished for was that they felt guilty that they were much older than other parents, but they were so grateful to finally have a child that it became impossible to say no.

When Mom was sixteen, she lost her parents, and when she was seventeen, she met my dad. The need for security, both financially and emotionally, and the need for the life that she'd had before her parents died made her cling to my dad like he had been sent from God.

I have always felt she does love me, but children, by nature, always take more than they give. Growing up, I saw the love in her eyes, but I could also see that resentment rode a very close line to that love.

When I say that I'm not shocked my mother strayed or even that she strayed so close to home, I mean it. I'd expected it.

What I had not expected was to bear the brunt of it. We had moved to Galway for my dad's job; we'd picked a house because my dad and I loved being so close to the water.

I can tell now, looking back, that sacrifice and my mother are like oil and water. They will always eventually split.

I've often wondered if she went after Sebastian just to prove she could still get what she wanted.

Don't get me wrong; I feel guilty, having these thoughts about her.

Just like with Killian, my own resentment runs a close race with love, but understanding as much as I do about her doesn't mean I forgive her.

The struggle between empathy and anger is hard. To have compassion for someone when you lie in the wake of their destruction seems counterintuitive. It would be so much easier if I could lay everything at her feet, ignore her past, and hold tightly to righteous anger, but I'm so tired.

Being angry all the time is exhausting, and I just want to move on from it all so badly.

I think some part of her feels shame for what she did, but despite what my dad said earlier, she did leave me.

Later that night, I'm in bed, scrolling on social media, and despite my better judgment, I go to Killian's page. His page is littered with photos of his team, Tanner, and his mom. I've been totally erased online, and I don't know why I do this to myself. It's like emotional flagellation.

Locking my phone screen, I set it on the charger and pull my covers up. I hate that anytime I feel emotionally vulnerable, I miss him the most. He doesn't feel the same, and the sooner I erase him from my life, the quicker I can move on.

My gauzy white curtains do very little to block the sun from glaring into my room and disturbing my sleep. I need to wake up anyway because Sunday morning means the Kings are at the diner, having breakfast.

A Sunday tradition I used to join in on is now an excuse to get into their house, clean, and get out without disturbing Their Majesties.

I slowly roll over onto my feet, wincing at the stabbing in my abdomen. Thankfully, Dad left prescription-strength Motrin on my nightstand along with a fresh water bottle.

Smirking at his obsession with hydration, I swallow down the pills and head into the bathroom to brush my teeth and get dressed. By dressed, I mean, pulling on some track shorts underneath my current sleep shirt, which happens to be an old practice shirt of Killian's from his eighth-grade team. It's all I can manage at the moment.

This shirt is definitely something I should have gotten rid of, but ended up keeping out of spite because it is extremely comfortable after multiple washes. And, yes, fine, I also like having something of his.

Leaving my room, I pause at my dad's door, shoulders sagging in relief when I hear nothing but silence. He is going to be so pissed that I still went to work, but we need the money. Now more than ever, considering a trip to urgent care was not cheap.

I creep down the stairs, grab my set of house keys off our hook by the front door, and head to the kitchen, only to pull up short at the sight of my dad and Killian sitting at the counter, whispering to each other.

Killian spots me first, eyebrows slamming down in anger, which, of course, alerts my dad. Rolling my eyes at the impending argument, I close the distance between us and grab one of the bananas out of the fruit bowl in the center of the island.

"Glory Jane, you cannot be serious. You need to get back into bed and relax."

"Dad, I'm not an invalid—"

"Uh, you literally are—" Killian cuts in but mimes zipping his lips when I shoot him a glare.

HARD FEELINGS

"I don't even know why you're here. Shouldn't you be at the diner with your mom?"

His mouth quirks in amusement at the blatant hostility in my tone. "I was coming over to tell your dad that I spoke with the Watts family, and they will cover all the medical costs from the injury Britney inflicted."

"Okay, well, you told us, so you can leave now."

"Glory …" My dad sighs, dragging a hand down his face.

"I'm sorry, but have we forgotten what an abominable dick he's been to me?" I cry out, instantly wincing and wrapping my arm around my ribs. Killian makes a move toward me but stops when I hold out a hand. "You've done enough, and I think you should leave."

"Now, wait a minute—" my dad begins to protest, but I bite into my banana and make for the back door.

"Fine, I'll leave instead."

I'm embarrassed to admit that I slam the door after me, but he shouldn't have even been let into our house. My sanctuary.

Killian could have emailed my dad. Sent a postcard. A smoke signal from his house.

Logically, I know my dad isn't siding with Killian, but my pain does not behave logically.

I feel weak, emotionally and physically, so of course I wouldn't want someone who's used me as his emotional punching bag for the last few years around me.

I'm just protecting myself, I rationalize as I hurry up the path to Killian's house.

Five

I let myself into the Kings' monstrous home with the code I've been assigned since I was a little kid and hurry into their kitchen to find the list Elizabeth left for me.

It's much shorter than usual, so she must have heard about what happened yesterday. Grumbling, I notice nothing she asked me to do will have me bending over or exerting myself, and I should be thankful, but I'm just resentful.

The Kings' home is a mix of the modern and old world. It's been in the family for generations, so you can see much of the history still in the home, but it's been updated along the way.

There's gorgeous wood paneling in the den with a gigantic stone fireplace taking up almost the entire side of one wall. A large TV hangs over the mantel, and a massive cloud sofa, where Killian and I used to camp out during movie marathons, dominates the room, inviting you to come relax.

Every time I'm near this room, nostalgia hits me, and my heart aches because, now, I'm here as the help instead of part of the family. I fluff the pillows instead of relaxing against them. It's a cruel twist that has me hurrying by and into the kitchen.

A large island that fits eight comfy counter stools glistens spotlessly clean; neither Killian nor Elizabeth is known for their cooking and eat at the diner more often than not. My favorite spot in this room is at the banquet, framed by large windows overlooking the lake. You can see my house from here, and it's where we ate our pizza every Saturday whenever I slept over.

Sucking in a painful breath, I put my headphones on and cue up the playlist I share with Cassidy. Our music tastes are so different, and I typically find myself laughing at her K-pop songs and female rap, intermingled with my singer-songwriter and alternative music.

"This Is the Last Time" by The National pumps through my headphones, the tempo providing the perfect soundtrack to my chores. Snorting to myself at how appropriate this song is, I sing along loudly while wiping down the already-clean kitchen counters.

I am well aware this job is a charade. Elizabeth is, in addition to being a paragon of society, a meticulously clean person. Something she passed down to her irritating son.

I spend my Sundays wiping down clean counters, vacuuming spotless carpets, and walking the garbage cans down to the end of their driveway. I collect the fifty-dollar bill out of the mailbox and head home in time for Dad to have lunch ready, where I exchange money for a sandwich.

I have a lot of things in abundance, but pride is not one of them. First, it was something my mother and this town stripped away, and then what was left was taken from me when I saw my father struggling to find work and fill our fridge.

It kills him—I know it does—but what option do we have? At least until I graduate, we're stuck. Dad hasn't confirmed it, but I'm certain the second I leave for college, there will be a For Sale sign on our front lawn, and we'll leave this town in our dust.

I opt for walking down their driveway and using the street instead of my normal cut through the woods. I should have done that to begin with, but an angry Glory is a dumb Glory.

At least the walk down their driveway is going down the giant hill their house sits on. I definitely would not have been able to make it up.

I huff and try to breathe slowly through my nose, but, wow … yeah, I think I was a bit too overzealous this morning.

My right arm clutches my ribs protectively as I sweat, causing goose bumps to pimple my skin. Damn, I should have called my dad to pick me up. I'm not even halfway down to the mailbox, and I'm exhausted.

Swallowing against nausea, I stop to try to get my breathing under control.

It's then I hear the distinct crunch of a car going over gravelly pavement.

"Fuck!" I whisper heatedly, trying to wipe the sweat off my brow and pretend I'm not about to totally keel over.

Elizabeth's black Audi SUV comes into view and squeals to a stop the second she sees me.

"Glory Purcell, what in the *hell* are you doing?" Elizabeth slams her door shut as she exits and marches toward me, looking like an L.L. Bean ad.

I did have a small fantasy of parent-trapping her and my dad during those first few weeks after my mom left. I was convinced it would work, except for one thing.

HARD FEELINGS

Her demon son.

"I sent Killian down this morning to tell you he'd pick you up and take you home."

Damn, I really need to unblock that fucker from my phone.

"I kinda ran out of the house this morning without really stopping to speak to him," I admit sheepishly. Repeating how childish I acted this morning is so cringe.

"Come on, young lady. I'm driving you home." Elizabeth loops her arm around my back and hustles me toward the passenger side.

I settle into the lush leather seat and let out a slow breath in relief. My anxiety ratchets up with thoughts about what my injury means with my scholarship and if I never get better. Little insidious observations, like how my ribs didn't hurt this bad yesterday or maybe I'm more hurt than I thought.

I swallow convulsively against the lump that sits in the back of my throat.

"Glory?" Elizabeth's gentle voice pulls me out of my spiral, and I open my eyes to see her worried expression. "Honey, are you okay? Should I take you to the clinic?"

My eyes sting at her motherly concern, and I try not to let the grief that this is coming from someone other than my own mother overtake me, so I nod and turn my head toward the window, watching the edge of her driveway disappear.

"I'm so sorry, Glory." Exhaustion heavy in her voice, Elizabeth pats my knee. "I know this has been tougher on you than anyone else. But Killian, he—"

"Elizabeth, I appreciate your position here, but I can't talk about Kill—" I wince as my voice cracks. "What's done is done. You've done what you can for me; it's more than we could have imagined, and … we're so grateful."

I keep my eyes pinned on the tree line as we head toward my house.

"I'm just going to say this because I believe you need to hear it. I love you, Glory Purcell, and I'm sorry for my part in your pain. I didn't think it was as bad as *this*. I'm ashamed of this town, of my son's part in it, and the people we used to call friends. You're innocent in all of this, and I hope, when you leave, you never think of this place ever again."

Blinking back tears, I look at her and see the resolution on her face.

"Thank you," I say finally and clear my throat, suddenly exhausted. I just want to curl up in bed and binge-watch *The Office*.

Dad's gone by the time I get home, the note on the island saying he drove into Clayton to get my pain meds filled at the pharmacy.

Ready to relax and empty my brain of everything that's happened in the last forty-eight hours, I kick off my shoes and grab some water and a bag of chips before crashing on our couch in the living room.

I barely make it through one episode before I pass out.

Of course, anxiety loves to show up in my dreams, so they're filled with me not going to California and having to work for the Kings for the rest of my life, like some modern-day Cinderella, except there's no prince.

I dream of my mother starting a new family with her new husband, and they're so happy. I go to visit her and meet my new sibling, but the doors are locked, and I can't get in.

But it's not either of these nightmares that wakes me up; it's the sudden silence of the TV shutting off.

Wincing, I sit up and open my eyes, only to find Killian staring at me less than an inch away. I don't scream, which isn't surprising. He used to wake me up like this all the time when we were kids, determined to scare me but he never did. Somehow, I always knew he was there, and it used to piss him off that he could never get the jump on me.

We stay like this for a handful of minutes, just staring at each other, neither of us blinking until, finally, I can't take the silent staredown any longer.

"What are you doing here?" I ask, surprising myself at how casual I sound.

Killian sits back next to me and kicks up his sock-covered feet on the large ottoman in front of the couch with a familiarity he shouldn't have after these last few years.

"Mom said she caught you on your way home and you looked like you were in a lot of pain."

Grabbing the remote, I click the TV back on. "Don't know why that concerns you."

"Glory."

"Killian," I mimic.

"Glowy—"

My head whips toward him. "Don't call me that."

Hearing his nickname for me—something from when we were children and he had a hard time with his *r*'s—shatters me.

Our staredown resumes, and I let him see everything this time—all the hurt, disappointment, guilt, shame. The rage.

Seeing it reflected back to me has me breaking first again … dammit.

"I fucked up," he admits softly, and I can hear the sincerity.

For what seems like the millionth time today, I find myself blinking back tears.

"I fucked up, Glory, and I broke the most precious thing in the world to me."

HARD FEELINGS

"I don't care, Killian," I whisper fiercely.

"Well, I do!" he growls, clearly frustrated with me.

Fuck him. He doesn't get to be frustrated with me.

"And why is that all of a sudden, hmm?" I turn toward him, practically spitting fire. "Because you finally see what your indifference has done to me? The lengths people will go to, to do something in your favor? For your attention? I don't care if you didn't do anything to me yourself. That's not an excuse, Killian! And I don't want to hear your apologies."

A sharp pain stabs behind my eye—one of the warning signs of an impending migraine. I wince and close that eye reflexively. I figured with everything that'd happened, one would come, but I wish it weren't in front of someone who I didn't trust with my vulnerability.

"What's wrong?"

"Just leave, Killian." I sink back into the pillows, exhausted, and close my eyes.

Any arguments he was about to make are interrupted by the sound of my dad's car driving up our gravel driveway.

"I'm going to fix this," he whispers to me and gives my hair a gentle tug.

"Don't bother." My protest comes too late as the sound of the back door shutting announces his departure.

My dad comes in a second later. "Hey, honey. How're you feeling?"

Dad comes around to sit on the ottoman in front of me and frowns at the clear pain on my face.

"My head," I whisper as the migraine starts to come on like a freight train, drowning me in enough pain that I don't even feel my ribs anymore.

"Okay, kiddo, let me get your meds. I have your painkillers, or you can take your shot. Which would you like?"

The shot for my migraines knocks me out, and oblivion sounds perfect right now.

"Shot," I croak and give him my hand so he can help me stand.

I feel a hundred years old as he helps me up the stairs and into my room. I crawl into bed as Dad pulls my blackout shades shut and turns on my white noise machine, the volume so low that I can barely hear it. My senses get unbelievably sharp when I have migraines, so what seems low is actually perfectly loud to me.

"I'll go grab your ice eye mask and your shot. Drink this." He points to a glass of Gatorade. Dehydration is the enemy when I'm having an episode.

I'm barely awake when he comes back and administers the shot. I feel him kiss the sensitive skin of my forehead as he places the mask over my eyes.

I don't even think of Killian as I slip into sleep; all I can focus on is praying that when I wake up, I'm no longer in pain.

31

Six

When I wake up, I have no idea how long I was sleeping, but if the pillow marks on my cheeks are any indication, it's been at least a couple of hours. My head feels better. Thankfully, I caught the migraine at the earliest signs before it got too bad, so I don't have the full episode hangover I usually have.

Hobbling into the bathroom to take care of business, I catch a glimpse of myself in the mirror and wince.

God, I look pale. Or rode hard and put away wet, as we like to say in the South.

My blonde hair is a mess, one side of my curls totally flat from where I lay on them, skin pale and pasty. My gray eyes are dull, bloodshot, and watery. I'm just thankful we don't have school tomorrow because, *Jesus* ...

Nurse Dad must have heard me moving around because he is already knocking on my door and poking his head in.

"Hey, you hungry?" he asks softly before swinging the door open when he sees I'm up.

I'm not, not at all, but I know if I don't eat, that will only make things worse. "I could eat."

"I've got some lentil soup going if you want to join me. The sun is almost down, so you can come downstairs without it paining you."

"I think I'm okay now, Dad. I got the shot before it got worse," I reassure him, knowing he gets panicky when I'm sick.

My dad used to turn into such a mother hen when my mother had a migraine, but it's an entirely different level for me.

He nods, relieved. "Okay, I'll go get you a bowl. Want to join me downstairs?"

I give him a thumbs-up and move stiffly out of the bathroom and follow him downstairs.

Moving like I'm decades older than I am, I grab the bowl of soup he prepared for me and groan as I take a seat on one of the barstools at the kitchen island.

"How are your ribs?" Dad asks, watching me carefully as he takes a spoonful.

"They hurt more today than yesterday," I admit, twirling my spoon around in the bowl. "I'm stiff."

"I think I should stay home on Tuesday too. We've got your follow-up appointment anyway. We can get McDonald's on the way home!"

I laugh softly at his enthusiasm. You know you live in a small town when a trip to McDonald's two towns over is an adventure, but he looks so excited that I agree easily. One more day before I have to go back to school.

I try not to let the anxiety of returning to school send me into a tailspin. There's no way the entire school doesn't already know what happened. The only thing that spreads faster than fire in this town is gossip.

My phone is silent, except for Cassidy and Marcus, both of them checking in on me periodically. I am tempted to unblock Killian just to see if he's texted me, but I throw that thought away immediately. No need to torture myself.

Dad begins talking about an interview for a contract job that'll keep him busy for a couple of months.

"It'll bring in more than enough money, so you can quit your job and focus only on school and soccer. It's crunch time now, kiddo."

"You don't have to tell me that. With this setback, I feel like I'm starting this season a month behind everyone else. That's great news though. I'll let Elizabeth know," I tell him, feeling a strange sort of sadness at the thought.

Without the excuse of cleaning, I'll have no reason to ever step foot in the house I spent half my childhood in again. Subconsciously, I rub the ache that thought causes in my chest.

I know this year is the calm before a lot of change in my life and in my dad's, but this seems …

"You okay?" Dad asks tentatively. "You don't have to quit if you don't want to. I just figured—"

Feeling silly, I quickly reassure him, "No, no, you're right. It's a good idea, and I'll appreciate having a solid rest day on Sundays to get a head start on school stuff for the following week."

Yawning widely, I dig in and we eat in companionable silence.

I should probably call Cassidy to see what the gossip is. The downside of having no real social media presence is getting left out of the loop on nearly everything.

It's also the upside.

HARD FEELINGS

As if I put the Bat-Signal out for some hot gossip, my phone starts ringing with Cassidy's assigned ringtone—"Mooo!" by Doja Cat.

It never fails to make me laugh, and to be honest, it's the only reason my phone isn't always on silent.

I scoop one more massive mouthful and gesture at my phone to my dad. He waves me away, grabbing my empty bowl, and I answer the phone.

"Are you sure you're not psychic?" I greet her, laughing lightly as I make my way out to the deck out back and settle into one of the Adirondack chairs facing the lake.

"I've been saying!" Cassidy laughs.

"So, spill 'cause I'm sure your phone's been blowing up," I demand, chewing on my thumbnail in dread.

"Well, you'll be shocked. I'm sure you know it's all over town that Bitchney Watts tried to take you out and Killian stepped in."

"Cool. Killian gets to keep his sterling reputation. I'm sure no one is talking about how she did all that in his name or for his attention or whatever."

"Girl, let me finish because, shock of shocks, Killian has put the word out that if he even sees you with anything other than a smile on your face, there will be consequences."

I blink, my stomach slightly dropping. "I just want to be left alone, period."

"It's better than some pick-me girl trying to break your damn ribs!"

"Who does he think he is, honestly? No high school boy should have this much power; it's weird."

"It's also the way it is, and, yeah, it's weird. I feel like we're living in a high school drama on TV or something. Who do you think would play me?"

"Madelaine Petsch, duh," I say without hesitation.

"She's so hot." Cassidy sighs.

"And I'm sure you think that for other reasons than she looks exactly like you."

"There's nothing wrong with loving yourself." Cassidy laughs. And, well, she's right.

Cassidy has more confidence than anyone I've ever met. Surprisingly, it's genuine. Amazing what happens when you grow up in a family with parents who have high emotional intelligence.

Can't relate.

"What does 'consequences' even mean? He's going to beat everyone's ass? He sounds like some teen Mafia boss." I circle back to the point of this conversation.

"I'm not sure, and I don't think anyone wants to find out. People get a lot of popularity by association, and none of the vapid idiots we go to school with want to lose that."

41

"Hmm …" I stare at the sun setting behind the waterline, mulling that over. "He came by here."

"Who, Killian?" Cassidy gasps.

"Yeah, he was here this morning, talking to Dad and then again this afternoon."

"Dude …"

"I know. I think he finally sees the damage he's caused."

"And?" she prompts.

"And nothing. This doesn't change anything. My sole focus is on graduating and not fucking up my scholarship to UCLA." It's all that matters.

"Why does it feel like senior year is never going to end?" Cassidy asks after a beat, wisely deciding not to push this at the moment.

"Because you want it to." I shiver slightly and decide it's a bit too chilly to be outside in shorts and just a hoodie.

I head upstairs, putting Cassidy on speakerphone. "Hey, you're on speakerphone," I warn her so she doesn't say anything my dad could potentially hear.

He knows how it is in town, but I don't think he has any idea how bad it's gotten for me at school. I've done a good job of letting most of it roll off my shoulder, and it helps that I have a team of girls ready to throw down on my behalf, but that doesn't mean some things don't eat at me.

Case in point: my ribs.

Dad doesn't need to worry about that on top of everything else. If anything, he'd pull me from school immediately and ruin my chances at UCLA.

"Gotcha. Hey, so, listen, the real reason I called is because Tan and I are heading to the dollar theater. They're having a Will Ferrell movie marathon, and since there's no school tomorrow, I figured you'd be down?"

Tanner and Cassidy both love Will Ferrell, and normally, I would, but, "Thanks for the invite, Cassidy, but I had a headache earlier, and I just want to chill. I'm probably going to bed after we hang up, honestly."

"Aw, you okay? Want me to bring you something?"

I smile at her thoughtfulness. "I appreciate it, but I'm all set. I feel fine now, just drained."

"Okay, Glo. I'll come over tomorrow and hang in bed with you. We'll have a *Gilmore Girls* marathon."

"Deal. Love you. Bye!"

"Love ya!"

I set my phone on my nightstand and decide to forgo taking a shower before bed. The idea is exhausting. I head to my dad's office, knowing he's already tucked away in there, working, and say good night.

HARD FEELINGS

I know just because we dropped the subject tonight doesn't mean it's over with Cassidy. Killian crossing our invisible boundary and coming into enemy territory is huge.

Sighing heavily, I climb into bed and turn on my white noise maker, hoping it distracts my brain from the racing thoughts.

Fucking Killian.

seven

The next two weeks pass in agonizing slowness. Having to attend every practice and game without playing has been brutal. My girls are kicking ass though, but I miss it more than anything. Mainly, I just want to put an end to the sympathetic glances from my teammates and the anxiety that, in two weeks, I'll have somehow forgotten how to play.

Irrational, but anxiety is an irrational bitch.

Other than my being a supportive teammate and torturing myself with worst-case scenarios, Killian has been true to his word. Everyone has seemingly backed off. I've even gotten a few *heys* and *I'm sorry that happened to yous*. All of these are totally disingenuous, given the fact that they are not entirely altruistic, what with Killian's displeasure hanging over them, but it's better than sneers and mumbled insults.

Killian has given me space, too, though probably not intentionally. He's also super busy with football, and with both our seasons active, we barely see each other.

Something that used to fill me with peace is now making me jumpy. If I know anything about Killian, it's that he's a dweller and a fixer. Two things that don't bode well for my plan to skate by the rest of the year, unnoticed.

I've tried my damnedest these last few years to be a duck, calmly gliding toward graduation without letting anyone see how hard I'm paddling under the surface.

I've operated the last few years, thinking that if I act unaffected, I will *be* unaffected. Hence why I'm running across the country the absolute second that stupid diploma hits my palm. I laugh to myself—yeah, totally unaffected.

"Something funny, Ms. Purcell?" Mrs. Kinde, my English teacher, interrupts my inner dialogue.

I sit up, tucking my hair behind my ears self-consciously, and shake my head. "No, ma'am. Sorry."

I have the hardest time paying attention in English, not because I hate it, but because it's the last class of the day, which means practice is after. Today though, I go back to the doctor to get the all clear.

Please, please, please let me get the all clear.

Dad had to run down to Atlanta for some business, so he won't be home until late tonight—a reason that he tried to use to move the appointment, but I refused. I do not want to go another day off the field than I have to.

Cassidy can't miss practice, so Marcus said he'd give me a ride. I snicker, remembering Cassidy's face when I told her that. She knows I would never go there, but, damn, did she seem jealous of us spending time together.

There's a sharp knock at the door that jerks everyone's attention, and Killian pokes his head in.

"Apologies for the interruption, Mrs. Kinde, but I need Glory. I'm taking her to her doctor's appointment. I have the note from her dad here." He casually walks the rest of the way in, like it's totally normal for a student to come to check another student out of school.

I glare at that permission slip to see if I've somehow gained the power to light objects on fire with my mind in the last five minutes, but unfortunately, I have not.

"Glo, let's go." Killian smirks at his little rhyme and walks out of the room without even waiting for me to put up a fight.

I try not to snarl at him using my nickname in front of all these people. I'm not stupid; I know what he's doing.

"You're okay to leave, Glory. Good luck at the doctor. We've missed you on the field." She smiles and hands me the note after I grab my bag and walk up to the front of the class.

I glance at the note and see my dad's scrawl, explaining that Killian is my ride.

Exiting the classroom, I stare at the smug prick leaning against the lockers across the hall.

"How'd you manage this?" I ask, heading toward my locker to stuff my books away.

"I overheard your dad talking to my mom." Killian falls into step with me, his body radiating heat next to me, indicating that, yet again, he's in my space.

"Since when do our parents talk?" I snort.

"Since some misguided girl decided to try and take you out because she thought it would put her in my good graces." He says this without a hint of arrogance, which is good for him and his nuts. If anything, he sounds embarrassed by it.

HARD FEELINGS

We reach my locker, and I make quick work of shoving my books in and grabbing my backpack, but before I can swing it onto my shoulder, Killian lifts it out of my hands and slings it over his right shoulder.

Closing my eyes, I take a deep inhale, praying for patience, and shut my locker door.

Do not snap at him. You are unbothered.

Refusing to meet his eyes, I start heading toward the senior parking lot. "I'm shocked you admitted it."

"I'm done lying to myself about a lot," he says quietly, and I can hear the pain and conviction in his voice.

Halting at the doors leading outside, I turn to find his eyes are already locked on me as he braces himself, as if I were about to roundhouse him in the beanbags, with an uncertain, small smile on his lips.

And he looks so much like my Killian at that moment—my once-quiet, anxious best friend who always wore a slightly timid smile, waiting for reassurance—that it feels like I just physically got socked in the stomach.

"Why are you doing this?" I whisper, throat so tight with emotion that it's difficult to speak.

"Because you're going to leave, probably forever, and I can't—" His voice cracks, and he breaks eye contact before continuing, "I can't let you go with this being the last memory you have of us. You were my best friend— more than that, you were everything to me—and the guilt and anger I have over ruining that guts me. I spent so much time and energy not thinking about you that it made me blind to what was going on. Knowing I'm the cause of that, Glory? God, it fucking *devastates* me."

He breathes heavily, eyes shiny, and it makes me want to cry. Here it is— the apology I always wanted. The accountability. And yet all I feel is sad. We wasted so much time, and he ruined my high school experience.

"I don't know if I can forgive you, Killian," I tell him honestly and angrily swipe the tear that slipped out.

"I haven't done anything to earn that yet, Glory."

"Then, what do you want?"

"Today? To give you a ride."

He pushes the door open and heads out to the parking lot, and I stall for a couple of seconds before following.

Killian's car, a souped-up matte-black G-Wagon, sticks out like a sore thumb—or rather, a giant dollar sign.

Slinging our bags into the trunk, Killian walks around to the driver's side and unlocks the rest of the doors.

When we were in middle school, we used to dream of all the adventures we'd go on together once we got our licenses.

I was obsessed with the idea of going down all the roads we would pass while in the backseat of my parents' car. My imagination would run wild with

47

the thoughts of us just deciding to turn down a road and what we could discover.

The reality is much more disappointing.

Killian pushes the Start button once I settle into the lush tan leather seat and starts fiddling with the AC.

"This okay? Or do you need more air?" Killian asks, but I'm distracted by my sudden need to roll the window down.

This is the closest we've been in years, and he overwhelms me. His scent surrounds me, familiar and intoxicating, yet he seems so unaffected by me.

"I'm fine," I reply shortly, turning my body toward the door and resting my chin on my palm to stare out the window.

Killian clears his throat, and we drive off. He's going grandma slow, but I refuse to comment.

The first ten minutes go by in absolute silence, which I'm fine to punish him with.

It's working too, if his compulsive throat clearing is any indication.

However, the fourth time in as many minutes is enough for me to finally break. "Can you put the radio on or something?"

"Sure!" His voice cracks in relief, and I stifle a laugh.

Wonder what the girls at school would make of this uncertain, vulnerable Killian.

The National comes through the speakers, and I glance at him quickly. They've been my favorite band since forever.

"Since when do you listen to them?" I ask, turning the volume down on the radio and watching the muscle in his stupidly cut jawline twitch.

"Can we not do any more heavy stuff today?" Killian asks, keeping his attention laser-focused on the winding roads.

I laugh sarcastically. "Uh, no. I think we've skirted issues enough, don't you?"

He sighs heavily and cuts me a quick glance, clearly annoyed with me. I just raise my brow in challenge.

"Dammit, Glory, fine. If you need me to expose every embarrassing feeling I have, then sure." He takes a deep breath, his grip tightening briefly on the steering wheel before relaxing. "I listen to them whenever I miss you ... which happens to be often."

If he thought I'd melt at his confession, he's wrong. I'm honestly furious more than anything right now.

"Are you going to say anything?" he prompts after a beat.

"I don't think you want me to say anything right now," I mutter, returning my attention to the pine trees racing by as we inch closer to the doctor. This already-long trip is going to feel ten times longer if it continues to be fraught with emotional confessions.

HARD FEELINGS

"Uh, no, I think I've had enough of your silence, Glory. I'm trying here, please."

"Killian, your version of trying is the bare minimum of being a decent human being. You called off your brainless army from making my life hell, and you're giving me a ride to the doctor. The bar is not on the floor. Our friendship meant more to me, and if you want to mend what you tore apart, I'm going to hold your ass accountable."

My breaths rush in and out of me like I've been running sprints.

"You're right," he concedes quietly.

"I know I am. Dick," I shoot back, and he laughs.

"Let's start small. What's one thing you miss that I can give you?"

I think for a moment, pretending to take my time when the answer is immediate in my head. "I want you at my games. I miss your support, Killian. It's my last season here, and I don't know if I'm—" I cut myself off, scared that somehow verbalizing my biggest fear will make it true.

"Done. Of course, done. And let me tell you something right now, Glory Jane. Bruised ribs are not going to ruin your future. You did not somehow forget how to play in the last few weeks. The doctor is going to green-light you, and you'll be right back on that field, where you belong."

"I know; I know. I don't know why I'm so scared."

"Because it's important to you, and the fear of losing what you love can be paralyzing." He says this knowingly, but I don't press him. I'm not sure I can take any more emotional vomiting today. "Hey, we're here."

Nerves strip my mouth of moisture, and I start swallowing compulsively, stalling a bit while Killian parks and turns the car off.

"Come on, Glory. It'll be okay. I'll even hold your hand if you're so scared," he teases.

Growling, I shoot him a glare and exit the car, walking slowly toward the squat brown building.

Killian swings his tree-trunk arm over my shoulders, jostling me into his side. "It's going to be fine, dude. Relax."

I nod but leave his arm where it is. I'm too freaked out to shove it off me.

EighT

"So, you're all clear?" Cassidy squeals loudly, nearly bursting my damn eardrum.

The doctor gave me the all clear, and I was so relieved that I nearly cried on the spot. When I made it back to the waiting room, Killian whooped the second he saw my face, startling the shit out of everyone else quietly waiting their turn.

After I got the news, I spent the entire trip back to town calling my dad and Coach and chatting about next steps.

The house was empty when I got home, which was somewhat deflating. I wanted someone here to celebrate the good news with and to tell me everything would be fine again when I stepped out onto the field. I wanted Cassidy, so I called her immediately, knowing she'd share my excitement.

"Yes, I can be back on the field tomorrow. Coach wants me to sit out this weekend's game. I've got some conditioning set up outside of usual practice, but I should be good to play soon."

"I—" Cassidy begins, but it's cut off by loud laughing in the background. "Ugh, do you care if I come over? Killian is here, and he and Tan seem determined to be as loud as possible. It's driving me nuts."

"Yeah, sure. Dad's not home, so it'll just be us. I'm a little lonely anyway; I feel like I need to be celebrating."

"Okay, I'm going to pack a bag. Be there in five!" Cassidy hangs up before I can respond.

I throw on some soccer shorts and my dad's old college sweatshirt. It's soft, it hits below the middle of my thigh, and it's one of my most prized possessions. I sniff it a bit and smell the laundry detergent my family has been using since I can remember, and I find myself getting a little teary.

I'm going to miss my dad so much. He's everything to me.

My front door slams shut, announcing Cassidy's arrival and startling me out of my thoughts. Removing the scrunchie from my wrist, I tie my hair up in a knot on top of my head and grab my glasses off my nightstand before heading downstairs.

I enter the kitchen just as Cassidy dumps a bag of junk food onto the kitchen island. "Jeez, dude, are we doing the ten-thousand-calorie challenge or something?"

Cassidy grins. "You wanted to celebrate, and short of going cow tipping—something I feel you'd rather not do—we're going to have a party night, like we used to!"

Emotion bubbles up inside my throat, nearly choking me with how much I love my friend.

"Glo, what the heck?" Cassidy laughs but sounds concerned as she crosses to me and yanks me into a tight hug. "Everything's okay, dude."

I sniffle against her shirt. "I'm just feeling overwhelmed. A lot has happened in twenty-four hours."

Cassidy pulls back and heads for the chips, aggressively ripping them open. "Yeah, about that … what's this I hear about you and Killian being friends again?"

I'm momentarily shocked before my skin starts to heat up, anger lighting me on fire from the inside out. "Excuse me?"

Cassidy nods knowingly before plopping down on the couch. "Oh, yeah, Killian came straight over after dropping you off, practically glowing. He couldn't wait to tell Tanner about how he told you how he feels and you forgave him and y'all are friends again."

"I haven't forgiven him! I accepted a freaking ride to the doctor. What the fuck?!" I yell, squeezing a Twinkie so hard that the cream shoots into the bag.

"Mmhmm." Cassidy crunches a chip, watching me pace in front of her.

"Told me how he feels? He literally admitted to being a jackass and wants to make it up to me. I explicitly said I didn't forgive him! Does he not understand how fucking awful the last few years have been for me? Does he not understand what consequences are? What an entitled prick!"

"Preach, sis!" Cassidy points a chip at me in agreement, and I grab it out of her hand and shove it into my mouth, chewing furiously.

"Just because I agreed to a cease-fire doesn't mean we're good. My father and I have been ostracized. He lost his job, for God's sake, and I was bullied! And he thinks he can do the bare minimum, and suddenly, it's all good?"

"Wait, so what happened? Because that's exactly what he thinks."

I flop down beside her. "Cassidy, I said he has to prove it. Like showing up to my games, being the friend I used to have. He has to work for it. I gave him some direction, but I don't even know what it's going to take for me to

HARD FEELINGS

forgive him, if I ever can. The only reason I'm even entertaining it is that it's my last year here and I wouldn't mind enjoying it. It would be nice to leave here with closure."

"Welp!" Her eyebrows shoot up. "That's entirely different than the impression he was giving Tan. I think he's taking that inch you gave him and stretching it into a mile."

I growl, muttering under my breath.

"I'm going to say something, and I need you to remember I ride or die for you. Maybe he's just happy you're speaking to him again."

"Cassidy! I never stopped. He is the one who changed everything," I point out, completely frustrated. "How the fuck is this getting turned around on me?"

"Okay, yes, you're correct. I'm sorry for making it sound like I was suggesting otherwise, but that's not really what I meant."

I take a deep breath to calm myself down because I'm getting pissed off that I'm so pissed off. I freaking hate how much he gets under my skin, and he's not even here!

"Explain," I demand once I've gotten myself under control.

"Um … " She eyes me cautiously. "Well, right now, you're terrifying, so I don't really—"

"Cassidy!"

"Okay, fine. I'm just saying that while this is absolutely a shitstorm of his own making, that doesn't mean he didn't miss you."

I nod because, yeah, Killian said as much himself.

"I don't want to talk about him anymore. He's living in my head rent-free, and it needs to stop. I need to focus on school and soccer." I grab the remote to turn the TV on.

"Topic changed. Actually, I need your help. Can you read my essay for Stanford?" Cassidy grabs her bag and yanks out her laptop.

"Sure!"

Unlike me, Cassidy is a legitimate genius. I don't say that to be self-deprecating or out of false modesty. I am a C-average student at best. I've just never had much interest in school. It's been soccer for as long as I can remember, and believe me, I've heard all the arguments.

The likelihood of me going pro is small. Even if I did, my lifespan as a pro female athlete would be short. I know I need to have something to fall back on, but I don't know what I want to do, and I am not even sure what I'm good at outside of soccer.

It's my whole identity, which is sad, I suppose. Dad says I don't need to have everything figured out right now and that I should take a bunch of different classes during my first two years of school before declaring anything.

I'm trying not to let myself stress.

Besides, my scholarship stipulates that I need to graduate with a certain GPA, so I need to focus on not reinjuring myself and then graduating.

Cassidy is dead set on getting into Stanford and then trying out for their women's team, but just as I've always wanted to be a pro athlete, Cassidy has always wanted to be an electrical engineer, ever since we went to the science museum in Atlanta.

She wants to save the world. I want to kick a ball down a field for the rest of my life. As Dad always says, it takes all kinds.

Cassidy passes me her computer after she pulls up her essay and settles back into the couch, turning on *The Kardashians*.

Her essay is about her inspiration, Edith Clarke, the first woman professionally employed as an electrical engineer and the first female professor of electrical engineering in the United States. She helped build the Hoover Dam, invented the Clarke calculator, and was a badass in general.

I smile, remembering our ninth-grade Halloween costumes. Cassidy dressed up as Edith with a little skirt, suit, glasses, and pinned hair. I went as Alex Morgan, obviously, which essentially consisted of me in a US Women's number 13 jersey. Real creative.

"Cassidy, it's great. You can feel your passion leap off the page. Maybe you should be a writer instead." I carefully pass her laptop back to her before settling back.

"Well, I'll be that as well when I get papers published in academic journals," Cassidy says so matter-of-factly that I have to marvel at her confidence.

"How the heck are you so confident?" I laugh because she says this like it's a foregone conclusion.

"How the heck are *you*, my friend?" she shoots back with an arched brow.

I laugh lightly, wishing I were more confident on the inside.

"Are you going to send it?" I ask quietly after a moment of watching Cassidy squint at her screen.

She glances over quickly, chewing on her lip, and nods. I reach over and grab her hand, giving it a squeeze of encouragement.

Cassidy exhales noisily and hits Submit on her application. It's early to be sending in an application, but she's hoping to get not only a scholarship, but early acceptance as well.

Coach is working with her to get a tape together to submit to the team at Stanford on the off chance she'll get invited to a summer clinic.

I try not to get too excited about it, not wanting Cassidy to feel any unnecessary pressure, but I would give anything for us both to be in California this coming summer.

We lapse into a comfortable silence. It's one of my favorite things about our friendship—our ability to be silent but undeniably present. To be so

HARD FEELINGS

comfortable with someone that just having them next to you settles something deep inside you.

It's part of the reason why I want her to come with me at the same time. Not that she will be any closer to me, but I unfairly consider Cassidy my support and comfort. I like the idea of still being able to be chaotic and jump in a car and drive to see her.

She's gotten me through these last few years and listened to me as I cried over Killian and my mom. Wiped my tears after we lost games. Defended me and encouraged me to show up every day when the world seemed to be content to shove me down.

I so desperately want great things for her. She's the best person I know.

"I love you, you know," I say quietly, not looking at her, but the feelings of pride and gratitude swell in my throat, making it impossible not to say something.

"Right back at ya, Glo."

Nine

practice is brutal. The football team distracts me. I'm worried about being good, so I start overcompensating by doing too much footwork. Something my coach hates and has no issue calling me out for in front of the whole team.

Really, everyone in the vicinity hears her chew me out.

It's mortifying to feel curious eyes on me. It's embarrassing to have witnesses to my meltdown. During the entire ninety-minute practice, I can feel Killian's eyes on me. Cassidy is watching with equal intensity, and I know I'm going to get interrogated by her the second she gets me alone.

Coach blows the whistle, dismissing us to the locker room, and I speed-walk ahead of the team, hoping to shower and change before anyone can corner me.

"Purcell! I see you sprinting, and I hope it's straight into my office because you're not leaving today without a conversation."

I stop immediately, shoulders climbing to my ears, and exhale.

"Actually, Coach, can I talk to you first? I've got to leave ASAP, and I need to ask about my tape," Cassidy cuts in as she reaches me and throws an arm around my shoulders. "You owe me."

I nod, thankful for the extra ten minutes to myself.

Heading to my locker, I take out my ponytail and throw my hair up in a high bun instead. Grabbing my shower gel and towel, I head for the stall and rinse off quickly. Our showers only spray cold-ass water—something that normally has me weighing the options of showering here or at home, but now has me feeling grateful. It's bracing, and it shocks my racing thoughts so I can think normally or at least organize them into coherence.

I'm in and out in five minutes since I didn't wash my wavy, thick hair, which will revolt at not getting properly washed, and I'm changed into my Galway High sweats before most of the team has finished showering.

Cassidy pats my shoulder as she exits Coach's office just as Coach yells for me to come in.

Frick.

"Take a seat, Purcell," Coach says as she stands in front of her whiteboard, writing the focus of the next practice in her sloppy handwriting.

Capping the whiteboard marker, she turns and faces me. Sitting guiltily in front of her desk, I try dutifully not to notice that her current roster for the game on Friday lacks my name.

Coach snaps her fingers in front of my face. "Yo, Purcell. I've been talking to you for the last five minutes. Have you heard a word I've said? What's going on in that head of yours?"

"Most recently? Contemplating the misogyny at this school. In general? How long do you have?" I smile big.

"How about we start with, what the hell was that at practice?" She lifts a dark brow and sets her laser *tell me what I want to know now* gaze on me.

Things to know about Coach Mira Li: The first-gen Korean American badass put this town on the soccer map by joining the US Women's National Team straight out of high school, making her the youngest teammate in USWNT history. Every girl who has ever wanted to play soccer for Galway High idolizes her, including me.

When she tore her ACL before her first ever game with the national team, we mourned with her, and instead of becoming bitter, she found her second passion, coaching—and thank God she did. She has developed a high school program that has had more girls move on to play at D1 schools than any other high school in the state.

I know for a fact that she gets offers every year to coach collegiate, but she turns them down. She loves what she does, and it's because of all this that I know she knows what's going on in my head and she won't give me some bullshit platitudes.

Yanking my hair out of its bun in frustration, I find myself confessing, "I had some pretty big anxiety about this first practice. I know—*I know*—I was only out a few weeks, but this is everything to me. It's the only thing that has ever made sense these last few years; it's my ticket out of this town and hopefully my path to a future that will give my dad and me the financial security we so desperately need."

"You're scared," Coach confirms, nodding as she takes the seat next to me.

"Terrified," I whisper, staring at the ceiling to force back the tears that want to sneak out.

HARD FEELINGS

"I get it, Glory—you know I get it—but you're one of the lucky ones. Showing gratitude will help tremendously to regain your confidence. What will not work is pushing yourself with extra practices or showing off."

"I know." I nod, and I do. I do know.

"You know how I feel about playing around with the ball like that. Tricks work in modicum, but sitting there, juggling and doing all kinds of stupid shit that might look good, is worthless if a defender knocks you on your ass and boots it back down the field."

"Less is more," I say, quoting her old adage.

"Less is more." Coach nods, smiling before getting serious. "I know that scared the shit out of you, but you've got to get your head on straight. The head takes longer to heal than the body. Figure it out, Glory, or you'll ruin your chance before it gets off the ground. That's all. You can leave."

"But"—I glance at the roster again—"I thought—"

"I was hesitant to even have you do a full practice, and after tonight's performance, there is no way I'm ready to have you play a game. I don't care if the doctor says you gained extra powers. Show me you trust yourself, and I'll trust you to play a game."

Feeling properly chastised and pissed in general, I head out to the lockers to grab my bag. I text Cassidy that my dad's picking me up so she won't wait around for me, then head back out to the field.

Most of the lights have been turned off, putting the field into muted darkness, the only light coming from the moon and the school building a couple hundred feet away.

I storm out to the middle, dropping my bag at my feet before sitting next to it. I grab the Bluetooth headphones Cassidy and Tanner got me for my sweet sixteen and settle them over my ears before getting my phone and putting on my Angsty Girlies playlist. It's shared with Cassidy, naturally, and I see that she's added some new songs.

Lying down, I rest my head on my bag and stare at the sky, trying to make out the stars.

When my anger fades and the sense of loss wins, the only thing I can think to do is visit the place I feel most at peace. The damp grass seeps through my sweat, chilling my skin and providing something for me to focus on when the sadness wants me to drown.

My headphones blare "She Used to Be Mine" from the *Waitress* soundtrack, and though my face is relaxed and my body is sinking into the ground, tears stream down my temples and into the hair that my mother gave me.

Her absence is a constant thing. It's in between my father and me when we eat at the kitchen island instead of the breakfast nook. It's the silence when we turn on *Veep* for the hundredth time, where there would normally be a playful complaint.

It's in the talks my coach has with me, giving me the comfort and hard facts that I need instead of her.

Damn, this song has me in my feels.

And double damn … maybe I should take my dad up on therapy.

I'm not sure how long I've been out here. I've replayed this song four times at the minimum, but apparently, the football team's practice wrapped because Killian collapses next to me.

You'd think for someone who smacks his body around on the daily, he'd be better at falling gracefully, but no. It's like someone slings a bag of potatoes on the ground.

"Jesus, Killian, be careful before you pancake me!" I complain, ripping the headphones off my head as I sit up.

Ignoring me, he mimics my setup and lies down, raising a brow when I continue to glare down at him.

Huffing an annoyed breath, I resume my position but leave the headphones off, already anticipating another annoying conversation.

We're silent for a while, long enough for my body to relax, and I begin to enjoy the same comfort of just being as I had with Cassidy last night.

"You want to talk about it?" he murmurs, keeping his gaze locked on the sky.

"Hell no," I reply shortly.

"With me or in general?"

"You think you deserve to hear my every thought?"

"If I thought I deserved it, do you think I'd ask?" he counters.

Pursing my lips, I concede, "Fair. And, no, in general, although you would not be in the top five of who I'd talk to about this, so don't get cocky because you caught me in a weak moment."

"Believe me, Glory, if there's one thing I'm certain of, it's that I'm going to have to work for every inch."

I sigh gustily. "My head game is fucked. It's been one thing after another since school started back up, and getting injured was a knock to my confidence. I'm stressed out, and that brings up a bunch of shit I'd rather not deal with."

"I get that. You know a lot of us feel that way; you're not alone."

"I'm not worried that I'm alone in feeling this way. My problem is, I do not know how to work through any of this. It used to be soccer, but with getting hurt and then my scholarship in the balance, it's no longer my source of solace."

"I know you don't want to commiserate with me on this, but I'm having that exact problem."

"Shit's fucking hard right now," I admit.

"It fucking sucks!" Killian yells to the sky, startling the shit out of me before turning his head and smiling at me. "Come on, Glo. Scream it out."

HARD FEELINGS

"No!"

"Do it!"

"This sucks! It sucks balls! I hate it here! Fuck this place!" I scream, then start laughing hysterically, Killian cracking up next to me.

"Ah shit, y'all have finally lost your minds," Tanner says above us.

Killian and I both scream, surprised by his sudden appearance.

"God, Tanner, we need to put a bell on you. How the hell are you so big and don't make a sound?" I ask, taking his hand when he offers it.

Killian hops to his feet easily, showing off that agility that's going to land him a spot on any team he wants next year.

"Years of practice from scaring the shit out of Cassidy. So, why are we screaming outside in the dark together?"

"Just blowing off some steam," Killian explains, slinging his bag over his shoulder before grabbing mine.

"Interesting. Normally, I like to blow off steam in a different way and with someone I don't consider family." Tanner grins lecherously.

I pretend to gag as Killian groans, "Bro!"

"Just saying! Anyway, you need a ride, Glory?"

"Nah, I got her," Killian answers before me, which earns him my hundredth glare of the evening.

"Wow, I had no idea you were so good at throwing your voice, Glo," Tanner teases, like the little shit he is.

"Me neither, but I guess he's right. Doesn't make sense for you to drive all the way to my place before doubling back home." I shrug. And also, I told Cassidy I got a ride from my dad.

"Well, isn't this just like old times?" Tanner grins, bouncing on his heels.

"Dude," Killian warns sharply.

"Let me make something clear since you seem to be under the impression all is forgiven," I say casually to Tanner, whose smile drops instantly. "You know exactly what I went through. You were there. Why you think I'd just bend over the second Killian opens his eyes is beyond me. Just because I'm allowing him to try and make amends does not mean amends have been made. What I don't need is for you to trivialize the last four years with snarky little jokes, got me?"

Killian grows tenser and tenser with each word that leaves my mouth, but I don't spare him a glance.

Tanner nods solemnly. "You're right; I'm sorry. I'm just ..." He pauses, clearly struggling to put it into words.

But I know what he means.

"I get that it's been tough, being in the middle, but not picking a side didn't make you a saint in this, Tanner, so I'm asking you to stay the hell out of it."

I don't wait around for his response, instead heading for the parking lot, leaving Killian to follow.

Guilt already assails me for coming down so hard on Tanner, but it kind of hurts; he's never been on my side exactly, but now, it feels a bit like he's decided where he stands. And it's not with me.

"Glory, wait!" Tanner yells a second before I'm yanked into a tight hug. I hesitate before wrapping my arms around his waist. "I've always felt like I should've done more. I'm racked with guilt over it."

That's the complicated thing though. Tanner stepped in constantly. One time, when I was walking home from practice sophomore year, some of the older kids decided it would be funny to chase me down on their bikes, heckling me.

It was terrifying.

I was fully on my own, on back roads, with three guys who were bigger than me physically in every way. Understanding my true defenselessness was incredibly humbling.

I'd done a lot to shield myself from the mental and emotional bullshit, but this was the first time it ever escalated to something potentially physical.

Being closer to Cassidy and Tanner's house, I pivoted off the road and ran through the woods because if there was one chance I had at getting away, it was by running. I might be small, but I'm fast as fuck.

Tanner was outside, shooting hoops with his dad, when I came tearing through the woods that backed up to their driveway. I don't remember much of what I said. Cassidy grabbed me and pulled me inside before I could explain everything, but I do know Tanner took off in the direction I had come from, and his dad called the cops.

The next day, those idiots were suspended, so I didn't get to see the damage done to their faces, but I definitely heard about it.

It sent a clear enough message through the school that any physical threat to me would be handled swiftly.

The outright name-calling and bullying died down quite a bit. There was still some of it, but nowhere near the level it used to be. Mostly, what stuck around was the ostracism from nearly everyone at that school, except the soccer teams and Tanner.

Which, honestly, was preferred. I wouldn't want to be friends with people who were so spineless anyway.

Tanner tightens his grip, bringing me back to the present before letting me go.

"I've got your back forever, Glory. You're the sister I've always wanted." He smiles at his oldest joke. The one that, if Cassidy were here, would earn him a punch on the shoulder, but gets a teary giggle from me instead.

"Everything's just really raw right now. I don't want to be pressured into something that's not healthy for me."

HARD FEELINGS

"I understand, and I'm going to keep my mouth shut about it until you want to talk about it. Listen, I gotta run, but you're coming to the game this Friday, right?"

I groan. "Tanner, I've been to one game in, like, four years. I don't want to."

"You're coming! I need your support. Now that you're sticking the middle finger to all the bullshit and Kills put the smackdown on all the shitheads, you'll actually enjoy yourself."

I roll my eyes at how easily he has me. "Fine, but then you have to come to ours."

"Shake on it?" Tanner grins, this time so widely that his dimples wink at me, and I know what he wants.

"Ugh, fine, but, Tanner, we're not in middle school anymore."

"Less talking, more booty shaking," he demands before putting his hands on his knees and, honest to God, twerking. I must say, it's absolutely worth making an idiot out of myself just to see a six-foot-one football player twerk. "Love ya, Glo Worm!"

"Love you too, Tan Tan."

I watch him amble toward his pickup, shaking my head before spinning on my heel to see where Killian is skulking about.

I spot him easily, near the only car left in the lot, as Tanner peels out, and I start making my way toward him.

"How much did you hear, you dirty little eavesdropper?"

"All of it." He smiles as he climbs inside at the same time I do. "I love that you guys are so close. It feels good to know you've had someone in your corner like that."

I bite my lip to hold back a sharp retort and decide to just stay quiet. He's been so nice lately, and every time I snap at him, it makes me feel like a jerk.

Which then makes me mad because I'm not the asshole in all this.

So, instead, I nod and connect my phone to AirPlay to listen to some music.

"You ignoring me now?" Killian asks, amused.

I sigh heavily. "Killian, come on. I'm just tired."

"Fine, but if you're letting me try to make amends, that might need some active participation on your part; otherwise, this is dead in the water."

I eye him warily. "What do you want?"

"Sunday breakfast is back on. Mom's orders." He glances at me, the glow from his dash screen highlighting how angular his face is.

Since I happen to love Betsy's Diner, I agree, "Okay, Sunday breakfast is back on."

"Want to shake on it?" He smirks.

"Shut up." I laugh.

Ten

Any awkwardness I was expecting at my first Sunday breakfast since letting Killian back in was absent. In fact, it was more shocking how easy it was. Elizabeth kept the conversation flowing by asking about school and soccer and how my dad was. Killian filled her in on where he was with his application and the tapes his coach was helping him put together to send to the University of Georgia football program.

After that initial Sunday, Killian and I fell into an easy rhythm. Somehow, it just became a natural assumption he'd take me home after our practices.

True to the guy's word, every football game I attend means Tanner and Killian will also be at my games. Anytime we don't have games the same night, I go with Cassidy to the football games.

Outside of the ten-minute ride home from practice, most of my interactions with Killian have been with others providing a buffer. Something I'm unwilling to change at the moment. It always seems to go wrong when we're alone together. Either he wants to talk about shit I'm not ready to talk about or I snap at him.

Luckily, the twins are more than happy to continue to hang out as a group. Seeing their easiness further highlights what Tanner mentioned a week ago. I see it even with Cassidy. Though she loudly takes my side in all of this, she's definitely more relaxed now.

I struggle with feeling guilty about that, but I've never put pressure on either of them to stop talking to Killian. They were friends with him before I moved here.

"Hey! Earth to Glory." Cassidy knocks her shoulder into mine, bringing me back to the present.

I realize Taylor, our goalie, asked who I'm rooming with. Coach told her to take down the room assignments.

I smile, embarrassed to be caught in my head again, and turn my attention back to the convo at our lunch table. Boys and girls from the soccer team crowd the table, talking excitedly.

Our senior trip to Atlanta, where we're going to attend an Atlanta United FC practice and game, is happening this weekend. Everyone is pumped, especially since it's an overnight trip.

Plans to sneak out after lights out are already in the works. We leave after school today—something I'm equally eager about and dreading.

It's going to be the closest I've been to my mom in over a year. Anytime she's come to Galway to visit—when her conscience gets the better of her—I've done my best to ice her out.

I must have done it so well the last time because she hasn't made an attempt to even talk to me about visiting since. All communication goes through my dad, apparently. I try not to let that bother me, but with my eighteenth birthday right around the corner, it's difficult not to.

As if looking like my mom isn't enough to give the kids in this town something to talk about, being born on October 31 certainly doesn't help.

Being called a witch is probably the least offensive insult that's been hurled my way. Cassidy and I decided years ago to embrace it. Every year now, we dress up like witches and watch *Practical Magic* while passing out candy.

"I'm rooming with Cassidy, of course," I answer Taylor's question, and she types on her phone.

"Me too." Marcus grins cheekily, coming up behind Cassidy and me to loop his arms around our shoulders.

"You wish." I laugh as Cassidy shoves his arm off her shoulders.

"In your freaking dreams, Marcus Gary Tyler," Cassidy says haughtily.

Marcus winces as the rest of our team echoes, "Gary," and laughs.

"Dammit, Cassidy, why the fuck did I give you my full name?" He groans, squeezing in between us, forcing me to scoot over or he'd be in my lap.

"Marcus," I complain, but secretly, I'm trying not to high-five him. It's a bold move, but he called me last night, explaining that he was going to shoot his shot with Cassidy this weekend.

"It's the hair. It hypnotized you." Cassidy smirks, shrugging her thick braid over her shoulder with a wink.

Marcus practically vibrates in his seat, and I want to tell him to chill out before he embarrasses himself, but I also find his blatant worshipfulness endearing.

"Tyler, why are you sitting so close to my sister?" Tanner playfully glares as he and Killian walk over with their trays.

HARD FEELINGS

"Hoping she ends up liking me by osmosis." He grins, and Tanner laughs before wishing him good luck.

"Speaking of Biology"—Killian locks his eyes with mine—"a little birdie told me you need a tutor."

I cringe in my chair at the immediate, undivided attention. "And?"

"Just so happens I have an A in AP Bio and am willing to share the knowledge in my gigantic brain with you."

"Cassidy can help," I counter.

"Uh, no, Cassidy cannot," Cassidy interrupts, leaning around Marcus. "Dude, I'm in all AP classes. I love you, but you're on your own. My class load is bonkers."

"I'm surrounded by geniuses," I mutter, picking at the crust of my sandwich. "Okay, fine, Killian. I'll allow you to tutor me."

"Oh, wow. Wow. Tan, did you hear that? She's going to *allow* me to tutor her. What an honor," Killian says sarcastically.

"Don't let this go to your head, Killian," Tanner warns with a grin.

"Okay, okay, carry on." I wave them on as they continue trolling me.

"For real though, do you have a second? I need to ask you something." Killian nods toward the doors leading to the outside lunchroom courtyard.

I shrug at Cassidy's curious stare and grab my bag to bring with me since lunch is almost over anyway.

Killian grabs it and slings it over his shoulder—a new habit he's picked up since he found me out on the field a week ago.

At the beginning of the year though, he, Tanner, and one other player started sitting inside, so they could eat fast and head to the field house to go over tapes from games. I used to be able to watch them through the doors.

So, of course, when his old lunch table sees him coming, they all perk up, excited to see him. It's when they see me peek out behind him that most of those grins drop—mainly on the cheerleaders' faces. I almost correct the jealous, knowing looks they send my way, but I don't.

Let them make their assumptions, especially if it keeps them away from me.

"Hey, Kills, you joining us for lunch?" one of the guys asks hopefully.

"No, I need the table. Move." Killian doesn't raise his voice as he says this, but the underlying steel has goose bumps crawling up my arms.

I nudge him with my shoulder, somewhat shocked by his rudeness. Everyone gets up from the table wordlessly, and the glares that are sent my way level up to outright hate.

"Don't look at her; look at me," Killian barks, seeming to grow larger in front of me so I'm completely hidden behind his massive back.

I wait until the door closes behind the last person before addressing him. "Jesus, Killian, that was a little harsh."

Killian leans against the table as I take a seat next to him.

"Really? You're defending those assholes?" His heavy brows lift in surprise.

"No, but—"

"I have no respect for people who have bullied you and gone through the amount of effort they did to hide it from me," Killian growls.

"But they were your friends," I point out softly.

"They were never my friends," Killian counters sharply before wiping his face in frustration. "That's not what I wanted to talk about, Glory."

Killian sits down next to me, back to the table so he's facing me. He pauses, uncertainty clear on his face, and I wave him on in impatience.

"I wanted to check on you because I know you're leaving for Atlanta, and ... I don't know." He pauses, jaw ticcing. "I just wanted to make sure ..."

My heart constricts painfully because I know what and why he's asking.

"It's been on my mind. I haven't visited her there, and I haven't seen her in months. I know it's stupid; Atlanta is a huge city, but I just worry about running into her. If she's eaten at a restaurant that I go to or if she's walked the same street. I'm so mad at her, but I—" I cut myself off, struggling to put into words everything running through my head. It's hard though when I don't even understand what I'm feeling myself.

"I haven't seen my dad in almost four years," Killian admits quietly, and I jerk in shock.

"Wait, what? I thought you saw him all the time! Do y'all talk?"

Killian focuses his intense attention on me, and I almost turn away from the emotion burning in his eyes.

"When my dad left my mom, I was a constant reminder of him to her. Listening to her cry killed me, Glory. She couldn't look at me for weeks. It didn't really endear my father to me."

"I get that; I'm my mother's twin," I tell him bitterly.

"I know," Killian says, and I hear him.

A buzzing fills my ears as everything starts to fall into place because, of course—*of course*—Killian would hate his reflection as much as I hate mine. He would do anything to protect his mother, as I would my dad.

I drop my head into my hands, groaning, "Killian, what the fuck has happened to us?"

His head drops to my shoulder, and he just breathes for a moment. I feel my throat constrict with emotion. God, the best intentions somehow always, always fuck things up.

"So, that's why I'm asking, Glory, because I get it. Have you unblocked me yet?" he asks, sitting back up.

I meet his gaze sheepishly. "No."

He rolls his eyes. "Unblock me."

"I will."

HARD FEELINGS

"Now, please." He lifts a brow when I still don't reach for my phone.

I don't want to explain to him that unblocking him will feel like the last brick in the wall I've built around myself, concerning him. It gives access … but maybe I don't need to worry about it anymore. Every day, I understand him a little more, and while our relationship will never be what it was, I can try.

I can at least try.

I pull out my phone and ignore him hovering over me as I click on his name, which I changed to Traitor. Killian snorts at the name as I unblock him.

"There. Happy?" I say a little combatively as I shove my phone back into my backpack.

"Thrilled," he says sarcastically. "You can call me if things get weird or if you want to talk."

"Since when did you become Oprah?"

"Can you stop being defensive for a single second?" Killian asks sharply.

I bristle even further, and seeing the fight on my face, Killian holds up his hands in surrender.

"Okay, listen, in the spirit of being vulnerable, I have something for you."

I eye him warily as he reaches into his backpack and pulls out a thick notebook.

He hands it to me quickly, and I notice his cheeks getting redder.

"Is this your diary, Killian King?" I tease lightly, holding on to it.

Cursing under his breath, he rubs his neck. "Sort of, and please refrain from giving me a hard time about this, but my mom said that if I want to repair this with you, I need to be honest."

Flabbergasted, I ask, "You talked to your mom about this?"

He nods. "And Tanner and Cassidy."

My eyebrows shoot up at that last one, and Killian laughs, embarrassed.

"Yeah, that went about as well as you're imagining. That girl loves you, Glory."

"I know." I swallow nervously. "Killian, you don't have to—"

"I do. I really do," he interrupts.

And seeing this giant guy look so earnest and self-conscious is the final crack in my wall.

"All right. Thank you."

"Listen, I've got to run, but call me, okay? I want to know how you are …" He hesitates and looks like he wants to reach for me but thinks better of it. Giving me a brief smile and an awkward wave, Killian leaves.

This is the Killian I know. The one who is deeply shy and caring, who can be awkward but so funny that he'll make you pee your pants. Who will do anything—*anything*—for those he loves.

69

It's why I've had such a hard time with how he acts and is perceived at school.

I open the journal to the first page and gasp.

Dear Glory ...

"Glory!" Cassidy says as she slams through the doors, startling me so badly that I almost fall off the bench. "What's that?"

"Nothing!" I say quickly, shoving the journal into my backpack.

"Uh-huh, really convincing."

"What's up?" I ask, standing up.

"We gotta go. Coach wants the girls' team to bring their bags to the locker room. She's checking for contraband." Cassidy wiggles her eyebrows.

"Ugh, okay."

We have fifteen minutes before our next class, and the locker rooms are all the way inside the gym.

After I stuff my bag in my locker, I sprint to the aforementioned Biology class, where I am barely skating by with a C. I stop in front of the classroom door and try to slow my breathing, so I don't walk into class, looking a mess. Cassidy continues speed-walking, shouting that she'll save me a seat on the bus. Her class is right by the pickup spot.

The final bell dings out as I enter the classroom. Ms. Fitz is writing on the whiteboard as I walk in and spots me before I can sneak to the back lab table.

"Miss Purcell, a minute?" Ms. Fitz asks, capping her marker and nodding to her desk in the corner.

Sighing, I follow her over, ignoring the curious stares from the rest of the kids. It's bad enough that I waited this late to take this class, as I've now got a bunch of juniors and a couple of sophomores in here with me, but to also need help with it? Ugh, embarrassing.

"I asked one of my AP students if they could help you out. You need to do well on this midterm, Glory, or I'll have to tell your coach you're not maintaining your average. You know we have to report your grades to UCLA in order to keep your scholarship."

"I know. Killian caught up with me at lunch."

I nervously twist my shirt as she smiles.

"Good! I'm sure he'll be a great help. Mr. King does extremely well in my class." She practically glows as she says this, and it takes Herculean effort not to roll my eyes.

HARD FEELINGS

"Okay," I drawl and make a move to leave.

"I know you won't let me down. Now, take a seat. We're studying organelles of plant cells today!"

"Yippee," I mutter as I make my way to my seat.

I slide into my seat and do my best to pay attention, but all I can think about is Killian's journal.

I don't know if he kept one before or if maybe this is something that started post our friendship breakup. What I do know is the absolute second I'm alone, I'll be reading it.

Eleven

The ride to Atlanta is less than two hours, and thankfully, my team is a great distraction. In seemingly no time at all, we arrive at the hotel, drop our bags in our shared room, and change into our Galway sweats before heading to the practice facility.

The manager greets us outside the building while Coach Yi and Coach Kent, the boys' coach, shush the excited chatter. A hum of energy seems to run just below the surface of my skin. I'm already constructing the fantasy of joining a professional team and coming to a place very similar to this one.

Cassidy loops her arm through mine as we follow the manager through the doors. "You've got stars in your eyes, Glory."

I squeeze her arm and let out a little squeak. "I've been dreaming about this trip since freshman year, dude."

My phone vibrates in my back pocket. Pulling it out, I see it's my dad, asking if we made it okay.

"Take a pic of us." I hand the phone to Cassidy since her arms are double the length of mine.

It's perfect because we're in the locker rooms with all the black, red, and gold.

Ugh, dream of dreams.

"Smile!" Cassidy grins at the camera, and I'm smiling so big that it's full-on Joker.

I hit Send to my dad and forward the pic to our group chat—a new experience for me since unblocking Killian.

Tanner responds first.

Look at y'all cheesin'.

Followed by Killian.

Glad you made it.

Okay, for a first text from him in years, it is a little underwhelming, but not everything has to be fraught with angst.

"Glory, come on. We're heading to the cardio room," Cassidy calls out as everybody exits.

Shoving my phone back into my pocket, I take one last look around, imagining what my own locker room will look like with my jersey hanging up. If little girls will take tours of the facility one day and take pictures in front of my jersey.

One day.

I hurry after everyone, and we enter a room with two rows of exercise bikes facing a giant window looking out onto the field.

God, this is so freaking cool.

"You're drooling." Marcus laughs quietly next to me.

"Don't mind me, just imagining my future." I laugh lightly, not at all embarrassed to be gawking.

"I see it for you, Glo. Maybe it's because since you were little, you were walking around, talking about *when* you play professionally, as if it were a foregone conclusion," he teases.

"Hey, visualization and speaking it into existence is a thing." I shrug, eyeing Cassidy as she hops onto a bike, only for Coach Yi to hiss at her to get off. Chuckling at her antics, I nod her way to Marcus. "How's it going, Romeo?"

He groans. "Dude, I'm so far gone on her, and she won't give me the time of day. It's getting embarrassing. I think it's time to call it."

I consider this.

"You're going to hate me for agreeing, but maybe it's time. Us spending more time together and you outright letting her know you want to go out with her haven't been working."

He nods, his shoulders sinking. "Yeah."

Seeing the sad look on his face has me hugging him. "I'm sorry, Marcus. I love you both and want you to be happy, but she's made it clear. You shouldn't continue to put yourself in the position of hurting yourself. And who knows? Maybe you moving on will spur her into action."

"Yeah, just what everyone wants. Someone to want them the second they stop giving them attention. Super healthy."

Wincing, I give him one more squeeze before releasing him. "You're going to find someone who appreciates you. I just know it."

"What about you?"

HARD FEELINGS

I laugh mockingly. "Marcus, I'm persona non grata. I've given up on the idea of dating anyone in Galway. Saving all that for college, I guess."

"How about this? If you're still single by prom, you and I will go together."

"Lord, has it come to this? A singles pact?"

"Don't turn your nose up at it. We'll have fun together. What do you say?" He holds his hand out to shake on it.

"Okay, you've got a deal, but just know, you'll probably be third-wheeling with Cassidy and me," I warn him while grasping his hand.

"We can go as a group. Band all the singles together. It'll be a protest." He laughs. "But I'll do the stupid photos with you and get you a corsage if you want."

"Stop. Your enthusiasm is overwhelming," I murmur sarcastically.

"Glory!" Cassidy calls out from across the room as everyone starts to leave. She eyes Marcus and me shaking hands before nodding her head toward the exit.

Marcus and I chat about UCLA as we head out to the stands, where we can watch the practice. He ditches me for his friends, and I grab the seat Cassidy saved for me.

"What was that all about?" she murmurs, sliding her sunglasses on.

Grabbing the hat I snuck into her bag before we left the hotel, I slap it on. It's definitely cooling off, but sitting in direct sunlight still sucks.

"Nothing, just chatting about school."

"Hmm," Cassidy hums skeptically, but I'm already zoning out as my attention is drawn to the action on the field.

I know most of us wish we could be down there, playing with them, but I'm happy to just sit here and watch. Their feet are so fast, the agility and speed, the freaking endurance … I'm just in awe.

Cassidy snickers, and then my phone vibrates. Distractedly, I pull my phone out and see that she sent something in the group chat.

"Oh God, what did you do?"

"Just capturing visual evidence of your lady boner."

The photo of me she sent has me leaning forward, elbows on my knees and my attention totally focused on the men on the field. Okay, yes, I do look thirsty. My cheeks are flushed, my hair unruly under my hat, and, yeah, I wish it were a better angle.

And, of course, Cassidy sent it with three water drop emojis.

"Dude, why would you send that to your brother and Killian? Ugh," I groan.

"I just think you look cute, all intense, and maybe others should see it."

"Who? Tanner?"

"Ah, yes, the obvious choice." Cassidy nods.

I lean back in my chair, arms crossed defensively. "What are you suggesting, Cassidy? That Killian would care?"

"I think Killian cares a lot. Like *a lot*, a lot." Her phone buzzes, and she cackles when reading the text. "And there's proof."

Suddenly feeling like I'm going to puke, I lean over to see her screen.

"Look, he texted me privately and asked who you were looking at like that. I'm telling you!" she squeals.

"Cassidy, we're just trying to be friends," I protest even if the thought of him getting even a little jealous does fill me with a modicum of joy.

The schadenfreude kind.

"Glory, you know I love you, but come on."

"Cassidy, you know I love *you*, but worry about your own love life," I reply sharply.

She puts her hands up in surrender before continuing to text. I go back to focusing on the practice below, but I'm aware of her texting the entire time.

Later, when we're back in the hotel room after dinner, Cassidy and I each shower and chill on our beds. Any plans to sneak out were ended the second Coach Yi said whoever went out would be benched every game until the holiday break.

There's no way I'm risking that.

I'm polishing off some Wendy's fries from dinner, silently praying Cassidy falls asleep soon so I can sneak Killian's journal out of my bag. It's across the room, taunting me right now, when all I want to do is clutch it to my chest like a little freak.

"Want the rest? I think I'm done for the night." Cassidy yawns loudly and tosses her bag of fries over to me before spooning the last bit of her Frosty into her mouth. A Frosty with fries is one of our friendship traditions.

Watching her turn her reading lamp off and flop onto her stomach, I wonder silently if I'm a witch and I have a super gift for manifesting.

Snickering at myself, I turn the volume of the TV down. Cassidy falls asleep in under ten minutes, so I know I've got to kill some time. Grabbing my phone, I flip onto my side, away from Cassidy, and open Instagram.

Late-night scrolling is a horrible habit, but as someone always seemingly on the outside, it's been my only way in for so long. Cassidy reads me the riot act about this often, and she's right. I know she is. People only post the best version of themselves. It's not real; it's curated.

HARD FEELINGS

But sometimes, the smallest voice inside me wins, and I wonder if she only says that to make me feel better.

This time though, instead of the lack of notifications, I see thirty-seven. Momentarily shocked because my phone is usually dryer than the Sahara, I click on the notifications and see that Killian has liked every picture I shared. Thirty-seven photos aren't a lot, especially compared to other kids I know, but I'm more of a lurker than participator online.

Feeling embarrassed and grossly happy about it, I send him a direct message.

You bored?

It doesn't take long to see those three dots jumping. I grip my phone tighter, heading into more unchartered territory with him.

Oh, the opposite. So many pictures of soccer practice to like, so little time.

I snort at his sarcasm. He's right though. I don't really share much else than soccer stuff.

Didn't you have a game tonight?

I'm on the bus home now.

Oh.

I stare at my phone, a little lost as to how to carry on a conversation with him. With Tanner or Marcus, it's easy. There aren't years of bad history we're trying to overcome, so there's that, but it shouldn't be this hard, right?

I can practically feel you overthinking through the phone.

Don't you find it weird? I feel like I don't know how to talk to you anymore.

I'm just happy you're talking to me at all. We'll get there, Glory. Just keep talking to me.

I change the subject to somewhat safer topics.

Did you win?

I wait a few minutes, staring at my phone, but he doesn't reply. Glancing at the time, then at Cassidy, I realize it's safe to grab his journal.

I tiptoe to my bag, grab it, then climb into bed. Clicking the flashlight on my phone, I huddle under my covers and open it to the first page.

Dear Glory,

I have so much hate inside me. Hate for my dad, hate for your mom, but most of all, hate for myself. You wouldn't understand. In fact, I know you don't because I've never explained it. I just shut you out.

Our first day of freshman year was something we talked about constantly, and I did my absolute best to ruin it for you. Not walking to school together, ignoring you in the halls, tripping you at lunch, and laughing as you fell on your lunch tray. Ruining your new outfit, one I knew you and Cassidy had spent hours picking out.

When you started to cry and Cassidy cussed me out, I walked away a lot calmer than I really felt. Tanner followed me, shouting at me, confused by how I was acting, but I didn't answer. I went directly to the restroom and threw up. I fell apart in that stall with Tanner holding me together. I begged him to understand, to watch out for you when I couldn't. He was so angry with me, Glory.

I hope I can explain why one day, but I don't think I'll get the chance.

Breathing sharply through my nose, I try to stave off the tears. I remember that day vividly. I begged my dad for money I knew we didn't have so I could have a cute first-day outfit. He gave me some money, not enough to buy anything new, but enough to get a full outfit from the thrift shop.

Cassidy and I spent hours sifting through multiple shops, begging her mom to drive us closer to the city to the rich neighborhoods so we could shop their castoffs. I was so proud of that outfit; I felt confident for the first time in ages after everything went down. I felt like I was walking into the school with armor, and he destroyed it so easily, laughing as he did so.

It was the first time I'd ever experienced anything other than love from him, and it devastated me. It set the tone for the years to come and let everyone know I was fair game.

That familiar embarrassment and rage come over me. I don't know what Killian hoped to accomplish by reminding me of all this shit he had done to me, but at this moment, I can't read any more, and I don't want to talk to him for the rest of the weekend.

I close his journal and shove it in my backpack. Turning off the bedside lamp, I wipe my face and try to remember I'm not that girl anymore, but she's still inside me, and she's so hurt.

HARD FEELINGS

As much as I'd like to say I've moved on or I refuse to let this affect me anymore, some scars are so deep that the ache never leaves you. I'm so tired of holding on to this, but I don't know how to forgive.

Twelve

I wake up, feeling conflicted but happy for the distraction of the day. We head down to the hotel dining area for the free breakfast. This is my second time in a hotel, but it's something I found to be the coolest thing ever when I was younger. Grabbing a yogurt and a banana—I don't want Coach coming after me for nutrition—to go with my waffle, I sit with Cassidy and Tia.

"What's the plan for today?" Cassidy asks over a mouthful of cereal.

"Coach says we have to load our luggage in the van before we head out. Checkout is at eleven, so before that …" Tia murmurs, half-asleep over her muffin.

"I was thinking of walking along the Beltline and then meeting everyone over at Hard Rock," I share.

"It's embarrassing that we're going to eat at Hard Rock; we're not tourists," Cassidy grumbles.

I snicker. She's a bit of a food snob.

Tia wakes up. "It's close to the stadium, and it has something for everyone."

"At least it's not The Varsity," Cassidy concedes, and I laugh full out.

The first time we came to the city together, she was so intent on trying The Varsity but ended up getting sick off it for the rest of the day.

She was so sick that we left early, and she still gags at the sight of hot dogs.

"Fine, I'm down to meander. I think the boys are heading to Ponce City Market to stare at girls. Happy to miss that. I'll spread the word." Tia stands up, already texting the team, and heads up to her room.

I continue eating my way through breakfast, lost in thought.

"You're quiet this morning." Cassidy leans back in her chair.

"I'm quiet every morning," I point out.

"What were you reading last night?" Cassidy asks casually.

I inhale sharply in surprise and start to cough as I choke down a piece of waffle.

Blinking furiously, I croak, "A book."

She gives me a *yeah, no shit* look and says, "Given your reaction, I'm assuming it's spicy. Are you finally reading that enemies-to-lovers book I recommended to you forever ago?"

Considering her, I decide to tell her the truth. If I tell Cassidy that this goes into the vault, she'll die with this secret.

"It's, um ..." I clear my throat. "It's Killian's journal."

Cassidy's eyes widen. "Excuse me? Mr. Tall, Dark, and Pissy keeps a journal? Are you sure you even want to read it?"

"Cassidy, this stays in the vault, okay? The only reason I'm telling you this is because I don't have anyone to process it with."

"I mean, you could process this with Killian since he wrote it," Cassidy counters in a moment of blunt criticism.

"I don't trust him yet, Cassidy."

"He's letting you into his deepest thoughts and feelings. I know I'm safe, but I really think if you want to move past this, you need to talk to him."

She's right. I know she is, but—

"And you don't know how badly I want to know what's in that journal, Glory. Let me tell you, being responsible right now is killing me, but I really think y'all need to figure this out together."

Sighing, I sink my head into my hands, and she scoots away from the table and picks up her trash.

"You coming?" she asks.

"I'll be there in a minute."

Grabbing my phone, I open my messages with Killian. Thumbs hovering, I chew my lip, struggling to put into words what I'm feeling.

How was the game?

I roll my eyes at myself. I'm going to ease into this. I mean, it's eight in the morning. No need to just open with, *Hey, I read the first entry in your journal, and it stirred up all the anger and shame I'd thought I shrugged off years ago, so thanks for that.*

My phone begins to vibrate, startling the hell out of me, and I nearly throw it across the room when I see it's Killian calling.

Bucking up my courage, I answer, "Okay, aggressive much?"

"Calling people is aggressive now?" Killian's humor-filled voice rumbles in my ear. He continues before I can answer, "And to answer your text, we won. Scouts were there, too, and I played really well."

HARD FEELINGS

He says all this matter-of-factly, like he's reporting the weather. It's odd because the Killian I know spoke with passion about football. He's the only person who got my love of soccer.

"Why do you sound weird?" I blurt out.

"Glory, the absolute last thing I want to talk about is my game when you've had my journal in your hands."

Wanting a more private space for this conversation, I tell him to hold on and head outside to the courtyard and curl up on one of the loungers by the pool.

"I told Cassidy, but she said I need to talk to you about how it made me feel."

Killian's quiet for a moment, and I wonder if he's pissed. "And how did it make you feel?"

I bite my lip to stop the awkward, uncomfortable laugh that wants to escape, but when Killian snickers, the dam breaks, and I giggle.

"Are you my therapist now?"

"Shut up." He laughs and then falls silent, clearly waiting for my answer.

Clearing my throat, I decide to leap. "I felt angry and embarrassed all over again. Shame and sadness. Frustration because I'd thought I moved on from this." Swallowing convulsively, I whisper, "I'm so pissed at you, Killian."

"I handled this so badly. I don't think you'll ever forgive me, and it's killing me, Glory. I feel like I can't breathe from what I allowed to happen to us," he whispers hoarsely, and I close my eyes, cheeks wet because I don't know what to say.

"I'm trying," I tell him.

"I know." He sighs heavily. "What time will you be home?"

The game is at one o'clock, and we've got almost a two-hour drive after that.

"Probably around dinnertime. Why?"

"Want to run with me tonight?"

I don't even have to think about it. "Yes."

"Keep reading, Glory. Keep talking to me about it, no matter how you feel. I want to know. Promise?"

"Promise."

The afternoon flies by in a whirlwind of excitement. The feel of seeing a game live, surrounded by close to seventy thousand fans, is an energy I cannot describe. It feels like fire in my veins, adrenaline and wonder, all wrapped up in my love of this game.

I've never felt more determined to have this for myself.

I'm exhilarated by the time we get on the bus; if the chatter from the rest of my team and the boys is any indication, I'm not the only one walking away stupidly in love.

It's not the same feeling as playing—nothing will ever beat that— whether I have a crowd of ten or ten thousand, but it's close.

I want to call Killian right now and try to describe it, knowing I'll fail to really put it into words, but he'll get it anyway. He was the one who always had the words to describe how I felt.

My mom used to call him my translator.

I settle into my seat near the window toward the back of the bus, and Cassidy drops down next to me and starts chatting with Kimmy, one of our defenders. Now that she knows about the journal and is uninterested, I don't feel weird about reading it in front of her.

Reaching into my backpack, I pull it out and tug my headphones out as well. I cue up the playlist Cassidy made me, called Glory's Pacifier. She thinks she's funny. It's filled with angsty, emotional music—which, again, does a better job of naming what I feel than I ever could—and I settle in.

> *Hey, Glory.*
>
> *Today was the first game of yours I didn't attend—at least officially— since you started playing your first year here.*
>
> *I wonder if you felt my absence. I fucking did.*
>
> *I did come though; you just didn't see me. I was on our rock. You were nothing but a speck from that height, but I'd know where you were with my eyes closed. Do you feel the same way?*
>
> *I sound pathetic. I know you'd make fun of me if you could read how sappy I sound, but you won't ever read this. I think you'll hate me forever. I've made sure of it.*
>
> *Your hair was in a ponytail, and it flew behind you like a blonde flag. I followed it down the field as you made your first attempt at a goal. The cheer that rose up told me you were successful, but I had known you would be.*

HARD FEELINGS

I miss keeping my hands busy with your hair, Glory.

Now, my hands are empty with only a memory of the weight of it, heavy with curls, and the sound of you whispering your hopes for the future echoes in my ears.

Ah fuck, I need to stop.

Closing my eyes, I try to breathe through the rush of emotion. My heart squeezes as I suppress the tears that want to come.

This is not the place, Glory. Suck it up.

I can feel his heartache.

Once I'm under control, I turn to the next entry. The date indicates it was the summer before our sophomore year.

Glory,

I don't know if I've ever really understood envy until now. I know that makes me sound like a prick, but I've never wanted something I couldn't have before.

Until you.

Now, I find myself envious of your friendship with Cassidy. Wishing it were me you told all your secrets to. I don't know when it changed; I thought I was good at hiding my feelings for you, but my mom knows me well, and when everything went down, then came an obvious reminder. Her for him. You for me. And no one for my mom.

Those first nights after they left were horrible. I'd never heard my mom cry before. It was disconcerting to see someone who was so strong, such a solid presence in my life, crumble.

It's hard enough that every time I look in the mirror, I see him, but knowing she does too ... it kills me. Every tiny flinch when she sees me feels like a sucker punch.

I felt a lot of self-hatred in the beginning. I know she tried to hide it, to separate me from him, but I saw the look in her eyes.

She resents my feelings for you, the obvious longing I have when she sees me look toward your house. A habit every time I leave or come back, always checking to see if you are home.

Something she used to smile over, like a secret she only knew, has turned into an accusation.

"You're just like him," it says.

I can't be him, Glory. Do you understand? I can't.

God, Killian.
I do understand. I get it. God!
What did he think I saw every time I looked in the mirror?
Pausing "My Enemy" by CHVRCHES, I snort at how appropriate that song is.
You know what? I'm going to text him.

I wish you had talked to me. Why didn't you just talk to me, Killian?!

"Damn, dude, what are you going to do? That boy is in love with you."

Startled, I slam the book shut and turn to find Cassidy with her head resting near mine, clearly having read everything I just did.

"I thought you were being responsible?"

"I gave you solid advice, but I'm only so strong. I mean, you're reading it right next to me. My eyes fell on the page. They just straight-up betrayed me, and next thing I knew, I was reading."

"Cassidy," I groan, knocking my head against the headrest. "What the hell am I going to do with him?"

"What's stopping you from forgiving him? Not for his sake, but for yours?"

I try to put it into words. "I've held on to this anger for so long; it's become a form of safety for me. The idea of letting it go, being vulnerable again ..."

"Babe, it takes a lot less energy to love someone than to hate them. And you are working so hard to hate him. Vulnerability is not weakness; it's strength. And besides, if you forgive him, it's not like everything will go back to normal, but it will give you a starting point to rebuild, if that's what you want."

I turn to look at her, shocked. "How did you get so smart?"

Cassidy laughs bitterly. "From the errors of others."

Grabbing her hand sympathetically, I lean my head on her shoulder.

People walk around, weaponizing their pain, like the person who wounded them is the only victim, but there are always unintended casualties, and more often than not, it's the people you vowed never to harm who end up hurt the most.

Thirteen

Dad is waiting at the pickup spot at school when our bus pulls in, happily waving at me like I just got back from war.

Laughing sheepishly, I wave back. He's such a dork; I love him so much.

"Tanner wants to take the boat out tomorrow. Want to come?" Cassidy asks as she grabs her duffel from above.

"Are y'all fishing?" I scoot out after her.

"He is. I'm going to be reading, but come hang. It's peaceful on the water, and you didn't go out with us much this summer after you got back from camp. It's going to be cold soon—"

Laughing, I cut her off, "Dude, you don't have to sell it. I'm in."

"Cool. I'll text you when I'm on my way. Around ten-ish?"

"Sounds good," I agree, and we bump knuckles before she heads toward her mom.

Dad is so excited that he's practically bouncing on his heels. "How was it? Tell me everything."

He grabs my bag from me and throws it into the back of our truck as I get in.

I talk the entire way home, doing my best to describe everything, how it's charged something inside me. I'm not even worried about playing after my injury anymore. Coach even commented that if I perform well enough at practice this week, I will start at Friday's game.

It's like I needed the reminder of how much I love the game, enough to overcome every fear I've had about losing it or not being good enough. If I can just remind myself of how it feels to play, it'll chase away doubts.

And, yes, I can clearly see the parallels between this and Killian. My inner dialogue is not subtle.

Dad tells me he went to Killian's game and sat with Elizabeth, much to my absolute shock. Mainly because the only time Dad shows up at public events like that is for my games, and even then, I know it costs him.

"Really?"

"Yeah," he admits sheepishly and runs his hands up and down the steering wheel nervously. "She came over Friday night and asked me if I wanted to join her."

Utterly flabbergasted, I practically yell, "Are y'all dating?"

Dad barks a laugh and looks at me incredulously. "No, Glory. We're friends. We have a lot in common, as you can imagine."

Laughing lightly at his sarcasm, I relax a little. "Are you, like ... okay?"

"Like, I am," he responds, clearly laughing at me.

"Dad, stop. This is wild." I sink back into my seat.

"With you and Killian on your way back to being friends, we wanted to ... I don't know ... make sure we weren't causing issues too. I've seen how hard it's been for you."

Ha, if you only knew.

"And Elizabeth knows she's messed up too. It's nice to be able to talk to someone who understands, you know?"

Actually, I don't know ...

"Is this going to be weird for you?" he asks, worried at my silence, and I turn to look at him.

"I am sincerely okay with this. I really mean that. It's just that a lot is changing again, and I'm trying to keep up."

We pull into the driveway, and the catalyst for all this upheaval is standing at the end of it. Sucking in a breath, I can't believe it's only been twenty-four hours.

Killian's legs are braced, arms crossed, like he's about to go fight, and to be honest, maybe he is. My emotions seem to have a hair trigger these days.

His black athletic shorts and plain white T-shirt set off his black hair and honey-colored skin. Killian has a beautiful skin tone, thanks to his Brazilian father. His stern expression though? That's all Elizabeth.

Considering how I've ignored the buzzing of my phone for the last hour or so, I can't say I blame him.

"Are you going somewhere?" Dad asks, looking at Killian curiously.

"For a run. I'll be home for dinner though. Want me to bring a pizza?" I ask, shooting for nonchalance, like Killian showing up at our house is commonplace.

Dad gives me a thumbs-up before exiting the car and smacks a hand on Killian's shoulder as he passes, carting my bag inside.

I sit in the car for another minute. I'm not technically being a chicken ... okay, I'm fully being a chicken.

Killian raises a brow, as if to say, *Are you coming?*

HARD FEELINGS

Sighing loud enough for him to hear me, I get out of the truck.

"Did your phone die?" he asks as I make my way toward him. "I'm guessing by the way you're walking toward me, like I'm about to scold you, it didn't."

I shrug, struggling to say something.

Killian gives me a break and nods toward the house. "Hurry up and change. I'll be on the back deck."

I hurry upstairs and grab some Nike running shorts and a hoodie. There's enough of a chill in the air that the hoodie is necessary. Shrugging it over my sports bra, I throw my hair up quickly, grab some socks, and meet Killian downstairs on the deck to slip my shoes on.

Belatedly, I realize I didn't check a mirror to see how I looked. That thought is quickly followed by one wondering why I would care. This is Killian.

And maybe that is why ...

"Were you waiting long?" I ask, slipping into my beat-up running shoes.

Killian's staring at my hoodie, and I glance down, realizing it's the Galway High JV Football hoodie he received after making it through early tryouts in eighth grade. He let me borrow it when we went to see a movie, and I meant to give it back, but then ... everything happened.

"You still have it," he says, a little astonished.

"Yeah, I ..." I stop myself from apologizing like a weirdo and shrug.

"I would have thought you'd put it on an effigy and burned it." He reaches down to pull me up beside him.

"I was tempted, believe me. I had it all planned. I'd steal a dummy from the thrift shop a town over. Dress it up, build a raft, and send it off on the lake, Viking funeral style."

Killian's lip twitches at my dramatics, and I give him a small smile back.

"What changed your mind?" he asks, tugging on the strings near my neck.

Heat rushes through my cheeks at his proximity, and I blurt out, "Is this you flirting?"

Killian's eyebrows shoot up in surprise before he lets loose a slow smile. I wonder if his ... yep, there go his stupid dimples. When we were little, I was so obsessed with his dimples, jealous of them really, that I used to stick my thumbs in them and grab his cheeks.

I was a weird kid. And why am I thinking about this right now? My cheeks burn with embarrassment.

His stupid grin spreads wider. "No, this is not me flirting. When I flirt with you, you'll know."

"Why? Because you're so good at it?" I grouse, grabbing the hoodie strings out of his hands and taking a step back.

He tugs at the end of my ponytail instead, rubbing the strands, before he lets it go and looks back at me.

"No, it'll be because there won't be any misunderstanding of my intentions with you, Glory. But we aren't there yet."

"What's that supposed to mean?" I demand.

"Are we running, or are we talking?" he asks, jogging down the stairs.

Grumbling, I jump off the deck after him. He sets a mild pace, easy for me to follow. I know he could go much faster, but he's adjusting his pace because of my much shorter legs.

For someone so big, he's incredibly light on his feet.

He guides us along a familiar path, one I've run countless times, around the lake and through the woods. We have just enough light left for it to be safe. It's the same route I ran when he mowed me down all those weeks ago.

We run in comfortable silence, my breath syncing with his, and I let my mind drift.

Before long, I realize where we're heading—toward our rock. I haven't been up here with him in years.

He slows as we break through the tree line and reach the rock. It's a giant piece of limestone that sits at the edge of one of the foothills surrounding our school. Up here, you can see the entire town laid out in front of you. Our school is on the left. Staring down at it makes me think of Killian up here, watching me play.

Killian speeds up a bit and leaps up before turning and offering a hand. Grabbing on to him, I let him pull me up next to him, and we sit. We stretch our legs out, catching our breaths, and stare down at Galway.

"How often did you come here?" I ask quietly, thinking of his journal entry.

"Every time you had a game and I didn't." He exhales sharply.

Rubbing my chest over my heart, I blink away the sting. "Killian, all this wasted time."

"Glory, I know I hurt you. I know I did. But I was hurting myself just as badly."

"I can appreciate that you think so, but it's different, Killian. The entire town turned on Dad and me. My high school experience has been a nightmare. Those are memories I'll never get back. And you—" I take a deep breath. "You stole my best friend away. You were everything to me— *everything*—and you took that away from me at the worst possible time. I needed you so badly—" I'm cut off as the words get caught in my throat and Killian makes a gruff sound before picking me up and setting me on his lap.

I cry for the first time in years, letting out all the pain I've been holding on to. It's ugly and loud, the pain so large that it feels like I can't catch my breath.

HARD FEELINGS

Killian continues to rock me, his cheek on my head, whispering that he's sorry over and over. I can feel his tears on my hair, but I can't stop. I cry for the kids we were and the adults we had to become too early. I cry at the injustice of all of it, the pain we caused each other and ourselves.

I let out the anger, shame, and utter devastation at being let down by the people I loved most, knowing I'm finally safe to do so.

I don't know how long we sit there as we grieve, but when I finally finish, exhausted, I return his hug. He shifts me so we're hugging more comfortably, and I squeeze him so hard that he grunts, breathing him in without a single ounce of embarrassment.

"No more," I whisper against his skin.

"No more," he whispers back, relief in his tone.

After some time, I crawl off his lap and sit comfortably next to him, leaning on his shoulder.

We're quiet as we watch the sun set.

Once it sinks behind the mountain, Killian stands and pulls me up into one more hug, holding me tightly, but not enough to hurt my ribs.

"I'm still going to read the rest of your journal," I warn him as he lets me go and hops down off our rock.

He laughs and turns his back to face me. "Want a ride?"

Smiling because I've missed his piggyback rides, I eagerly hop onto his back. He barely moves as I latch on to him like a spider monkey.

"Are you going to be able to carry me all the way back?" I cross my feet around his waist and rest my chin on his shoulder.

Killian snorts. "Don't insult me."

"I'm bigger than I used to be and mostly muscle now."

"So am I," he counters, and I giggle.

"Did you know your mom and my dad are buddies now?"

"Good," Killian says firmly.

"Good? You don't think it's weird?"

"No, I think it's nice. They have each other now."

His words echo my dad's, and I sigh, letting it go.

"Yeah …"

"My birthday is coming up," he says conversationally, and I tense slightly. "What about it, King?"

"Tanner is throwing me a party."

"And you want me to come?" I frown, not really a party person.

"You're the only one I want there."

"Ugh, Killian, don't beg. It's embarrassing … for you," I tease.

He pretends to drop me, eliciting a squeal, and laughs loudly. God, I missed his laugh.

"Come on, Glory. I know you don't like parties, but I want you there."

"Fine, fine."

"Are you going to hang with Tanner and Cassidy tomorrow? Tanner told me he and Cass were going out onto the lake." Killian asks after a moment, and, yeah, he's not out of breath.

In fact, feeling his body move under mine is doing weird, confusing things to me.

"Glory?" he prompts, and I drag my mind out of the gutter.

"Yeah, I'll be there," I confirm softly, staring off toward the house lights peeking through the trees as we approach the beach.

"I can drive us."

"Cassidy has me."

Killian's shoulders stiffen at my answer.

"Killian, why is that a problem?"

When he doesn't answer, I wiggle until he sets me down, and I turn him so I can see his face.

I flick his nose playfully. "Talk to me."

Rolling his shoulders, he sighs heavily, "I don't want things to go back to the way they were tomorrow."

Understanding dawning, I tug his shirt until he leans down so we're eye to eye. "You have to trust me too, Killian."

His lips twitch at my stern tone, and I narrow my eyes so he knows I'm being serious.

He rubs my hair affectionately before standing up straight. "Okay."

We reach the point where the path splits.

"I'll see you tomorrow, okay?" I walk backward, his silhouette darkened by the sinking sun behind him.

"Night, Glory," Killian says but doesn't head home.

Glancing over my shoulder, I see he's still watching me as I head out of sight.

Rubbing my chest, I realize more might have changed tonight than I'm prepared for.

FOURTEEN

Yesterday was the first day that I fully relaxed in years. The four of us out on the water was normalcy I hadn't had in so long. It was like no time had passed at all. Tan and Cassidy bickered constantly. Killian was right next to me, always touching some part of me. Whether it was his knee knocking into mine, his hand messing with the ends of my hair, or his arm slung around my shoulders.

I could practically feel the anxiety coming off of him, though he pretended to be just as relaxed as everyone else.

Cassidy, of course, kept giving me crazy eyes. I'd filled her in somewhat when I got home after the run, but I don't know that I could have predicted Killian's behavior.

He acted like I might disappear right in front of him, even insisting on driving me home from the lake later that afternoon.

Speaking of which, this morning, I can already hear him downstairs with my dad.

I grab my phone and text Cassidy.

Hey, Killian is here. I guess he's taking me to school???

Cassidy texts back immediately.

Yeah, dude. Apparently, old bestie was ready to duel the new bestie over this one. I decided to let it go since I'm shipping y'all.

Jesus. Shooting her an eye roll emoji, I shove my phone in the back pocket of my jeans and grab my Galway High hoodie before jogging downstairs.

Sure enough, Killian is sitting at the kitchen island with my dad. They chat easily with each other, and it's a scene that, if the few years hadn't happened, would have been a given.

Of course Killian is at my kitchen table. Where else would he be?

"Uh-oh, plotting against me first thing in the morning, Glory?" Killian grins as I come into the kitchen, noticing my eyes narrowed at him.

"Sorry." I smirk, grabbing my smoothie out of the fridge. "Habit."

"I'm so glad you kids are hanging out again. I know Glory has missed you something fierce, Killian."

"Ugh, Dad, come on," I groan, pulling the hood of my sweatshirt down past my eyes.

Killian grabs my sleeve and pulls me to his side. "Don't be embarrassed, Glory Jane. I promise I missed you more."

Feeling unsettled at his honesty, I groan louder and shrug Killian off so I can grab the rest of my breakfast.

Glancing at Dad sheepishly, I notice a slight reddening in his eyes, and I turn away at his blatant emotion. I know he feels guilty, not that he should, about Killian and me.

Uncomfortable, I grab my backpack and nod toward Killian. "We gotta go. I have a study group before homeroom."

Killian stands up from where he was leaning against the counter and follows me out toward the door.

"Oh, hey, Glory? I have a job down in Dahlonega, so I might be late, picking you up after practice."

"Don't worry, Dad. I'll catch a ride with Marcus. I've got something to talk with him about, anyway," I call out as I head outside.

Killian stiffens beside me at the mention of Marcus, and I frown at him.

"What?" I ask, opening the passenger door and attempting to haul myself into the seat. "Jeez, Killian. Did you have to get it lifted too? I feel like I need a ladder."

Killian snickers behind me and grabs my hips, helping me into his car.

Closing the door, I watch him walk around to the driver's side, eyeing how he shrugs his shoulders like he's shaking something off.

"I can take you home," Killian says quietly as he starts the car.

Tugging my seat belt on, I shake my head. "You'll still be at practice. Besides, Marcus and I need to discuss what we're doing for senior night. We both signed up to plan it this year."

"That's not happening for months."

Shrugging, I plug my phone in so I can bring up Spotify while we drive to school.

"Marcus is taking me home," I repeat firmly.

I'm not doing this coddling shit. He's going to have to trust me when I say we're okay. Gluing himself to my side is not the same as trusting me.

HARD FEELINGS

Killian growls under his breath, clearly annoyed.

"Moving on," I continue, settling on my morning playlist and turning the volume low enough so we can chat. "What're the details for your party?"

"My house after the game. I already told Tanner it can't get wild or go late; I have game tape to review the following morning."

"Killian, it's your eighteenth birthday; shouldn't you allow yourself to let go a little?"

I study him from the passenger seat. He's got one hand loose on top of the wheel; the other is resting on the gearshift. He appears at ease at first glance, but I notice the whites of his knuckles as he grips the gearshift. I see the muscle jump in his jaw.

"Killian," I prompt.

"I don't want all those fake fucks celebrating my birthday when they went out of their way to ostracize you. They hurt you, Glory." Emotion bursts out of him, and I'm a little taken aback.

Killian has always been demonstrative, but I've never seen him so angry.

Grabbing his hand, I squeeze it tightly. "Fuck them, Killian. They don't get any more of you. Stop giving them energy. If you don't want them there, don't have them there."

"You say it like it's simple."

" 'Cause it is," I say wryly. "It's amazing how unburdened your life is when you care only about the opinions of those who truly love you. Starve the haters and clout chasers."

Killian shoots me a lopsided smile, looking so ridiculously gorgeous. I blink a few times, startled. I've been noticing it more and more. I mean, I knew he was hot, but it was something I always thought of spitefully. Never in appreciation and certainly not actually finding myself thinking he was attractive in a way that could affect me.

Killian pulls into the senior parking lot and gives me a funny look. "You okay? You went quiet."

I open my mouth to respond, but screeching tires cut me off. Megan Thee Stallion blares as Cassidy pulls in beside us, grinning from ear to ear. Tanner, miserable, sits low in the passenger seat, clearly wishing he were anywhere else.

"She drives like a maniac," Killian grumbles as Cassidy hops out and yanks my door open.

"Morning!" she sings and grabs my backpack so I can jump down. "Jesus, Kills, didn't really think through the lift kit for when you'd be driving our little pixie around, huh?"

"I thought about the fact that I'm six-five and growing," he says dryly, coming around the rear of the car.

Tanner comes over and rubs my head affectionately. "Killian told me you're partying with us on Friday."

Cassidy spins toward me, surprised. "You are?"

I shrug my backpack on, slightly uncomfortable with everyone's undivided attention. "Yeah. I mean, I don't know if we have the same definition of partying, but I plan to show up."

"Spend the night with me. We can leave early and have a girls' night. Then, I can take us to conditioning on Saturday."

I bump knuckles with Cassidy and say a quick good-bye as I head to the library for my study group.

The rest of the day and week fly by as we prep for midterms, and before I know it, it's Friday, and I'm heading to Cassidy's with my overnight bag.

She takes one look at the sleeveless, cropped white Nike tank top, oversize green flannel I stole from my dad, and slightly baggy jeans that show a sliver of my stomach and groans.

"This is your first high school party, and you look like you're going to see a Nirvana cover band. You kill me."

I glance down at myself and shrug. I'm comfortable.

I roll my shoulders as I follow her upstairs. The tension in them and the tingling on the back of my head are hinting at something that I would really rather ignore.

"Hey, do you think I could put a little blush on you? You look a kinda pale." Cassidy's eyebrows draw together as she leans closer. "Wait, are you okay?"

"I feel a migraine coming on. I'm just going to pop half a dose of Excedrin and drink some electrolytes. It'll knock it on its ass."

I throw my bag on the end of her bed.

"Are you sure? We can skip tonight and just chill here."

That is probably the best move, but I don't want to miss this. Not only because it's Killian's birthday party, but also because it's one of the high school experiences I've yet to have.

"I'm sure."

The medicine and the sports drink dull the oncoming pain enough that I'm not really worried anymore. I'm tired of these headaches ruining things for me.

Cassidy finally gives up on trying to get me to change my clothes and does some light makeup on me. I leave my hair down, mainly because anything pulling on my scalp right now is a really bad idea.

HARD FEELINGS

Same with the perfume, instead going for the tantalizing scents of deodorant and the peppermint oil I always keep on hand. Rubbing it on my temples and inside my wrists, I pray I can at least hang for an hour.

"You smell like Christmas." Cassidy grabs my hand as we head downstairs to get something to eat before the game. "What are you feeling?"

"Can we just get something on the way?" I need the familiarity of riding shotgun with Cassidy and listening to music. Anxiety creeps along my skin and sets my nerves on edge.

"Girl, what do you mean, on the way? There's a McDonald's two towns over; you want that?"

"Yeah." I pass my wallet to Cassidy to stick in her purse. Pocketing my phone, I head outside.

"Dude, what's the rush?" she says, running out the door behind me.

Aggravated with myself, I huff and stare up at the sky. I can already hear the crickets starting up as the sun sinks behind the trees.

"I'm nervous," I admit, tugging on her door handle impatiently.

"No one is going to start shit with you. Not now." Cass unlocks the car and we climb in.

"I know. That's not it." I chew on my lip, wondering how much I want to admit. "Killian's kinda hot, Cassidy, and I don't really know what to do with that."

Her reaction is instantaneous and humiliating. Covering my face with my hands, I groan at her laughter.

"You're telling me you just noticed this?" She arches a brow as she backs out of the parking space.

"No," I sigh. "I knew that objectively, but I wasn't, like, *attracted* to him."

Cassidy hoots triumphantly. "This is my dream, you know? I've read enough enemies-to-lovers to know one when I see one."

"We were never enemies," I argue.

"It was Galway's version of the Cold War," she contradicts. "Y'all are so cute together. I mean, Killian is broodier right now, but he's all sunshine and golden-boy vibes, and you're quieter and so focused on soccer. You balance each other. I've seen more of the old you and the old Killian this week than the last few years."

"You don't think it's a bad thing that we've slipped so quickly back into a routine?"

Cassidy considers this for a moment.

"I don't know what the right answer is here, Glory. What's your concern?"

"Am I an idiot to have forgiven him so quickly?" I bring my knee to my chest and rest my chin on it.

"Are you happy?" she counters.

"Yeah," I admit quietly.

"Then, that's all that matters. Killian knows he messed up. I believe him when he says he'll never fuck up like that again."

"Never is a long time."

"So is almost four years without your soul mate."

I roll my eyes. "You are so dramatic."

We pull into the drive-through lane. I don't have to say anything; Cassidy orders our food, knowing exactly what I want. Even if she constantly gives me shit for eating a fish sandwich.

"Heinous." She pretends to gag, and she hands me the bag.

"You want your fries or nugs first?"

"Fries, duh. They aren't good cold."

I divvy up the food, and we fall into companionable silence as we head toward the school for Tanner and Killian's game. I eat slowly, hoping to not upset my stomach, and play car DJ for us.

Music is one of the only things that calms my mind when I get too deep in my head. When Killian wasn't around to help me put my feelings into words, I found lyrics that could describe them.

I've always wished I had some kind of musical talent, but when I tried out for band freshman year, I was too impatient to sit through learning an instrument. My talents are out on the field and being able to always set the vibe with good music.

"I forgot to tell you," Cassidy says over a mouthful.

"Hmm?" I nibble on a fry. Lord, there is nothing compared to salty, fresh McDonald's fries.

"Guess who got tickets to go see Charli XCX in Atlanta on Halloween."

"Wait, shut the fuck up!" I squeal, slapping her on the shoulder.

"Happy early birthday, Glo!"

"Stop it!"

"Oh, we're going. It's general admission and I figured we can split a hotel or something and stay the night. It's at The Tabernacle, so we can get there early, grab some dinner—"

I lean across the center console and nearly strangle her in a hug.

"Glory! I'm driving!" she yells, but she's laughing.

"Thank you, Cassidy. Thank you so much."

"I know if you could do one thing for your eighteenth, it would be to go see a show. She just announced her tour last month, so it was perfect."

I get a little choked up, realizing this is probably going to be one of the last birthdays of mine we get to celebrate with each other.

"Now, why are you crying?" She smiles at me fondly, rolling with my mood swings.

"I'm going to miss you so much, Cassidy. I know you joke that Killian's my soul mate, but I know it's you. You're like a sister to me; you're—" I

HARD FEELINGS

struggle, trying to put into words what it has meant to me to have her unwavering support by my side from the moment we met in third grade.

Killian's always held a special place in my heart, but Cassidy has always had the other half. I was devastated when he left me, but if Cassidy ever did, it would absolutely destroy me.

"I just love you so much," I finish.

Cassidy glances over, her eyes bright with unshed tears, and says, "We need to come up with meetup dates for when we're in California before you leave in June. We've got plenty of time, but I just want something concrete on paper."

"Duh," I agree before settling back into my seat.

Senior year is weird; we're on top of the food chain and beyond excited to have one foot out the door. Then, it'll hit me that nothing will be the same in a few months.

I don't know that I'll ever come back here. No more hanging on the lake with Cassidy and the boys. No late-night drives around town when we're bored and we can't sleep. No more runs with Killian. We're growing up, and it's a wonderfully painful experience.

Suddenly, my desire to leave as soon as possible wanes a little. I'm glad I'm going to the party tonight.

No more missing out on things, I promise myself. I want to experience as much of this last year as I can.

I finish eating by the time we pull into the school parking lot. Damn, it's packed. Crumpling up my trash, I grab Cassidy's, and we head toward the field entrance.

Tossing the trash in the can by the bleachers, I go to head toward my normal spot, but Cassidy grabs my shirt and yanks me back.

"Uh, no. No, we're not sitting all the way up there. You're sitting with the rest of our team, and you're going to cheer for Tan and Killian."

She takes my hand and pulls me along, refusing to let go until we're seated with the soccer teams.

Marcus calls my name and heads my way, picking me up in a huge hug. "She's finally come down from her tower."

I roll my eyes. "Please don't make a big deal out of this."

He sits next to me, and we begin chatting casually about what we should do for senior night. He suggests renting out one of the rooms at the dollar theater and showing some of our teams' favorite soccer films—*Bend It Like Beckham* and *Goal!* Okay, so there is kind of a shortage of good soccer movies, but those two are classics.

It's about two hundred to rent a theater, but it also gets us free popcorn and drinks. It's well within the budget, so I'm sure our coaches will go for it. We could make it a pajama theme.

Cassidy nudges me, pulling me out of my conversation. "They're about to head onto the field."

Sure enough, "Enter Sandman" by Metallica starts to play. The cheerleaders line up, shaking their pom-poms, and the players start to run on the field.

The bass of the song and the cheers as everyone stands on their feet vibrate the bleachers, and I have to admit, the energy is infectious.

Killian runs out, a head taller than everyone around him, his face fierce. The black smudges underneath his eyes add to his ferocity as he searches the stands.

I notice his eyes flick to the top of the bleachers, where I used to be, and Cassidy screams his name, drawing his attention toward us.

When his eyes lock on my own, I feel a jolt through my entire body. I clap along with everyone else, feeling a bit bewildered at how my body is reacting to him in his all-black uniform and formidable glare.

Then, he smiles, and I recognize my Killian behind the face of this badass.

"Damn," I mutter softly to Cassidy, and she snickers.

"Welcome to the reason everyone comes to these things." Cassidy snorts.

Our team wins the coin toss.

Hands gripping his pads, Killian stands on the sidelines, chewing on his mouthguard. Jesus, why is that sexy? I shift, feeling a little hot even though it's definitely cooled off now that the sun has set.

Tanner is a wide receiver; his long legs eat up the ground so fast that I'm shocked, and the ball sails right into his hands. Cassidy yanks me up with the rest of the crowd. I stand on the seat so I can see over everyone's head just in time to see Tanner easily bring it in for a touchdown.

Cassidy screams, "That's my brother!" and grabs me into a hug.

I laugh, caught up in her joy, and cheer for Tanner as he runs to meet his team, waving at us as he passes.

Then, it's the other defense's turn, and I find myself biting my thumb as Killian stalks onto the field.

He kneels down, staring at the big dude opposite him, and it's jarring to see guys almost as big as Killian.

This dude is built like freaking Godzilla.

The other team's quarterback calls the hike, and suddenly, Killian's ramming himself into the guy across from him. My eyebrows shoot up when Killian lifts him clear off his feet and shoves him back an entire foot.

"Holy effing hell," I whisper.

"Yeah, dude. Your boy is a freaking beast," Marcus says under his breath, eyes on the field.

They reset; this time, Killian's a little farther on the outside.

HARD FEELINGS

"He's going to go for the QB. Watch," Marcus tells me.

Sure enough, the ball is spiked, and Killian's on the move, moving much faster than someone his size should be able to.

He tackles the QB before the ball ever leaves his hands, and our side goes nuts again.

Killian jumps off the ground, light on his feet, and looks my way before pointing at me.

"Uhh," I stutter, not loving him directing attention at me.

"Oh, he's starting some shit with his fangirls with that one," Cassidy says, nodding to the girls leaning on the fence separating us from the field.

A couple of the girls glare at me, and I stare back stonily.

I refuse to give them anything, especially after the bullshit Britney pulled.

Unfortunately, it's like this for the rest of the game. Killian continues to point toward me after his biggest hits and stares at me, basically letting everyone know whom he's playing for.

"I wish he wouldn't do that," I mutter as Killian walks off the field.

"He's claiming you, Glo," Marcus comments, humor evident in his voice.

Bristling, I turn to glare at Marcus.

"Hey, don't get mad at me; I'm an innocent bystander."

I shove his shoulder playfully, and he grabs me around the neck, giving me a noogie.

"Glory Purcell!" Killian's yell cuts through all the noise, startling me into shrugging off Marcus's arm.

Once he has my attention, he taps his fingers over his heart, and I gasp. We used to do this when we were really little. It was like our secret message to each other.

You got me? it says.

Anytime we were launching on an adventure or needed reassurance, we'd tap over our hearts. Killian would do this during his peewee games. I used to do this when I left for soccer camp. I'm near positive we stole it from a movie, but still.

The emotion on his face suggests this means something else now. He's been showing all night how he feels for me in front of everyone. Breath hitching, I make the gesture back, tapping my two fingers against my own thudding heart.

I got you.

His shoulders relax, and I can practically hear his thoughts, telling me everything is different.

"Please tell him not to kill me," Marcus jokes but puts a little more distance between us.

"I haven't seen y'all do that in ages," Cassidy tells me, her tone suggesting she understands the significance.

I oddly feel like I might cry. Everything is changing so fast … or is it going back to normal?

"I don't know what I just did," I tell her, slightly panicked.

Cassidy gives me a side hug. "I have a feeling it's a little too late to worry about it now. You just gave that boy the green light."

Shit.

Fifteen

The game ends with another W for our school, and Cassidy drags me down the field to celebrate. Tanner reaches us first, grabbing us both in a big hug, lifting us off our feet while we squeal. Then, I'm in Killian's arms.

His face nuzzles into my neck, and I feel him take a deep inhale, breathing me in before pressing a kiss to my temple. A friendship kiss. Right? Friends do that. I've seen it ... somewhere. Maybe.

"Are you going to wait for me?" he asks as he sets me back down, but Cassidy answers for me.

"No, she's coming with me. I need to go home and change." She threads her arm through mine, gently tugging me away from Killian.

"Drive safely, Cassidy. None of that flooring it out of the parking lot."

"Yes, Dad," she says, rolling her eyes.

"I'll see you soon, ba—" Killian catches himself, clearing his throat. "Glory."

Uh, what the fu—

"Oh my freaking God, Glory Jane Purcell, he was about to call you baby," Cassidy hisses in my ear as she yanks my attention toward her.

I give him one last look over my shoulder to find him still watching me, frustration clear as he rakes his hand through his hair.

"What the literal heck is happening right now?" I ask, a little shrilly.

"This is a legit CW show; I'm watching this unfold right in front of my frickin' eyes. Wow. I mean, wow, dude. I got the hots just from watching him watch you." Cassidy waves her hand, as if to cool herself off.

"Cassidy, I'm five seconds away from a panic attack," I warn her.

"He looked like he wanted to lick you right up."

"Cassidy—"

"Glory," she mimics, unlocking her Jeep as we reach it.

"We just agreed to be friends again; I mean, don't you think this is moving too fast?"

"Maybe for you. Seems like this is the direction Killian has been heading since the beginning."

Rubbing my forehead, I take some slow breaths. I'm starting to feel my temples pound in time with my heart.

My phone vibrates with an incoming text.

You okay?

Killian. Of course he knows I'm freaking the eff out.

This is a lot to process, Kills. I'm trying to keep up and not freak.

He doesn't respond for a full minute, which escalates my anxiety.

You called me Kills.

I bite my lip, contemplating how truthful I want to be.

That's who you are to me.

Shit, was that too honest?

I'll see you soon, Glory.

Great. A response, but not the one I was looking for.

"Hey, I'm going to be super quick and just run in to change. The boys are heading straight to Killian's after. Everyone's probably already showing up, so we'll be somewhat fashionably late. Are you good with waiting in the car?"

"Sure, but where will Elizabeth be? She's cool with this?"

Cassidy grins at me as she pulls into her driveway. "It's so cute that this is your first high school party."

"Don't patronize me, butthole."

"Tanner said she went to Atlanta for a girls' weekend."

"Oh, so she doesn't know?" I chew on my nail.

"Glory, you need to chill out. Nothing is going to happen; no one will destroy the house. Your dad knows you're spending the night at my house. It'll be fine."

I really am being a worrywart.

"Okay, you're right. Go get changed. I'll chill here."

I sink into my seat and rest my feet on the dashboard, bringing up my phone to check Instagram.

HARD FEELINGS

Feeling like I'm going to regret this, I open the app and freeze when I see I have twenty new requests to follow me. I click through and realize it's mostly the football team and their circle.

Hovering over Accept, I decide I'll think about this later and click on the hashtag for our school. Of course, there are tons of pictures from tonight's game, but I zero in on a picture of me in Killian's arms.

I study us in the first pic I've seen since we were in middle school. Killian's brows are pinched tight, as if in pain, but in contradiction, he's smiling so big. I'm laughing over his shoulder.

We look happy.

I screenshot the picture and save it to my photos, and like an idiot, I begin to read comments. There isn't a lot, and for the most part, they are innocent, except for one.

Like mother, like daughter.

Rubbing the ache in my chest, I close the app and bring up the photo again. I get why Killian did what he did. I live in fear of being compared to my mom in this way. It's absolute bullshit that the comment exists at all.

It doesn't matter.

We're working our way back to being friends; I'm not going to allow shit people say to get in the way of that.

I lean against the window and sigh at how good the cold glass feels against my head. Fuck. I just have to make it at least an hour. I can do this.

Cassidy's front door slams, and then she runs to her car in a cute pink bodycon dress.

"You okay?" she asks, hopping into the driver's seat.

"Yeah," I say unconvincingly and change the subject before she presses. "You look so hot, Cassidy. Dressing up for anyone special?"

"Yeah, myself." She flashes me a saucy grin, and we're on our way.

The music greets us first; loud, thumping beats vibrate through the night as we turn into his packed driveway. Seeing all the cars gives me a slight twinge of anxiety because it suggests how outnumbered I am.

"How are the neighbors not calling the cops?" I wonder out loud.

"Two reasons: one, Killian rarely has parties, and two, he's a King," Cassidy says as she parks.

Curling my lips slightly at the privilege, I get out and follow her up the steps to the front door. People litter the front yard, red Solo cups in hand, staring at us as we walk up.

Cassidy eats up the pavement, long legs stomping the ground like she's on the runway, and I scurry behind her.

I grab her hand nervously as we enter, shocked at how humid and packed it is inside. The bass slams into my head, and I wince as my senses get a little overwhelmed.

Cassidy seems to notice and nods toward the bar.

I'm not much of a drinker. I don't like losing control, and while I sometimes indulge in foods that aren't good for me, alcohol is another beast altogether. Not that I begrudge others, but I don't do things to myself that could fuck up how I play.

This time though, I happily grab the beer from Cassidy and sip it. I gag a little. Nothing like warm beer, surrounded by body heat.

Cassidy grabs my hand again and pulls me toward the backyard. I'm thankful for the fresh air as we settle in loungers around the pool. I haven't been out here in ages.

The Kings' backyard is something straight out of *Architectural Digest*. Massive pool with fantastic outdoor furniture. Lanterns add a glow to the landscape, giving everything an ethereal vibe.

I set my beer down on the ground next to my lounger and stretch out. Resting my hands on my stomach, I try to breathe through the nausea. I don't know if I'm going to make it an hour. This migraine is coming on fast.

I'm about to let Cassidy know I might have to leave earlier than expected when Tanner comes outside and yells our names.

"Come on! I need y'all for table tennis." He waves us toward him, and Cassidy hops up and grabs my hand to pull me along.

My head feels two steps behind my body as she weaves us through the throng of people and heads down to the basement.

I look for Killian and still don't see him. Is he hiding?

Tanner is downstairs with some football players, our QB taking up one side and Tanner on the other. Tanner grabs Cassidy immediately, to no one's surprise since she kicks ass at table tennis.

"Fine, the twins versus Glory and me." Travis points at me as I make my way over to him.

One game. These are Killian's friends; it's imperative I make a good impression. I can do one game.

"Should we give them a handicap?" Cassidy smirks at her brother.

"Because he has Glory?" Tanner laughs. "You know, for someone who is such a great athlete, it'll never fail to make me laugh how little hand-eye coordination you have."

"Hey!" I protest. "I have superior eye-foot coordination. We don't handle balls with our hands that much."

Travis laughs, and my face heats up as I realize how that sounded.

"I don't know about you, Glory, but I always handle balls with my hands." Cassidy wiggles her eyebrows.

"Shut up, Cassidy." Tanner gags. "Let's play. First to ten."

HARD FEELINGS

I'm okay for most of the game. By okay, I mean, I'm not puking. I'm terrible at table tennis, even worse when I'm trying to battle the beginning of vertigo.

I swing hard at Tanner's serve and miss, my momentum knocking me into Travis hard. I stumble, and my vision goes fuzzy for a second.

He laughs, tucking me into his body to steady me, and I feel bile crawl up my throat.

"I'm gonna go to the bathroom," I mumble and head off in that direction, ignoring Cassidy calling after me.

Just get to the bathroom, Glory. Just get there.

I bump into people as I head upstairs from the basement.

"Oh my God, she's fucking wasted."

Someone laughs, and I lean against the wall in the hallway that leads to the bathroom.

Fuck, of course there's a line.

I close my eyes and try to breathe.

The pain is starting to get unbearable. I'm covered in a light sheen of sweat, and I have to keep my eyes closed because if I open them and see the room spin, I'll collapse.

A pained moan escapes my lips, and I decide, *Fuck it, I need in that bathroom.*

Pushing past people, I stagger my way toward the closed door.

"Someone, go get Killian," I hear someone yell.

I want to protest, but the words seem huge in my mouth. I can't get them out.

"Glory!" I hear Cassidy yell, and then I fall.

I hit the floor with a thud, and shocked laughs echo around me.

So loud. Everything is so fucking loud. I open my eyes to see if Cassidy is actually there or if I am hallucinating it.

Jesus, everything hurts.

I try to breathe because crying will not help the pressure in my head, but I feel my tears soak into my hair.

"Damn, what the fuck is she on?" I hear someone ask above me before there's the telltale flash of someone's phone.

"Did I just see you take a photo of her?" Cassidy growls from above me, and I relax slightly.

She's here. She's got me.

"She's not on something, you asshole! She's sick!"

"Cassidy," I whisper and lift my hand up with my eyes still closed.

"Everyone, get the fuck out of my house!" Killian roars, and I whimper at how loud the sound is.

The pounding in my head muffles the sound of people leaving, but knowing they're leaving relaxes me further. I do not like feeling vulnerable in general; I hate it in front of people who would relish in witnessing it.

"I'm going under," I whisper to Cassidy, and she squeezes my hand reassuringly.

"What the hell is wrong with her, Cassidy?" Killian's panicked question is the last thing I hear before I slip into blessed darkness.

I'm not sure how long I've been out, if it's minutes or hours, but when I do wake up, I'm in a dark room—thank God. The room is cold—another blessing—except for the furnace next to me.

Carefully, I turn my head, hoping the vertigo has calmed enough that it doesn't spin me into outer space, and see Killian next to me, asleep.

I pat the bed and find my phone, squinting at the harsh light as I check the time and see it's past three in the morning. Fuck, I've been out for hours.

I turn the brightness down and text Cassidy.

Where are you?

I hear the buzz in the room and lean on my elbow to see her camped across the room on a blowup bed.

"Cassidy," I whisper, and she shoots up and then crawls to my side of the bed.

"Oh my God, Glory Jane, that was a bad one. We almost took you to the emergency room to get you a migraine cocktail. Why didn't you tell me you weren't feeling okay?" she whispers furiously.

"I didn't want to miss my first party and Killian's birthday," I whisper back, feeling stupid. "Did you give me a shot?"

"Yeah, and almost got my arm bitten off by the Hulk over here. He freaked when he saw the needle."

"Did you tell him what was going on?" I ask nervously.

Cassidy shoots me a look. "What was the alternative? Tell him to mind his business? Yeah, dude, good plan. You'll have some explaining to do when he wakes up; he's super worried."

Sighing, I sink back into my pillow.

"On that note, I'm heading to the guest room across the hall to get some real rest. We've got, like, four hours before we have to be up. Are you even going to be able to hack it at conditioning?"

"I'll have a little hangover, but I need to show up. I'll take it easy though," I promise as I get out of bed quietly so as not to disturb the goliath sharing the bed with me and follow Cassidy to the bedroom door.

Cassidy kisses my forehead. "You'd freaking better, or I'll rat you out to Coach."

HARD FEELINGS

I gently shut the door behind her before turning back toward Killian. He's still asleep, which is good because I already know I'll be slipping back to sleep the second my head hits the pillow.

We can deal with this in the morning.

sixteen

My phone alarm chimes loudly in the quiet of Killian's dark room. It startles me awake, scaring Killian in the process.

It's then that I notice I'm being spooned. Killian radiates heat behind me, and it's so warm that if I didn't have to get up, I'm sure I'd be able to fall back asleep easily.

Killian rolls onto his back, his arm still under my neck, and stretches, letting out a loud groan that has heat flooding my cheeks.

I continue to stare at the wall, not pretending to be asleep—because, duh, I just jerked like I got electrocuted—but clearly avoiding him.

"Glory," Killian warns and makes the decision for me by rolling me easily into his chest.

I muffle a squeak as my face smashes into his chest, and, wow, Killian has chest hair. That is so weird! I remember pretending to shave our beards with Popsicle sticks in my dad's bathroom. Obviously, I wouldn't have a beard … at least hopefully, but I was jealous Killian would be able to. And here he is with actual body hair. Puberty is wild.

"You're, like … a man, Killian." And, yeah, that sounded as dumb out loud as it had in my head.

"Yeah, that's typically what happens with puberty," he says dryly and tilts my head up so I'm looking into his eyes.

Killian looks adorably sleepy. His eyes are soft, and pillow marks crease the right side of his face. For the first time, I find myself imagining kissing him. We're so close that it would take little effort to meet his lips with my own.

Something must show on my face because Killian's eyes flare with an emotion I don't feel like touching with a ten-foot pole this morning.

"We're going to talk, Glory," Killian tells me, and I barely refrain from rolling my eyes at his stern tone.

"It was a migraine, Killian. I get them sometimes."

"That seemed a lot more serious last night than your nonchalant tone suggests."

"I'm not being nonchalant." I scoot out of his arms and rest on the pillow next to his so our heads are close, like when we used to have sleepovers when we were little. "This has just become my new normal."

"When did this start?" he whispers.

"About the time everything fell apart. I got one before my first period. Ever since then, it's been figuring out what's triggering and how I can avoid it. I fucked up last night and didn't listen to my body, so it got more out of hand than normal."

"Why?"

"Why didn't I listen to my body?" I confirm.

"Yeah."

I stare at him, memorizing what big Killian looks like. He is not so different from little Killian; he's still the same boy. I can be honest with him even if it's embarrassingly vulnerable.

"Because it was my first high school party and your birthday party," I admit softly.

Killian sits up and runs his hands through his hair in frustration. "Glory, my real birthday is today. I wouldn't have given a shit if you weren't able to come because you didn't feel well. I'll always want you to take care of yourself first."

I sit up too, crossing my legs next to him.

Before I can continue, Cassidy pokes her head into the room. "We've got ten minutes before heading out."

Groaning, I get out of Killian's amazingly comfortable bed and pull the covers up on my side behind me. I grab my gym bag and head to his bathroom to change quickly.

Killian's room has changed just as much. Gone are the Star Wars–themed bedding and his spaceship decals on the walls. They've been replaced with light-gray paint, a soft navy comforter, and some really great black-and-white shots of him playing football. The photos are definitely all Elizabeth. She is responsible for most of the photography in their house and some in mine as well.

There's a desk, where I imagine him writing in his journal or working on his laptop, and I see a picture of us sitting there. It's taken from behind, so you just see our silhouettes. Also Elizabeth's work. We look like we were maybe eight or nine, given I was almost the same size as Killian.

I clear the sudden lump in my throat.

HARD FEELINGS

"Listen, I know you might have more questions, but I need to head to conditioning. I thought, later, we could celebrate for real? We could have a movie night, like we used to?"

I lean on his bathroom door and stare at him, still sitting on his bed, covers around his waist. He looks indecent, and if I hadn't felt his sweatpants earlier, I could easily believe he was naked.

Killian looks at me under his lashes and nods. "I'd love that."

Nodding, I close the door and quickly change into my workout leggings, a long-sleeved shirt, and a hoodie.

I slip my slides on my sock-covered feet and throw my hair up. Digging in my bag, I search for my toothbrush and curse when I can't find it. My medicine gives me horrendous dry mouth, and I want nothing more right now than to brush my fur-covered teeth.

Cracking the door back open, I catch Killian shrugging on a white T-shirt, and, damn, even that's hot.

Embarrassed by my thoughts, I keep my eyes on the floor in front of me and ask, "Do you have an extra toothbrush? I forgot mine."

Killian's feet come into view, and I marvel at how freaking large they are, a literal Bigfoot here in Galway.

"This is very domestic, Glowy." Killian's amusement has my damn cheeks reddening again.

Feeling a little struck dumb at the sight of him smiling down at me, both dimples popping, I don't move immediately to let him through, which has him picking me up like a little kid and sitting me on his bathroom counter.

"You can't just move me around because I'm small and you're big," I complain even though I'm secretly thrilled at having his hands on me. Shit, maybe the migraine drugs are still making me loopy.

"Really? 'Cause I think that's exactly what I did?" Killian kneels between my thighs, and I gasp, only for him to open the cabinet beneath and pull an extra toothbrush out.

My blood pounds in my ears as he steps close to me and hands me the toothbrush. Killian bites his lips, and I narrow my eyes. He knows exactly what he's doing.

Being this close to him has me off my game, and I lash out, hoping to make him feel even the slightest like I do. "Cassidy said you almost called me baby last night."

Killian leans closer, forcing me to crane my neck up to meet his gaze, and he tugs on my hair lightly. He's always had such a thing for my hair.

"Do you want me to?" he says in a low voice, his mouth brushing against my temple, making me shudder.

My breathing picks up to a near pant, and I realize if he stepped a little closer, the only thing separating our most intimate areas would be my thin black leggings and his sexy-ass gray sweatpants.

"Hmm?" My eyes close as he nuzzles my neck. I tilt it to give him more access, and even though he's doing nothing but breathing on me, my skin breaks out in goose bumps. Guess I have a neck kink.

"Do you want me to call you baby?" he whispers, and I feel his lips brushing against my skin this time.

His voice, low and gravelly, saying the word *baby*, does something to me in places I never thought he'd affect me. My body is a living pulse, and I shift restlessly, my hips tilting without my permission, as if seeking friction from him.

I have to stop this.

Too much, too fast.

"Glory," Killian moans slightly, obviously as affected as I am.

He cages me in with his arms, and all I want to do is wrap my arms and legs around him and bring him into my body, but, no, this is way too soon.

Get a grip, Glory!

Cassidy's best-friend Spidey-Sense must be on high alert because she again barges into his room, yelling my name.

Startled, I jerk back, nearly slamming into the mirror behind me.

"Killian, back up," I say desperately, needing distance more than I need my next breath.

He shudders, trying to get control, and leaves without another word.

I hop down and face the mirror. My face and neck are beet red, my eyes are feverish, and my lips are red and swollen from my chewing on them subconsciously.

I quickly splash some cold water on my face and speed through brushing my teeth. I do not need Cassidy bumping into Killian's boner on her way to drag me out to her car. I run downstairs, effectively avoiding bumping into Killian, Tanner, or Elizabeth, and rush outside to hop in Cassidy's Jeep.

She takes one look at me and squeals. "Oh. My. God! Glory Jane Purcell, you are horned up!"

"Stop!" I whisper furiously, looking around, like Killian might jump out of the bushes. "Let's go, Cassidy. I'm freaking out."

I sink into the seat and cover my face. When I reach to turn on the radio, she slaps my hand away.

"Oh no. Uh-uh. You're opening that trap of yours and spilling."

"I think I like Killian. More than a friend."

Cassidy snorts. "Yeah, no shit."

"Cassidy! Be serious." I take a deep breath and try to slow my racing heart. "Is this too soon? I mean, we just got back to being friends."

"Glory, listen carefully. You were always going to end up here if you reconciled."

"You don't know that," I scoff, shifting uncomfortably in my seat.

HARD FEELINGS

"Do you honestly think that I didn't realize you had a crush on him in middle school?" Cassidy shoots me a disbelieving glance.

"People have crushes all the time!" I protest.

"I'm just saying. Y'all were always in this freaky little best-friend bubble; it started to change in middle school, and who knows what would've happened if Killian never shit all over it?"

"Anyone ever tell you, you have a way with words?" I ask dryly.

"Fine, maybe you didn't have a crush, but I know for sure that Killian did. He used to talk to Tanner about you all the time. It was gross, at least to middle-school me."

I quietly digest that information and promise myself to read more of his journal when I get home this afternoon before—

"Fuck!"

"What?" Cassidy says, startled by my shout.

"I told Killian I'd come over tonight for one of our movie nights. It's his official birthday, you know."

"Need Tan and me to run some interference?" she asks immediately, and for the millionth time, I thank the universe for bringing me such an awesome bestie.

"You know I love you, right?"

"I'll take that as a yes." She laughs.

Conditioning lasts for two hours, and I find myself trying not to puke several times. Typically getting my blood pressure up after a migraine makes me feel dizzy, so I really should have known better. Cassidy drops me off at home, and I shower and go straight to bed. My body needs way more sleep than I've gotten in the last twelve hours.

When I wake up, the sun is low, and grabbing my phone, I see it's later in the afternoon.

Damn, I slept for, like, five hours.

Hearing voices downstairs, I shrug some sweatpants over my panties and a large cardigan over my cropped tank top. I slept on wet hair, so it's a mess that'll take me too long to fix, and I'm too curious to see who's downstairs to wait much longer.

I jog down the stairs, and the voices go silent.

Suspicious now, I call out for my dad and head into the kitchen.

Sitting there, like she never left, is my mother.

I do my best to hide my reaction, my poker face honed after the years of shit I've taken from this town because of her selfishness.

"Hey, Glo baby." She smiles at me—an exact replica of my own smile.

I ignore the stupid nickname she gave me as a child and instead turn my attention to my father.

He's sitting across from her at the island, and I notice him shuffling a stack of papers in front of him.

"What is she doing here, Dad?" My tone is hard, unyielding, and reflective of the wall I've had to build because of *her*.

"Glory," he sighs, and I walk farther into the room and peek over his shoulder.

Petition for divorce.

My breath stalls in my throat. Of course.

I glare at her over my father's shoulder, resting my hand on him in support, and ask, "Why now?"

Oddly enough, they've been separated this entire time. You'd think my dad would've filed immediately, but I think hope kept him holding on for longer than he should have. Also, divorce is expensive, so what's changed?

My mother stands up and moves around toward me, and it's then that I notice her stomach. Her *pregnant* stomach.

"Honey—" She reaches out toward me, and I recoil, eyes focused on her *fucking* stomach.

"How could you be even worse? How could you do this to us?" I whisper, hating how my voice cracks. "Did you both come up here together? Finally asking for a divorce after you ran away and left us to deal with the wrath of this entire town because you're ready to cut ties with us forever in order to start your new family?" My voice rises until I'm yelling at the end.

Tears flow freely, and I hate it. I hate that I always cry when I'm angry. I hate that I'm crying in front of her now.

She flinches but holds my glare.

"Do you even know what it's been like for me these last few years? For having the unfortunate reality of looking exactly like you? Dad lost his job, and we were treated like pariahs because no one had anyone to punish for you and Sebastian hurting the town's golden family. We have *struggled*, and we have been in *pain,* but I'm so happy you were able to start over without a single repercussion."

Dad stands up and draws me into a hug, and I grip him tightly.

"You don't understand, Glory. I never meant for any of this to happen. I didn't mean to hurt you or your father. This has hurt me too, Glory. You think I enjoy missing out on so much of my daughter's life?"

Shoving out of my dad's arms, I face her again. "Yeah, I do! Where have you been? Where have you *been*, Mom?"

She tucks her hair behind her ears—a nervous habit I have as well—and my heart feels like it's breaking all over again. How can I be so much like her and nothing like her at the same time?

HARD FEELINGS

"I am in so much pain," I say hoarsely, slapping a hand over my chest. "You have broken me irrevocably."

Dissolving into tears, her hands cover her face as she shakes her head, trying to deny it. My dad grunts like I delivered a blow. I've done a good job at hiding this, I think. Fueled by anger and a survival instinct to ignore the wound until I was to safety.

Don't think about it; don't think about it. If you don't think about it, it doesn't hurt.

"Please, Glory, I want you in my life. I want to be in yours. You're going to have a little sister who needs you," she cries.

If she touches me, I might say something I'll never be able to take back.

"Right now, I'm having a hard time even stomaching the sight of you," I tell her flatly, and again, she flinches like I slapped her.

I wish I could say hurting her makes me feel good, but it doesn't. It makes me hate myself more for turning into someone I'm not.

I feel like I'm going to scream, cry, puke, and collapse, all at the same time.

"I need to go," I whisper, backing away from them.

Dad grabs my hand, tears in his eyes. "Please don't go right now, Glory. You're too upset. We can talk this out."

"How are you okay with all of this?!" I rip my hand out of his.

"This was always going to lead to divorce, Glory."

"I'm more referring to the fact that she gets to start over fresh while we continue to pick up all the pieces she smashed on her way out," I counter sharply and give her one more glare. "Oh, I'll want to be in my future sister's life. If for no other reason than to be there for her when you inevitably disappoint her as well."

Ignoring them yelling after me, I run out of the house and head on the familiar path to Killian's house.

I need him.

If his dad is delivering the final blow to Killian and Elizabeth, he'll need me too. Elizabeth filed for divorce the absolute second Sebastian walked out on her. No way was she ever going to let him back into her life. But this news? This will destroy her.

I wince as I run over the dirt path, realizing I forgot my shoes, but I run faster than I ever have.

I'm barely halfway there when I hear someone crashing through the woods toward me. I stifle a sob, knowing exactly who it is.

The moment he comes into view, I stop running and nearly fall to my knees, crying.

Killian is in the same outfit I saw him in this morning, and it's jarring somehow to think it's the same day. This morning with him, where a new possibility took shape, seems like a lifetime ago.

His face is a picture of the same devastation I feel. He doesn't stop running until he's directly in front of me, and then I'm in his arms, legs around his waist, face buried in his neck, and sobbing.

He sinks to his knees, rocking us both, trying to calm me down. I hear his pulse thundering as he fists my sweater in his hands. I wish I could crawl inside him and hide forever, protected and loved in a way my own mother could never manage.

"Glory, Glory." He repeats my name over and over, like a mantra.

"She's pregnant," I whisper against his skin, and his grip tightens.

"I know," he whispers back, just as heartbroken.

"Is he there now?"

"Yeah …" he sighs, and I know he's worried about his mother.

"What kind of asshole does this on your freaking birthday?" I hiss, pulling back to look into his eyes.

His lashes are wet, but he won't let them fall. Killian always tries to be the strong one, the one who always takes care of everyone else.

Who takes care of him? It used to be me. It should be me now.

He gives a sad smile and a small shrug, and it breaks my heart all over again.

"I'm sorry your dad is such a dick."

"I'm sorry your mom is such a massive letdown."

I let out a watery laugh, and Killian rests his forehead on mine.

"What are we going to do?" I ask desperately.

"Be there for her; she's going to need us," Killian vows, and I know who he's talking about. Our little sister. His big-brother instincts are kicking in already.

Oh, ugh …

"We're going to be stepbrother and stepsister." I wrinkle my nose, and Killian laughs, giving it a quick kiss that has my pulse pounding for other reasons.

"Cassidy would be swooning; she loves a stepbrother romance."

"How do *you* know that?" I raise a brow.

"Maybe I snoop a little when I sleep over. Maybe I also read a little too," he confesses, red tinting his cheekbones.

Aw, embarrassed Killian. I've missed him. Something about this giant dude blushing makes my insides melt.

"Killian Sebastian King," I tease and laugh when he groans at his full name, "are you a romance reader?"

"Please shut up," he begs before shifting me so he can get more comfortable but keeping me in his arms.

My laughter dies as quickly as it came, and I lay my head back on his chest, sighing gustily.

HARD FEELINGS

"We should go back, huh?" I ask, slightly defeated and exhausted by all of this.

"I think so," he says in the same tone of voice.

"I think I need to talk to someone." My voice is small. I'm uncertain by the idea of it. My emotions feel so huge, and I've locked them down so tightly; I'm afraid of what could happen if I start to not only acknowledge them, but also work through them. I might never stop crying.

"I talk to someone," Killian confesses quietly, and I lean back to look at him. "I've had horrible anxiety since I started playing seriously. Plus, the pressure of taking care of my mom, not wanting to disappoint her in the same way, hurting you, and the family business … it's a lot. More than I could handle by myself."

"Why have you never said anything?"

Killian shrugs. "I don't really know. My mom got me in touch with him when she witnessed me having a panic attack before my game. He's helped a lot. I know it's scary, Glory, but I think it'd help you so much. I will always be there to listen and support you, but all of this is bigger than what I can help you with."

I crawl off his lap and stand, rubbing my face furiously, feeling completely overwhelmed.

"My dad really wants me to too."

"It's not a bad thing, Glory."

"I know. I know it's not." I step back as he stands up and tucks me in for one more hug. "I need to go back."

"Are we still on for tonight?" he asks hesitantly, and I immediately reassure him.

"Now more than ever, Killian. We need to salvage this birthday. Between me screwing up your party and then our parents taking a big ole deuce on this afternoon, we need to turn this ship around."

Killian laughs and plants a big kiss on my forehead. "Text me after you talk to your dad."

"I will," I promise and turn to head back, taking my time.

SEVENTEEN

Both of my parents are waiting for me when I return. My dad immediately pulls me into his arms and rocks me. He's shaking slightly, and I know this is a lot for him; I might have also freaked him the eff out. Just a little. To be fair, it's the most he's seen me talk about my mom since she took off.

He wraps an arm around my shoulders and walks me over to the couch, thoughtfully sitting between my mom and me. I might be on my way to working toward a new normal, but that doesn't mean I am anywhere near forgiving her.

"I want to be there for *her*"—I emphasize the last word and watch my mom's face brighten with hope—"but right now, I want nothing to do with you."

Her face falls just as quickly.

Good.

Turning to my dad, I meet his worried eyes. "I think I'll take you up on talking to someone. I need help with undoing all this damage." I look over his shoulder at the nuclear bomb that is my mother.

Her eyes drop to her hands, and I notice her knuckles are white.

For a brief moment, I feel guilt for lashing out, and anger swiftly follows. She deserves this. I shouldn't feel guilty for expressing myself.

The roller coaster of emotions that has happened within minutes tells me that, yeah, getting help is probably the right idea.

Dad gets excited and tells me he already has some recommendations his own therapist gave him, and I try not to roll my eyes because of course he does.

Mom leaves shortly after, promising to call me regularly to fill me in on what's happening with her pregnancy, and I try not to scorn her for only wanting to call me to talk about herself.

I stand at the front window, watching Sebastian's car pull up in front of our house. He hops out and rushes toward her, clearly playing the role of a worried husband well. He grips my mom's elbow to support her walking toward the car, like she all of a sudden forgot how to walk.

Sebastian must feel my gaze on him because he looks right at me as he shuts my mom's passenger door and gives me a bashful little wave.

What a douchebag.

I give him the finger.

Turning away before I can see his response, I head upstairs and grab my cell. Four missed calls from Cassidy. The twins must have gotten a heads-up that our lives just imploded once again.

Sitting on my bed, I call her back.

"Glory!" she answers, out of breath, worry clear in her voice.

Dammit, here come the tears again.

"Can you come over?" I ask, voice wobbly.

"I've been waiting. Yes, of course. Tanner already left for Killian's. I was practically out the door, ready to head over in a few minutes, whether you called me or not. Should I bring a change of clothes? Tanner said he was sleeping at Killian's; he doesn't want to leave him alone."

"Yes, please."

"Oh shit, you're being so polite. Okay, I'll be there in five. Do you need me to stay on the phone with you?"

I cry a at how she obviously cares about me. It just hits harder in the wake of everything that just happened with my mom.

"Okay, okay, I'm going to. Let me fill you in on what happened with Tara and Gage."

Cassidy begins telling me all about the book she's reading, and I curl up in my bed, thankful to be distracted.

In no time, I hear her bursting through the door, yelling, "Hello," at my dad as she stampedes up the stairs.

I don't move as she opens the door, holding myself so tightly so as not to break again.

"Shit, babe," Cassidy whispers and practically climbs on top of me to give me a giant hug.

She's so much bigger than me that she squashes me into the bed, and my tears turn to laughter.

"I know I shouldn't call women bitches, especially a pregnant lady— which, by the way, what the absolute fuck?—but your mom is a *bitch*, dude."

I giggle, and Cassidy moves to lie down, facing me.

HARD FEELINGS

"Are you okay?" she asks and then immediately winces. "Never mind. Stupid question."

I flick her nose. "I will be. I told my dad I wanted to talk to someone."

Cassidy holds my gaze, not an ounce of judgment on her face. "That's good, Glory!"

I sit up, wiping under my eyes. I need to go downstairs and grab my ice roller. My eyes feel almost swollen shut.

"We need to turn this day around. For Killian," I tell her, trying my hardest to rally.

"What are you thinking?" She sits up.

"We make his favorite cake, order enough pad thai to feed two football players and us—"

"So, a fuck ton." Cassidy laughs.

"But first, I need to do something about my face."

"You look fine." Her voice gets high—a clear sign that she's a lying liar who lies.

I give her a dubious look. "Can you place the order for dinner?"

"It's, like, a thirty-minute drive from here; when do you think we'll be able to pick it up?"

I glance at my phone again and wince at the time. We need to get moving.

"Set pickup for six. That'll give us time to make his cake and for me to de-puff."

"Do you have the stuff to make a birthday-flavored birthday cake?" Cassidy asks knowingly, and I curse.

"Shit, no. My health-nut dad would never. Damn, okay, let me change, and we'll run to the grocery store."

We're out the door in ten minutes—de-puffing will have to wait—and we arrive at our small local grocery store. I hope they have a box of his favorite brand. It used to crack up his parents when they asked Killian what flavor he wanted for his birthday cake and his answer was birthday cake–flavored.

Vanilla with sprinkles every year.

Cassidy triumphantly holds up the blue box and tosses it into the cart like she's attempting a free throw.

"Should we get snacks?" I bite my lip, heading toward the chip aisle.

"Duh. All his faves?" She grabs a bag of spicy cheese puffs—her favorite—and tosses it in.

"Yeah. Ours too. Killian likes some freaky shit." I grab a pickle-flavored bag of chips and hold it up to her. "Case in point."

We end up with a cart full of junk, and I have to laugh. There is no way we're going to eat all of this, but it'll be fun to try.

We rush home, and I put on my ice mask as we make his cake. Something Cassidy finds hilarious. The cake comes out looking insane. Somehow lopsided, smothered in white frosting with sprinkles and a giant blue dick drawn on the top, courtesy of dear Cassidy.

We change into our pajamas—oversize T-shirts and ratty, old sweatpants—and get ready to leave.

Running upstairs, I head to my dad's office to give him a quick kiss good-bye. He's typing away when I come in.

"Tell Killian I said happy birthday. I already told Elizabeth I'll join y'all for Sunday breakfast at the diner."

Heart warming at the thought of us all together, I give him a big squeeze and tell him I'll see him later.

A little over an hour later, we're pulling up Killian's driveway.

We text the boys to come help with all the bags, and they both come out, also in their pajamas. It's a requirement for movie night.

"Holy shit, y'all went crazy," Tanner exclaims when Cassidy opens her trunk. There are at least eight bags of just junk food, a couple liters of Coke, and a to-go bag of Thai food.

"Calories don't count on movie night," Cassidy tells us as she elbows Tanner out of the way. "Here, Killian, carry your cake and do it carefully. Glory and I spent a lot of time on that thing."

I snicker as his eyebrows shoot up, and he smiles at me.

"Thank you, guys. You didn't have to do all this."

"Um, yeah, we did," I counter, grabbing dinner and following him up the stairs to his front door, leaving the twins arguing behind us. "How's your mom?" I whisper, looking around for her.

"She hasn't left her room. I think finding out your mom is pregnant was harder than signing the divorce papers."

My heart sinks at that. Elizabeth had a hard time getting pregnant, miscarrying several times before she had Killian, and that was after several rounds of IVF before she was able to carry successfully to term. She always called Killian her miracle baby.

"God, I hate them for that alone," I say furiously. "Let's not talk about them anymore. Tonight's about you."

We set everything on the kitchen counter, and I pull him into a hug. "Happy birthday, Kills."

"Thanks," he whispers against my hair.

"Well, look at you two," Cassidy crows as she comes around the corner, bags loaded on each arm.

Groaning, I pull out of Killian's arms and take some off of her. "Please don't start."

"I just need everyone to know I'm officially shipping you two. Team Gillian for life."

This time, it's Killian who groans. "Don't give us a name. Jesus."

HARD FEELINGS

"Sorry, Team Gillian it is. I'm getting shirts made," she teases, and I laugh.

We bring the food into the living room. Their couch is large enough that all four of us can stretch out comfortably. We pile all the food on the giant coffee table the sectional surrounds and begin to dig in.

Since it's Killian's birthday, he gets to pick the first movie, and it is, of course, *The Empire Strikes Back*. I hide a groan because even after the years of us being apart, he's still so predictable.

I am not a Star Wars kind of girl. It's also two hours long.

I pull my knees up and use them to rest my pad thai on. Cassidy and Tanner are movie talkers, and normally, that would annoy me, but their constant commentary is hilarious and makes the time go by fast.

At the end of the movie, we decide to do cake and sing to him. Elizabeth comes down, and I try not to wince in sympathy at the sight of her face.

It's clear she's been crying, but I commend her for rallying for Killian. When she joins us at the kitchen island, I sidle over to her and give her a hug. She pulls me tight against her side, and I bite my lip to avoid tearing up again.

Lord, what a day.

I glance up and see Killian watching us with an intense look on his face, and I offer him a small smile.

Tanner sticks candles all around the dick, outlining it and giggling to himself.

"Beautiful cake decoration, ladies," Elizabeth says dryly as she moves over to Killian's side and pulls him into a hug. "Happy birthday, baby."

"Thanks, Mom," he replies solemnly.

"Okay! Make a wish!" Tanner replies, backing away as he lights the last candle.

"We haven't sung yet, idiot," Cassidy scolds and counts us down.

We all sing "Happy Birthday" to Killian, and for a moment, it's the most normal my life has been in so long. It's these little slices of normalcy that make shit like today easier.

"Make a wish," I tell him, smiling as we finish.

Holding my eyes, Killian leans over and blows the candles out. How can that be sexy? I think something might really be wrong with me if him blowing candles out makes me want to kiss him again.

"What did you wish for?" Elizabeth asks.

Killian shakes his head. "It's a secret," he says so slyly that it makes me blush.

"I think I know," Cassidy teases me as she passes out dishes for everyone, and I smack her butt.

We move back to the living room, stomachs swollen with food and soda. The twins lie on either side of the sectional with Killian and me in the middle. Less than an hour into Tanner's pick, *The Hangover*, the twins are passed out.

125

Killian sits like a live wire next to me, and though so much has happened since this morning, it's all I can think about.

What almost happened …

Checking my phone, I see it's almost one in the morning. His mom is definitely asleep. The only people awake are him and me. A strange awareness enters my body, and I fixate on the fact that we could go up to his room, totally undetected, and finish what he started this morning.

As if reading my mind, Killian stands up and offers me his hand.

I take his, wincing at how hot mine feels compared to his. "Sorry," I apologize like a weirdo, but he just gives me this knowing smile.

"Come on. We need to talk without the cheering section." He smiles fondly at Cassidy.

I let him pull me up and lead me upstairs to his room.

Swallowing my nerves, I follow him in and sit on the edge of his bed, back ramrod stiff.

"Glory, relax. We're not doing anything you're not ready for," he assures me, sliding into the opposite side of the bed, where he slept last night.

"I'm not a virgin!" I blurt out and then cover my face, mortified.

Killian curses viciously before growling, "Can you please come over here? I don't want to be staring at your back for this conversation."

Wincing at my own word vomit, I crawl under the covers and lie down, facing him.

He stares at me intently, as if memorizing my face, his eyes dropping to my lips for a moment before meeting my eyes.

"So, you're not a virgin?" he says a little too casually.

"I lost it last year at soccer camp," I tell him bluntly.

I don't regret that moment with Jason. He was attractive and attentive. We got along great, and he was kind. My first time was painful and awkward, but he made it better.

"What's his name?" he asks softly, his hazel eyes looking more gold in this lighting.

"I'm not telling you that," I retort firmly, a little annoyed. "Did you think I would wait for you? You hadn't spoken to me in over two years at that point."

Killian grumbles in frustration and reaches over to yank me closer. "I'm not mad at you. I have no right to be. I'm fucking pissed at myself because that should've been me. We should have been each other's first, and I ruined that."

"Killian, I didn't even know you liked me like that. I mean, I still kinda don't. You haven't said."

"Glory, I have loved you in one way or another since we were little kids. As we got older, I could feel that change. Before everything went down with my father, I was going to ask you on a date. Our first date."

HARD FEELINGS

Feeling a little heartsick for the both of us, I say, "So, ask me now."

"Glory Jane Purcell, will you go on a date with me?" he asks so seriously that I don't even have the heart to tease him.

I watch him carefully, cataloging this Killian so I can remember this moment years from now. The moment I decided to leap and let him catch me, to change our relationship for the second time in as many months.

I was right; we would never go back to the way we were, but maybe we could be something else. Maybe we could be this.

"Yeah, Killian, I'd love to," I answer, a huge smile breaking across my face, so large that I feel it in my soul.

He smiles back and asks me something else, "Can I kiss you?"

I raise my brow. "I'm not kissing you while we're in bed together before we have our first official date. Sorry, no."

He chuckles, tucking me into his side so I'm resting over his heart. "What about the first date?"

I yawn loudly before snuggling into him. "We'll see."

I sleep so hard that when I wake up, it feels like no time has passed at all. The cold air behind me lets me know Killian is already out of bed. Sitting up, I rub the sleep from my eyes and head downstairs.

Cassidy meets me at the bottom of the stairs, wiggling her eyebrows.

"Stop. Nothing happened." I slap her arm as I come up beside her.

"That's not what I heard. I heard you're going on an official date," Cassidy squeals, shaking my shoulders.

"Tanner and Killian gossip more than anyone else I know," I groan but wrap my arm around her waist. "And, yes, he asked me on a date, and I said yes."

"This is huge," she squeals again, excitement making her voice climb an octave most singers wish they could hit.

"Please do not put pressure on this. It's just a date," I plead with her.

"Fine, relax, but I get to pick out the outfit and help with makeup and hair," she counters. "This is your first real date, so we're going all out for it."

"Fine," I concede and follow her to the mudroom, where we dropped our overnight bags. "I need to brush my teeth. I didn't before bed, and they feel slimy from all the shit we ate last night."

"Same. I feel like all the spicy cheese puffs I ate have given me the ability to breathe fire."

"Girls, we're leaving for breakfast in ten minutes with or without you!" Elizabeth calls out, and we hop into action.

"Hopefully without you!" Tanner echoes right after, and Cassidy flips him off as we pass the kitchen to head into the downstairs bathroom to brush our teeth.

I don't feel the need to change, though I should at least put on a bra.

We're ready to go in less than ten minutes. We follow everyone out to the car and all hop into Elizabeth's giant SUV.

She's talking about the upcoming holiday season. Cassidy and Tanner sign up every year to run the cashier booth for the lot they sell the mature trees on. Killian usually does the heavy lifting, helping people chop them down and transporting them to cars.

"Glory, you are more than welcome to come work the season as well. We need someone in the gift shop," Elizabeth offers.

My season will be over in November, right before their busy season, and since I no longer clean for her now that my dad has steady income, I'd love the extra money to sock away in my college fund.

"I'd love that. Thanks, Elizabeth," I agree easily.

She catches my eye in the rearview mirror and smiles.

"Your dad is going to do some contract work for us as well. It's time the Purcells and Kings are back in business together," she continues as she pulls onto Main Street and parallel parks in front of the diner.

My throat is tight with emotion, and all I can do is nod. I wonder if Killian had anything to do with this. The meddling should annoy me, but I'm grateful someone cares enough to right the wrong.

I get out of the car slowly, feeling suddenly overwhelmed by the number of people at the diner. Most of the town is here, which makes sense since it's before church service.

One diner and four churches in our town. Only one place for all of them to come.

My steps slow as we approach the doors. I already hate all the attention on me.

Killian glances back from where he holds the door open for Elizabeth and the twins and frowns at my dawdling. Letting go of the door, he comes over and offers his hand.

In for a penny, in for a pound, I think before placing my hand in his.

He gives me a comforting squeeze, and I enter the diner on a Sunday for the first time in years. The familiar smell of frying bacon and brewed coffee hits me with nostalgia.

I hear my name called and glance over to see my dad holding the corner booth for us. If I were dramatic, I'd say that every patron is watching as we slowly walk down the aisle to the booth where my dad sits. In all actuality, it is just a few people watching and whispering.

Marcus shouts my name, waving from his seat with his mom, who gives us a bright smile as we pass them. Elizabeth bends down to give her friend a

HARD FEELINGS

quick hug before continuing on. I guess between the Tylers and the Kings, the Purcells now have enough clout to be accepted back into society.

It's so backward that it makes me want to climb onto a table and moon the entire diner.

I barely refrain. Don't want to scar my father for the rest of his life. Besides, that's more of a Cassidy response. I hold my head up, staring down at the group of girls whispering as we pass.

"What are we whispering about?" Cassidy asks loudly, stopping at their booth.

They sit up straight, mortification evident on every single one of their faces as they avoid meeting Cassidy's eyes.

"That's what I thought," Cassidy says smugly as she closes the distance between her and me.

"Cassidy," I warn but can't help but laugh.

She is a lioness when it comes to protecting those she loves.

I slide in next to my dad, who leans over and gives me a hello kiss on the forehead, and thus begins a shockingly normal breakfast with family and friends.

In fact, the next couple of weeks slide into a new normal so seamlessly that I don't question it at all.

Killian drives me to school, and on days when I don't have practice or a game, he drives me home as well. We run on Saturday mornings, and he helps me study on Sundays.

My midterms come and go, and I do well enough to maintain my GPA. I attend all of Killian's home games, and vice versa.

I try not to get annoyed. We're both so busy between sports, work, and school, but it's been three weeks.

"Purcell! Look alive," Coach Yi yells from the sidelines, and I realize the rest of the team is heading inside for strength training.

Whoops!

I hurry to catch up. My eyes connect with Killian's immediately, and I feel the now-familiar heat rush through my body. He sets his weights on the rack and sits wide-legged on the bench, sweat glistening on his skin, making it glow golden under the fluorescent lights. Or maybe that's just the lust goggles I have on.

He stands and makes his way over to me. A couple of his teammates smirk as he passes, earning them a severe glare, and they turn their attention elsewhere. Grabbing my hips, he gently pulls me into him, and I guess I should be grossed out by how sweaty he is, but I'm just as sweaty from my earlier cardio.

Besides, he smells delicious. Whatever cologne he's wearing, combined with his own scent of evergreen from working on the farm this morning, really does it for me. He always smells like Christmas.

"Hey," he says quietly, and I fight the urge to kiss him.

"Hi." I mimic his private tone.

We haven't been super demonstrative at school; we're not even technically dating, but being this close to him now feels like we've been teasing each other for weeks.

Killian inhales deeply, as if drawing me in, and his eyes go heavy-lidded with the same desire I'm feeling.

"About our date," he begins, and I interrupt with, "Finally!"

He laughs. "I'm sorry. I didn't forget; it's just been—"

"Crazy busy," I finish for him.

"Yeah." He sways slightly toward me before shaking his head and taking a step back. "You have a game on Thursday, and we have a bye week, so how about Friday?"

"What are we doing?" I ask eagerly.

"It's a surprise," he tells me, then chuckles when he sees me frown. "I promise you'll like it."

"What should I wear?" I bite my lip, hiding a grin when his eyes zero in on my lips again.

"Something comfortable."

"So, not a tight, short dress and heels?" I tease.

Killian groans. "Shit, maybe I can change our plans."

I laugh and give him one more squeeze before heading over to spot Cassidy.

This is going to be fun.

EighTeen

The day of our date, I'm buzzing with excitement the moment I wake up. I feel like I should be nervous, but we've slipped into this state of complete comfort with each other. I know it'll be just us hanging out ... with maybe some kissing.

At least, that's what I'm telling myself.

It's Friday afternoon, and we thankfully don't have practice after last night's game, so I can head home to get dressed. I smile as I shove the books I don't need for homework into my locker.

We played great last night. It's such a thrill to win in general, but when the whole team is on point? It's a type of synergy I don't experience anywhere else. It's like we're all speaking a language only we understand through movement.

It shows how hard we work together. It makes me so proud to be a part of this team. We have only a couple more games before the fall season is over. Then, it's only one more season before we graduate. The tune of my internal countdown clock has changed. The more time passes, the more I begin to understand how much I'm going to leave behind.

It's so weird; I've been so focused on getting the hell out of this town that I didn't stop to think about whom I'd be leaving behind.

Most of the girls are staying in state. Only Marcus and Cassidy will be heading across the entire country with me.

Rubbing the ache in my chest, I head toward the parking lot, intent on meeting Cassidy at her car for a ride home. Killian has to stay to discuss something with his coach, so I'm hitching a ride with her.

Cassidy was so bummed when I relayed the wear "something comfortable" suggestion from Killian. Since we could be hiking for all I know, I'm in charge of the clothes I wear, but I'm giving Cassidy carte blanche on hair and makeup.

When I push through the doors, I see most of the parking lot is empty, and Cassidy is sitting on the hood of her car, cross-legged, texting on her cell. She glances up when she hears me walking toward her and gives me a giant grin.

Because it's impossible not to smile back at Cassidy, I give her one in return even though I'm slightly terrified of what she has in store for me.

"What's up, my little peach?" She hops down and unlocks her Jeep.

"You tell me, Dr. Frankenstein. What do you have planned for me?"

Cassidy laughs evilly. "Well, for one, we're going to do something with that mop of hair."

Grabbing the ends of my hair, which reach the middle of my back, I stare at the split ends and wince. Okay, yeah, I don't remember the last time I got a haircut.

"No color, right? Just a haircut?" I ask cautiously.

"Yes, and we're plucking your eyebrows. Just a little. You've got a great natural shape, but there are a few hairs that have been bugging me," she says as she gets behind the wheel.

"Jeez, Cassidy, don't hold back." I laugh.

"How do you feel about self-tanner?"

"I feel it's unnecessary when it's October," I reply 'cause no.

Who's going to see it anyway? Killian? He doesn't care.

"Fine. Okay, so hair, eyebrows, and some makeup." She nods to herself and drums her fingers on her steering wheel in excitement. "This is going to be so fun!"

I laugh and turn up the radio, smiling as Cassidy starts belting out Charli XCX's "Move Me."

The lyrics make me think of Killian, and I pull out my phone to shoot him a text.

Cassidy is giving me a makeover, so prepare yourself to be shocked.

"Are you pumped about the concert?" Cassidy shouts over the music.

I turn the radio back down so she doesn't bust my eardrums out. "Yes, totally. What's the plan?"

"We leave Friday after school and drive down. I got us an Airbnb in Old Fourth Ward. It's a cute-as-hell carriage house."

Joy bubbles up inside me. "This is going to be the best birthday. Thank you so much, Cass!"

"Don't thank me yet. The boys caught wind of the plan and are trying to get tickets to a Falcons game. They've got a home game that weekend too."

"That's okay."

HARD FEELINGS

"And they want to come out with us on Saturday."

"Do they even like going dancing?" I ask, confused.

Cassidy gives me a side-eye. "I think it's more of not wanting us to go out without them. Or rather, you."

"What does he think is going to happen?" I laugh incredulously, knowing she means Killian.

"Dude, I think Killian spends a lot of time thinking up scenarios where you drop his ass for someone else. Y'all are in that weird in-between stage in your relationship, where you're not technically exclusive."

"So, you're saying he's insecure?" I ask, brows furrowing.

"Yeah, and I think he's feeling a little possessive. He'll get over it."

"He'd better. He can trust me."

"I don't think it's you he doesn't trust."

I roll my eyes at that. Guys can be so strange sometimes.

"Fine, they want to crash my birthday weekend. The more, the merrier." I shrug.

"I didn't think you'd care too much, but I wanted to give you a heads-up."

"As long as we get bestie time, it's fine."

We pull into her driveway, and she rushes me upstairs into her bathroom. It's a Jack-and-Jill she shares with Tanner, and it's easy to see which side is hers.

I love Tanner like a brother, but he's a slob.

Cassidy catches me grimacing and nods in sympathy, as if to say, *This is what I have to put up with. Gross, right?*

She stands behind me, checking my height compared to hers, and says, "Okay, you get your hair wet. I'm going to grab a stool from downstairs. You're too short for me to cut your hair without some help."

Shrimp status strikes again, I think as I give her a thumbs-up.

Stripping off my shirt, I bend over her clean sink in my sports bra and rinse my hair under her faucet and soak it. Grabbing the towel Cassidy left me, I squeeze some of the water out of my hair, letting it hang heavy down my back.

I'm wiping up the water I got on the counter when Tanner's door swings open on the other side of the bathroom, scaring the living shit out of me.

Seeing it's Killian standing there, I cut off my screech and slap a hand on my chest, willing my heart rate back down.

"Jesus, Killian, whatever happened to knocking? The door was closed." I glare.

Killian's eyes are hot as they rake over me, up and down, and it's then I remember I'm in leggings and a sports bra. My chest flushes red under Killian's eyes, and he steps inside the bathroom, shutting the door behind him.

133

"Cass will be back any minute," I warn him as he closes the distance between us, forcing me to stare up at him.

Killian doesn't say anything as he runs a hand down my wet hair. "It's so much longer when it's wet."

I lick my lips nervously. "Water weighs my curls down."

Killian turns his lust-drunk gaze back on me, and I swallow convulsively.

"How married are you to the idea of our first kiss happening during our date?" he asks, his voice like gravel.

"Cass—" I breathe, already panting at the thought of him just taking it. Goddamn.

"I can be quick," he promises. When he reads the acquiescence on my face, he lifts me up onto the counter so I'm closer to his height.

"That's disappointing," I get out right before our mouths connect.

Killian's full lips are firm yet soft as they tease mine, gently at first, then more forcefully when I gasp in surprise. He tastes like peppermint and something so distinctly him. My hands move up his chest until they're wrapped around his neck, bringing our chests tightly together.

He flicks his tongue against my top lip, as if requesting permission, and I moan, scooting forward until he's between my thighs before opening my mouth to give him access.

He eats at my mouth like he's starving, and I'm helpless to do anything but follow his lead, tugging on his hair as he fuels my arousal.

Damn, Killian knows how to kiss.

I try not to think about all the practice he's gotten, but good Lord. Kissing Jason was nothing like this. It was sloppy, clumsy, and neither of us knew what we were doing. We were kids, kissing. Trying things out.

This is an entirely different ball game.

His stubble scratches against my skin in a way that tells me I'll be wearing his whisker marks on my cheeks later, but all it makes me want to do is rub against him like a cat.

I can feel him harden against my thigh, and my core clenches as I imagine what it would feel like to have him inside me. My hips shift toward him reflexively at the thought, and Killian's answering groan vibrates against my lips.

"Glory … baby," he whispers roughly before yanking me to the edge of the counter, giving me that heady pressure right where I need it.

I always thought being called baby would be gross and infantilizing, but there's something about it coming from Killian that just sets me on fire.

He feels big, and it makes me want to do things we are in no way ready for, but … *wow*. Girls used to say Killian King was king-sized, and before, that would make me want to barf. Now, I want to shake his hand and congratulate him.

"Don't run with scissors, Cassidy!"

HARD FEELINGS

"Don't stand in the way of sharp objects, Tanner!"

Hearing the twins, I rip my mouth from his and rest my forehead on his chest, trying to catch my breath.

Leaning back, I realize he hasn't moved a muscle. His chest pumps with his breaths, color high on his cheeks, and his delicious mouth is swollen from me. His hair looks crazy, and his eyes are glazed with arousal. In short, he looks completely indecent.

"Killian, you need to back up and get out of here," I whisper furiously, trying to move him out of the way by sliding forward, and he hisses when my body brushes against his erection.

I glance down and wince in sympathy. His jeans are doing nothing to hide his massive hard-on. Biting my lip, I look back up apologetically.

"Okay, you actually need to go before she gets in here," I plead when he continues to stand there, dazed.

Eyes on mine, he adjusts himself, tucking his hard-on behind the waistband of his jeans, and, holy effing hell, *that* was hot.

Killian tugs my hair, tilting my face up to him, and he drops another quick kiss on my lips. He inhales deeply before stepping back and putting distance between us.

"Better than I imagined," he says softly before turning toward Tanner's room. "I'll see you later, Glory."

Sinking against the counter, I blow out a noisy breath. *Wow.*

Cassidy comes bounding back into the bathroom a moment later, coming to a halt when she sees me flushed and mussed, standing suspiciously bewildered.

Setting down the stool, she raises a brow at me. "Why do you look like you just got your shit rocked?"

Dropping heavily onto the stool, I meet her gaze in the mirror. "Killian just barged in here and kissed the ever-living shit out of me."

"What?!" Cassidy screeches.

Laughing, I cover my face, equally embarrassed and happy.

Cassidy hugs me from behind, resting her chin on my head, and she squeezes me. "I'm so happy for you."

Her sincerity brings tears to my eyes, and I turn to wrap an arm around her for a hug. "I want this for you too, you know. You deserve someone who loves you just as fiercely as you love others."

Cassidy steps back and grabs a wide-toothed comb to detangle my curls. "It'll happen, but not until after I get my master's."

I roll my lips between my teeth to prevent the words *you can't control everything* from coming out. Cassidy has blinders on. I did too, and look where I am now.

We try to plan so much of our lives, but the more you hold tightly to the vision you have for yourself, the more life pushes back.

Whatever life throws her way, I've got her back.

"Do you trust me?" Cassidy asks, snipping the scissors in the air with a slightly maniacal gleam in her eye.

"Uh, in any other situation, yes, but—"

"I've watched, like, ten YouTube videos on how to cut curly hair. I swear I've got this. Nothing drastic," she promises.

I bite my lip. "Okay, go for it."

She sections my hair, chatting idly about one of the girls on our team finding out her boyfriend was texting another girl. I pretend to listen, but I'm staring nervously as chunks of my hair fall to the floor.

"Cass, please remember my hair shrinks when it's dry." I wince as another lock falls to the ground.

"Trust the process, Glory."

Ah, Jesus, okay. I close my eyes, figuring it's better to just let this be a surprise.

Cassidy doesn't cut for very long before she starts styling it. This is a bitch on my hair, but I trust her. After all, she's the one who helped me figure out how to actually do my hair.

"Turn toward me and flip your hair down," Cassidy orders, attaching the diffuser to the hair dryer.

Doing as ordered, I let her dry my hair. How come this always seems to go faster when someone else does your hair?

Before I know it, she's running oil through the strands. It's an abbreviated version of my normal routine, but when I flip my hair back, I notice she's added some layers and face-framing pieces.

There's so much more movement rather than just hanging there. It softens the angles of my face and somehow makes my eyes bigger.

"Cass, I love it!" I squeal.

"See! I told you. I have many talents." Cassidy turns me toward her and pulls out her makeup bag, "Now, I know this is a casual date," she says with some disgust, making me laugh lightly, "but I want to do a little more than your normal natural makeup look."

"You're batting a thousand, my friend; have at it."

Twenty minutes and some cleanup later, I'm back in her car, going home to get changed. Killian was gone by the time we left, having only stopped briefly after giving Tanner a ride home before heading out.

Tanner wolf-whistled as we left, making me blush like an idiot.

HARD FEELINGS

It feels weird to put so much effort into my appearance for someone who has seen me at my absolute worst. I mean, we both got chicken pox together in fourth grade. We were flu buddies in seventh.

Once you've seen someone lean over and yack into a trash can, I feel like the illusion is gone.

But at the same time, I feel really pretty, and I realize this is more for me than Killian. Cassidy was right that the makeup is subtle and natural-looking, only serving to bring out my features. I've never paid much attention to my appearance. I know I'm not ugly, but my resemblance to my mother became something to hate about the same time I started actually becoming self-aware in that way.

It's left me feeling conflicted about how I look.

More to talk to my therapist about, I guess.

I began going to therapy about a week after my dad suggested it, following the meltdown I had when my mom decided to implode my life for the second time.

It was a rough start. I found myself unable to talk about things without bawling my eyes out. It was more than a few sessions before I was able to coherently express myself.

I feel better though. It's nice to have a subjective ear, and I didn't realize how much I just needed someone to listen. Nothing groundbreaking yet, but I don't hate going.

Cassidy pulls into the driveway, bringing me back to the present, and suddenly, the butterflies that have been absent all day arrive.

I run my sweaty hands up and down my thighs and hesitate getting out of the car.

Cassidy, picking up on my nerves, flicks my nose to get my attention. Wincing, I rub my nose and glare at her.

"It's going to be fine. This is Killian we're talking about. Probably the most romantic guy I know."

"He told me how he sneaks your books to read," I admit, smiling.

"Yeah, I might have mentioned that he could learn a thing or two."

"Okay." I blow out a breath. "Okay, I'm going to go."

"Call me the second you get home tonight, Glory Jane," she says as I get out of the car.

"I swear I will. Cass, I feel like I'm going to puke," I confess nervously.

"It's going to be totally fine." She pauses, picking up her phone. "How about this? I'll set an alarm for eight, and I'll call you. If things are going south, we can make something up, and I'll come get you. If you don't answer, I'll assume it's all good."

"Okay, it's a plan."

"Have fun, Glo!" Cassidy calls out as she backs out of the driveway.

I glance at my phone and see he'll be picking me up in less than forty-five minutes. *Shit!*

Booking it inside, I call out a quick hello to Dad. He knows about my date tonight but promised not to make a big deal out of it. We're hanging out tomorrow anyway. He said he'd take me to the sporting goods store to look at new turf shoes in exchange for my helping him clean out the garage, but only if he doesn't embarrass me by demanding to take pictures or interrogating Killian.

I rip my closet door open and am immediately overwhelmed. I normally dress casually, but I want to look cute, especially with the new hair and the glowy look that Cassidy did with my makeup.

I grab a pair of asymmetrical waistband jeans and a fitted, long-sleeved white crop top. Now, something to put over the top since it's getting down to the forties tonight.

Ah, perfect, I think as I spot the plaid fleece shacket.

I pair this with my white Air Force 1s and video-call Cassidy for a 'fit check.

There's a whoosh sound, and Cassidy's eager face greets me.

"Hey, okay, let me set the phone up so you can see," I speak quickly, checking the time and realizing he's going to be here soon.

I set my phone on my bedside table, leaning it against the lamp, and back up, doing a little twirl and picking up my foot so she can see the shoe.

"Love! You look comfortable but still put together. Are you going to wear any jewelry?"

I don't have my ears pierced—or at least, not anymore. It got annoying, always having to take them out or tape them down when I played. Easier just to let the holes close. I'm not a big jewelry person anyway but—

"I have that gold chain you got me for Christmas last year," I tell her, heading over to my bulletin board, where it's dangling from a thumbtacked picture of the two of us.

"Oh, that's perfect!" she exclaims as I put it on.

I huff out a breath and give her a wide-eyed look.

"It's going to be fine, Glory. Relax."

"I wasn't nervous until today." I laugh, tucking my hair behind my ears.

The doorbell rings, interrupting whatever I was going to say next, and I jump.

"Glory, oh my God." Cassidy laughs. "This is so adorable! But you need to chill. It's Killian. Hair-braiding, romance-reading, gags-at-bananas, and totally-gone-for-you Killian."

"Football-star, town's-prodigal-son, rich, hot, and has-the-power-to-crush-me-again Killian," I counter but take a deep breath.

HARD FEELINGS

"He might be all those things, but you're Glory mothereffing Jane Purcell. Bad bitch on the soccer field, full ride to UCLA, strong, intelligent, and able to handle whatever comes your way."

"Okay, okay, you're right. I'm a bad bitch," I say, sounding completely the opposite.

"The baddest!" Cassidy echoes. "Call me literally the second you're home."

"I will," I promise, then squeal before ending the call.

I grab my little cardholder, phone, and house keys before slipping them into the pocket of my coat.

As I run down the stairs, I hear my dad talking softly to Killian and slow to a halt just out of sight.

"I've missed you too, son," my dad says in a choked voice, and I hear back slaps. "You know I love you, but you'd better take care of her."

"I will, sir."

"You can come out now, Glory," Dad says, and I flush from head to toe.

I peek around the corner, and they are both facing me, grinning at my eavesdropping. Rolling my eyes, I come all the way into the room. Killian thinks he's quick—or at least, he's trying to be with my dad standing right there—but I see the brief cataloging look.

He bites his lip, and I know he approves.

Feeling warm, I glance over at my dad, and he's got that classic James Purcell sentimentality thing going on. He is the least successful person I know at hiding his emotions, and I love him for it. Even when it mortifies me— kind of like right now.

"Dad, stop." I laugh, walking over to him to give him a big hug.

"Give me a break. This is your first date. You turn eighteen next week. This is a lot to process." He lets out a watery chuckle.

I give him a hard squeeze before pulling back. "Home by ten?"

"Make it eleven."

"Wow, a whole extra hour, Dad?" I tease.

"Get out of here and enjoy it. We've got a seven-in-the-morning start time tomorrow."

I grab Killian's hand and wave good-bye to my dad.

"What are y'all doing at seven tomorrow?" Killian asks, unlocking his car.

"Dad's got me cleaning out the garage in exchange for some new turf shoes." I stand back as Killian opens the passenger door for me. "Pulling out all the stops, huh?"

He rolls his eyes at me, closing my door before getting into the driver's seat.

Killian leans close to me. "You deserve it."

My heart warms, and all the nerves slip away. This is Killian.

"Did you get your Biology midterm back yet?" Killian asks, backing out of my driveway.

I barely prevent myself from chewing on my thumbnail. Killian has been helping me here and there, and that's in addition to the class study group I attend in the mornings. I have to maintain my GPA, but this class is kicking my ass.

"I should be getting it back next week."

"I'm sure you aced it, Glory."

I snort. "Killian, I'm an average student, and I'm not embarrassed about it. My efforts have always been geared toward soccer."

"Do you know what you want to major in as a backup career?" Killian asks curiously.

Again, I'm struck by how much time we've spent together over the last couple of months, yet there's still so much to catch up on.

"I'm interested in being a sports agent, so I might major in sports management. I just love the idea of being that someone who gives a little girl in the middle of nowhere some hope that her dreams aren't unrealistic."

"I love that, Glory. Do you have an agent?"

"No, I asked my coach, and she said it's not necessary right now but that I should definitely look into it down the line."

I try not to look too far down the barrel of my future; it gets extremely overwhelming.

"Have you already declared for Georgia?"

Killian's shoulders visibly tighten. "Not yet. Georgia is coming for me pretty hard though."

"Yeah, I figured you'd be dead set on UGA," I say conversationally.

It's obvious he's got a lot on his mind, but I would have thought he'd be clear about going to UGA.

"A lot has changed," he says simply. "Here we are."

I look to see we're pulling into the back gate at the farm. The back entrance is reserved for employees only. When you pull through, you're greeted by rows and rows of evergreen. It smells amazing. To the left is a path that brings you to the front office, where the gift shop and apple cider stand are.

For Christmas every year, they hire a Santa Claus and have a little picture station. Pretty Christmas lights line the main building and the stand, giving everything a soft glow.

I haven't been here in years.

Killian turns right, toward the delivery truck and ATVs.

"Where are we going?"

If we were doing something at the farm, I think for sure it would be at the front.

HARD FEELINGS

Killian parks next to the truck—an old, bright red Jeep truck with wood siding and *King Family Farms* in a cute white font on the sides. It looks just like the red truck ornaments you can find every Christmas.

My mom used to say that King Family Farms was like walking onto the set of a Hallmark movie, and I can't disagree.

"Come on. We're going to switch to the truck," he says, grinning at my questioning look.

We get in the truck, and we're off again, this time heading into the forest of Christmas trees. It's pretty dark out, the truck's headlights guiding the way.

"Are you going to off me?" I joke as we go deeper into the middle of the trees.

"If I were going to kill you, Glory, I wouldn't have announced to everyone that we were going on a date and then come to my family's farm to do it."

"Ah, so you admit to at least thinking about it!" I laugh, only to fall silent when I see one tree lit up, complete with decorations. "How the hell did you manage to get lights working all the way out here?"

Killian laughs. "Long-ass extension cords and a generator."

He maneuvers the truck so the truck bed is facing the tree.

"Stay here for a second," he says before hopping out.

The truck rocks as he climbs into the back. I refuse to look; he's going to all this trouble to surprise me, and I'm going to let him.

A couple of minutes later, he opens my door and holds out a hand.

"Close your eyes," he whispers in my ear before kissing my cheek.

Obligingly, I let him lead me around to the back. The smell of fire has me smiling. There are few things I love more than the smell of a campfire in the fall. Giving my hand a squeeze, Killian tells me to open my eyes. A loud gasp leaves my mouth as I take in the scene before me.

He has a small fire going in a clearing with decorated trees surrounding us. I walk to the nearest tree and discover three gifts in front of it, beautifully wrapped. Moving closer, I see that the decorations on the tree aren't simple bulbs or garlands; it's little pictures of us.

"Killian," I choke out as emotion overtakes me.

"It's all the stuff we love. See," he says quietly, coming up beside me and pointing out some of the figurines. "And it's us."

There must be a hundred of them, cataloging the years of our friendship. Us at each other's birthday parties, us in matching pajama sets for Christmas, me in a much smaller version of Killian's jersey as I cheer him on at his game, the two of us fishing, sharing a milkshake … all these little moments.

"Killian, this must have taken you forever," I whisper, overwhelmed.

"It was fun." He blushes. "I didn't realize how many pictures our parents took."

I turn to take him in fully and realize he's also decorated the back of the truck. He put some padding down with a fluffy, huge blanket. Pillows surround the sides, and it looks like the perfect place to curl up and watch the fire. I notice a little cooler on the side and quirk a brow at him.

"You really thought of everything, huh?"

He heads over to it excitedly. "We've got cider and stuff to make s'mores. Mom made us some sandwiches—wait, should I admit my mom helped me with this stuff?"

"I think it's cute," I tell him, coming up to hug him from behind, my arms barely making it around his thick waist. Feeling a bit like a tick on a dog, I laugh at myself.

"Are you making me the little spoon?" He grins as he turns around and faces me.

"I tried, but I don't think it worked." I smile back, and he drops a quick kiss on my lips.

"Here," he says, lifting me to sit in the back of the truck. "I can't wait any longer for you to open your presents."

"I didn't realize presents were a thing on a first date."

"I have lots of birthdays and Christmases to make up for, Glory." Killian grabs the presents and heads back to the truck.

He's got on dark jeans and a dark green sweater. It complements his coloring, and with the fire making his skin glow and hair shine, he's stunning.

"You look beautiful, Killian," I tell him softly as he walks toward me.

"That's my line, baby," he says as he closes the distance to give me another kiss.

When he hops up next to me, I sit cross-legged, facing him as he sets the gifts between us.

"Which should I open first?" I ask, wiggling my fingers over them eagerly.

"This one." He hands me a flat box, and I shake it, putting my ear to it and laughing when he rolls his eyes at me. "Just open it. I can't believe I forgot what a production you make out of opening presents."

Smirking, I decide to torture him and slowly peel off the tape, carefully unwrapping the paper. It's one of those simple white boxes kids hate getting for Christmas because it usually means clothing. Intrigued, I open the box and see it's a Glory-sized version of his jersey with his name on the back.

Stomach in my throat, I look at him, and he's watching me intently.

Getting a jersey like this from a player means only one thing: he's claiming you as his. Being a girlfriend of a player means a lot at our school.

For Killian to want me to wear this …

"You want me to be your girlfriend?" I ask quietly.

"I would be honored if you were," he replies sincerely.

"So, we're really doing this then?" I hug the jersey to my pounding chest.

HARD FEELINGS

"Yes, if you want to."

"Jeez, I must be a better kisser than I thought," I joke, slipping my jacket off so I can pull it over my shirt.

Killian relaxes the second it goes on, and for a moment, I realize how much power I had. *Have.* For so long, I've felt like such a casualty from the wreckage of our parents' decision, then a victim of this town. The only power I've felt is in not letting them see how much it hurts and dominating on the field.

"What would you have done if I'd said no?" I ask curiously.

"Nothing. We'd be exactly as we are, as we were. Best friends. You mean everything to me, Glory. I'd like to be in your life in whatever capacity you want."

"I was hoping you'd say something like, *I'd have kicked that tree and cried from utter devastation,*" I say lightly despite how heavy with emotion this conversation is.

"Glory, I would kick every single tree on this farm," he says seriously, but his eyes are filled with humor. He picks up a smaller box and hands it over. "Open this one."

I take the box and open it, revealing a gorgeous necklace with a bar with stamped coordinates on it.

"It's the coordinates for Galway. I know you must hate it here, but I want you to take a piece of me with you when you go to college. We met here. Our friends are from here. I like to think it's not all bad, Glory."

"No," I whisper, running my thumb along the numbers and letters, "it's not. I've been realizing how much I'm actually going to miss this place the closer we get to finishing the school year."

"Now, you'll always have a piece of it with you."

I lean forward and give him a kiss. Killian takes me into his arms and settles me on his lap, letting the kiss go deeper before pulling back.

"Can I put it on you?"

I nod and turn in his lap, lifting my hair so he can secure it.

My fingers go to where it rests against my chest, and I feel grounded the second I touch it. "I love it, Killian."

"I'm glad." He nuzzles my neck before kissing my cheek again. "One more."

I lean forward, deciding to stay in his lap, and grab the heavier box. I don't wait to savor; I just rip this one open and pause at the gorgeous leather-bound album with both our names embossed on the outside.

I trace our names with my pointer finger before opening it and seeing larger copies of all the photos he put on the tree. "Killian, this is ..." Tears clog my throat as I flip through pages of us.

Seeing him in so much of my life for so long is overwhelming. He's been there for almost everything. He knows me better than anyone. We get older as I flip, and I begin to pay more attention to how Killian looks at me and I at him. I can see how much he loves me. It's beautiful to see how much he cares, how he always cared.

Hugging it to my chest, I laugh as I cry harder. "I'll treasure this forever, Killian."

"There are blank pages in the back, so we can add pictures. I know it's a little old-fashioned—"

"It's perfect," I assure him quickly. "Man, do girls cry this much on first dates?"

Killian laughs and gives me another kiss before lifting me out of his arms. "I can fix that with some s'mores."

I lean back against the pillows and watch him.

My heart is so full. I just have to make sure the way I feel is louder than the voice in my head, asking if I can trust these feelings.

NineTeen

That night changed everything for us. We had already been on our way, but it made everything official. We were together now. When I got home that night and called Cassidy, we both squealed and gushed over the thoughtfulness of his gifts.

I always knew Killian felt so much, but to have physical proof made me feel cherished.

The following week at school, Killian went above and beyond, letting people know I was his and he was mine. It was a version of Killian this school hadn't seen before.

Now that I think about it, I don't think I've ever seen him in a relationship or show outward affection to a girl at our school besides Cassidy.

Boyfriend Killian is tactile and demonstratively affectionate. Every hello or good-bye is said with a kiss, he's always touching me in some way, and I feel surrounded and protected by him.

It's the night before my birthday, and I'm curled up in bed, watching TV, while Killian is at practice. They have a game tomorrow that Cassidy and I will miss since we're heading to Atlanta a day earlier than them.

I'm scrolling through social media, and I smile at the picture Killian posted after our date. It's just a simple shot of us snuggling in the truck, the fire setting our faces aglow. He's dropping a kiss on my head, his eyes crinkled in a way that shows he's smiling, as I grin hugely into the camera.

It's the same photo I use as my lock screen on my phone. Ugh, yes, I am now a part of one of those lovesick couples Cassidy and I use to gag at.

My phone buzzes, and a notification drops from the top of my phone, blocking out the top half of the picture.

Please tell me you're packed for tomorrow.

Shit, Cassidy. I am not.

Doing it now!

Rolling out of bed, I dig my overnight bag out of my closet and wrinkle my nose when I realize I never unpacked from the last time I used this that weekend I went with the team to see an Atlanta United game.

I grab the clothes out and throw them behind me near my laundry basket and gasp as I find Killian's journal. I have been looking everywhere for this thing!

If I crack it open, I know I'll just sit here, reading it, and not pack, so I toss it onto my bed. That can be my motivation to hurry this the hell up. Turning the bag upside down, I shake it out and toss that onto my bed as well.

Standing, I shove my hands into my lower back and stretch as I consider my closet. I don't have many going-out outfits, but I grab something I know will work. Cassidy is always giving me something she thinks I should wear in an effort to get me out of my usual comfort clothing or soccer clothes.

Shoving my sweaters to the left, I pull out some of my Cassidy-approved options. There's a sleeveless coffee-colored bodycon dress with a mock neck. It hits above my knees. This, paired with my thrifted black leather jacket, will be perfect for going dancing. I can take the jacket off if I get hot, but the dress is still long enough that my legs will be warm.

It's chilly at night, so if Cassidy thinks I'll be rocking ass and tits out, she's out of her mind.

For the concert, I grab some ripped jeans and my black bodysuit and call it done. I can pair both with my cool platform black boots. They're grungy, and they make me three inches taller, so obviously, a winner. It also means I don't have to toddle around in heels.

I have not practiced enough to wear heels. Cassidy tries, but I'm just more comfortable in Vans or soccer shoes. Nothing wrong with it. I can be sexy in my style too. Sometimes, I think Cassidy tries to fill the void of my mother, pushing me to explore more traditionally girlie things, but it's just not me.

I lay the outfits out on the floor with the shoes and send pics to Cassidy. She immediately responds with a thumbs-up.

Folding them carefully to avoid wrinkles, I grab some pajamas, an extra sweater, and some panties and pack them all into my bag. I can pack toiletries tomorrow morning after I use what I need.

Okay, done!

Hopping back into bed, I stack my pillows behind me so I can get comfortable and grab Killian's journal.

HARD FEELINGS

Glory,

I almost beat the shit out of Tyson Carrington today, but Tanner beat me to it. He told me what they did, chasing you through the woods. Scaring you. I swear to God, I felt like I had been lit on fire.

I've never been so angry in my life.

Tanner told me it's taken care of, and that kills me too. Someone else is protecting you, when it should be me.

The next day at school, I made sure people knew if they laid a hand on you, I'd break every finger of that hand.

You'd be so shocked at the violence I feel when thinking someone would scare you like that. It shocks me too.

I wonder if I'll ever begin to care less. I hope so. I hope I'm able to forget you.

But for now, you haunt me, Glory.

My hand reaches for my phone to call you constantly. I want to tell you all the little things about my day, and I realize I can't. I feel like I have to learn how to walk again.

I'm so lost without you.

I exhale shakily; I can feel his anger and pain come off the page. This is the shortest passage I've read of his, nothing clams Killian up more than anger.

He's always been so good at expressing himself, except when he's mad. In fact, all negative or deemed negative emotion is difficult for the entire King family. They are so conscious of the eyes on them at all times; the pressure to always be so strong and unperturbed must weigh heavily.

I flip the page and see it's nearly six months later between the last entry and this one.

Hey, Glory.

You're sixteen today. You've talked about this day forever. I think all the movies make it seem like a bigger deal than it is. Mine was a month ago, and the only thing I noticed was, you weren't there.

147

Tanner told me that he and Cassidy were taking you to the hibachi restaurant in Crestwood, and I was tempted to convince my mom to go out to dinner there, just so we could run into each other.

But I know that would only piss you off because you hate me now, and part of me is glad.

For a while, you gave me nothing, barely noticed my presence, but recently, I've been on the receiving end of your anger, and, God, is it horrible to admit I'm happy about it?

I'd rather have your anger than your indifference.

Tanner thinks you're mad because I told the new guy to back off. I know it's wrong to feel so possessive of you.

But I can't help it, Glory. I covet you, but I can't have you. Not without causing people harm, and I'm beginning to wonder if that pain is worth it.

Doesn't matter anymore anyway. You hate me, like you should. I understand.

I hate myself too.

"Oof, Killian," I murmur to myself.

Yeah, I remember that he scared that guy off. I was furious.

One of the few people who had moved to this town in the last decade, who had no preconceived notions of me, had shown interest in me.

And it was reciprocated, which I think was the actual problem Killian had.

Austin was a genuinely nice guy, and we had a lot in common. We both played soccer, and he became fast friends with Marcus—if Marcus gives his stamp of approval to a guy, then he's a quality dude.

Austin's interest lasted an entire day. I was so sure he was going to ask me out, but he walked right by me in the hall after eating lunch with me the day before despite my calling out to him.

Marcus was the one who got the truth out of him and told me Killian had warned him off me.

I'm getting mad all over again.

"Okay, that's probably enough of that for today." I close his journal and tuck it inside my nightstand drawer for later.

Maybe reminding myself of all this shit isn't for the best, but I do enjoy getting inside Killian's head. It's helping me understand his perspective more—even if it reminds me how I felt.

HARD FEELINGS

My phone rings, and I see it's Killian.

"Hey," I answer, settling back into my pillows. "How was practice?"

"Hey, baby," Killian greets, and, man, I still haven't gotten used to the nickname. Every time he says it, it sends a little thrill through me. "It was a light one because of our game tomorrow. Just working out some new plays."

"Hmm."

"What are you doing?"

Glancing at where I stashed his journal, I say, "Well, I finished packing for this weekend and was reading some of your journal."

"Fuck, I forgot you had that," he grumbles, and I can feel his discomfort. "What did you read?"

"Oh, just how pissed you were at Tyson and his dipshit friends. Then at Austin for having the audacity to not hate me on sight, like the rest of this town," I tell him more casually than I'm actually feeling.

"You sound mad," he says tentatively.

"Hmm."

"That's the second time you've hummed at me instead of giving me an answer," he calls me out, annoyance in his voice.

"I'm just trying to process this stuff, Killian. It's like living it a second time."

"Maybe reading it isn't the best idea …"

"Why? So then you don't get held accountable for the immature bullshit you pulled?" I snap and then instantly feel like shit.

"I'm coming over."

"No, don't."

"You're mad at me; I want to come over and make it okay," Killian argues.

"And I'm telling you, I need space. You need to respect that," I tell him firmly, and I can practically feel his anxiety spike through the phone. "Killian, just because I'm mad doesn't mean we're breaking up."

"Why would you even say that?" he bites out.

"Because anytime I'm angry or out of your sight for too long, you freak out. You don't trust me, and it's starting to actually tick me off."

"I do trust you, Glory," he argues.

"Hmm."

"Stop humming at me!"

"Look, we will be fine. I just need to untangle my feelings right now. Having you near me always scrambles me up. Let me sleep on it, and I'll see you tomorrow."

"First thing in the morning, Glory. Don't blow me off. I'm picking you up, and if you're still mad, we're going to hash it out."

We hang up, and I toss my phone on my bed before turning over.

149

The next morning, I'm up and ready to go way before Killian arrives to take me to school. I'm downstairs, eating my birthday pancakes, which are just pancakes with multicolored sprinkles in them and a metric ton of whipped cream, when he knocks on the door before opening it.

My body stiffens as I fork another huge bite into my mouth and force myself to relax.

He stands at my back like an anxious, giant black cloud, and I decide to take pity on him. Turning around, I don't even need to stand up to hug him—he's that close; I'm able to just wrap my arms around him.

Killian immediately encloses me in his arms, exhaling like he's been holding his breath since we talked last night.

"Happy birthday, Glory," he whispers against my hair before giving me a kiss on the forehead.

Got to keep it clean in front of my dad, who is looking anywhere but at us.

"Thanks, Kills." I turn to my dad. "Dad, you can look. We just hugged."

He looks over at us sheepishly and shrugs, as if to say he can't help it.

"Run me through the plans again," Dad orders, resting his elbows on the counter.

"Cass and I are driving down tonight. I already sent you the address of the Airbnb. We'll text you the second we arrive. The concert is tonight, but we should be back at around eleven. Cass wants to get up early on Saturday and work out before walking to a cute little breakfast place."

"What are your plans for Saturday?" Dad asks, and I know it's part grilling me and part genuinely curious.

"I don't know yet; we're winging it. Killian and Tanner are coming down for a game, so we'll probably do some shopping before meeting up with them later."

He nods his head, but I can tell something is on his mind.

"Dad, spit it out."

Killian sits down on the stool next to me and slides my forgotten pancakes over to himself. Opportunist.

"Uh, your mom texted, and I might have told her you'd be in town," he confesses.

Killian's fork hovers halfway to his mouth, his eyes shooting over to me.

I take a deep breath because the instant rage that consumes me is too much for this early in the morning. At least I'll have plenty to talk about with my therapist on Monday.

HARD FEELINGS

"Dad, she hasn't texted me once since she was here last." I shoot for calm, but it comes out between gritted teeth, so I think I failed.

Killian's hand drops to my thigh and squeezes.

"She's scared of you, Glory."

I scoff. I scoff so hard that I'm surprised it doesn't propel me into outer space.

"She's just hoping you might be interested in coming to an ultrasound appointment on Saturday morning. It's early in the day, so you can still grab lunch with Cass."

"How can you talk about all this with her? She cheated on you and got pregnant by that asshole. No offense, Killian."

"None taken," he says dryly.

"Glory, I'm talking with your mother because she's *your mother*. I'm also tired of being pissed off. I'm ready to move on. We're getting a new start soon, and I'm not giving her the power to overshadow that," Dad says pointedly.

I stare mutinously at the counter, counting the flecks in the granite in front of me. Something he said strikes a chord though—probably for the wrong reasons. He's taking back his power through forgiveness, and I know that's what my therapist wants. I'm considering this out of spite, which ... is the opposite of forgiveness.

"Fine, but she needs to reach out to me and send me the details," I counter.

"I'll tell her."

"And this is Killian's sister, too, so she needs to at least extend the invitation to him," I continue, and Killian's hand tightens on my thigh again. I don't know if he wants to go, but I definitely know the invitation won't be coming from his dad.

Dad glances warily at Killian before nodding.

"Is that weird ... for y'all?" Dad asks tentatively.

I laugh loudly. "Dad, this whole situation is off-the-charts weird!"

"Thanks for asking, Jamie, but we're working through it," Killian adds, and I raise a brow.

"Wow, *Jamie*. Aren't you two buddy-buddy?"

Killian shrugs, forking the final bite into his mouth, and Dad just smiles. I'm happy. Dad is there for Killian now, and it brings me joy. At least my mom is showing some interest in me in her own emotionally damaging way. Killian's dad would like nothing more than to erase his previous life from his memory. He already changed his freaking name back to Ramos from King.

"We gotta go," Killian says, glancing at his watch.

I stand up and head over to my dad, giving him a big hug. "I'll text you when we get on the road and when we get there."

"Thank you." He gives me a quick squeeze and then lets me go.

I grab my backpack, which Killian takes from my hand and slings over his massive shoulder, and I take my overnight bag instead.

Once we're outside, Killian grips my hand. "Are you okay with meeting your mom?"

"I mean, no, but whatever. I'm not going to let her corrupt my baby sister either. Were you okay with me throwing your name in there too? I didn't even ask."

"I want to be a part of her life too. Will it be awkward? Yes, but I'll get over it. We'll have each other, and I'd much rather deal with your mom than my dad. I'm more likely to knock him on his ass than talk to him."

Killian opens my door, and I hop in. He slings all our bags into the backseat.

"Are your parents talking?" I ask, clicking my seat belt in place.

Killian lets out a single loud, "Ha!"

"Damn, I thought maybe he'd not be a prick."

"Oh, he's being a prick. He's fighting for more alimony."

"Are you serious?" I ask, incredulous.

Killian nods, then glances over. "Our fight seems stupid now."

"Killian, we weren't even fighting."

"You seemed pretty pissed last night," he points out.

I huff, "I was. I read all that, and it brought up old stuff. I'm working through it, and I'm doing it for us because I want there to be an *us*. What I have a bigger issue with is you thinking I'm going to run every time we disagree."

"I'm also working on that."

"Good."

"I just sometimes wonder what the hell you're doing with me. I don't deserve you."

"Then, I guess you'd better try because I don't think that. That is all you."

My phone buzzes, and I see Tanner and Cassidy wishing me happy birthday in the group chat, trying to outdo one another with the funnier GIF.

Laughing softly, I put my phone away. "We're going to be fine. This is new territory we're navigating. Let's not make it harder with insecurities. Unless I do something to validate these concerns of yours, tell that voice in your head to shut the fuck up."

Killian chuckles. "I will."

I lean over and kiss his cheek, giggling when he turns to meet my mouth briefly.

God, there is something so soothing about driving down some mountain roads, the music low. The leaves are bright, like shades of fire, and the air is cool, but there's still some fog.

HARD FEELINGS

I want to stay like this forever. I grab Killian's hand off the gearshift it was resting on and bring it to my mouth, pressing a kiss there before holding it in my lap.

We're going to be fine.

TWENTY

On the way out of town, Cassidy stops at the gas station for snacks and drinks. She's a strong believer in *if you're in the car for over thirty minutes, you should get a snack*.

It's a philosophy I've happily adopted. Do we need four bags of chips, two candy bars, and two giant sodas? Probably not, but it's my birthday, and we're heading into Atlanta during rush hour, so why not?

We deserve it.

Wiping my fingers on my leggings because I'm classy, I grab my phone and shoot off a text to Dad as we merge onto the highway.

"Can you let Killian know in the group text?" Cassidy asks as she spies what I'm doing. "Tanner is in protective twin mode. Kill two peacocks with one text, right?"

Snorting, I do as she asked. Tanner is two minutes older than her, and he never lets her forget it.

"What is he going to do with you all the way in California?"

"Ha! I didn't tell you. He's trying to get into the University of Washington."

"Wait, really? Why?" I ask, dumbfounded.

It's been Tanner and Killian's plan forever to go play together at UGA.

"It's not for certain yet. He's still applying to UGA. He's not getting scouted there though, so he'd have to be a walk-on, which is not likely, considering UGA's football program. I think that reality is hitting him hard."

"Damn, I feel like shit. I need to be a better friend to him."

"I think he finds it hard to talk to you and Killian because you two are, like, the biggest sports stars at our school. I mean, you already have a scholarship and signed a letter of intent," Cassidy says without a hint of jealousy.

Not that she would be. It's never been her dream to play professionally. She'd be happy to play in college or not.

It would be the end of the world for me. I wonder if Tanner is feeling the same way.

"Yeah …" I trail off, uncertain.

"So, your mom …"

"Damn, Cass. From one sad topic to the next."

"I can't help it! Car rides make me chatty."

She's not kidding. I can't count how many times we've driven around town—there's not much else to do, honestly—and just listened to music and talked about deep shit.

Groaning, I sink further into my seat. "Yeah, she wants me to go with her to the ultrasound appointment tomorrow."

"Dude, I cannot believe she's pregnant."

"You're telling me."

"How far along is she anyway?"

"I don't know. I was too shocked that she was pregnant at all to find out." I chew on my thumbnail.

"So weird. Weirder still that you and Killian are going to have a shared sibling," she says slyly.

"Cassidy Ann, this is not like one of your books."

"Puh-lease. This is exactly like one of my books. If for nothing else than the absolute stink of angst that wafts off you and Killian."

"Stink of angst?" I laugh.

"I can practically see little stinky squiggles coming off you and Killian when y'all are in the same room. It's either that or you're trying to undress each other with your minds."

"We're not that bad, are we?" I ask, blushing furiously.

"Uh, yeah, you are. You sent a freshman girl into puberty the other day just with how hot you two were together."

"Ew, Cass!" I squeak in disgust.

"I'm just saying." She holds up her hand in surrender.

"Say less." I pretend to gag.

We amicably chat the rest of the way, snacking on food and repeatedly listening to the entire *Crash* album in preparation for tonight's concert. Cassidy is convinced Rina Sawayama will be a surprise guest for their song "Beg for You" because she is in town, according to Cassidy's Instagram stalking.

Atlanta traffic adds an extra hour to our travel time, but we turn on a tree-lined street with large, old homes, and soon enough, we're parking on

HARD FEELINGS

the street in front of a gorgeous home. There's a little gate leading around the back to the carriage house we're staying in.

There's no time to enjoy everything because we're two hours away from the doors opening for the concert, and we want to eat and get there early since it's general admission. We're ready and out the door fast, snapping a photo of how hot we look and posting it. My phone buzzes with a notification that Killian likes my photo, and I can't resist teasing him.

Wow, liking a pic two seconds after posting. Someone's thirsty!

He replies instantly.

Have you seen yourself?

Grinning, I tuck my phone into my jeans and focus on spending time with Cassidy. I know she was a little worried about Killian and me getting together and if it would absorb all my time, like we've seen happen with other girls on our team.

But she's my ride or die.

We joke about retiring and buying townhomes right next to each other when we're older.

It's nights like this, just the two of us, that I'll cherish when I'm feeling lonely at college next year.

"Whatcha thinkin' about over there?" Cassidy asks as we walk down the street to the pizza place we spotted on the way in.

"Nothing much. Just that I love ya." I wrap an arm around her waist when she wraps one around my shoulders.

"Aw, I love you too, Glo."

The rest of the night is one of the best nights I've ever had. Halloween has brought the entertainment out—that's for sure. People show up to the concert in costumes—something Cassidy and I kick ourselves over for not thinking of.

After, we both collapse into bed, exhausted at the end of the night, and sleep for what feels like five minutes. I wake up to my phone buzzing under my cheek. Groaning, I open my eyes and smack my lips. Grimacing at how dry they are, I realize I'm fully on my stomach, face lying on my phone, with a sore throat, indicating I was snoring.

Damn, I sleep like the dead.

"Glory, answer your phone!" Cassidy grumbles next to me in the bed.

I roll over, getting out of bed, and move out into the tiny kitchenette.

Seeing Tanner's name flash on my screen, I answer quickly. "Why didn't you call Cassidy?"

"Well, good morning to you too, sunshine!" he greets in a singsong voice.

"Tanner," I groan, not awake.

"Open up. We're here."

"Where?" I stand up straight.

"Outside, dude. Open up. It's cold!"

I hang up and open the door and see Tanner waving from the gate.

Hurrying down the stairs in my bare feet, I open the gate, asking, "Where's Killian?"

"He's parking. I'm going to wake up Cass. Let's go to breakfast."

"Tanner, what the hell time is it?" I ask, at a loss. His energy is off the charts.

"Almost ten!" he calls out over his shoulder.

"Ten?" I mumble, running my hands through my hair to get it off my face.

"Hey, baby," Killian greets from behind me, and I turn in time to have him pick me up.

Hugging him, I wrap my legs around his waist and nuzzle his neck. "I'm not awake yet."

"Tanner tried calling Cass, but she must have her phone on silent. Since I'm coming to the doctor's appointment, we left pretty early," he explains, climbing the stairs.

"No! This is a no-cuddling zone," Tanner says as he rips the blankets off Cassidy before going over to sit on the couch.

"Tanner, you dick!" Cassidy cries out.

"We need to eat. Glory and Killian need to go soon. Time to wake up, Sleeping Ugly!"

"Asshole!" she screeches but sits up, shoving her hair off her face to glare at her brother.

Killian sets me down with a kiss, and I sigh, heading over to my bag to grab some clothes. I change into a sweater and put on the jeans I had on last night before finishing getting ready. Cassidy is knocking on the door as I'm brushing my teeth, and we trade places.

The manspreading happening on the couch leaves me with two choices. I can either crawl back into bed, which means I'll probably get horizontal and fall back asleep, or I can sit on Killian's lap. Deciding Tanner can just get over it, I head over to Killian, who immediately tucks me into his side.

Yawning, I lean against him and absorb his warmth.

"How was the concert?" Killian asks, rubbing my arm.

"It was awesome. We had such a great time, but, man, we crashed when we got back here. I can't remember the last time I slept this late."

"What are y'all doing for the rest of the day?"

"After the appointment, Cass and I are going to walk around Ponce City Market. She's in charge of finding a place for dinner. The game should be over by then, right?"

"Kickoff is at one thirty, so, yeah, thereabouts."

HARD FEELINGS

"I can't believe y'all want to come dancing with us tonight," I muse.

"Killian promised to be my wingman, so I'm into it," Tanner says without looking up from whomever he's texting on his phone.

Cassidy exits the bathroom, and we head out to breakfast. My nerves eat at my stomach, so I can't really get much down.

Half an hour later, Cassidy is dropping us off outside my mom's doctor's office, and I'm desperately trying to swallow past the giant lump in my throat.

"Tanner and I are just going to walk around the mall down the street. Shoot me a text when you're done." Cassidy turns from the front seat.

I stare out the window, chewing on my lip nervously.

"You don't have to do this if you don't want to, Glory," she says, but I shake my head.

Yeah, I definitely do. I want to.

I give her what I hope is a convincing smile that I'm all right and hop out of the car.

Killian follows at a slower pace, and I can practically feel the awkwardness and anxiety wafting off the both of us.

What a pair.

We enter the lobby, and I look around for my mom, only to jump when she yells my name across the room.

Killian grabs my hand, and we walk over.

My mom looks beautiful pregnant. Her white-blonde hair is long, and she's let her natural curls go wild. Her skin is glowing, she's smiling, and all I can wonder is if she was this happy when she was pregnant with me.

"Killian! James told me you'd be tagging along." She smiles, and then she takes in our hands. For a brief second, a look crosses her face, but I choose to ignore it.

"I hope that's okay. I'm happy to wait out here."

"We're not doing transvaginal ultrasounds anymore, so as long as you're okay with seeing my pregnant belly, I'm happy to have you in the room."

I blush to the roots of my hair, hearing her say *vaginal* in any context, and she laughs at my embarrassment.

"I forgot how much of a prude you are, Glory Jane."

I have to physically bite my tongue not to clap back at her. And I'm not a prude; I just don't love hearing my mom say anything in relation to her vagina in front of my boyfriend. It's weird!

Killian squeezes my hand, grounding me, and I breathe deeply through my nose.

"I'm not a prude," I say simply, sitting down but leaving a chair between us.

My mom's smile drops a fraction, and I'm simultaneously pleased and feeling guilty.

"Mrs. Purcell?" A nurse comes through the door, looking expectantly at us, but all I hear is buzzing in my ears at the name they called.

She won't be a Purcell for much longer.

I follow them in a daze, keeping a death grip on Killian's hand, and watch mutely as they get her set up.

"Is this your daughter? The resemblance is uncanny," the nurse says conversationally as she squirts some gel onto my mom's stomach.

My mom hums noncommittally, her eyes and focus glued to the screen.

I can feel immense pressure behind my eyes at the love clearly on her face—something I haven't seen reflected at me in far too long.

"There she is!" the nurse cheers, and my mom's face blooms into a smile of pure contentedness.

A quick thumping sound fills the room, and I realize it's my little sister's heartbeat.

My heart feels like it's trying to meet its pace, and a weird buzzing fills my head as darkness edges around my vision.

I have to get out of here.

"Killian," I call out, my voice high and reedy, and then I'm running.

Ripping my hand out of his, I ignore my mom's startled yell, and I run through the halls.

Where the hell is the exit?

There.

The second I'm outside, the tears start, and I'm sobbing harder than I have in so long. I run to the side of the building and find a wooden lunch table under a tree.

Just get there, just get there. Come on, come on.

"Glory!" Killian yells as he closes the distance between us, and then I'm in his arms as a loud keening sound escapes me.

"Why doesn't she love me like that, Killian? She's so happy, and it makes me so angry. I needed her! Killian, I needed her so much." I cry harder, gasping.

"Glory, I need you to slow down and take a breath. You're starting to hyperventilate."

"She doesn't love me, Killian. She doesn't. Did you see how happy she is? Why wasn't she happy with us? What's wrong with me that people find it so easy to leave me?"

"Baby, please, you're killing me." He pulls me tight to his chest, and he's surrounding me. "Take a deep breath. Come on, with me. Deep breath in."

My inhales are short and quick, but I follow the rise and fall of Killian's breath until my breathing calms down, the tears with it, until I'm drained.

I give him my whole weight, knowing he has me.

"She's okay. She just needs a minute. We'll be back soon," Killian tells someone, and I hide my face in his shoulder, embarrassed.

HARD FEELINGS

"I can't go back in, Killian," I murmur, deep mortification replacing the panic.

"You don't have to."

"Sorry," I tell him, still hiding.

"Don't apologize. It's a lot, Glory. She asked a lot of you to come here."

"I wanted to be here for *her*," I say, the last part meaning our sister and not my mom.

"You will be, but that doesn't need to come at the expense of your well-being." He leans back to look into my eyes. "I will never understand our parents' decisions, and I don't have to, but you need to believe me when I say, it has nothing to do with you. This is on them."

I search his fierce gaze, the stoic, hard line of his mouth. He's pissed off on my behalf, and it warms something inside me. We're a team, he and I. I'm not alone. I have my chosen family and my dad.

But—

"Glory, don't think it," he interrupts my thoughts, and I rip my eyes away from his.

Sometimes, having someone who can read you like a book is a pain in the ass.

"I hate her," I whisper angrily, knowing it's a lie. I just desperately wish I did.

"All this anger has become comforting to you, but it's not comfort, Glory. You've just become used to the pain that you don't know what it's like to live without it anymore. I know how scary the thought of letting it go is. I promise you, when you do, you'll get yourself back."

"How do I forgive this?" I ask hoarsely.

"Because you love your mom and you want to be in your sister's life. You're mourning the version of the mom you needed. The hardest lesson I learned in all this was that I had to let go of the idea I had of my parents and realize they are just as deeply flawed as the rest of us. They are not perfect. They fuck up, sometimes epically." Killian sighs sadly. "My dad will never be who I need, and it fucking sucks. Just because we're blood doesn't mean we have to be in each other's lives. Sometimes, the kindest thing they can do is leave."

At least my mom is trying to have some sort of relationship with me even if she's doing a terrible job at attempting it.

"I'm so sorry, Killian. You deserve so much more than what he has given you." I hug him to me tightly, as if I can absorb his pain.

"I know, and I'll be okay. I hope you don't mind me borrowing your dad sometimes," he jokes, but his voice cracks, belying his pain.

I guess just because you forgive someone, it doesn't mean it doesn't still hurt.

"Of course, only if I can have Elizabeth sometimes."

"We'll work out custody later." He laughs, and I lean back so he can give me a kiss.

I've come to learn a lot about the kisses Killian gives. There's the one where it feels like he's trying to consume me, one where he kisses me slowly, as if committing the moment to memory, and one like this. They are so gentle that they bring renewed tears to my eyes because it's love. There's so much love in his kisses that it overwhelms me.

"Come on."

As we head back to the front of the building, I draw up short at the sight of my very worried mom.

Killian kisses my forehead. "I'm going to go call the twins to come get us. You can do this, Glory."

I nod mutely, not taking my eyes off my mom as she closes the distance between us.

"Glory," she sighs. I watch her hesitate to hug me, and it kills something inside me. "Are you okay?"

I shrug, unable to speak, for fear of crying again, and I'm so sick of crying over this that it's unreal. Therapy has just turned me into a watering pot, but I guess it's better than shoving my mother's betrayal so far down inside me that it burns like acid whenever I think of it.

"I'm trying, honey." Her voice wavers, and I nearly break.

"Were you this happy when you were pregnant with me?" I ask in a small voice and watch the devastation on my mom's face.

"Glory, when I was pregnant with you, I felt like the luckiest person in the world. I felt like I could do anything, being your mom. You are such a gift."

"You could do anything but stay."

She sighs and looks at the ground. "My leaving had nothing to do with you."

I scoff, and she steps closer, angry now.

"Listen to me, Glory Jane. It had nothing to do with you. It didn't even have anything to do with your father. It was all me. You did nothing wrong."

My face crumples, and she pulls me into her arms.

"You did nothing wrong, Glory. Nothing."

"Why didn't you come back? You just disappeared from my life, and I needed you so much, Mom."

She pulls back, wiping her eyes, and rests her hands on her stomach.

"Shame is a powerful thing. It eats away at what you think you deserve until you believe you deserve nothing. It paralyzes you, destroys your self-worth, and in the end, it hurts those around you. I know I have a lot to make up for, and I likely never will, but I would be so grateful if you at least gave me the opportunity to try."

"I don't know if I can go back to what we were," I admit.

HARD FEELINGS

"And that's okay."

"I'm trying to forgive you. For *her*. For me. But I'm so angry with you. This all feels like you trying again with a new family. I feel like you're replacing me, and I'm—"

"Glory, no. Never. I know I've royally messed up, and I do hope I can do better by your sister, but that doesn't mean I'll stop trying with you even if you don't need me anymore. We don't need to go back to what we were; we can be something else. Whatever you decide that looks like."

I nod, stepping back when I see Cassidy pull into the parking lot.

"I've got to go," I tell her.

"Okay. Here, take these." She hands me two ultrasound photos. "I got one for you and Killian. I'm so happy you both decided to be in the baby's life. She's going to need both of you."

"Maybe you could tell your future husband not to be such a fucking asshole to his son," I tell her as I take the photos.

"Sebastian is ... complicated."

"Hmm." I wave at Cassidy, letting them know I'm coming. Killian hovers outside the car, eyes locked on me, and I know he's cataloging every expression and movement in case he needs to intervene. "Killian is amazing, and his dad is missing out."

My mom's eyes are sad as she nods. "We both are."

"I'll talk to you later. Thanks for this." I gesture at the photos.

"Bye, Glory," she says softly and heads toward her car.

I watch her leave, feeling heavy with sadness, guilt, and anger—a confusing cocktail.

I walk to the car. Killian searches my eyes for distress, and I give him a halfhearted smile in response.

All I want to do is nap.

We pile into the car. The twins, picking up on the heavy mood, do most of the talking, hoping to cheer us both up, but we remain quiet.

I lean my head against Killian's shoulder and pull my phone out of my pocket to text my dad.

I love you, Dad.

He texts back almost immediately, and I imagine him pacing the house, waiting for me to contact him. He knows where I've been this last hour, and I'm sure he's been worried.

Are you okay? I love you too, honey. So much.

I'm okay, just wanted to let you know.

Okay, I'll see you soon. We'll get Barkley's when you get back.

163

I smile. My dad's comfort food is Barkley's Doughnuts. It's a twenty-minute drive outside of town, but he takes us whenever we are having a rough day. We listen to music together and just drive, eating apple cider doughnuts. We don't need to talk; just being with each other is enough.

But the doughnuts don't hurt either.

Twenty-one

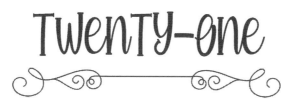

I had to practically shove Killian out the door to go to the game. They had gotten tickets through UGA and were meeting some of the current players and coaches. Tanner was over the moon at the opportunity to be in box seats. He wouldn't stop talking about all the free food.

Killian looked like a solemn statue in comparison, but after I swore a hundred times that I was okay, that Cassidy had me, and that we'd see each other later, both of them were out the door.

I fill Cassidy in as we walk around Ponce City Market, and I'm happy to report that I'm able to talk about everything without crying about it.

She's sympathetic and supportive, but my best friend is always the last one to forgive someone who's hurt me. I'm the same way when someone hurts Cassidy. We protect each other. Even so, she's excited about this baby, too, and we decide it'll be fun to pick out some cute little baby outfits while we're here.

For lunch, we sit down at one of the adorable restaurants inside Ponce City Market, and Cassidy whips out her Pinterest board for dorm room ideas. She's going with her family for a school tour of Stanford over the Thanksgiving holiday and is excited to see what the dorms look like so she can start ordering stuff.

She hasn't officially heard back yet, but she took her SATs and ACTs months ago and got nearly perfect scores. I'm sure she'll get in, but I can see it's still worrying her.

"Are you planning to apply to any backups?" I ask her.

Cassidy shrugs and shakes her head.

"Cass, you should, just in case. I'm sure you'll get into Stanford, but—"

"You didn't."

I don't want to point out that I didn't need a backup because I already got into my school—well, at least, contingent on me not flunking the rest of my year.

I stare at her until she looks up and rolls her eyes at me.

"Fine. I'll think about it. I've just been Stanford or bust forever. You get that."

"I do. I totally get being single-minded, but it can be blinding."

"I hear you. I'll look into it."

I let it drop and just hope she hears from them soon.

"Do you know where Killian will end up?"

"I'm guessing UGA. I don't know," I say nonchalantly because I've become an expert at not thinking about what's going to happen to us next year.

"He hasn't said anything? Even with Tanner potentially not going?" Cassidy asks, confusion evident.

"Does he know Tanner is applying elsewhere?"

"Glory, those two share a brain. Killian knew Tanner was thinking about it before Tanner even admitted it out loud."

"We just don't …" I trail off.

"Talk about the future?" Cass finishes for me.

"We literally just started dating; we're taking this slow," I tell her.

"Hmm."

"Cassidy …" I warn.

"I just think it's a giant elephant in the middle of your relationship, and maybe you should talk about it."

"He knows where I'm ending up, and he would never abandon the family business. It's their entire legacy. Besides, he's a shoo-in for UGA. His dad is an alum. And the school literally invited him to the game they're at now."

"Okay." She holds her hands up in surrender.

"We'll be fine," I continue.

"I'm sure you're right."

Cassidy brings up her phone again and lets it go, but now, it's a freaking worm in my brain.

He knows I'm going to UCLA. He's going to UGA. That has been the plan since before we were together, since before our parents split. Cassidy asking suggests there's another possibility, but there's no way. The farm is everything to the King family.

We'll be fine.

By dinnertime, we still haven't heard anything from the guys. The game ended about a half hour ago. Cassidy is getting hangry, and I do not want to deal with the She-Hulk when her blood sugar gets low.

I text the group chat.

HARD FEELINGS

Where are y'all?

Tanner responds.

The UGA coach invited us to dinner. Text us when you get to the club, and we'll meet you there.

I relay this to Cassidy as another text comes in.
Killian texts, and I already know the ribbing is coming.

See you soon, baby.

Then Cassidy.

Bye, baby!

Then Tanner.

I'll see you soon, baby!

Fuck off.

Laughing quietly at Killian losing it, I put my phone on the coffee table.
"Let's get ready for tonight. I've booked us a table at eight."

"You go ahead and take the bathroom," I tell her after I slip my dress on and grab my phone again to put on our playlist.

"That's Where I Am" by Maggie Rogers comes on, and I dance around, clapping to the beat. When it gets to the bridge, Cassidy leans around the bathroom door and sings into her hairbrush.

Laughing, I sit in front of the floor-length mirror and start my makeup. Thanks to Cassidy, I can at least pull off a heavy liner. I keep it simple at that with some mascara and red lips.

Dabbing some of the lipstick onto my fingers, I use it as a blush on my cheeks, and I'm done with my makeup.

My hair is another thing entirely. The waves are still intact, but it's going to get hot in the club. I decide to do two French braids down the sides. It makes me look more put together than I expected.

Standing up, I take in how I look. Rubbing my hands down the front of the dress, I feel more feminine than I have in a while.

"Uh-oh, look at that smile. Is Killian getting lucky tonight?" Cassidy grins as she comes around the corner in a short black dress with cutouts on the sides. Black sets off the red of her hair, which she's straightened into a glossy waterfall, reaching halfway down her back.

"You look hot as hell, dude," I tell her, changing the subject.

"Oh, I know." She smirks.

"Are you sure we can get into this club?" I ask, grabbing my small wristlet and tucking my phone inside.

"Eighteen to party, twenty-one to drink," she tells me, not looking up from her phone. "Okay, Uber will be here in twenty."

We breeze through dinner. Cassidy is so excited about her trip to Stanford in a couple of weeks. She has an entire itinerary planned of things to do. It makes me wish I were going on a college visit.

I chose UCLA from pictures, but it would be cool to actually go before I moved there. I haven't been anywhere other than Georgia. Moving across the country for the first time outside my home state seems pretty ambitious.

Maybe I could save from working at the farm and convince Dad to go for a visit.

By the time we reach the club, there's a line outside, and it makes me glad I wore a jacket as we stand, shivering.

We wait a good forty minutes, and when we get inside, we still haven't heard from the guys. Cassidy shoots them a text, letting them know we're here and to come find us when they get here.

But all thoughts of them disappear as we enter the dark nightclub. Lights flash, giving us glimpses of the dance floor. Tables, filled with people and there's a balcony above, where even more are chatting. On one end, a bar, the entire length of the building, is slammed, and on the other is the DJ booth.

The bass of the music vibrates through my body, and my heart rate picks up as Cassidy laughs joyously and grabs my hand, rushing us to the middle of the dance floor.

Cassidy screams excitedly when the DJ starts playing her current favorite song and begins dancing, tugging me along with her.

It's hot and humid, and I'm already regretting this jacket. Deciding I'd rather just hold it, I slip it off and nearly groan in relief.

The song isn't halfway over before two random guys move towards us, getting way too close. There's a truth universally acknowledged that if two women are dancing in a club, they must want some dude's junk grinding on them. *Not.*

Cassidy and I try dancing more wildly, hoping our flailing limbs will ward them off, but judging by the glassy look in their eyes, they are barely conscious of what's happening around them.

We move around the dance floor, hoping to lose them, but they follow.

"Y'all are playing hard to get!" Beer breath fans my cheek as the one in the backward black baseball cap leans close from behind me.

"Maybe you should take that as a sign!" I yell back over the music and make hard eye contact with Cassidy. I'm about done with this place.

"I am, baby." He laughs, pulling me close and grinding against me from behind.

HARD FEELINGS

I cringe, upset, hearing him use that nickname—something that means so much when coming from someone else. His sweat is all over me, and I just want to go home and shower at this point. Cassidy successfully shoves off her creep before marching toward us, coming to a halt when she spots something behind me.

"Cass, what are you doing? Help me!" I yell, trying to shove this guy off me, but he's like a pervy octopus.

Suddenly, he's ripped off of me, and I spin around to find Killian towering over the both of us, his hand gripping the back of the guy's neck as he says something into the guy's ear that has him paling considerably.

Killian's furious eyes are locked on mine, and I nearly collapse in relief. Maybe I do need to take Dad up on his offer for me to take some self-defense classes before I leave for college. Fucking sucks that I'd have to, but I'm barely five foot three, and though I'm mostly muscle, I clearly don't know how to protect myself.

Instead of just letting him go after scaring the shit out of him, Killian keeps his grip tight on the guy's neck and walks him to the front door, making sure the bouncer ousts his ass.

Tanner shows up and sticks by our side until Killian gets back, pointing to a table they secured.

Happy to take a minute to sit, Cassidy and I hurry to the table with Tanner dogging our heels.

"You okay?" Tanner asks me, and I nod.

Cassidy slides in next to me, and I lean against her, grateful to sit. To be honest, my head is starting to pound, and I know Cassidy wants to party until the sun comes up, but I'm ready to go.

This isn't my scene, and it's been an emotional day. I just want to curl up in bed and watch TV.

Before I can say all this to Cassidy, Killian arrives like a pissed off magician.

"Glory, let's go."

"Killian, no!" Cassidy whines. "We were having fun before all that."

"Were you?" he asks, raising his brow at her. "Glory, do you want to leave?"

I hesitate, looking at Cassidy, who drops her head back in defeat and slides out.

She pulls me into a hug. "This is not how I wanted tonight to go."

"I know, and I was having fun with you, but today has been ..." I trail off, pulling back so she can see me. "I'm just exhausted."

"Ugh, fine. I'll hang with my stupid brother."

"You're the stupid one," Tanner counters, staring at a blonde girl by the bar.

"Cass, Tanner has the key to the hotel room. It's two queen beds. Are you good there?" Killian asks, pulling me toward him.

"Yes. Go and be in love."

"Text me when you're safe at the hotel." I make her promise before leaving.

Giving Tanner a death stare to make sure he knows not to ditch his twin, I let Killian lead me out of the club.

"She'll be fine," Killian assures me, reading my mind.

"I feel bad," I tell him.

"I give it maybe fifteen minutes before they both get sick of that place, head to McDonald's, and go home to watch *What We Do in the Shadows*."

"That was extremely specific." I laugh lightly as he heads toward his car. I can't believe he was able to find parking.

"It's their new obsession," he says as he opens the passenger door.

I plug the address in for the Airbnb and settle back.

"You're fine with me coming back and staying with you, yeah?"

I turn to watch him, his face illuminated by streetlights, and notice the stubble on his chin and the tightness of his jaw. He looks upset and tired.

"Yeah, Killian. I want to be with you," I tell him simply, and it's true.

When everything gets crazy, he grounds me. There's no one else I'd rather decompress with.

We're quiet on the ride home, our minds elsewhere, and really, all I want right now is a shower. I can still smell that guy on me, and humidity, plus makeup, is always a recipe for a breakout.

Killian follows me up the stairs to the carriage house entrance, and I plug in the code, letting us in.

"I'm going to take a shower," I tell him and head into the bathroom, already peeling off my jacket and toeing off my shoes.

I kick the door closed as my dress comes up over my head and turn the shower on.

I throw my hair up into a giant knot on top of my head and step inside, grateful for the hot water.

Never one to take long showers, I'm out once I'm clean, and I grab a towel, only to realize I didn't bring in my pajamas.

Shrugging, I wrap the towel around me and open the door to find Killian stripped down to his black boxer briefs, lying on the bed, watching TV. He's turned off all the lights, except for the bedside lamp.

I raise a brow. "You got comfortable."

He glances over, sitting up straight when he sees I'm just in a towel. He licks his full lips, taking in my bare legs. Drawing his eyes up to meet my amused gaze, he grins sheepishly.

"Figured I'd go ahead and set the mood."

HARD FEELINGS

"What's the mood? Married couple at the end of the day?" I tease, bending down to grab my oversize T-shirt when I realize I don't have any clean underwear. "Um ..."

"You okay?" he asks, leaning back to rest his hands on his freaking eight-pack.

I'll be sleeping next to you ... without any underwear on.

"Yep!" I wince as my voice cracks, and I head back into the bathroom. *This is fine, Glory. It's fine.*

I towel off. Stealing some of Cassidy's lotion, I rub it all over me before shrugging on my shirt. I smell delicious, and I'm very aware of the fact that I am completely nude under this shirt.

And it's turning me on way more than it should.

Taking my hair down, I detangle it and run some hair oil through the ends. Okay, and now, I'm fully primping. Snickering at myself, I brush my teeth and apply moisturizer.

Deep breath, Glory.

I open the door to find Killian standing there.

"Can I borrow your toothbrush?" he asks, sliding by me.

That should gross me out, right? Is it weird that it doesn't? I tell him yes and then crawl into bed under the covers. I see he turned on one of my favorite shows and smile. There's something so comforting about someone knowing me so well.

Killian finishes up in the bathroom and joins me in bed, pulling me toward him until I'm half on top of him. My thigh drapes across his lower belly, right above the areas I desperately need to stop thinking about, and my cheek rests on his pec.

"Were you jealous when you saw that guy dancing with me?" I tease him softly, remembering the fury on his face.

"Glory, you looked like you were two seconds from ripping his face off. I'm not jealous of some handsy asshole. Now, if you were cuddling up with someone, giving them that soft look you give me when you're happy? Yeah, I'd be fucking jealous."

I move so I can rest my chin on my stacked hands and stare at him. Killian's eyes are on the TV, hands behind his neck. He feels huge beneath me. Sometimes, I forget our size difference until we're close like this. He makes me feel so delicate. I know I'm small, but I don't feel petite on the field. I feel like a battering ram.

Killian must feel my eyes on him because one of his large hands drops on the back of my upper thigh, and his eyes flick to mine when he feels my bare skin. Maintaining eye contact, he runs his hand higher until he reaches my bare ass.

Lust heats up his eyes, and his nostrils flare when he realizes I'm naked underneath.

"Glory, are you wearing any underwear?" he asks hoarsely, keeping his hand on my ass.

A sly smile creeps over my face that turns into a laugh as he flips us over and settles between my legs.

I run my hands through his hair, cupping his cheek before bringing my lips to his. Our kiss is slow, lips clinging to each other before diving back for more. He settles his weight on me, keeping some of it on his elbows, but it feels amazing, cradling him with my thighs.

Killian breaks our kiss before nuzzling my neck, pressing a hot kiss to the thrumming pulse there before leaning back.

"Do you want to?" he asks, flexing his hips into mine.

Instead of answering him, I lift my hips, gasping when I feel him hard and straining against his boxer briefs.

So hot.

I hold his gaze as I pull my shirt over my head and toss it to the ground. I lift my chin, refusing to allow an ounce of insecurity to enter this moment. I know my body isn't everyone's type. I'm muscular with small breasts. I don't have curves for days, and I'm still rocking the remainder of a deep farmer's tan from this summer.

But watching the lust and adoration on Killian's face as he takes me in for the first time has me believing that while all those things might be true, in his eyes, I'm the most beautiful woman he's ever seen.

He leans down, pressing a kiss over my heart, his stubble tickling my breast, eliciting a gasp.

I'm extremely sensitive there, and he looks victorious at discovering that. He lowers his mouth again, this time dragging his tongue across the stiff peak of my nipple before closing his mouth over it and sucking.

My core pulses, like it's got a direct line to my breast. I shift restlessly, needing more. Killian's hand drifts down between my legs, and he groans at finding my curls damp with how much I want him.

He strums a finger along my seam, and my head falls back.

"Please, Killian."

"I've got you, baby." Pressing one more lingering kiss to my breast, Killian moves down the bed until he's kneeling on the floor at the end and drags me down toward him, lifting my thighs over his shoulders.

Heart pounding, I shift away, nervous.

"Has anyone ever done this for you before?" he asks, looking downright deviant as he stares at the most intimate parts of me, licking his bottom lip.

"No," I groan, shifting closer but then pulling away.

I don't know how I feel about this. I'm slightly embarrassed at him being so close to me, not sure how I smell or taste, but judging by his ravenous look, he doesn't care.

HARD FEELINGS

"You're going to love it," he promises, leaning close enough for me to feel his warm breath against my most sensitive area.

Gasping at just the thought of it, I have a feeling he's right. I will.

Killian drags his tongue against my pussy before sealing his mouth over my clit and sucking. It sends me over the edge so quickly that I can't catch my breath. Killian watches me triumphantly, a little cocky at how fast he made me come, and adds a finger.

My hands fling to the sides, grabbing the comforter, sheets, anything to ground me as he tortures me with his tongue and fingers.

The heat takes longer to build this time, but I'm almost scared at how big it feels. My thighs shaking are the only warning I get before it crashes over me. I come so hard that tears escape, and I slam my hand over my mouth to stifle the incoherent scream, but he reaches up and pulls my hand away from my mouth.

"I want to hear you, Glory," Killian tells me, giving my clit one last kiss before standing up.

I stare at his erection greedily. He adjusts himself so the tip of his cock peeks out from his waistband. Watching at me, he palms himself, shuddering at the feel, and it makes me hungry to do that myself.

Widening my legs, I beckon him closer, inviting him in.

Killian shucks his briefs, grabs a condom out of the pants he discarded, and rolls it on. He stands there without an ounce of modesty. He's totally comfortable with his body, and it shows. He's all solid muscle, stacked under deliciously tanned skin. His black hair is mussed from my hands, his lips swollen and glistening. His chest pumps with his breaths as his heavy cock hangs proudly between his legs. He looks otherworldly, intimidating, and so incredibly sexy that I can't quite believe this is happening.

But it's the look of pure admiration in his hazel gaze that really lights me up. It's difficult to believe that this is my Killian, that he's my man.

Mine.

That thought makes me feel somewhat feral.

He stays where he is, seemingly as lost in thought as I am, so I get on my knees and move toward him. I can meet him halfway on this.

Happily.

I wrap my hand around his erection before bringing our mouths together, our kiss more frantic as a result of the storm he created. I suck on his bottom lip before leaning back.

"Killian, I need you," I whisper before biting his jaw gently, smiling when his hands flex on my ass before dragging me closer.

Feeling him hot and heavy against my stomach is driving me nuts.

"Now," I whine, lying back down as he crawls over me.

He reaches between us to line himself up against me and meets my eyes. "Are you sure?"

Instead of answering, I flex my hips, bringing him in slightly and making us both moan. Killian slowly works himself in, watching me closely for any discomfort. I only slept with Jason a few times, and that was a while ago. Killian is big, so the fit is tight and uncomfortable.

When he fully seats himself inside me, I let out a huge breath. "Give me just a minute."

Killian holds himself still, teeth gritted, as my body adjusts and begins to clench around him. He leans down, kissing my breasts, and soon, I crave the friction and fullness he provides.

When I undulate my hips, Killian gets the signal to begin moving. He slowly rolls his body, drawing out the sensations, and we both groan. It's nothing like the jackhammering Jason did.

I raise my knees toward my chest, bringing us closer and providing more friction where I need it.

"I'm not going to last," Killian gasps.

"It's okay."

He gives me more of his weight as he thrusts into me and brings his lips to mine, kissing me so sweetly that it brings tears to my eyes. We stay like that, close and staring at each other as he chases his release. I'm not going to come again—it's too soon, or so I think—but I'm still so fulfilled by the idea of giving him pleasure that I don't even care.

The intimacy is almost too much, and I find myself tearing up from the love on his face. I whisper his name, and he rests his forehead against mine. Killian reaches between us, finding my clit, and I'm so sensitive that just that touch has my entire body jerking. It takes him no time to bring me to the edge, and if I cared, I'd be a little embarrassed at how quickly he's able to make me come, but I'm just grateful. My body spasms, squeezing him tightly as I sob his name. Killian begins to pulse inside me, and I hug him to me as he begins to come, crying out my name.

When he stops moving, he rolls us until I'm on top, resting heavily against him. I press a kiss over his heart before settling my head on his chest, smiling at his pounding heart. It matches the pounding of my own.

This is so different from what I had with Jason. Feels so much more ... everything. This is what it should be, feeling loved and adored as the other person shows you how much they care.

I never knew.

TWENTY-TWO

That weekend changed everything. We were cemented as a couple. I'm not big on public displays of affection, mostly because people can't keep their opinions to themselves and a lot of this town made up their minds about me a while ago. No need to give them kindling for their gossip. But I can't keep my hands off Killian, and vice versa.

Everyone at school has backed off, but I still get looks, indicating how much they think I don't deserve Killian. I do my best to shut out the noise, and for a while, it's easy.

We're both busy finishing up our seasons and then working at the farm. Thanksgiving comes and goes in a blink. Dad and I kept it simple; neither of us likes Thanksgiving food, so we treated ourselves to some Thai and a Christmas movie marathon.

Everything is so easy that I can't help but wait for the other shoe to drop. My therapist says that I need to work on trusting people and myself. I need to remind myself that I survived some absolute bullshit. I will be fine either way, but letting these anxious thoughts take hold will only manifest everything I'm worried about.

We're a week away from Christmas now, and I just finished my last final. Right now, the one thing that's on my mind is making sure I pass all of them. The idea of shitting the bed now, after working so hard to secure my place at UCLA, makes me want to vomit.

Speaking of vomit, Cassidy finally got her early acceptance from Stanford. We were at her house when her mom walked in with the mail. She ripped it open, and her only reaction was to get sick at the kitchen sink. Then, she started to cry. I didn't realize how much this had been weighing on her, but I'm so unbelievably happy with where we're both going after this school year.

Winter is cold and wet in Georgia, and it seeps into your bones. I'm grateful that I'm working in the gift shop instead of hauling trees to people's trucks, like Killian. Though that side of the business has slowed. It's mostly kids coming to say hi to Santa and parents buying little King Family Farms trinkets in the gift shop.

I'm wrapping up the final customer's gift now. It's a cute little replica of the red truck that Killian drove us in a couple of months ago, and just thinking about how that was actually a couple of months ago has my hands pausing as I tie a bow.

It's shocking how fast time goes by.

I finish the wrapping and turn to the customer, smiling. "Thank you for shopping at King Family Farms!"

They leave happy and full of the Christmas spirit, and I lock the front door behind them. When I turn around, Killian is sitting on the counter, smiling at me.

"I'm getting glimpses of the future," he says, seeing me decked out in my King Family Farms gear.

I cock a brow. "The only glimpses you should have of me in the future is my making the US Women's National Team before I'm thirty."

He chuckles and hops down, helping me clean up and finish closing the shop up. We're meeting Cassidy and Tanner at the diner. It's only seven, but I only had a small snack for lunch, so I'm ready to put away a giant stack of pancakes.

Killian sneaks a kiss as we head outside to his car.

"You know, you still haven't told me what you want for Christmas, and I'm running out of time," he says as he climbs into the driver's seat.

I fix the air vents so the heat is blowing on my hands. Killian seems completely unaffected by the temperature change, but maybe that has something to do with his mammoth size because I'm shivering so hard that I can almost hear my bones clanking together.

"Jesus, Glory, maybe I should get you a thicker coat and some gloves."

He grabs my hands and rubs them in his, and I sigh thankfully.

"I won't need a thicker coat in Southern California," I tell him.

Killian freezes for a moment and then gives my fingers a kiss before letting them go in order to drive. We're quiet after that because neither of us is ready to acknowledge that I'm leaving after this coming semester.

"Are you ready to go to your mom's?" Killian asks as we pull onto Main Street.

"Ugh," I groan loudly. "Yes, and no."

"It's just for Christmas Eve."

"I know …" I drawl. "Are you sure you can't come?"

HARD FEELINGS

"Mom already bought plane tickets. We haven't seen my grandparents in over a year; I think my mom would actually kill me if I backed out," he says apologetically.

Killian is heading to Florida to visit his grandparents, the twins are heading to Boston to visit their cousins, and I'm heading to Atlanta to visit my mother. Nightmare vibes. We haven't really spoken since that day at the doctor's, but my guilty conscience and my therapist convinced me to go down. Originally, it was going to be for the entire week of Christmas, but there was no way. I know myself; I wouldn't have made it without starting a fight.

Besides, I am not ditching my dad on Christmas. The compromise is that I will go down for the twenty-third, stay for the day of Christmas Eve, and then come home that night.

Tonight at the diner is our version of a friends Christmas since everyone is taking off soon. The next time we all see each other, it'll be a new year, and the official countdown until we leave will begin.

Unfortunately, seeing my mother soon preoccupies my thoughts for most of our dinner and while hanging out with Killian after.

"It's going to be okay, Glory." Killian hugs me to him as we lie together on his couch.

We've been watching Christmas movies for the last hour since we got home from dinner. The twins were excited to go to Boston and kept most of the conversation flowing, thankfully, and they didn't seem to notice I was a million miles away.

Killian did. He's like a bloodhound for my moods.

Knowing we won't be seeing each other for the next two weeks threads a sense of urgency through me, and I turn in his arms so I'm facing him. Our parents sensed the change in my and Killian's relationship and instituted a *no closed doors* rule. It's made it difficult to be together in the way we want to.

"What are you thinking?" Killian asks, voice deepening from the look on my face.

"Killian, it's been a while, and we're not going to see each other for weeks. I miss you," I whisper, shifting in order to straddle his hips but keeping us both under the cover of the giant down throw we've been using to keep warm on the couch.

Killian's hands drift down and grab my ass, pulling me harder against him, and I drop my head between his shoulder and neck to stifle my moan.

"I've missed you too. My balls are so blue; it looks like I have frostbite," he groans, undulating underneath me.

I glance toward the stairs, and Killian answers, guessing my thoughts, "She went to bed hours ago. You have to be quiet though, Glory. You think you can do that?"

He licks up my neck, and I moan again.

"I'll try."

"Stand up," he orders, shifting so he's sitting instead of lounging and shoving his pants down his legs.

Biting my lip to keep quiet at the sight of his hard cock straining against his lower stomach, I kick my pants off, dragging my panties along with them, but keep my oversize sweater on, just in case.

"Fuck, that's hot," Killian curses, staring at the apex between my thighs. "I can see how wet you are."

I climb onto his lap, dragging my core along his cock, teasing us both, before taking him in my hand. I roll my thumb along his tip, spreading his pre-cum before bringing it to my mouth and licking it off.

Killian's eyes nearly roll to the back of his head. "I swear to God, that'd better be the last thing I see before I die."

Laughing softly, I position him where I need him and sink down slowly. It's a tight fit, especially because it's been a while since we've been together, but I feel like I've been edging forever so I'm more than ready for him. Everything he does gets me hot.

Watching him hauling those trees into the backs of people's trucks. Not to mention, watching him chop them down. He just does it for me in every way.

I whimper, just thinking about it.

"You're killing me," he groans, his big hands grabbing the ends of the cushion, knuckles white from the effort to let me take my time getting comfortable.

"You're so big," I say, somewhat accusatory, but groan loudly when he's fully seated inside me.

"Shh," Killian admonishes, "or I'll have to cover your mouth."

My muscles clench around him at that idea, and my head tips back, my long hair teasing my ass as I begin to move.

"Fuck, baby," he growls. "That's it."

God, I've felt so empty inside without him. It's a near-constant ache, and I want to take my time, but Killian has other ideas. He leans up and takes my nipple into his mouth, and I have to bite my lip to muffle a scream.

I must do it poorly because he settles his hand over my mouth, and there's something so erotic about him having to force me to be quiet. It's so good that I can't help but be loud, unafraid of waking up his mom upstairs.

Maybe I'm kinkier than I thought.

"You're so fucking hot." He runs his mouth along my jaw before leaning back to watch himself disappear inside me.

I can feel the heat building, coiling tight as I chase my orgasm. Collapsing on him, I bite down on his shoulder as it rips through me. I'm grinding down

HARD FEELINGS

on his lap, legs shaking, as it seems to go on forever. Killian holds me tight to him, staving off his own orgasm.

When I catch my breath, I lean back and give him an open-mouthed kiss. His lips are swollen from him biting down in an effort to quiet his own moans, and I suck on them before letting my tongue dive back in, eager for his taste.

Killian rips his mouth from mine. "I'm gonna come."

I can feel him pulsing inside of me and know he's close to his own orgasm. Climbing off his lap, I shift down to the floor on my knees and take him into my mouth.

"Fuck," he whispers tightly, his head falling back. "Glory, Glory." He chants my name, and I feel him swell and know he's got seconds before exploding.

I bring my hand to his base and apply pressure as I tongue his tip, tasting his salty cum before swallowing him down. Killian's hips leave the couch with the force of his orgasm; he covers his own mouth in order to stifle the yell that wants to escape.

I swallow, and it's more than I expected. Sitting back on my heels, I watch his chest heave as he stares back at me, totally blissed out. Standing, I pull my panties back on, followed by my sweatpants, and toss Killian his.

"Hey," he says softly, and I glance over before curling up beside him, "are you okay? We didn't talk about using protection."

"I would've stopped us if I wasn't okay with it," I murmur sleepily.

He kisses my forehead. "I'll be sure to keep condoms on me at all times. Just in case my girlfriend decides to jump me again, I'll be prepared."

Snickering, I lean up and kiss his jaw, loving that he didn't push to always go bare. We've talked about birth control, and I've tried going on the pill before, but it messed with me too much. I lasted three months before coming off. Killian knows this and respects our need for condoms. Neither of us wants children anytime soon, if ever, if I'm honest.

"Come on, baby. Time to get you home."

He stands up, giving me a hand, and I sleepily follow him out to the car.

He buckles me in, kissing me quickly. "You're so snuggly after you come. I can't wait to be able to curl up with you after instead of rushing off."

I smile contentedly and settle in for the drive home. Neither of us speaks until we are pulling into the driveway.

"I'm going to miss you," I confess, rolling my head toward him.

Killian leans forward and captures my mouth in a languid kiss. I can feel everything that he's not saying. His anxiety over how I'm going to feel, being away from him and with my mom and his dad, sadness over spending our first Christmas together away from each other.

I soothingly rub my hand along his jaw and let our lips cling together before pulling away. "I promise to video-chat every night, okay?"

He presses one last kiss to my forehead, inhaling deeply before pulling back. "Okay. Text me when you get there."

"I will."

As promised, I send a brief *here* to Killian. Technically, it's true. What I leave out is that I've been sitting in the driveway for ten minutes, letting my dad's car idle. His car is an older Honda, which functions perfectly but seems out of place in this neighborhood. The houses aren't huge; in fact, they are cute little storybook homes along a tree-lined street with tidy yards, but something about it has me thinking that I stick out like a sore thumb.

Probably all in my head, right? I do feel a bit like an interloper despite the invitation.

Their house is decorated for Christmas, and I have to swallow back bile at seeing it like this, remembering all the years we celebrated together before she left. The drapes swish in their bay window, and I know I've been spotted.

My mom opens her front door and stands there, smiling, happy to see me. She's gotten bigger since I saw her last, but that's not what captures my attention. It's the giant Killian look-alike behind her, hand on her shoulder, smiling at me like he's not a scum-sucking, cheating deadbeat fucker.

Narrowing my eyes at him, I climb out of the car and grab my overnight bag. His smile drops a few degrees.

Good, I think. *Just because you knocked up my mom doesn't mean I have to be nice to you.*

My mom moves forward, knocking his hand off her shoulder as she comes closer to greet me.

"Hey, Glory!"

She hesitates in front of me, unsure of what to do. Take the bag? Give me a hug? Kiss on the cheek? She settles for patting my shoulder, and I have to physically hold back the awkward laugh that wants to break free.

"Hi," I say softly, staring at her, feeling totally unsure how to engage with her. I gesture toward the house. "Should we go in?"

"Yes! Sorry. Yes. It's just a shock to see you here. I'm so happy that you are. I'll show you to your room."

"My room?" I ask, hesitantly following her inside.

Sebastian has disappeared. Excellent.

The inside is as cute as the front. It's smaller than our place back in Galway, which is surprising. Really would've thought she'd demand a mansion, but I guess their location in Grant Park is top tier, so what more could you ask for?

HARD FEELINGS

I follow her upstairs, down a short hallway, to the door on the other end of the master bedroom.

Please, God, let me not hear anything even remotely icky …

I shudder at the thought.

Mom opens the door, and I'm surprised to find a nicely decorated room. It has a queen bed with a white bedspread, and wood and white fixtures, giving it a calming vibe.

It's the pictures on the dresser though that capture my attention. Somehow, she snagged senior pictures of Killian and me both. Killian is in his uniform, kneeling with his helmet. I'm similarly in my own uniform, a soccer ball tucked under my arm. What a couple of jocks. I laugh to myself.

"So … what do you think?" Mom asks, twirling the bottom of her shirt in her fingers. A nervous habit I seem to have inherited.

"It's really nice," I tell her, tossing my overnight bag on the bed.

Her shoulders sink in relief. "Good. Sebastian and I wanted to keep it neutral for when Killian or you were here, but we wanted to make sure you knew there was a place just for y'all."

"Thank you," I say, shifting awkwardly on my feet.

"Okay, well, I'll let you get unpacked. I've got lunch almost ready. Come down whenever you want." Mom clasps her hands together. "I'm happy you're here, Glory."

She leaves, sucking the tension out of my body as she does so, and I collapse back onto the bed.

It's just one night, Glory. One freaking night. You can do this.

My phone buzzes, and I see Cassidy sent a photo in the group chat of her and Tanner in lobster bibs, giant smiles on their faces and a massive amount of seafood in front of them.

I type back.

Jealous!

Cassidy hearts the message.

Man, I'm missing her already. Sitting up, I grab my bag and unpack my toiletries, walking across the hall to set my little bag on the sink. Realizing I'm officially unpacked, I head downstairs, knowing if I don't, sooner or later, someone will come looking for me.

Sebastian and my mom are seated at a small table in a bay window, chatting happily together when I arrive. Of course, the talking ends, and I'm left awkwardly getting myself some chili and salad, sitting between them both.

"What were you talking about?" I ask more casually than I feel, but anything is better than listening to the sounds of chewing.

"We were deciding on what we should name the dog we're going to get when your sister is a bit older," Sebastian says, and my spoon pauses halfway to my mouth as I glance over to my mom.

"You hate dogs," I remind her.

"I don't hate dogs, Glory," she scoffs, taking a bite of her salad.

"Uh, yeah, you do. I begged for one every year, and you told me no because you didn't want an animal in your house."

"Glory, stop it," Sebastian interjects.

I glare at him. "Maybe you should mind your business. Seems to be a huge character flaw of yours, getting into other people's business."

"Glory!" my mom yells, astonished, and I guess she would be. I never talked back ever when I was younger.

"Why now, huh? Why get a dog now? What's so different between this life of yours with him and my new sister and the one you had with Dad and me? The math is the exact same."

"Glory, please, can we not fight? It's Christmas," Mom begs, and I decide to relent because I'll be damned if I'm considered the bad guy here.

"Well, since it's Christmas," I say sarcastically but drop it, putting my attention on finishing my lunch.

There's a long pause, broken only by the sounds of utensils clinking against porcelain. I stare hard at my food, as if it holds the answers to letting go of this anger. It doesn't.

Nothing does.

And I need to find it. God, I need to find it. I'm sick of this. The bitterness is a collar around my neck, claiming me as its own. When it tightens around my throat, the only thing that escapes is vitriol. It crawls under my skin, making it difficult for me to accept affection. It's also a lie because underneath its vicious armor is hurt. A hurt so deep with no way to heal, every wound freshly salted with every interaction, or lack thereof, with my mother.

I can see she wants to make it better. I know all I have to do is let her try, but then stuff like this happens, and I'm back to that abandoned little girl who needed her mother.

"Glory ..." My mom rests her hand on my arm, startling me out of my thoughts, and I turn to see the concern on her face.

"What?"

"You drifted off." She smiles tentatively.

I blink and realize I need to make this effort if I ever want to move on.

"Sorry." I stare at her. "What were you saying?"

Mom's eyes move back and forth as she tries to read my face. "Want to make some cookies? You can bring some back to your father. Gingerbread is his favorite!"

HARD FEELINGS

It will never fail to surprise me, the ease she has as she speaks about my dad, but I find the idea of doing something for him comforting, so I agree, and we're off.

We spend the rest of the afternoon together, and oddly, I find it not terrible. There are definitely new boundaries in place, but it feels okay. I let go of the anger about them getting a dog. None of it really matters anyway because I want my sister to have all these things.

It's the most normal day I've had with my mom in years, and that's exactly what I tell Killian while I'm upstairs, changing into my pajamas before dinner.

"Well, that's good, right?" he asks, adjusting the screen of his laptop so I'm not staring at his chin.

I tug his practice shirt over my sports bra and tug on my flannel pajama pants. "Yeah, it's just weird."

"How's my dad?" he asks hesitantly, and I'm infuriated by Sebastian's lack of courage all over again.

"He's made himself scarce all day. I did give him shit though at lunch."

"He's probably scared of you." He smiles, his eyes crinkling at the sides, and I briefly picture him older, his dad's age, with beautiful laugh lines I want to kiss. "What are you thinking about? You've got horny eyes."

"Kissing your laugh lines when you're older." I snicker, slapping a hand over my face.

"You're such a weirdo." He chuckles, and it's so good to hear, especially after talking about his dad, that I don't even care that it's at my expense.

"I'm sure you've thought weird stuff about me too." I raise a brow, pulling my hand away from my face. I can feel the heat in my cheeks.

"Sometimes, I imagine saying naughty things to you in public just so I can see those pretty cheeks blush," Killian says, his voice dropping an octave, which has me biting my lip.

"Yeah?" I shift the phone as I sit back against the pillows on the bed. "Like what?"

"Glory Jane Purcell, are you asking me to have phone sex with you in your mother's house?"

Before I can answer, my mom knocks on the door and pokes her head in. "Come on, slowpoke. We're starting the movie!"

Killian starts cracking up as I jump a foot in the air, nearly dropping the phone.

"Be right there!"

Mom raises an amused brow at me before saying loudly, "Hi, Killian. Merry Christmas!"

"Merry Christmas, Caroline!" Killian calls out, and I want to sink into the floor.

"Come down before the pizza gets cold," she tells me and gives me a look that means to wrap this up now before shutting the door.

I bring the phone up to see Killian laughing silently. "Well, you got your fantasy. I'm pretty sure this blush is forever burned onto my cheeks."

"How's it been?" he asks, his laughter dying down.

I glance away, shrugging. "A little hiccup when I got here. We're okay now."

"It's going to take time, Glory. Don't beat yourself up."

Breath hitching, I glance up to prevent more tears. I'm so sick of freaking crying. "I know."

"I miss you, baby," he says softly.

"Miss you too," I sigh. "I'll talk to you later. I should go before she comes back up."

I hang up and tap my phone against my head. I'm not exactly hiding that Killian and I are dating, but I also haven't brought it up. Mostly because he and I are adults and it's up to us who we date, but also because I'm dreading hearing their thoughts on it.

"Glory, come on!" my mom shouts from the bottom of the stairs.

Tossing my phone on the bed, I head downstairs.

Just a couple more hours, Glory. You can do it.

TWENTY-THREE

My last semester as a high school student begins like any other, except for the overwhelming feeling of nostalgia tingeing every moment. Walking down the hallways, sitting in class, lunch with friends, every time I step on the field, it is a countdown to the last time I will do any of it.

Soccer has a longer season than football, so I've been keeping busy most of this semester. I stacked my classes to be somewhat easy, and so far, I'm not having a problem with keeping my grades up.

Mom is due in a couple of weeks, and she's huge. Well, I guess she's normal, but she's so petite that she looks all belly. It's weird to think I'll have a baby sibling at eighteen. I'm actually excited about it, and being excited about it has gone a long way to mending my relationship with my mom.

She'll never be what I need, but I don't need her in that way anymore. We're more friends now, if anything, and it's okay. I'm adjusting and working with my therapist on setting boundaries. Not everything has to be a fight. I don't need to walk away from every interaction, feeling guilty, bitter, or pissed off.

Sometimes, when I leave, I feel neutral, and that progress is so important to me.

It's why I'm at the baby supply store a couple of towns over, helping Killian pick stuff out for our new sister. He's going to visit them this weekend by himself since I'll be heading to California with my dad, who I still cannot believe surprised me with tickets for Christmas.

So, for my last spring break in high school, I'll be going to college. I've never been on a plane; I've never even driven anywhere farther than the distance from Galway and Atlanta. It's not something I thought I'd be intimidated by until Dad handed me the ticket.

He's beyond excited, which is also why he can't stop texting me to tell me to get home at a decent time. We're driving to Chattanooga in the early morning since it's the closest airport to us, and he's terrified we're going to miss our flight.

I'm starting to see where I inherited some of my anxiety from, I think as I quickly text my dad back.

"He's still freaking out?" Killian asks, a confused look on his face as he stares at breast pump attachments.

Rolling my eyes, I shove his shoulder so he walks toward the clothes in the back. "You are not buying my mom a breast pump."

"I wasn't planning on it." He laughs and hooks his arm around my neck, bringing me into his side. "I'm just … imagining how it all works."

"Stop imagining my mom's boobs, ya freak," I tease, wrapping an arm around his waist.

Killian pretends to gag. "Not who I was imagining, but thanks for the boner-crushing image."

"You're welcome, and, yes, he is. Oddly enough, his freaking out is preventing me from freaking out, so I'm grateful."

"I can't believe I'm missing your first time on a plane," he grumbles, and I smile into his shoulder.

Killian has gotten oddly territorial about my firsts. I think it's because he missed so many of them when we were apart, so the idea of missing more drives him batty.

"There are so many plane milestones to still experience. A cross-country flight in basic economy at five in the morning with my dad doesn't sound like you'll be missing much."

"Are you getting a tour when you get there?" Killian asks, tossing some plain white onesies into the basket I'm holding.

"The assistant coach is meeting us to tour the facilities, and then there's a kind of student-athlete ambassador who's going to take us to tour the campus. I'm going to see my dorm building, so that's cool. I haven't gotten my roommate assignment yet, but they try to keep the players together, I heard."

I hold up a bib that says *Milk Drunk* and show Killian.

"Obviously." He nods to our basket.

I toss it in, echoing, "Obviously."

"We haven't talked about college much, and it's already March. You don't find that weird, Glory?" he says a little too casually, and I really can't believe he's bringing it up in a baby store.

"I'm not sure what we need to talk about."

"We're not breaking up." Killian pulls me up short and rests his hands on my shoulders to make sure I'm focusing.

"Why would you even say that?" I ask in shock.

HARD FEELINGS

"Because a couple of the guys on the team are breaking up with their girls, and I'm just letting you know we're not doing that."

"First of all, if I want to break up with you, I will, but lucky for you, I don't. We're not like them, Killian."

He lifts me up by my elbows and smacks a hard kiss on my lips, tearing a laugh out of me as he drops me back on my feet.

"Glad we got that out of the way. Let's get some diapers." I point toward the back wall of the store. "You haven't mentioned anything about UGA. Have you gotten your room assignment?"

Killian stalls and looks around before pulling me into an empty aisle. "I haven't committed to them yet."

My mouth drops. "Excuse me, what?"

"I haven't committed to them."

"Killian, you've been talking about going to UGA since I've known you."

"Things change ..." He trails off, searching my eyes.

"Where would you go?" I anxiously tug on the bottom of his shirt. I haven't really asked him about college because I assumed nothing had changed. Killian knew my plans, and I knew his. "Killian, how are you only saying something now?"

"You haven't brought it up either," he points out, grabbing my hand from his shirt.

"Because I assumed you'd be going to the school you'd talked about since we were children! Is it because of your SAT scores?"

Killian smirks, winking that sexy little dimple at me, and I simultaneously want to slap it off his face and lick it.

"No, baby, I got a nearly perfect score on my SATs and was nominated for All-American this year."

I roll my eyes at his cockiness.

"I'm just considering my options," he says, turning away to check out diapers.

"Are you going to tell me where you're considering?"

"I will when I have a strong candidate. There were several offers; I'm doing my due diligence."

"Mmhmm." I head towards the checkout having decided we've gotten enough.

"Don't be mad," Killian calls out, trailing behind me.

"I just don't understand where this is coming from," I say, as he sets the basket on the cashier counter with a smile.

"It's been on my mind for a while," he admits, "which you would know if you kept reading my journal."

"Wait, you knew about this before you even gave me the journal?" I step back as Killian moves in front of me to pay the cashier.

My phone rings, distracting me, and I see it's my mom.

187

Rubbing Killian's back to get his attention, I point to my phone and head outside the store to take the call.

"Hey, Mom."

"Hey, honey! What are you up to?"

"Helping Killian pick out some stuff for the baby. He's bringing a little gift down with him."

"Oh, that's so nice of him!" She sounds enthusiastic, but given the octave of her voice, I know something is wrong.

"What's wrong?" I glance toward the doors and move farther away.

"Nothing—"

"Mother."

"Fine, okay. We're getting closer to my due date, and the doctor was asking about my birth plan, and it had me thinking ..."

I glare at the parking lot, willing her to finish her freaking sentence.

"It would be really nice if you were in the room with me."

I blink rapidly. "Wait, you want me in the room with you while you give birth? Am I even allowed? What about Sebastian?"

"Sebastian will be in there with me, too, and, yes, you're allowed."

"Wow, I wasn't expecting—"

"Hey, Whorey!" Tommy Gaines yells from the back of a black pickup truck.

"Mom, I gotta go." I hang up before she can say anything and glance behind me to check where Killian is.

"Looking for your boyfriend, Whorey?" Tommy is belligerently loud as they pull up in front of me.

Since it's the Friday before spring break, I knew there would be a little partying, but the sun has barely even set, and Tommy is off his fucking face already.

"Go away, Tommy."

"What, you think you're hot shit now because you're fucking King and heading to California, leaving this all behind? That's the plan, right?" Kyle, one of Tommy's little asshole friends, sneers.

Kyle's the younger brother of Tyson, one of the guys who chased me all those years ago and got his ass beat by a freshman Tanner.

"Killian is right behind me. Do you really want to run your mouths right now?" I ask, taking a step back as Tommy hops out of the truck bed.

"Yeah, I think we do." Kyle opens the door, and I try to hold my ground, but I'm starting to freak out a little bit.

What the hell is Killian doing in there?

"Ever since you started dating King, you think your shit doesn't stink, but I can smell the trash on you." Kyle backs me up against the brick column in front of the store, Tommy blocking me in from the side.

HARD FEELINGS

Between the truck and them, I'm barely visible, and I'm extremely aware of it.

"Back off." I try to sound strong, but I'm scared.

Kyle is clearly holding a grudge, and Tommy is a drunken idiot.

"Your little bitch boy, Tanner beat the living shit out of my brother, then had his daddy go to the cops and report him. That went on his record, bitch."

"I doubt it's the first time he's had harassment reported against him," I tell him.

Kyle slaps the brick next to my head, making me flinch as he leans close. The stench of beer is heavy on his breath, and I lean back as far as I can, digging my head into the brick.

Kyle's hand settles on my neck, and I swallow nervously, staring into his eyes. "Your tattletale mouth and your boyfriend's family made it so he couldn't get a job in this town."

"He can't get a job in this town because he's a drunk—something you seem to be working toward too," I point out, biting back a gasp when his hand closes tightly on my throat.

"Kyle!" Tommy yells a second before Killian appears over his shoulder.

He doesn't look at me, instead focusing on Kyle, and leans close to his ear.

"Take your fucking hand off of her," he says in a dark voice, rage emanating from every uttered word.

Kyle blanches and immediately drops his hand, stepping back to give me space.

"Glory, go get in my car," Killian tells me, handing me his keys but still refusing to look at me. I think that's the only thing preventing him from killing Kyle. If he saw how scared I was …

"Killian …" I say his name nervously, not wanting him to do anything that could jeopardize his future.

"Glory, get in the goddamn car. Now!" he barks.

I quickly grab his keys and the bags he dropped on the ground and hurry to his car.

Tossing the bags in the back, I sit in the passenger seat and watch Killian. Tommy reaches into the back of the truck and grabs a bat. Killian's focused on Kyle, so he doesn't see Tommy, so I roll the window down and yell his name.

He turns in time to catch the bat as Tommy swings it at him. I let out a horrified scream, covering my mouth as Killian yanks the bat away from Tommy and throws it down the sidewalk.

Hands shaking, I crawl over into the driver's seat and pull the seat up so I can reach the pedals. I'll run these fuckers over before I let them jump Killian. Hurrying, I start the car and try not to scream again as Kyle swings at Killian.

Killian hits Kyle, knocking him out with a single punch, and I flinch at the brutality of it. He turns to Tommy and says something that has Tommy backing up with his hands up.

Killian turns toward me as I drive toward him, and he hops into the passenger side as I pull up beside him.

"Killian," I say tearfully, watching him as he pulls his phone out, his knuckles busted.

"Hey, Carter," Killian greets, and I realize the Carter he's talking to is the freaking sheriff.

Killian gives him a brief rundown of what happened, promising he and I will come in to give a statement soon and to let them know Kyle and Tommy were both drinking and driving.

Shaking, I drive toward my house, zoning out as I listen to him finish up the call.

"Slow down," Killian orders, his voice still tight with barely constrained rage.

I ease my foot off the gas pedal as we exit the small town. We are surrounded by woods on either side as we twist our way back up and over the mountains. My hands are trembling so hard on the steering wheel that it makes the car weave, and I will them to stop, but the adrenaline is coursing through me violently.

"Pull over." Killian points to a scenic parking lot off the side of the road. It's empty at this time of day, and the sun is setting behind the trees, already rendering it useless for tourists traveling through.

I shift the car into park and turn to Killian. He's holding himself so tightly that I can see nearly every muscle in his body is flexed. His jaw is clenched so tight that I'd be surprised if he didn't crack a tooth.

I've seen a lot of versions of Killian over the years, but I've never seen him so enraged before. I'm not afraid of this version, but I don't know how to defuse the situation. Purcells are not the best at navigating emotions. That's always been Killian's expertise.

"Are you okay?" he asks hoarsely, still not looking at me.

"Killian, why won't you look at me?" I ask softly, unbuckling my seat belt and turning toward him fully.

"Because I'm barely holding on by a goddamn thread, and if I see one mark on you, I'm going to lose the control that allowed me to walk away from Kyle without beating him unconscious."

"I'm okay," I promise.

"You're not fucking okay, Glory. You're shaking so hard; it's rocking the car." He's seething, and I realize he's not going to calm down unless I do something.

HARD FEELINGS

I climb over the center console and settle myself in his lap, leaning forward to press kisses to his jaw. "I'm okay, Killian. I'm okay," I continue to repeat until his arms come around me, crushing me into him.

He buries his nose in my hair and inhales deeply. I close my eyes and rest against him, his heat seeping through my simple T-shirt dress and black tights, warming me until the shaking begins to stop. His body shudders against mine, and he presses a kiss to my shoulder, my neck, and my cheek before pulling back and framing my face.

I let him tilt it, inspecting my neck where Kyle grabbed me, and seeing no bruising, his eyes finally begin to clear.

"See?" I tentatively smile, but it only lasts a second before I'm trembling again.

"I'm not going to let anything happen to you, Glory," he promises, but he misunderstands why I'm scared.

Of course, I was scared for myself. Kyle and Tommy aren't as big as Killian, but they don't need to be to wield their physical strength against me. That will always be a fear of mine, and I'm even more determined to sign up for self-defense classes. What really got me was how close Killian came to being hurt.

"Tommy was going to hit you with a bat," I whisper tearfully.

"But he didn't. We're fine."

"I'm so sorry, Killian—" I begin, but he cuts me off.

"No. Do not apologize. This is not your fault. Kyle and Tommy made their decision. Just because those idiots hold you responsible for their actions does not make it true."

My lip trembles, and I know he's right, but this town has held me responsible for perceived grievances. It's difficult to shake it off.

"Stop. Baby, stop," he begs and leans forward to kiss my tears off my cheeks before capturing my mouth in a frenzied kiss.

The emotional aftermath of what almost happened sweeps us both up, and my kiss turns frantic with need.

"Killian, I need you." I bite his bottom lip, rocking against his hard-on, trapped in his jeans between us.

"Jesus," he groans and pushes my skirt up. "I can feel how wet you are beneath your tights."

"Hurry," I beg, pulling his shirt up and over his head.

Killian pushes the seat back to give us more room and reaches into the center console to pull out a condom. Snickering, I help him unbutton his jeans.

"I can't believe you have that in your car," I comment, biting my lip as he pushes his boxer briefs down, revealing his erection. I moan quietly at how hard he is, pre-cum already beading at the tip of his cock.

"I'm never going anywhere unprepared after that night on my couch," he tells me and rolls the condom down his length.

I hover over his tip, hips undulating impatiently as he fondles me through my tights.

"Just rip them," I tell him impatiently, and Killian's face goes dark with lust. I gasp as he hooks his fingers along the seam over my pussy and rips my tights open. Cool air greets my warmth, and I clench in anticipation.

Killian's hands go to my hips, and he holds me still as he pushes in only slightly. My head tips back at how good it feels, thighs flexing with my need to sink all the way down and ride him. He inches his way in slowly, driving me insane with the need to move.

"Killian, if you don't—" I'm cut off with a gasp as he drives all the way in, fully seating himself inside me. The sensation has my eyes rolling back and my nipples stiffening against the thin cotton of my dress.

He leans up, capturing a stiff peak in his mouth, and the feel of his tongue over the fabric feels indecent. I'm not wearing a bra, and I don't really need to, so the heat of his mouth penetrates the thin fabric. The firmness of his tongue, wetting the fabric of my dress, provides just the right amount of abrasion against my sensitive nipple that I feel a rush of wetness flood where we're connected.

Killian leans back as I ride him, grasping him as I rise and then sink back down. The friction is heavenly. His heavy-lidded gaze watches me work us both, and I try to memorize him in this moment.

His curly, dark hair is mussed from my hands. Full lips swollen from my kisses, golden skin flushed high with color, and the look in his eyes … I've never felt more beautiful, more coveted than when he looks at me like this. His hazel eyes are more golden, his gaze adoring as he watches me.

"Glory," he groans, hands settling on my hips as he stares into my eyes.

This level of intimacy would be too much for me if it were anyone else. With Jason, I couldn't even do it with the lights on.

But Killian? I want him to see me as much as I want to see him. It's imperative we have no barriers between us.

Everything that's happened before, more than just Kyle and Tommy, flashes through my head. Happy tears well, reflecting more emotion than I've ever found myself able to articulate. Apparently, the only thing I know how to do anymore is cry.

Killian immediately gets concerned and tries to stop me, but I shake my head and lean down to give him a kiss before whispering against his lips, "I love you."

He makes an almost-feral sound, as if struck by those words, and begins to pump himself inside me furiously. I cry out, holding on for dear life as he rushes us toward our orgasms.

HARD FEELINGS

"Killian," I scream as my entire body clenches tightly before shuddering as wave after wave crashes over me. It seems to go on forever, my body shaking on top of him as he chases his own release.

He tips over the edge after me, yelling, "Fuck!" as he jerks inside me.

The car falls silent as I stare out the fogged-up windows, smiling at how quickly we lose it with one another.

I've told Killian I love him countless times throughout my life. When we were younger, those words came easily to both of us. But I haven't said it since we've been together, definitely not when we reconciled.

It's always been there. Even when he hurt me, it lurked under the pain, but I held myself back from saying it because I knew the next time I told him those three words, the meaning would be different.

I'm *in love* with him. I love the man he is. He's kind, protective, and wise, and he makes me a stronger, more confident person. He pushes me to be better and, at the same time, allows me to be perfectly myself, loving me as I am all the while.

Killian's eyes widen at my confession, and he stills. His look of utter disbelief has me laughing through the tears.

"I love you, Killian. I love you so much," I say again, holding my breath as his chest pumps with his emotion.

Killian lets out a gruff sound before pulling me to him so my front is touching him as he hugs me tightly.

"Your lack of response is freaking me out." I try to lighten up the overwrought turn of events, but it's actually freaking me out how quiet he's being.

He pulls back and gives me an incredulous look. "You have to know I love you."

"I'm finding out that I need the words." I smile softly, my heart pounding at hearing him say it.

"Glory Jane Purcell, there hasn't been a moment since we met that I haven't loved you. I don't remember when it changed, but it grew deeper and sank so far inside me that I cannot imagine not loving you for the rest of my life. You mean everything to me. I love you beyond measure, in ways I can't find words for, but I hope, one day, I can show you."

"Sap," I choke out before resting my head on his chest.

My phone rings, startling us both, and I grab it from the cupholder to see it's my dad.

"Ugh, absolutely the last person I want to think about with you still inside me." I gag and slowly lift myself off of him before letting the phone go to voice mail.

"Gross, baby." He winces as he tucks himself back into his pants after cleaning himself up.

I know it's another *get your butt home* call, so it's time to go. Gingerly, I get back into the driver's seat and pull my dress back down.

"Well …" I shrug and wait for him to click his seat belt in before backing up.

Killian laughs as I drive us back to my place.

When I pull into the driveway, I fully expect to see my dad pacing, but it's empty. I put the car in park and look at him. He's already looking at me, and we both smile a secret smile. Everything feels like standing in sunshine.

Hopping out of the car, I circle around, meeting him at the back.

"Are you going to be okay in Atlanta?" I ask, gnawing my lip.

In all of this, we never got a chance to discuss him going down to our parents'. It'll be the first time he's spent any real time with his dad since all of this began.

Killian thumbs my lip, pulling it from my teeth, and tugs gently on my hair. "I'm going to be okay, Glory."

"Have you talked to your dad at all since my mom's surprise pregnancy bombshell?" I wrap my arms around his waist, hugging him, when his face falls slightly.

"We've texted, but you know …" He shrugs.

"What does he think about you potentially not attending his alma mater?" I raise a brow because I know Sebastian will have something to say about that.

"He doesn't know," he admits sheepishly.

"Killian …"

He rests his chin on my head and sighs loudly. "I know. I'll tell them both soon, when I figure it out. My life has been decided for so long, Glory, and now, there are options. I owe it to myself to explore them."

Killian steps back, drops a kiss on my lips, and says, "All right, you'd better get in there before your dad's head explodes. Call me, okay?"

"I will. Love you!" I say and begin to walk away before Killian grabs my hand and spins me back to him, making me laugh as he kisses me again.

"I love you too." He smiles against my lips, and it might be my new favorite feeling of all.

TWENTY-FOUR

Stepping off the plane with my dad is a surreal experience. I can't believe we are here. I have been watching vlogs and following UCLA hashtags for years. I don't even remember when I first got stuck on going to UCLA. I just wanted someplace that was the opposite to where I grew up.

It's been sensory overload since we left. The plane ride, navigating LAX, experiencing an insane level of traffic, the people … I feel like my brain is going to explode, but it's all worth it to step on campus for the first time.

When the Uber drops us off at the entrance, Kimber, the student-athlete ambassador, greets Dad and me. She looks exactly how I imagined an LA girl to look. Sun-bleached blonde hair in beachy waves, long and lithe, effortlessly cool and so kind. I want to be her. And from then on, I feel like I'm walking around with heart eyes. Even Dad seems to be enamored with the campus.

We get a tour first, thankfully mostly on a golf cart since the campus is enormous. Of course, I get a selfie in front of Royce Hall. Dad falls in love with Powell Library. Kimber takes us over to Bruin Plaza, where the store is located, and Dad buys me my first official UCLA merch—an oversize sweatshirt that I already know I'm going to live in. He gets a pennant for himself to hang in his office. Kimber takes a picture of us in front of the giant bronze statue of the Bruin bear.

Finally, before she takes us to the athletic facilities, we stop over at the Hill, where all the dorms are located. I point out De Neve Plaza, where I'll be in Cedar.

The elation and joy I'm feeling come second to the pride bursting from my dad. I can't believe this is real and happening. Cassidy said the second she stepped on campus at Stanford, she felt a rightness and it made everything seem so real, and I have to agree.

I have nerves, of course. It'll be the first time I'll be away from my dad and Galway, surrounded by people I don't know, except for Marcus. I hope he's ready for us to be joined at the hip because I'm going to cling to him until I make some friends.

Having him here and Cassidy a few hours away makes it not so scary, but I'm sure I'll get lonely. Fortunately, that's a feeling I'm used to.

My head is spinning as we head back to the golf cart, where Kimber is going to drive us over to the athletic facilities and field. I send the pics I've taken so far to Cassidy and grin; she floods our text chain with GIFs and memes of excitement.

Cassidy texts back.

Are you freaking out?

My chest warms with how well she knows me and how I won't have that in a few short months.

How do you even make friends with people you haven't gone to school with since the dawn of time? Especially when you're not the most social …

Realizing my racing thoughts are answering Cassidy's question for me, I laugh at myself and answer her.

Uh, yeah.

It's going to be okay. Promise!

That's easy for her to say! She's like a people magnet and not just because she's legitimately stunning with hair you can see a mile away. She's got the most unique, comforting energy. You can't help but love Cassidy, and I feel like the only reason people like me half the time is because she's my best friend and she brings out the best in me.

Before I can pour every anxious thought into a text, the golf cart screeches to a stop, and I nearly fall out of it. Kimber has been so friendly, but, holy shit, she's a terror behind the wheel.

I glance up at Acosta Athletic Complex in awe. Dad wraps an arm around my shoulders, giving me a squeeze every so often as Kimber walks us through it.

There are students in there now, and to imagine myself as one of them has me equally thrilled and wanting to throw up. I've never allowed myself to consider the pressure of collegiate athletics or how I am going to balance a college workload at one of the top schools in the country. I remind myself of what will be at my fingertips, the support I'll have, access to tutors, and force myself to chill out.

No sense in worrying about something before it happens; I just need to trust the choice the recruiters made. They want me here for a reason and

HARD FEELINGS

believe that I can fulfill that reason. I tell myself this as we make our way out to the practice fields, and as soon as I step on the grass, I'm calm.

Kimber is telling my dad about some scheduling stuff we'll have to do soon, but I tune it out and close my eyes. Breathing in, I smell familiar scents of grass and baking concrete in the sun and smile. Everything else might be changing, but ... this feeling when I step on the field will be the same. It's everything.

By the time we leave, both Dad and I are overstimulated and extremely hungry. We both agree that as a rite of passage, we cannot come all the way to California and not try the infamous In-N-Out. We decide to go big and order a ton before heading back to the hotel to gorge ourselves and watch some TV.

We have all day tomorrow planned, doing touristy things, and I can't wait to just hang with my dad. I'm not sure how many more times I'll have with him just like this. He's eager for me to see the beach. I can't believe I live on the East Coast, but the first time I'll see a beach is all the way on the other side of the country.

The more I start to wrap my head around all this, the more I realize how much I haven't experienced for a multitude of reasons. I can't wait to try everything. Suddenly overwhelmed with gratitude, I turn to my dad, who's stretched out on his bed, chowing on animal-style fries, and smile.

"Thank you, Dad."

He turns to me, eyebrows high as he says over a mouthful, "For what?"

I laugh lightly at him. "Literally everything."

His eyes warm as he chews, and I can tell I've choked him up a bit. We've been through a lot together, and he's done the best he could. I know his biggest worry is how all this is affecting me, but I'm going to be okay, and I think he finally sees that. A lot of that is in thanks to him, and I'm so happy we're here now.

It's not until Wednesday night, when Dad and I walk like jet-lagged zombies into our home, mumbling to each other as we make our way upstairs for our respective naps, that I realize I haven't heard from Killian since I left.

I toss my bag on my bed, knowing if I set it anywhere else, it'll likely not get unpacked until I need to use the bag again. I decide to first wash the travel off. My entire body feels stale and, at the same time, extremely dry and oily.

After my shower, I braid my hair, not willing to go through my entire hair routine right now, and pull on my new UCLA sweatshirt and some Nike running shorts. Stepping out of my bathroom, I stare at my bed and let out a whine.

It's probably best to do all this now because crawling into bed will not help me get back on East Coast time. I dump my bag out and throw all the clothes into the laundry basket. I grab my toiletries bag and toss it on the bathroom counter and call myself unpacked.

Grabbing my phone, I plug it into the charger and sit on the floor beside my bed. I refuse to even sit on it because I know, within ten minutes, I'll be fully horizontal and fighting sleep. I call Killian, only for it to ring once before getting sent to voice mail.

"Uhh," I sputter before trying to call again.

Killian has never declined my call. Ever. This time, it goes straight to voice mail.

I send him a text, and after fifteen minutes of no response, I start to get a little worried. I decide to call Cassidy instead, who picks up on the first ring.

"Dude," she answers, and I'm already sitting up, nervous.

"Killian isn't picking up the phone, and he knew I was coming home today. Has Tanner heard anything about how it's been going down at my mom's?"

"Yeah, Glory, it's not great." She sighs into the phone. "Hold on, I'm putting you on speaker. Tanner's right here."

"Tan, what the hell happened?" I demand.

"Has he mentioned his plans for college?" Tanner asks hesitantly.

"Only that he's thinking about other schools besides UGA. He's just considering his options. He wasn't even mentioning it to anyone, so I don't—"

"Well, his dad found out," Tanner inserts.

"Okay, but found out what exactly?" I push.

"Glory, Killian is planning on following you to college," Tanner says bluntly, and I gasp so hard that I start choking.

"Are you okay?" Cassidy calls out.

"Yeah, I'm just …" I trail off in shock.

"So, as you can imagine, his dad had something to say about that," Tanner drawls sarcastically.

"I'm sure," I murmur and wince.

Sebastian is bitter about giving up his supposed dreams, even his last name, for Elizabeth. Add that to the fact that Sebastian is a UGA alum and has been on Killian's ass since birth about continuing that legacy, yeah … I'm sure Sebastian had quite a bit to say.

"Anyway, they got into it. Big time. Sebastian stormed off to God knows where, and Killian left, trying to make it home before his mom found out and went off the deep end."

Guilt gnaws at me. "Guys, I do not want him giving anything up for me. That's not fair to him."

"Killian doesn't see it that way," Tanner assures me, but that's beside the point.

"Killian doesn't see it that way now. What happens a year from now? Ten years from now?" I chew my lip. "So, he's at home right now?"

HARD FEELINGS

"Yeah, but I wouldn't go over—" Cassidy begins, knowing exactly where my thoughts are going.

"I'll call you back," I tell them, already slipping my feet into some sneakers.

"Glory, that's a bad idea. Emotions are high right now," Tanner warns.

"I'm not letting him make this huge mistake. Look at what happened to our parents. I refuse to repeat history," I tell them, and they both start talking at the same time. "Y'all, I will call you back later."

I hang up before they can interrupt again and head out, calling out to my dad that I'll be back soon.

The walk to Killian's house takes no time since I basically run the entire way. I reach their front door and wince when I can hear them yelling from outside. Debating whether to just let myself in, I decide to just do it. Elizabeth has said I don't have to knock, and although now would be the time I should knock, I let myself in anyway. Uncaring of what I might walk in on.

From the sounds of it, they are in the kitchen. I creep toward them, halting when I hear my name come up.

"You cannot be serious, Killian. Would she do the same for you? I don't even have to ask since she's not staying here. You don't think Georgia has a great soccer program?" Elizabeth says.

"She's following her dreams. I would never ask her to give them up. That's not love," Killian says calmly, but I can hear the strain in his voice.

I rest my hand against my throat, cringing a little because I already know what Elizabeth is going to say.

"What do you know about love? You're eighteen!"

"Do not diminish what I feel for her because of how old I am," Killian warns.

"Killian, sacrificing for the ones you love is all well and good, but eventually, you will give too much of yourself and you won't recognize who you are anymore."

I bite my lip as tears fill my eyes because I remember my mom saying the same thing. Sometimes, you bend too far, and you break. I don't want to be the reason Killian breaks.

"We are not like you and Dad, Mom."

"Killian, please." Elizabeth's voice breaks. "I can't lose anyone else. Please don't go."

"Mom, it's four years. You won't lose me." He sighs, pulling her into a tight hug.

"You don't understand, Killian," she cries, and I walk backward, heart breaking.

Letting myself out of the house, I cry the entire way back to mine, knowing what I need to do. I call Cassidy the second I'm home, and she tells me she's been waiting to come over. I don't even have to say anything, and she's already on her way.

She lets herself in and finds me staring blankly at my bedroom ceiling.

"What's going on in that head of yours, Glory Jane?" She crawls up beside me and rests her head against mine.

I let out a huge sigh and blink the tears out of my eyes, letting them trail along my temples and into my hair.

"I need to break up with Killian." I choke the words out, and Cassidy reaches down to grab my hand in hers.

"Is there any talking you out of this?"

I shake my head.

"Glory, why do you think you have to?"

"He's giving everything up to come follow me to school. His mom is devastated, and she's right; I wouldn't do the same. It never even entered my brain to consider going somewhere closer."

"Are we even sure he's thinking of following you? What if he just wants to go somewhere else?"

I turn my head toward her. "You don't find it weird that he's barely mentioned this to me? Or the fact that he never considered this until we started dating?"

"Okay, fine, the timing is suspicious."

"Besides, I refuse to be my parents or let him be his either."

"Lord, what are you talking about now?" Cassidy groans next to me.

"My mom sacrificed what she wanted, and look how that turned out. She never wanted to come to Galway."

"Okay, there are miles between what your parents did and deciding to go somewhere else for college."

"I hear you, but it starts somewhere."

"I support you, but I think you're making a mistake here."

"Cassidy, if you fell in love with someone in Galway, would you give up Stanford and stay?" I ask her point-blank.

"Glory," she groans.

"You wouldn't, and if you did, you'd come to resent that person."

"All I'm going to say is that, sometimes, when you fight so hard to not become something, you miss the fact that you're becoming a different version of it anyway."

I'm silent as I mull that over, but it doesn't matter. "I'm not willing to chance it."

"So, what do you think is going to happen now? You'll break up and be friends, share a sister, and everything will be fine?" Cassidy asks incredulously.

"Eventually, we'll get there. Before we were this, we were that." I refer to our friendship.

HARD FEELINGS

"And your parents got in the middle of that, and you're letting them do it again."

"Cassidy, enough. This needs to happen."

"Fine, but do you hear me?"

"I hear you," I tell her and squeeze her hand.

Some people think friendship is blind loyalty and support, but true friendship is being unafraid to voice your opinion, even if you disagree, and know that it will be received with respect.

"I appreciate what you're saying, but I have to do what I think I can live with."

"I appreciate *that*, but I think you're acting out of fear," Cassidy argues.

We both go silent. I'm exhausted.

This isn't easy for me. I don't want to break up with him. We literally just told each other how we feel, and that hasn't changed, not for me. By ensuring he has the future he deserves, I'm showing just how much I love him. I want the absolute best for Killian. He has sacrificed so much for his family and for me. I can't ask him to keep doing that when I'm unwilling to do so.

I hear what Cassidy is saying, but I'm just too afraid of what could happen down the line.

My phone rings, startling us both, and I jolt, almost afraid to see if Killian is calling me back. Biting my lip, I grab my phone and see it's my mom. She's probably calling to fill me in on what happened between Sebastian and Killian.

I answer the phone. "Hey, Mom."

"Glory," she wheezes, and I sit up immediately.

"What's wrong?" I demand as Cassidy shoots up next to me.

"The baby is coming. Can you get here, please?"

"Where is Sebastian?" I'm already slipping my shoes back on.

"He's on his way. He's calling Killian. He should be stopping by to pick you up any minute," she breathes, and I can hear the pain in her voice.

"Okay, okay." I panic, glancing around my room, at a loss as to what to do right now. "Okay."

"Glory, relax and just get here safely. Hopefully, by the time you arrive, you'll have a little sister."

"Okay," I say again weakly.

"It's going to be fine. Just get here. I gotta go. I hear Sebastian downstairs."

Mom hangs up, and open-mouthed, I stare at Cassidy, who's grinning widely at me.

"I'm going to be a big sister today," I say numbly.

Cassidy comes over and shakes my shoulders in excitement. "You're going to be such a fun big sister, Glory!"

"She's early. She's thirty-eight weeks, Cassidy."

"Almost thirty-nine. It's going to be okay. She's at a great hospital; all her scans have been good. It's going to be fine. All you need to concentrate on is getting to the hospital."

"Right. Okay. What the hell is happening today?" I ask hysterically.

"Glory, go tell your dad. Killian will be here any minute," Cassidy orders, and I instantly jump to do what she said. "I'm going to head out. Call me with updates."

"Okay. I love you," I tell her, voice wobbling with emotion.

Cassidy gives me a big hug. "Everything will work out."

I throw on something a little more appropriate for a hospital and head down to my dad's room, knocking when I see his door shut.

When he tells me to come in, I enter to find him sitting cross-legged on top of his covers, eating popcorn and watching TV. We're so alike sometimes that it's actually painful.

"What's up, kid?" he asks, wiping his hands on his sweatpants.

"Apparently, my sister waited just long enough for me to get home before deciding to come," I tell him, coming in farther. I've always hesitated to tell him too much about my mom's pregnancy. It feels weird to be excited about it in front of him, but at the same time, I know he's in such a good place right now.

"Is your mom okay?" he asks.

"Yeah, she seems more concerned with not having the baby at home and more about getting to the hospital." I fidget where I stand, picking at my cuticles.

"She'll be okay, Glory. You were a little early too. Your mom wasn't much further along with you when you decided it was time."

Nodding silently, I cross my arms over my chest and Dad smiles at me sadly before getting up and pulling me into a tight hug.

Everything is about to change again, I think, gripping my dad's shirt in my fists and telling him I love him.

"Love you too. I guess Killian must be on his way?" Dad asks.

As if he conjured him, our front door bursts open, and Killian yells my name from downstairs.

I hug my dad one more time before pulling back. A lot more is going to change than just my mom giving birth—way too much to unpack right now.

"I'll text you when we get there and then call you later. Love you!" I call out as I head down to meet Killian.

Killian is pacing in the foyer when I come into view, similarly dressed. He looks like I feel—tired, scared, and stressed.

"Hey, baby." He pulls me in for a kiss, and I feel the tension ebb from his body.

HARD FEELINGS

Willing myself to lock down every emotion that I've had over the last four hours, I kiss him back before pulling back and grabbing my phone and house keys.

"Hey, we really need to get on the road," I tell him abruptly, pushing him toward the door and locking it behind us.

The silent car ride would be awkward if we both weren't so far in our own heads. It's the longest couple of hours of my life, but soon, we're at the hospital and being pointed toward labor and delivery.

Killian grabs my hand, and I hang on to the lifeline it provides. My nerves are unbelievably frayed. Killian texted his dad when we arrived, so when we get off the elevator, he is already waiting for us.

"Did we make it in time?" Killian asks as we follow him down to my mom's room.

"She's getting ready to push. Glory, she wants you in there," he tells me as we pull up at the door.

I wring my hands, looking uncertainly at Killian. I feel bad he won't be in there.

"Go." He kisses my forehead—something that has Sebastian immediately heading into the room.

I'd be lying if I said I couldn't sense the tension between father and son, and I'm sure it'll explode again at some point, but the focus is elsewhere now.

"Okay, I'll come out and fill you in as soon as I can." I press a quick kiss to his mouth and squash the guilt of showing him affection after talking earlier about breaking up with him and head inside.

Entering my mom's room, I'm met with organized chaos. Sebastian wasn't kidding about getting here in time; she's already pushing. Spotting me, she holds her hand out, and heart pounding, I hustle to her side and squeeze her hand.

It feels so weird to be here. I've had months to wrap my mind around having a little sister and what this will do for my family. In many ways, I feel like I shouldn't be in here. My mom and I have a tentative truce, and we're definitely in a better place than we were a year ago, but it still feels like she should have someone else here.

Sebastian stands on the other side, lovingly encouraging Mom to push, whispering how strong she is, how beautiful she is, and the lump in my throat grows. It's this moment where I see Killian in Sebastian. It's hard to imagine he was able to do anything hurtful to Elizabeth, but seeing him with my mom, I know it's more complicated than I can understand.

I don't forgive them, but I don't need to right now.

My thoughts are interrupted by a loud wail as my little sister enters the world. Sebastian moves to the end of the bed and snips the umbilical cord. Breath stalling in my throat, I see her wriggly little red body briefly before she's hurried away by nurses to the corner, where they begin to check her over.

I glance at my mom, who's already staring at me, and we share a tear-filled smile.

"I saw her," I choke out, emotion overwhelming me. "She's beautiful."

Mom grins at me. "I'm sure when you saw her, she looked like something out of *Alien*."

I laugh lightly, nodding, but still. That's my sister!

Sebastian turns to us from where he's watching over her and smiles; all the tension leaves my mom's body. I know she was worried about her coming early, but Sebastian giving her that smile communicates that there's nothing to worry about.

After getting cleared, the nurse brings her over to my mom, and I watch them meet for the first time. My mom greeting my sister is beautiful and makes me think of when I was born.

I can see the love on her face, the awe, and I know she must have felt that way about me. Maybe her love isn't perfect, and maybe it hurts, but seeing her look at my sister reminds me that she does, at least, love me.

She loves the best way she knows how, and that's not what I needed back then, but maybe it's enough now.

I settle into the seat by the bed, giving Sebastian and my mom a moment with their new little family, and grab my phone to text Dad, telling him all is well.

Sometime later, Sebastian leaves to grab Killian.

"Do you want to hold her?" my mom asks, and I jump up, eager yet nervous.

"I've never held a baby before." I chew my lip but edge closer to the now-sleeping baby girl.

"It's okay; I'll show you." Mom waves me over and lifts her into my arms, telling me to support her head.

The first moment I saw my sister, I was in awe. Now holding her and staring at her perfect, innocent little face, I fall in love. She's so much smaller and lighter than I expected, adding to my nerves of holding something so precious.

I sit back in my chair and stare at her, promising all sorts of things to her in my head. Leaning down, I press a gentle kiss to her forehead, and that's when Killian walks into the room.

HARD FEELINGS

My heart feels wholly blown open as I meet his eyes, smiling wider than I ever have before. Killian's face softens dramatically as he moves his gaze to our sister, and I know instantly that there's a new little love in his life.

He moves to my side, crouching next to my chair so he can smooth a hand over the black fuzz on her head.

"She looks like you," I whisper so as not to wake her.

She has the same golden skin with black hair and Killian's chin. I haven't seen her eyes open yet, but I'd bet they are going to be hazel. Mom told me the baby's eye color changes over time, so we won't know for sure for a while.

"She's got your mouth," he says, watching her intently.

"Do you want to hold her, Killian?" Mom asks, and Killian immediately stands up and away from us.

Laughing lightly, I know precisely his thoughts right now, and if I was nervous about holding her at my size, I'm sure Killian the giant is even more nervous. Standing up, I nod to the chair, and Killian hesitates for a moment before taking the seat.

I repeat my mom's words about how to hold the baby, like I'm an expert now, and Killian chuckles at me under his breath as I hand her over. She looks even smaller in his arms.

God, the feels!

I feel like my tiny Grinch heart has expanded so fast over the last couple of hours.

"What is her name?" Killian asks softly, studying his sister like she might disappear if he looks away.

"That's actually something we wanted to talk to you two about," Sebastian says, sitting on the edge of the hospital bed and taking my mom's hand.

"We wanted to do something that honored both of you. You're going to be such a big part of her life—we hope anyway—so we want her to have a piece of you always."

I lean against the wall next to Killian and wait, breath stalling in my throat.

"What do you think of the name Korrie? We'll spell it a little differently, but it's a combination of both of your names."

My chin wobbles as I stare at my mom, and I glance at Killian, who is equally overcome with emotion. Likely more so, considering the argument he and his father got into earlier. I run my hand down the back of his head, scratching lightly in comfort before turning back to our parents.

"I love it." And I do. I think it's adorable, and I feel honored that she'll carry a part of me with her always.

"Me too." Killian's voice cracks, and he clears the emotion from his throat before turning back to our sister. "Hi, Korrie. I'm Killian."

I lean down next to them and trace her tiny little eyebrows. "Hi, Korrie."

I look up from Korrie to smile at my mom and Sebastian, who both have tears in their eyes. There are lots of emotions running wild in the room right now, but the one that feels the largest to me is gratitude.

"Thank you," I tell them both.

TWENTY-FIVE

By the time Killian and I get back to our parents' house in Atlanta, it's late, but I can't seem to stop myself from going into helper mode. While Killian heads upstairs for a shower, I clean the entire downstairs.

I need to keep busy; otherwise, I'm going to blurt everything out to Killian. If I stay busy, he won't see what's right under the surface. Sebastian is staying at the hospital for the night, but I'm hoping I can get everything in order before Killian and I have to leave tomorrow.

I'm pulling out ingredients for the only thing I know how to cook—something my mom calls kitchen sink casserole. I haven't had it in years, not since before she left, and right now, it's the only thing I want.

It was basically whatever vegetable we had in the kitchen, some chickpeas or whatever other meat alternative was available since my mom was a vegetarian, and some cream of mushroom soup.

When I hear Killian stomping down the stairs, I panic and start chopping carrots like it's my one and only job in the world and I'm shooting for employee of the month.

"Uh, what are you doing?" Killian asks, taking a seat at the kitchen counter.

"What's it look like?" I wave the knife at the mountain of carrots and potatoes I've already hacked up.

"Well, I was going to say cooking, but it looks like you're practicing your ninja skills."

"Ha," I mutter before dumping them into the casserole dish and grabbing the cauliflower. "It's kitchen sink casserole."

"Damn, I haven't had that in forever," he says, snagging one of the carrots and taking a bite. "What time do you want to leave tomorrow?"

"I want to stop by the hospital first, then go. As early as we can," I say, still not looking up.

"Glory?"

"Yeah?" I say, dumping the cauliflower into the dish. I'll have to cook some of this first, or it'll be too hard. Hmm, I need a pot. I start opening cabinet doors until I find a big pot.

"Glory, look at me." Killian's voice gets louder.

I just can't. I can't. I can't look at him right now because he'll know, and then I'll have to break both our hearts.

"Killian …" I plead and begin to fill the pot with water.

"Glory …" Killian matches my tone, but he knows something's wrong now. I can feel his body shifting from relaxed to tense behind me.

"Just leave it for tonight, please. Let's just leave it," I beg him, setting the pot on the stove and turning the heat on high.

"What is *it*, Glory? You need to talk to me."

And suddenly, I'm furious.

Turning away from the stove, I face him over the counter, arms braced in front of me.

"You need to talk to *me*, Killian." I slap a hand on my chest as his face shuts down completely. *Yeah, I got you.* "Why am I finding out all this shit about you going to school on the West Coast from everyone but you? Or that you already told your parents? Apparently, everyone knows, except me."

"We did talk about this, Glory," he points out, and I scoff.

"Killian, there were no specifics. You basically said you were thinking about exploring options. How did it go from that to you telling your parents you're not going to UGA?"

"I don't understand why you're mad. We'll be going to school together or at least near each other. I thought—"

"I'm not going to let you give up your dreams for me, Killian!" I wail, stepping back from the counter, shocked by the sound of my own voice. Its loudness echoes in the tiny house and stuns Killian into silence.

"What are you talking about?" Killian says softly, knuckles white from how hard he's gripping the counter.

"I can't ask you to do that. You've talked about UGA since I've known you, and now that we're together, you suddenly want to change course?"

"You're not asking me to do anything. I want to do this," Killian stresses, pressing a fist onto the counter.

Staring at him now, seeing the man he's become, I know he'd do anything for me. I know how much he loves me because it's the same love I feel for him. There's nothing I wouldn't do for him. Even if it means setting him free.

"I don't think we should see each other anymore," I say softly, tearing my eyes away from his.

HARD FEELINGS

"What the fuck are you talking about?" he growls.

Sucking in a breath, I hide my shaking hands behind my back and force myself to meet his gaze. Seeing the fury and the pain underneath his deceptively placid face, staring back at me, is almost enough to cower me.

"I think we're better off as friends." I force the words out of stiff lips.

"Friends." He laughs, but I don't know if I've ever heard a laugh sound so sad.

"Killian—" I cry, but he pushes away from the counter, cutting me off.

"I know what you're doing. Do you think I don't get it? You're so fucking transparent, Glory. I knew this was going to happen. I fucking knew it!" he swears viciously as he begins to pace.

"I refuse to let us be like them, Killian."

"Even now, you're letting them dictate your decisions. You're so sure this is how we'll avoid ending up like them." He hangs his head, and I dig my nails into my palm to stop myself from going to him. He nods to himself before looking back at me, all emotion wiped from his face. "Okay."

"Okay?" I ask, startled.

"Yeah, okay. Fine. Whatever." He walks off.

"Killian, don't be like this." I follow him out of the kitchen.

He takes the stairs two at a time. "I think you've made enough decisions for me in the last thirty minutes. I'll allow myself to be a little upset that my girlfriend is breaking up with me because she's afraid of turning into her mom, if that's all right with you?"

I flinch but don't falter. "I'm doing this for you!"

Killian comes back down the stairs, halting only when he's right in front of me. His hands frame my face as he studies me, his thumb grazing my lips. I try not to lean into his touch, but I can't help but savor it while I still have it.

"I love you," he tells me, kissing my forehead when I whimper, "but you interpret sacrifice as an obligation that you have to pay back when I would do anything for you if you'd only ask. Love is not transactional. It's not point for point. I need you to hear me when I say, I'm trying to find my own way too."

I shake my head as a tear crawls down my cheek.

Killian thumbs that away. "I know you, baby. I know what you think you're doing and why, and I also know that you haven't had a lot of experience with trusting people, so okay. If you want to be friends, we'll be friends."

Killian kisses me one last time before heading back upstairs. "For now."

"For now?" I call out, but he doesn't answer; he just keeps going up the stairs. "Killian? For now?"

I wait at the bottom of the stairs, so sure that he's going to come back downstairs and continue the fight or just storm out the door, but he does neither. In fact, none of this went how I'd thought it would.

Stumped, I head back to the kitchen to finish making the casserole, suddenly feeling so drained that I barely finish making it. Killian doesn't come out of his room for the rest of the night, and when I finally head to bed hours later, I hesitate outside his door. He's staying in the guest room, which leaves our parents' room, and I feel a bit icky about sleeping in their room.

The light under the door isn't on, so I guess that's it for that conversation. I don't know if he understands that we're broken up. He accepted it, but maybe not? Feeling confused, I head instead to Korrie's nursery and decide to sleep on the small twin bed in there.

My mom decorated it in a calm sage green with white furniture. A cute little mural of wildflowers covers the wall where her crib stands. Pictures of Killian and me, my mom and his dad, line the top of the dresser, and again, I feel overwhelmed with love for this new little person in my life.

I slip off my shoes and decide to just sleep in my underwear and hoodie, too exhausted to hunt for some pajamas from my mom. I'm out as soon as my head hits the pillow. I don't dream; it's just pure exhausted sleep from a day of heavy emotional overload and jet lag, so when Killian knocks on the door, telling me to get dressed, I startle awake.

"Coming!" I shout, quickly getting dressed.

I jog down the stairs, and Killian is waiting at the bottom of them, grinning when he sees me.

"You ready?" he asks, and I watch him warily.

"Yeah …" I answer hesitantly.

I follow him out to the car, feeling awkward as hell, and hop in when he unlocks the door. The silence as we head to the hospital is driving me nuts, and I can't hold back anymore.

"Killian, do we need to talk about last night?"

Killian's jaw tics, but he smiles as he stares at the road. It's the fakest shit I've ever seen. "What else is there to say?"

"I don't …" I struggle to put what I'm feeling into words, but it's difficult to speak over the lump in my throat. Therapy might have given me a new dictionary to describe what I'm feeling, but I still haven't overcome the roadblock of communicating my emotions to others.

"We're friends now, right?" Killian says, glancing over at me.

Studying him, I find it's starting to piss me off—how cavalier he's being about all of this when I feel like I ripped my heart out. "Yes."

Crossing my arms, I face the window away from Killian and try not to bite his head off. This is what I wanted; I cannot control how others react. It's unreasonable of me to be upset at Killian's lack of reaction. All of this might be true, but I also can't help that it makes me want to jump out of this car.

"Cool," he says as we pull into the visitors parking lot.

"What do we tell everyone?" I ask quietly, unclicking my seat belt.

Killian finally looks me in the eye, and as much as he wants to seem unfazed, I can still see that fury and pain in his eyes. It's even more disconcerting to see that while he forces another smile on his face.

"Exactly that. We're friends." He gets out of the car and slams the door.

Okay, so this is fucked. I hurry after him and decide not to bring this up again.

Korrie's even cuter in the morning. She's still a sleepy little girl, but it feels good to snuggle up with her. I promise my mom I'll be down to visit as soon as I can, definitely before I leave in less than two months.

The following month or so will be crazy with games, then playoffs. Outside of soccer, I'll be wrapping up the year, and I'll need to start packing. There'll be so much happening, and I can't help but feel when we go to school tomorrow, everything will be on the fast track. Maybe it won't be so terrible, seeing Killian every day and knowing I can't go up to him and touch him, kiss him, hold his hand …

"Are you okay, Glory?" my mom whispers to me as Killian and Sebastian take turns trying to make Korrie laugh.

"Yeah. Why?" I ask, barely succeeding in keeping the emotion out of my voice.

My mom glances over at Killian before looking back at me meaningfully.

I shrug, and this time, I fail. "I broke up with him. We're just friends now."

Mom's face falls, and she grabs my hand. "I'm sorry, honey."

I look up at the ceiling and blink away the tears that want to fall. Feeling eyes on me, I turn to find Killian basically glaring at me, and I spin around to my mom. "It'll be okay. It's for the best."

Mom nods, but it's clear she doesn't believe me.

I can tell she wants to push, but I shake my head. "Let it go. I'm not doing this here."

Mom bites her lip but nods. The look in her eyes tells me we will be revisiting this, but I just can't right now.

"Ready?" Killian calls out, practically one foot out the door already.

Ugh, God, this trip home is going to suck.

I hurry over to Korrie and give her one more kiss before following Killian. I pull my wire earbuds out of my purse before he even starts the car. I don't want to have any conversation, and thankfully, neither does he.

Pulling up my shared playlist with Cassidy, I see she's added a lot of new songs. Most about heartbreak. I hit play on "Heartbreak Anniversary" by

Giveon and curl up in the passenger seat, watching the trees pass as we leave the heavy congestion of Atlanta traffic.

Pulling my phone up, I text Cassidy about what happened. She promises to be at my house with snacks when we get home.

I know she's been expecting this.

In fact, seemingly, the entire school knew this breakup was coming because the weeks following are filled with a mix of *told you so* grins from girls who were praying for my downfall and covert glances from the guys who are wondering if I'm now fair game.

During all this, Killian has been the consummate platonic friend. We are not nearly as close as we were before we dated. In fact, I would say that he and Cassidy are now much closer than he and I are. It bothered me at first, but now, I just don't have the time to care. I also don't have the right.

The new dynamic in our little friend group has put me at odds with everyone, naturally, and I can't find it in myself to hold a grudge over it either. It's been a month of feeling awkward, but I'm so damn busy that I feel exhausted deep down in my bones.

Every night, I collapse into bed, surrounded by folded piles of clothes and little knickknacks I plan to bring with me to college. I'll take most of my clothes with me initially, but Dad is going to mail a box after I leave.

One of the saving graces in all of this is how close Marcus and I have gotten. I'm starting to feel more confident about moving out there, knowing I won't be totally alone. He received his room assignment and will be in the same building complex as me.

His camp doesn't start until a few weeks after me, so I'll be alone initially, but it'll be okay.

I'll be okay, I repeat to myself, like I have been all these years before, as I walk down the halls.

Prom posters plaster the walls, and I feel sick at the sight of them. Killian announced at lunch yesterday that he was taking Chelsea Konig, one of the cheerleaders, as his date.

I had to leave and hide in the restroom. Cassidy followed me, rubbing my back as I cried. At least I experienced that rite of passage. Apparently, Killian had wanted to come after me, but Cassidy had stopped him, and for that, I was glad.

He's moving on, as he should. I guess I underestimated how much that would hurt.

HARD FEELINGS

"Hey, Purcell!" Marcus calls out from behind me as I head toward the girls' locker room for practice.

Spinning on my heel, I greet him with a genuine smile. Something I'm still surprised I'm able to do, considering … well, everything, but I find it's not difficult with Marcus.

"I can't help but notice you're single and it's time for prom." He smiles as he pulls up in front of me, and I roll my eyes.

"God, we did make that pact forever ago, didn't we?"

"Are you saying you don't want to?" Marcus asks, pulling on the straps of his backpack.

"I haven't really been feeling like celebrating lately," I confess, and understanding dawns on his face.

"I heard about Killian and Chelsea." He winces.

I groan in embarrassment. "Is everyone talking about this?"

"Well … kind of."

"Great."

"Come on, Glory. Do not let this place get the best of you again. You've missed out on enough because of these assholes, don't you think?"

I study Marcus, and for what seems like the hundredth time since I've known him, I'm reminded of what a fantastic person he is. Doesn't hurt that he's hot as hell and he can hold his own against Killian's golden-boy reign over Galway High.

"You're right," I admit and decide to just say *fuck it*. Why shouldn't I go to prom? "Okay, I'm in."

Marcus brightens and lets loose that dangerously beautiful smile of his. "Seriously?"

"So seriously. Let's do this. You're right. Fuck this place."

"Hell yes, Glory. There's the killer on the field I know." He grins and pulls me into a hug just as Cassidy opens the door from the inside the locker room, nearly smacking into the both of us in the process.

"Marcus, why are you pawing at my best friend?" Cassidy asks, leaning against the doorway.

"No pawing, just a grateful hug. Glory here just agreed to come to prom with me," Marcus says as he steps back.

Cassidy gives nothing away as she glances between the two of us. "I thought we were going together?" Cassidy settles her hard stare on me.

I open my mouth, but Marcus beats me to it.

"We can all go together. A threesome!" he says, then grimaces when we both level a *are you for real* stare his way. "Sorry! Wrong word choice."

"Marcus has been an excellent friend to me lately; I don't see why he shouldn't come with us," I tell her.

Cassidy holds my stare before nodding. "Fine, but you're getting us both a corsage."

"Deal." Marcus grins before hiking his backpack up higher on his shoulders. "All right, ladies. I have to head to practice. I'll talk to you later."

I watch him leave, waiting for him to disappear before turning back to Cassidy, who's watching with a disapproving glare.

"What?" I ask.

"You know what," she says, following me as I enter the locker room.

"Actually, I don't know what," I tell her, spinning the lock on my locker.

"Killian is going to throw a fit. He's seen how close you and Marcus have gotten," Cassidy says, sitting on the bench in front of my locker as I shrug out of my clothes and into my practice gear.

I roll my eyes. "I don't care what Killian thinks. We're just friends—something he's been sure to remind me of almost daily. Besides, he's going with Chelsea; what does he care?"

"They're friends, and don't act like you don't know that," Cassidy points out, and I lock eyes with her.

"I didn't know," I confess, feeling slightly embarrassed. "It doesn't matter anyway. I'm not using Marcus to make anyone jealous. Before he asked me, I wasn't even going to go."

Cassidy gasps. "Tell me you're joking."

"I'm not." I balance my foot on the edge of the bench, tying my laces instead of meeting her eyes.

"Glory, come on. Why?" Cassidy asks, pulling on my hand when I try to ignore her.

Letting out a long-suffering sigh, I lean against my locker. "I just don't feel like celebrating anything. Killian's acting like everything is fine, and it's killing me, Cassidy. I know I'm the one who broke up with him, but seeing him take it so well ... I know I don't have any right to be upset, but it's like a knife in my heart."

Cassidy gets up and pulls me into a hug. "I think you forget what a great actor Killian is, Glo. Nothing is ever as it seems with him."

"It was with me. He's always been so honest with me about how he feels," I whimper, hugging her tighter.

"Glo," Cassidy sighs and pulls back. "Trust me when I say, he's hurting more than he lets on, okay? But none of this is a reason not to go to prom. It's a rite of passage."

"It's stupid," I protest.

"Okay, Ms. Nonconformist, maybe that's true, but I think you'd regret not going."

"I am going though, so let's move on."

"Fine. Want to go dress shopping after school today?" she asks as we head out to the field.

"I have a meeting with the financial aid officer after school today," I tell her.

HARD FEELINGS

Although my scholarship to UCLA will pay for nearly everything, there are still books. I know for a fact that I will not be able to spend money I don't have on expensive textbooks. The likelihood of balancing the number of hours I need to maintain my scholarship, tutoring to keep my grades up, being a collegiate athlete, and a part-time job will be near impossible.

"Okay, but we have to go this weekend. We don't have much time."

"When is prom anyway?" I ask, tightening my ponytail.

"You kill me, you know that? It's literally next Friday."

"Wait, seriously? Where has the time gone?" I ask, shocked.

"Dude, you've had your head so buried in the sand that this isn't surprising."

"Cass, I'm not keeping my head buried. I've been busy."

"Hmm, sure," she teases, and I shove her.

"Girls! Enough horsing around. Give me six laps around the field." Coach blows her whistle, and we're off.

I take off at a steady jog while Cassidy sprints off. Glad for the minute to myself, I take my lap and try to sink into the present. I've been trying to do this more often, like I'm imprinting time here on my brain.

Like practices with my team before we all scatter across the country with promises we know we likely won't keep, like staying in touch or meeting up over the holidays. Life has a way of separating people despite their best intentions.

Rounding the edge of the field for the third time, I slow for just a second at the sight of Killian sitting in the stands between the fields. Heart twisting, I turn away.

Everything will make sense when I leave, even for him.

TWENTY-SIX

Prom is an interesting concept to me. From what I've seen on television and in movies, it happens to be very different from what is happening at Galway High's senior prom. I seem to have forgotten while seeing all those gorgeous, highly decorated, hugely attended proms that we're in freaking Galway.

Not to say they didn't try to pull out all the stops. If there was ever a motto for this town, it would be, *We do the best with what we have.*

Our gym still looks like our gym, just with worse lighting. A couple of disco balls hang from the rafters, and streamers decorate every doorway. Instead of a DJ or a band, it's Mr. Yates, our music teacher, and his Spotify playlists.

Lucky for us, he has good taste in music.

A long table was placed under one of the basketball hoops and is littered with bowls of Kool-Aid with boys hovering over them, trying to discreetly spike them with bottom-shelf liquor and failing. Krispy Kreme doughnuts, little bags of chips, and cookies are interspersed throughout.

All in all, I'm glad I thrifted my dress. It didn't take much convincing for Cassidy to get on board. I mean, I'm here and in a dress, hair, and makeup, done by her, so I'd better not hear any whining from her while I sit high up on the bleachers and bite into a doughnut.

I stare down at my hundred or so classmates mingling in little clusters, laughing or hugging the walls, staring at everyone else. Marcus left to grab me a drink, sans alcohol, to wash down my second doughnut. Something I know is going to bite me in the ass later. Krispy Kreme doughnuts are legendary, but they are also sugar bombs in the stomach.

It's because I'm in this sugar coma that I don't hear Killian's giant ass clomping up the stairs until he's right beside me.

Glancing up, I swallow hard at the sight of him in a white collared shirt with a few buttons undone, tucked into his black slacks. There's something about that shirt disappearing behind his belt that makes me a little feral. I want to yank it out and lick the taut golden skin I know it's hiding.

His hair is slicked back, so he looks much older than his eighteen years. It's like getting a glimpse into the future. It's his eyes though, shining like gold coins in the soft lights flashing around us, that arrest me completely.

He takes me in; my dress is a simple light-green cocktail dress that hits me slightly above the knee with short lace sleeves and detailing around the bodice. Cassidy complained that it looked like I was going to an Easter service, but I thought it was cute. Simple white heels are on my feet, adding a few inches to my height and imbalance to my gait. I definitely should have practiced walking more in these.

Cassidy did my hair in another braid crown and wove some fake white flowers in it. My makeup is simple, and I feel beautiful in it. Cassidy said I looked like a fairy princess. Killian seems to agree as his gaze, now heated, meets mine.

I swallow my last bit of doughnut and lick my lips, drawing Killian's attention. He reaches out, and I freeze in place as he rubs a thumb along my bottom lip before bringing it to his mouth and sucking the glaze off.

My body heats so fast that I sway a in my seat, and I realize it's been over a month since I've felt his skin on mine. Something that feels criminal. I suck my lip into my mouth to see if I can taste a little bit of him, only to be disappointed when I just taste sugar.

"Dance with me?"

Killian extends his hand, and I hesitate, looking around for Marcus. I spot him dancing with one of the girls on my team before taking Killian's hand in mine.

His closes around mine tightly, as if he expects me to yank mine out and run away. Fair … since I feel immediately like running away the second I feel his hand swallow mine. Not for the reason he thinks though.

Being around him like this is overwhelming, like I've been in the darkness for so long, only to come outside into the light of day at noon.

I follow him down the bleacher stairs, ignoring all the looks shooting our way. Killian leads us toward the doors, and I realize too late that he's taking us out into the hallway, away from the prying eyes at our backs.

Before I can protest, mainly because I don't know if I can trust myself while alone with him, Killian pulls me into his arms as the opening chords of "Only You" by Cannons begin to play. It's such a perfect song for this moment.

HARD FEELINGS

His breath tickles the tiny strands of hair curling around my ear, making me shiver, and I cuddle closer. I rest my head over his heart and listen to the steady thump—a sound I've missed so much these last few weeks.

Killian's jaw rests against my temple as he nuzzles me; it's so tender that I feel my eyes smarting. I inhale deeply, taking in his scent. The sweatshirt I stole from him barely smells like him anymore. I'm ashamed to say that I caught my dad throwing a load of my laundry into the machine and freaked out at him when I saw Killian's sweatshirt in there. Dad watched in shock as I yanked it out and smelled it. I won't lie; I felt a little like Gollum.

It was embarrassing.

Having him so close to me now? I feel heady and overcome, and ... I can't do this. This was a mistake; it's too much to be so close to him like this.

Killian must sense my panic rising because he whispers, "Glory, please."

"Killian ..." I murmur in protest, matching his quiet tone. It feels like if we're too loud, it'll break the moment.

"Come with me. I need you," he says against my skin, rubbing his lips over my temple, and he pulls me in closer so I can feel the outline of his arousal against the thin material of my dress.

The shock of feeling him against me makes my knees buckle. I pull back to answer him, but he swoops in and takes my lips in a kiss so possessive that he brands my very soul.

I've missed this. God, I've missed this so much. One more time. It's okay, just one more time. To say good-bye.

When Killian pulls back, searching my face and seeing the consent, he leads me down the hallway and into an empty classroom.

"God, Glory, you don't know ..." he growls, lifting me into his arms and setting me on the edge of a desk.

"We have to be fast," I whisper, reaching for his belt.

Killian laughs sarcastically. "Not going to be a problem."

I raise a brow. "Not too fast though."

"Don't worry, baby; I always make sure you enjoy yourself."

I hide my face as I unbuckle his belt so he doesn't see what hearing him call me baby does to me.

Killian hisses as I free him and grip him, hot and heavy in my hand. I bite my lip so I don't say something stupid, like, *I missed you*, to his erection. Definitely cringe.

My thoughts are interrupted when he lifts up my dress to settle around my hips and kneels in front of me. Killian groans at the sight of my wet panties, and my face flames at how obvious it is that I want him.

My body is not bothering to play hard to get. She's been pissed since we broke up.

"I've missed you," he whispers, running a finger down the seam of my center, and I let out a laughing groan. "What's so funny?"

"I was thinking the same thing when I saw your dick but thought it was too weird to say out loud."

Killian looks up at me and grins. "Leave it to me."

"Leave it to you," I agree, smiling softly at him.

He reaches for my panties and drags them down my legs before pocketing them, shrugging when I give him a look. I don't want to know what he has planned for those later ... or maybe I do.

Killian grabs a condom out of his wallet and quickly sheathes himself, and I try to shrug off wondering why he still has those at the ready, but he reads my mind.

"Don't even, Glory. I haven't been with anyone since you," he says sharply before tugging me to the desk edge and lining us up.

"There's been no one for me either," I admit too, and a look of deep satisfaction steals over his face. Usually, I'd roll my eyes at his possessiveness, but at this moment, it feels comforting.

Killian groans as the tip of his cock teases my wetness and gives me an apologetic look as he seats himself inside me. "Ah shit."

"Just fuck me, Killian." I flex my muscles around his cock, gripping him tightly and making us both moan.

God, I've missed him. I've missed this fullness.

"Have you thought of me?" he whispers as he pulls out, only to slam back inside, making me slap a hand over my mouth to hold back the squeal.

"I always think of you," I gasp. My head drops back as I go nearly catatonic from how quickly my orgasm builds.

A rush of wetness and the deep pulls of my muscles contracting are the only warnings I have before I go over the edge. My body jerks as it begins, and I fling myself forward, hugging Killian to me and biting down on his pec to try and muffle the scream that's trapped in my throat. I moan wildly against him, my thighs shaking uncontrollably as my nerve endings light up from the delicious friction.

Killian slows his thrusts, letting me recover, only to speed up again when the twitching dies down.

"I've missed this, Glory. Fuck. The feel of you is tattooed on the inside of my brain. I can't even get myself off anymore; it's just not the same. It's never enough. This is what you've stolen from us."

I sob against him, overcome and already feeling another orgasm building. I'm too sensitive; it's been too long. Killian senses I'm close again and reaches between us to pinch my clit before invading my mouth and sending me over the edge again, this time following me.

He growls against my neck, telling me how beautiful I am, how much he loves me, how nothing and no one compares, and how fucking mad he is that I'm doing this to us.

HARD FEELINGS

I just whisper, "I'm sorry," over and over again, falling silent when we both come back down.

Killian leaves me, and the emptiness almost brings me to tears again. I watch him tie off the condom and flinch when I hear voices laughing out in the hallway. I can't believe we did this in school, just feet from prom, where our dates are.

Feeling ashamed, I hop off the desk and fix my dress. "This was a mistake."

Killian lets out a pained laugh, and I wince at the horrible sound.

"You're killing me, Glory," he says gruffly.

I nod. I know I am. I'm killing myself too.

"I'm so—" I begin, but he interrupts.

"Don't," he says sharply.

I cross my arms and turn away from him, unable to meet his eyes. "I need to get back."

"Sure, run off," he scoffs.

Spinning around, I cry out, "I don't know what you want from me here, Killian!"

"I need you to trust me." He slaps a hand against his chest.

"Glory!" Cassidy's voice calls out from the hallway, and I jump, running my fingers under my eyes to wipe away any tears or running mascara.

I glance once more at Killian, but he's turned away from me, arms braced on the desk where I sat only moments before. He looks defeated, and my heart squeezes because I know I did that.

"I am sorry, Killian. I'm doing this because I love you."

I wait for a response, but he gives me nothing. Until, that is, I reach the door handle.

"I know you think that," he says softly but makes no move to stop me from leaving.

The hallway is once again empty, and I blow out a relieved breath and head back to the gym. I spot Cassidy talking to Marcus and make my way over to them.

"*There* you are!" she exclaims as I approach, and her eyebrows shoot up when she sees me. "Excuse me, Marcus. Need to steal our date away for a minute."

"Sharing is caring!" Marcus calls out as Cassidy drags me over to an empty corner.

"And where have you been that your lips look swollen and eyes glassy, hmm?" she hisses, glancing back to the door just as Killian walks back inside, adjusting the cuff of his sleeve.

He glances our way briefly before making a beeline to Chelsea.

"Tell me you didn't!"

"Um …" I blush deeply at her disapproving stare.

221

"Glory Jane."

"I know. Believe me, I know. It was a huge mistake. I can't seem to stop making those lately." I groan and drop my head on her shoulder.

"It seems you've given yourself a hard enough time, so I'll stop."

"Generous of you. I appreciate it. Anyway, what were you hunting me down for?"

"You've danced with everyone but me at this prom, ma'am." She grabs my hand and tows me into the middle of the gym floor.

A slow song is just finishing, and Mr. Yates yells out, asking if we want a fast one or a slow one.

"Fast!" Cassidy and I shout in unison, much to the annoyance of the couples around us, but a cheer goes up as the guitar riff from "Brutal" by Olivia Rodrigo explodes over the room.

Cassidy and I scream along with all the other girls, who ditch their dates, and it turns into an all-girl mosh pit as we all start singing and jumping along with the lyrics.

I feel more connected to these lyrics now than ever before, more connected to everyone around me. It's one of those moments in life that doesn't quite feel real, but you want to stay as present as possible in order to remember it forever.

I'll cherish these three minutes of united female rage.

Cassidy asks if we want to leave on a high note, and I agree.

I don't see much of Killian after that—something that fills me with dread as we get closer and closer to graduation until we only have one week left. The last week of school is a pretty sweet deal for seniors.

We don't have to attend classes anymore; we instead spend the morning practicing the graduation ceremony and meeting with our counselors to get our final grades. We have our senior banquet for the boys' and girls' soccer teams.

It's like a slingshot to the end.

Cassidy has been over at my house every single day, helping me pack up my room and finalize the two suitcases I'm bringing. It seems weird to fit my entire life into two bags, but somehow, I'm able to do it.

Cassidy and Tanner let me tag along as they pick out their dorm decorations since I'm not really doing that. I'm going to pick out my bedding and other essentials when I get there. Cassidy and Tanner's parents are turning the summer into a massive road trip, stopping their way across the

HARD FEELINGS

country to first drop Cassidy at Stanford and then Tanner at the University of Washington.

It still blows my mind that Tanner isn't staying in state. Speaking of which, Killian has kept his mouth sealed shut about where he's going. Tanner doesn't even know, or if he does, he's not saying.

He's been gone a couple of weekends over the last few months on university tours, so I know he's still planning not to go to UGA. I go back and forth daily about whether I screwed up by breaking us up, and now, it just feels like it's too late to fix anything.

"Is your mom coming to graduation?" Cassidy asks, looking up from the Pinterest board she created for me to use as inspiration when my dad and I go pick out my dorm stuff.

I glance up from where I'm combing through Killian's Instagram, looking for any clue as to what he's doing. It genuinely kills me to be so out of the loop of his life, but I deserve it.

"Glory, you have to let it go." Cassidy grabs my phone and tosses it onto the bed.

"I can't help it," I mutter, rubbing my eyes. Sighing, I scoot over to where she's sitting on the floor with my laptop. "And, no, she's not coming. Probably not the best idea, all things considered. Sebastian isn't either. I'm going to head down after graduation and spend the weekend with them before I leave that Monday."

"I can't believe you'll be gone in five days," Cassidy whispers brokenly before resting her head on my shoulder. "Everything is about to change."

"Cass, I promise you, we won't."

"Everyone grows apart. It's so rare to stay friends through college." She sniffles, and I swallow the lump crawling up in my throat.

"It's about effort, Cass, and growing together. We'll be okay." We have to be because I do not think I could handle one more important relationship in my life failing.

She gives a watery laugh before wiping her eyes, embarrassed. "Sorry, it's just starting to hit me."

I grab her pinkie with mine. "I pinkie promise that after the first month of classes, we will set up a FaceTime date every week, and I'll commit to a weekend visit within the first semester."

"And text all the time," she counters, squeezing her pinkie against mine.

"And text all the time," I agree and let her pull me up with her as she stands.

"Okay, I need to head home. My mom's already texted me twice. You think your dad was bad about you leaving? She's freaking the fuck out at both Tanner and me going to school across the country."

"I'm sure." I follow her downstairs, knowing Dad is going to want to eat the second he gets in the door from work.

Dad pulls into the driveway about three minutes after Cassidy leaves. I'm searching the fridge for anything to eat, but we've done an excellent job of cleaning out the fridge before we go.

Since Dad is staying a whole week in LA with me, he doesn't want anything to go bad while he is gone. It's led to some pretty interesting meals.

"There is nothing in there. Please tell me you're hungry," he says, hooking his workbag on the back of one of the counter stools.

"What are you thinking?" I ask, closing the fridge.

"Thai?" he asks hopefully, and I smile.

"Sure. One last time," I say, grabbing my phone off the counter.

Dad's eyes immediately well. "You have to stop."

"Sorry, sorry!" I exclaim, wrapping him in a hug.

I hide my face in his shoulder so he doesn't see the smile. He's being so sweet, but good Lord, he's been crying at the drop of a hat for the last month.

"You keep saying *one last time* like you don't ever plan to come back here." He kisses my head before pulling back.

I shrug, not wanting to voice that I really might not. I can't handle the idea of running into Killian and seeing him with a girlfriend, going about his life without me. I want him to be happy—I really do—but I don't have to witness it.

Dad and I spend the next few days together. He's been glued to my hip, making sure I have everything packed. We have gone through the checklist so many times that I could probably recite it verbatim.

Then, before we know it, it's Friday, and I'm shrugging on my navy-blue graduation gown over the same dress I wore to prom. I stare at myself in my childhood bathroom, feeling overwhelmed.

Dad knocks on the bathroom door before entering. He's already tearing up, but this time, I have no smile to crack at his expense.

"Dad, stop." My voice wobbles as tears well in response to his.

"Do you need help with your cap?" His voice cracks before he clears it.

I nod, handing him the decorated cap. The top has my graduation year, a soccer ball, and Michael Scott's quote in white glitter.

Cassidy and I finished them last night.

Dad helps me pin it to my head before stepping back to take me in as I turn. He snickers at how giant the gown looks on me.

"It's the smallest size they had," I whine but end up laughing along with him.

HARD FEELINGS

"I can't believe it's here. We've been talking about this day forever, it seems. You've handled the last few years with so much maturity and grace. I am in awe of your talent and just so proud to call you my daughter."

"Dad," I exclaim, diving into his arms again. I breathe deeply, taking in the familiar scents of Gain detergent and coffee, of home.

"Okay, okay." He pulls back, wiping under my eyes before doing the same under his. "Get it together, Purcell, or we won't have any tears left for when we actually say good-bye."

I laugh and check to make sure my makeup looks okay in the mirror before following him downstairs.

"Okay, time for pictures." He has me sit out on our front steps, posing this way and that.

Cassidy and Tanner pull in, honking before Dad waves them over and makes us pose for some more photos.

"All right, I'll see you there." Dad waves me off.

"Send some of those to Mom, please?" I call out, climbing into the back of Cassidy's Jeep.

Dad gives me a thumbs-up as we pull out of the driveway.

"How many times did your dad cry today, Glory?" Tanner asks, turning in the passenger seat to grin at me.

I laugh, rolling my eyes. "I can't even be embarrassed. It's so sweet."

"And you've been crying just as much," Cassidy points out.

"Yeah," I sigh and rest my head against the window as we make our final drive to school, only to turn off onto Killian's street. "Wait, we're picking up Killian?"

"Yep," Cassidy says, pointedly ignoring me, and I make evil eyes at her in the rearview mirror.

I sit up and run my hands through my hair. We haven't seen much of each other this last week, and I—

Well, I don't want his last memory of me to be this sad girl.

Cassidy's Jeep rolls up Killian's driveway, and he must have been waiting for us because he's already outside, dressed similarly to Tanner in slacks and a nice shirt. His gown is on but unzipped, so it looks like a cool cape flapping in the wind as he walks toward us. Stubble dusts his sharp jaw, and dark circles mar his otherwise perfect face and ...

"Wipe your drool, Glo," Tanner says under his breath.

I whip around to glare at him before rearranging my face into what I hope looks like nonchalance as Killian climbs into the backseat with me.

Which is problematic, given his size. He can't help taking up so much room, apologizing when his knee knocks into mine. As spread out as he is, he still looks uncomfortable. I scoot over closer to the door to give him more room, but he frowns at me.

225

"You can't even sit next to me now?" he asks quietly, and my mouth drops open.

"I was giving you more room," I whisper back, but he's already turned toward his window.

"Cass, you ready for your speech?" Killian asks.

"Yep. Are you?" she counters, grinning at him.

Tanner turns, making a face at me that has me laughing. Cassidy is valedictorian while Killian is the lowly salutatorian. Something they've battled good-naturedly over all year.

Meanwhile, Tanner and I bonded over attending study halls until the very end, but we both made it. He must be thinking the same thing because he holds his knuckles out for me to knock mine into.

"Normies!" we say in unison before laughing.

"I thought salutatorians didn't give speeches?" I ask Killian, who still refuses to meet my eyes—the chicken. At least I'm trying here.

"Oh, they don't normally, but when you're *the* Killian King," Tanner teases.

"Tanner," Killian groans but laughs.

I lapse into silence as we pull into our high school for the last time together. My nerves make my stomach flutter, and I'm not sure why. Maybe it's because this is officially it.

Cassidy and Tanner hop out of the car the second we park, and I stay back a moment, nervously picking at my cuticles. I keep my eyes focused on my knees even though I'm hyperaware of the fact that Killian has stayed beside me.

The heat of his stare feels like when the sun comes out on a cold day. I feel it everywhere, warming me, only to remind me of how cold it is when I don't have his attention.

He sighs heavily, and I hear his gown shift as he moves to exit the car. I'm overtaken by the need to keep him in the car with me. Just a little longer. Just the two of us here, now, before what comes next.

You'd think I'd be better at being separated from him, but it still grabs me by the throat.

"Killian," I whisper urgently, turning enough to see his knuckles whiten on the door handle as he waits for me to do … something, anything, but whatever I'm going to say is stuck in my throat, driven back by shame and insecurity.

He laughs sadly before shaking his head and opening the door and slamming it behind him. I fold over myself, holding my forehead, and try to prevent myself from hyperventilating.

I suck in breaths too fast. It's all just way too fast. I flinch as my door swings open, and life floods back in.

"Get it together," Cassidy whispers to me, rubbing my back.

HARD FEELINGS

"I'm trying," I whisper back, sucking in a deep breath and wiping underneath my eyes.

Sitting back, I stare at where he sat a moment ago. Where he was with me a moment ago. Closing my eyes, I inhale deeply before exhaling one last time.

So, this is what heartbreak feels like.

"Okay." I unclick my seat belt and shift, avoiding Cassidy's stare as I climb out of her car.

We round her car, and I spot Tanner and Killian in front of us easily as families and seniors swarm the small parking lot. They stand a head above everyone else. Tanner has his arm around Killian's shoulders, saying something to him as Killian keeps his eyes on the ground, nodding along.

His shoulders are drooping, his gait lazy, but I know he's hurting. I just delivered another blow. I have to let him go. When I said all those months ago that we'd never be what we had been, I didn't think it meant this.

Sucking back a sob, I turn into Cassidy's arms, which wrap around me instantly.

"She's fine! Just emotional over graduation," Cassidy lies as someone walking by asks if I'm okay.

Fuck, that's embarrassing. Get it together, Glory!

"Glory, I'm sorry," Cassidy whispers miserably, and I know she understands that I'm finally getting it.

It's finally sinking in. There is no more Gillian.

I dig my nails into my palm, and the pain helps me focus a little. I cannot do this here. This place has had more of my tears than it deserves. I'm going to suck it the fuck up and walk across that stage as a giant *fuck you* to this town that has stolen so much from me, but it's never gotten my dignity.

I step back and nod to Cassidy. She wipes the tears from my face.

"Your eyes are a little red and puffy, but you can just tell everyone it's allergies," she assures me, and I snort.

"Please, the entire town knows what happened between us," I say bitterly.

"Fuck this place, Glory. Seriously. Everything you've wanted is in your grasp. You're getting out, you'll be playing for one of the top schools in the country, and you're in a better spot with your family. It's all happening. Try and focus on the good stuff. I know it's difficult, but you don't want to look back on this day and only remember crying over a boy."

I nod because she's right, but a tiny part of me whispers, *Killian isn't just a boy. He's the boy ... just not for me.*

TWENTY-SEVEN

I wish I could say I walked across that stage, middle finger high, and right out the door, never to think about this place ever again, but that's not how it went down. With our class of one hundred twenty graduating seniors, the actual ceremony was pretty short.

A small cheering section of Dad, Tanner, Cassidy, and my senior girls on the team yelled out as I crossed the stage. I returned the favor, hooting and hollering for my favorite twins when they got their diplomas. I cheered for Killian, too, but you couldn't hear it over the thunderous applause of everyone in the audience.

I love him, but good Lord. How he escaped without a gigantic ego was genuinely miraculous. Cassidy's speech was eyebrow-raising, naturally, as she railed against the lack of funding for STEM and female mentorship at our school, and Killian's was a much shorter show of appreciation to the town that cheered him on at every game and to his mom, who he believed he owed everything to.

He said that last part in such a biting tone that it had most people glancing at her uncomfortably, but Elizabeth was the queen of *you'll never see a tear drop in public, bitches* and sat there with a beautifully frozen smile on her face.

I worried I was part of that tension.

I avoided the after-graduation parties, instead borrowing my dad's car to head down to Atlanta immediately. Something I was internally glad about for once when I saw all the tagged posts Killian was in as he uncharacteristically got hammered.

I deactivated my account.

This last weekend at my mom's has ended up being perfect. I spend as much time with Korrie in my arms, inhaling her baby scent and taking as many mental pictures as I can. She's going to change so much in the time I'm gone, and I find myself, for the first time ever, thinking it would be nice to stay in the state if only to watch her grow up.

It's not until I go to leave and my mom hands me my graduation gift that I break. It's a beautifully framed picture of Killian with his arms around me as I hold little Korrie at the hospital, both of us practically glowing with love for each other and for our new little sister.

It also represents what I've lost, and my fragile little heart smashes because it's not just the past I mourn for; it's the future we could've had. Mom's face drops in shock as I break down in front of her, crying harder than I ever have before in the driveway of her house.

Apparently, I only lose it in public places.

It all tumbles out. Every insecure thought I've had about being worthy enough for Killian in conjunction with the betrayal and anger I've felt toward him, all the rage I've had in general, the abandonment … all of it.

And I'm so angry with myself because I thought I'd come such a long way in therapy. I thought I had moved on from all of this, but when you spend years hearing from everyone how you're not worthy, you start to believe it. I mean, why else would your own mother leave?

It's so difficult to untangle decisions people make from the effects they have on you. It's hard to believe that the decisions they are making now won't hurt you in the long run after they have in the past. It's even harder to believe they have absolutely nothing to do with you.

I don't trust myself anymore. I don't know how to trust others. How do you believe them?

"Oh, Glory." She pulls me into her arms and runs a soothing hand up and down my back until my cries slow and I stare listlessly over her shoulder at nothing, just so completely drained and grateful for the quiet in my brain now after letting it all out.

"I thought I was making the right decision with Killian," I tell her quietly.

Mom pulls back and stares at me, using her thumbs to wipe my tears away. "Glory, has it occurred to you that by breaking up with him to avoid what happened between your father and me that you just set it into motion anyway?"

I pull back, and my mouth drops open, a disbelieving squeak erupting out of me. "But … Elizabeth—"

"Glory, making decisions to please others and making decisions to avoid becoming others is not living *your* life. What do *you* want?"

That simple question haunts me the entire drive home. It haunts me the whole flight across the country, and it haunts me today. It never even occurred to me that I could end up like my mom by breaking up with Killian in order to save us from ruin later. I ruined us now.

My brain feels like it's exploded. Now, it's been months since I broke up with him, and it feels too late.

What have I done?

"Okay, kid, I think you have one more bag down in the car, and then you're unpacked," Dad says, collapsing on the unmade twin.

I set my second giant suitcase, filled with bedding, on it.

"I'll go get it if you want to start unpacking that suitcase," I offer, feeling slightly terrible that I'm making him help me when we're both so exhausted.

"Then food," he groans, leaning back up and running a hand through his hair before slapping his ball cap back over his unruly curls.

I might have gotten my hair color from my mom, but the texture is all Dad's.

"Deal. Jen was telling me about a taco truck down the street we can walk to."

"Tacos!" he shouts, clearly as delirious as I feel.

I head downstairs and grab the bag out of Dad's rental car. Jen, my new roommate, will be home in an hour. She's a local girl—something I'm dreading and also thankful for. She'll have all the recommendations, but she also has an entire friend group here, and I'm already cringing at being the weird, quiet tagalong, but whatever.

I'm determined to not be a loser here.

My phone buzzes in the back of my jean shorts pocket as I grab my little overnight bag out of the car. I close the door as I sling the bag over my shoulder and grab my phone, seeing a text from Cassidy.

What are you doing right now?

Brows furrowed, I text back that I'm finishing unpacking. Two seconds later, she's calling me.

"Hey," I answer.

"I'm honestly shocked that I have to tell you this, but then I remembered you *deactivated your freaking social media!*" Cassidy screeches in my ear, and I wince.

"I'm going to turn it back on. I just ... need a minute. Why? What happened?"

"Killian announced where he's going on his IG, and it's being covered on freaking ESPN, *dude!*"

My heart takes off when I hear his name. Not seeing him before I left for California hurt so bad, but he basically left for Atlanta the day I came back, and I was sure that wasn't a coincidence.

"Where?" I clear my throat when my voice breaks.

"He's coming to Stanford with me. Glory, he's going to freaking Stanford!"

"Please stop yelling."

I feel hot all over; I can feel the heat coming off of me. It's like that hot feeling right before …

"I think I'm going to faint."

"What?" Cassidy yells, and I sit on the ground right by my dad's rental and let my head fall between my legs.

All this, and he's still doing it anyway.

"This isn't happening," I mumble, mind whirling.

"Well," Cassidy drawls, "it is."

"How does he seem? Is he happy?" I chew on my nail.

"Eh, you know Killian. Still waters run deep, but he's not stealing books from my bookshelves, so I think that means he's doing okay."

"Cool," I choke out. "Cool, cool, cool. So happy for him."

"Yeah, you sound it," Cassidy says so dryly that I start snickering.

Then, she starts laughing, and soon, we're both wheeze-laughing.

"How's it going?" Cassidy asks, changing the subject, thankfully, when our laughter dies down.

"I'm almost fully unpacked. Dad and I are getting tacos in a few and then heading to the store to get some things. Jen and I made plans to get breakfast tomorrow."

"Is she already all moved in?"

"Nah. She doesn't have to fully be in yet because she lives here."

Cassidy is silent before asking quietly, "Is it scary?"

I know what she means. Being away from Galway, all new places, all new things. "Dad is still here, so it's not been bad, but I'm anticipating a freak-out when he leaves. I'm sure it wouldn't be so bad if I were starting in the fall with everyone else. I'd be so busy, but I've got two months of just soccer."

"You'll be super bonded with your team though."

"True." My phone buzzes in my hand. I check it to see Dad is wondering where I am. "Hey, listen, Dad is wondering where I went. He leaves in two days. Can we FaceTime then? I have a feeling I'm going to need a friendly face."

"Sure, babe. And listen, don't let this Killian news mess with your head, okay?"

I laugh sarcastically. "I'll try."

HARD FEELINGS

Later that night, my first night in my dorm room, I pull up my Sad Girl playlist on Spotify and finish unpacking. Dad is back at the hotel, making me swear to call him if I freak out, but I refuse to call my dad in the middle of the night to come get me, like I'm a little kid at a sleepover.

Besides, I won't have the luxury after another twenty-four hours.

Now that I'm on my phone, I bite my lip, and cursing my lack of willpower, I pull up Instagram. Two seconds later, I'm on Killian's profile, looking at his announcement post. He's holding up a red Stanford Cardinals jersey, smiling broadly with both his parents by his side.

Elizabeth's smile is so thin that it could cut a bitch. Sebastian looks proud, which is certainly a change of tune from what I heard last. I'm actually shocked they were able to be in the same room together without it getting nasty, but I'm happy for Killian.

I begin scrolling.

Wow, he's been a busy boy since graduation, I think bitterly.

It must be nice to be so beloved and not have a care in the world. I scroll faster, grimacing when I see a photo of him and Britney freaking Watts. Killian is standing by a firepit, chatting with someone, and she's leaning on his shoulder, laughing up at him.

They look cute, like a couple, and I want to reach through the phone and slap them both. Her? Of all people?

I go to send the photo to Cassidy to see if she saw this shit, but instead of hitting the arrow, I accidentally like the picture.

"Nooooo!" I wail, unliking it quickly and throwing my phone across my room.

I slap a palm on my forehead and pace back and forth. *Oh my God. Dummy!*

My phone buzzes with a notification, and I groan, terrified to look at it. Falling onto my bed, I grab it and wince when I see an Instagram DM from Killian. Feeling like I might puke, I open it and curse.

It's not what you think.

I'm sure it's exactly what I think, Killian.

I don't care. I liked it by accident.

Great job, Glory. Admit that you were doom-scrolling his freaking profile and liked a photo from two weeks ago.

Maybe I wanted you to care.

So, you did it to hurt me? Congratulations. You succeeded.

"Summertime Sadness" by Lana Del Rey starts to play, and I close the app, not waiting for him to respond. I think I preferred when we were just straight-up not talking about this.

Suddenly exhausted, I dump my bag onto my bed and grimace. I really need to make it a goal this year to unpack after trips, so I don't lug dirty clothes with me across the freaking country.

Grabbing the hoodie, shirts, and a pair of dirty knee socks that must have been a change of clothes from a sleepover, I toss them into the little hamper I have beside my bed and fold my bag up, pausing when I see a small brown Moleskine notebook fall out.

Killian's journal.

I can't believe I lost this thing again, but it somehow found its way with me. I pick it up and fan the pages under my thumb, contemplating if I even want to go there.

Maybe, someday, I will, but not today—and definitely not after that bullshit. I think I've heard enough from his stupid ass tonight.

I crawl into bed, and it's lights out the second my head hits the pillow.

TWENTY-EIGHT

Two days later, I'm saying good-bye to my dad at the airport, and I don't know who cries more—him or me. It's a quiet, tearful ride back to school in an Uber, and I'm thankful the first day of camp begins the next day. I need the distraction.

And distract it does. In fact, soccer from sunup to sundown with bonding activities scheduled for every minute we're not playing or sleeping does a lot to make the time go by.

Cassidy and I have a standing FaceTime date every Friday, but we text constantly. It's almost like having her with me. We make an effort to fill each other in on everything happening in our lives, all the new characters. She hates her roommate, and every time she talks about Nina, I thank the universe for sending me Jen.

Jenika "Jen" Carey is probably the friendliest, most laid-back, and most levelheaded person I've ever met. She makes me feel so calm and accepted; it's never weird, hanging out with her or her friends. Not like I dreaded. I was so worried it would be, but Jen has this innate ability to put people at ease and make them feel included. She has a standing family dinner every Sunday that I've gone to a couple of times whenever I particularly miss my family or the twins.

It helps to be around them. Plus, they love to feed me, which, being a broke college kid, is music to my stomach.

She's an alternate striker, but we'll see how long that lasts; she's got a deadly aim, and she might be one of the best at getting header goals that I've ever seen. She's another giant, to me, at five foot eight, and her vertical jump is crazy.

So, yeah, compared to Nightmare Nina, I really lucked out.

Jenika is studying for a test, so I head to one of the quiet study areas on our floor with my laptop for my call with Cassidy. The ringing of a video call chimes through my computer speakers just as I enter the room, and I answer as I settle into place.

Cassidy pops up on my screen, smiling, and I'm immediately grinning back. Cassidy is sitting on her bed, back against the wall she decorated with Polaroids of all our friends from home, plus a few new ones. It takes everything in me not to stare at the one of her and Killian. She's in a Stanford hoodie, and he's decked out in his football gear.

Cassidy hasn't made their friendship a secret, and I would never demand she not be friends with him. They've known each other outside of Killian and me being together since they were babies. Friends before I ever moved to Galway.

But I can't lie that it hurts still.

Cassidy sees where my attention has strayed, and her smile drops.

"You know he's still beating himself up about posting that photo," she says quietly, and I huff. "He's been up here once a week, pillaging my bookshelf."

"Give him some Colleen Hoover books. That'll teach him," I say bitterly.

Cassidy laughs. "You just want that man to cry."

I shrug and try to hold on to my anger but end up laughing. Revenge à la emotional torment from Colleen Hoover might be a bit too far, even for me. At least I didn't say Nicholas Sparks.

"Still odd how much he loves romance novels," I mutter, picking at my cuticle.

"Nah, I think he reads them because he misses you and misses being with you."

"Cass, come on," I groan.

"He's so happy here; I don't know what you're still waiting for. Make amends!"

I struggle to put it into words, but shame is an insidious emotion. It sinks its teeth into you, spreading its poison before you ever know you got bit. Soon, it infects every decision you make and every thought you have about yourself. It makes you ask yourself if you deserve someone instead of wondering if they deserve you.

"I feel like I've gone too far. The entire time we were together, I kept telling him to trust me, and I couldn't even do the same. I'm a hypocrite." I wipe my eyes, furious with myself.

"All I'm going to say is that you were able to forgive him for all the shit he had pulled. I'm sure he can get over you breaking up with him."

Cassidy glances over her laptop as her door opens, and her eyes widen in panic.

"What are you working on?" Killian's voice fills the silence, and I jerk, as if electrocuted. It's been so long since I heard his voice.

"I'm—" Cassidy's voice gets impossibly high as she glances at me on her screen before looking back at him.

"Ah," he says as if realizing what, or rather who, has Cassidy's attention. "I just wanted to return this one."

Cassidy leans up and grabs a book from him, flashing me the title of a very famous second-chance romance, and I simultaneously want to cry and roll my eyes.

"I'll get out of your hair." His voice gets quieter as I imagine him heading toward Cassidy's door, and before leaving, he murmurs, "I miss you."

Cassidy looks at me with a brow raised, and I smack my forehead lightly with my computer.

"I have his journal still," I confess, and Cassidy groans with evident annoyance.

"Glory, are you just torturing yourself? Like, I don't get it."

"I haven't read it in forever. It's sitting in my desk drawer. I just ... I don't know. It's like I'm scared to read it and have my fears confirmed, and I'm also afraid because it could confirm what a colossal screwup I am."

"First of all, don't talk about yourself like that. Why is everyone else allowed to make a mistake, except you? Why are you able to forgive everyone but yourself?"

"I'm working on it."

"I hope so! Go read the journal, Glory Jane," Cassidy orders in a mock stern voice, and I pretend to salute.

"I will," I promise and change the subject.

Later that night, I'm back in my room and putting away the laundry I just brought back when there's a knock on my door. Jen curiously looks up from the book she's reading as I open the door.

Marcus fills the doorway, his grin huge when he sees Jen behind me. I didn't think he'd ever get over Cassidy; he'd been over the moon for her for as long as I could remember, but a lot has changed since we left Galway.

Marcus and I have become even closer. It's difficult to make friends outside of student athletes. People just don't understand the workload and the focus. It's rare we get to socialize in general, and even when we do, it is usually not partying with the freedom other students have.

His crush on Jen was almost immediate, and, hey, I totally understand it. She's the freaking best, but I try not to take it too hard when he comes over to hang just so he can see her.

"Well, well, if it isn't Marcus Tyler darkening our door," Jenika says from behind me, and I snicker as I step back to let him into our tiny room.

"Please tell me you two aren't staying inside during our bye week," he says, turning my desk chair around to straddle it.

"What are you doing?" I ask, returning to folding my clothes.

"Not chores," he teases. "Party at the basketball house."

I look at Jen, and she shrugs. Marcus looks at me hopefully, tucking his hands under his chin, and I laugh.

"Okay, fine. My shift at the coffee shop starts at nine tomorrow, so I'm not staying late."

"We'll get you home by one, Cinderella," Marcus promises before standing up. "I'll be downstairs in the rec room."

Jen jumps into gear the second the door closes behind him, yanking her closet door open and throwing all her clothes on her bed.

Raising a brow at her, I ask, "Tonight's the night, huh?"

Lucky for Marcus, the crush goes both ways, but she's been working her courage up to ask him out. Not sure why she has been nervous because he's so obviously head over heels for her.

"It's happening. I can't watch those dimples and that smile flash my way one more time without kissing it off his face," she declares, grabbing a red minidress and smiling deviously at me.

"He doesn't stand a chance." I laugh, recognizing the dress as the one she calls the man-eater.

"Don't just stand there. Get dressed!" she says, whipping off her oversize SpongeBob shirt.

Sighing, I grab my black romper that ties at the waist and has cute little cutouts on both sides and my red Chucks. Once I've wrangled my hair into a single braid, I check my mirror to see if the makeup I still had on from my shift earlier this afternoon is okay and nod.

Jen is running some oil through the ends of her hair when I turn around. I let out a wolf whistle when she slips on her heels. Her lips are as red as her dress, and she looks stunning.

"Marcus is going to lose his shit when he sees you," I tell her, grabbing my crossbody purse to toss my phone, keys, and wallet in.

"Ready?" she asks, holding the door open.

"Yep!"

Marcus grabs his heart and pretends to stagger when he sees us coming downstairs, eliciting a giggle out of me and a pretty blush out of Jen. We take electric scooters to the edge of campus and call an Uber. The basketball house is about a couple of miles off campus.

238

HARD FEELINGS

When we arrive, people are milling in and out of the house. Marcus grabs Jen's hand, and she holds mine as he leads us toward the kitchen to grab drinks. I wave at some of my teammates who are dancing on the makeshift dance floor in the living room.

Marcus points to some beers as Jen grabs my hand and pulls me onto the dance floor. She snaps a picture of us dancing, and I roll my eyes as she immediately stops to post it online. She insists on tagging me even though she knows I don't check. I haven't been back on my social media since that stupid picture.

We dance for a couple of songs before joining Marcus at the ping-pong table, where everyone is playing flip cup. Jen points to the line for the bathroom and rolls her eyes before joining.

Marcus sidles up to me and leans his shoulder against mine. "What's up, Purcell?"

"Your chances, apparently, Tyler."

He turns, grabbing my shoulders in excitement. "What did she say?"

"Well, she didn't break that dress out for funsies."

"Awesome," he whispers, and I snicker as he settles back against me.

I'm quiet as I watch the chaos around me, so when the next song comes on, it takes a moment before I react. "Only You" by Cannons plays loud enough to be heard over the din, enough for me to hear. It's the last song Killian and I danced to at prom.

I turn and rest my forehead on Marcus's shoulder as emotion overtakes me.

"Glory ..." Marcus settles his hand on my head.

"It's our song," I whisper brokenly, and he pulls me into a hug.

"Hey, Glory, what happened?" Jen asks worriedly as she comes up behind me.

"Can we go?" I ask, wiping my face, embarrassed.

"Yeah." She nods, still studying me.

I take off, suddenly needing to be out of this house and away from that song more than anything. I hear Marcus whispering to Jen about Killian as I order the Uber. I vow to myself to read Killian's journal tomorrow.

Nothing could hurt worse than this.

Jen is still gone when I get back from work the following afternoon.

After dropping me off at the door, Marcus and she disappeared. I was both happy for them and grateful to have no witnesses as I cried myself to sleep last night, playing that song over and over.

It was pathetic.

I toss my backpack on the end of my bed as I toe off my sneakers and collapse into bed. The need for a nap is strong, but keeping the promise I made to myself last night is stronger.

I lean over, and my hand hovers at the handle of my nightstand drawer, hesitating for only a second before grabbing it. Stacking my pillows behind me, I open where I left off, surprised to see it's the last entry and only a few weeks before he and I reconciled.

> *Glory,*
>
> *Today was the first day you spoke to me in years. I'm not sure if you know that or not, but I do. I had that fucking little punk up against the wall for what he said about you, but now that my anger has gone, the only thing that lingers is that question you asked me. Is this who I am now?*
>
> *It ricocheted around my head, forcing me to take stock, and I hate the answer. I don't know who I am anymore. Maybe I never did. Every single thing I've ever done has been for my family, for my friends, for everyone else but myself. The only thing I've ever claimed for myself was you, and I tossed that away for the sake of others.*
>
> *I'm tired of carrying everyone else's wishes on my shoulders. I want to forge my own path, and I want you on that journey with me. I don't know if you'll ever take me back as a friend or as someone you just don't hate anymore, but I fear your apathy more than your hatred.*
>
> *What I do know is that I don't deserve you. I threw away what we had because of fear, obligation, stupidity, and shame.*
>
> *"You're just like your father," used to be such a compliment, growing up.*
>
> *Now, it's a vise around my neck, tightening until I can't breathe, until I am only a shadow of someone else. I know my mom doesn't mean it. Fuck, she's never even said it, but I see it every time she looks at me, and I just can't hurt her anymore.*
>
> *And so I hurt you, and I hurt myself.*
>
> *So, you were right to ask that question, Glory. I'm not myself. I haven't been for a while. If I ever was myself, it was only with you. You accepted every part of me with no expectations, except that I did the same for you.*

HARD FEELINGS

I'm going to take a chance on myself. I'm going to take a chance on you. You might never forgive me, but at least I'll be able to say I tried.

If nothing else, you'll know I love you and myself enough to do that.

Yours,

Killian

My hand shakes so hard as I reread his last entry again and again. God, I recognize so much of what he's going through. On the page, he articulates exactly what I feel so well that I want to call him and scream, *Exactly!*

I fan the pages, considering what I should do, when my eyes land on the pen next to my Chemistry notebook. I owe him at least this—my own words.

I move to sit at my desk and cue up the Killian playlist I created. My pen hovers over the paper; I'm not sure how to get the swarm of emotions out on paper, and then I realize I should just start.

Just begin, Glory.

I find writing to Killian is easier than talking to Killian. Everything I'm feeling just pours out of me in a way that I wonder why I haven't been journaling forever.

I write and write and write. The playlist has played four times all the way through, and the sun begins to set, washing my dorm in the warm glow of dusk.

Jen comes in, asking if I want to go grab dinner with her, and I shake my head. I wave her off when she promises to bring me back a burrito, and I know I'll make up for my rudeness later, but right now, I have to exorcise this shit from my brain before it corrupts me any further.

When I finally finish, my hand cramps painfully, and I've filled every page, front and back, of Killian's journal. I sit back and rub a trembling hand over my face, simultaneously exhausted and so much lighter that I feel like I could float.

With the plan forming in my head, I call Cassidy.

"Hey, Glo! I was just thinking of you," she answers cheerily.

"Cass, I need you to do me a favor," I begin and tell her my plan.

After we hang up, I head over to the bookstore to mail the journal to Cassidy's dorm. She's going to get it into Killian's hands for me.

Later, I hop on the computer and book my train ticket to Stanford. Our football team is playing Stanford next weekend, and I originally was not inclined to go. I thought it would be too painful, but not anymore.

Strange adrenaline courses through my veins because I know I'm going to see him soon and I wonder what he's going to think about everything I wrote. I bared my soul on those pages, but there's no one I trust more to read it than him.

Whatever happens, at least I tried. Just like he had. We are worth a shot, and I can only apologize to him a thousand times for not believing that sooner.

I still have a long way to go in terms of shaking off my past, but the first step to trusting someone is deciding to.

Twenty-Nine

The following week, I avoided my phone like the plague, instead throwing myself into soccer and midterms. By the time Friday morning rolls around, I'm thankful for the long train ride up to see Cassidy. I sleep most of the way when I'm not chewing my nails and worrying about the rest.

Cassidy assured me that Killian has been a freaking monk since we broke up. She told me that he got so drunk with her one night, confessing that some girl had tried to kiss him at a party and he freaked out. Since then, he hasn't even allowed another girl, except Cassidy, to touch him.

It shouldn't make me so happy to hear these things; he's totally free to do whatever he wants. We aren't together, and I have no right to feel any type of way, but I do. I was so fucking relieved when she told me this on the phone last week that my knees gave out.

When the train arrives, I grab my backpack and step off onto the arrival platform, shivering at the temperature change. Sometimes, I forget how huge California is.

"Glory Jane mothereffing Purcell!" Cassidy screams, and I spin around, catching sight of her waving at me through the throng of weary travelers.

Uncaring of the stares we get, I run to my best friend, laughing, overcome with love for her. I crash into her, knocking her back a step, and hug the living shit out of her.

She squeezes me back just as hard, and I feel the wetness from her tears on my shoulder.

"Stop. You'll make me cry." I laugh, but I'm already blinking away tears.

Before college, the longest we spent apart was a week at the most. I haven't seen her since June, and it's October. I step back and take her in, looking for anything that's changed, signs that she's no longer my Cassidy, but her familiar, beautiful, freckled face is smiling that mischievous smile at me.

"Oh my God, Glory, I've missed you so much. I didn't realize how much until I saw you." She sighs, hooking her arm through mine as we make our way to the exit.

"Same freaking page." I lean my head against her.

"Well, I hope you're fine with staying in tonight."

My shoulders relax in relief; the last thing I wanted to do after an entire day on the train was go out.

"What do you have in mind?"

"You're here for such a short amount of time; I can't find it in myself to be charitable enough to share you with my friends. Besides, Nightmare Nina is out of town. So, I thought we would have a classic night. *Gilmore Girls* and junk food?"

"Hell yes!" I agree because nothing sounds better, and since I can't wait a moment longer, I ask, "Did you give it to him?"

She nods. "He came by last night. I handed him the journal instead of a new book. You could've blown the boy over with a feather from the shock he was in."

"How did he seem? Happy? Mad?" I ask, chewing on my lip.

"I barely handed it to him before he grabbed it and basically ran out of my room. Left the door open and everything. It was like a cartoon. I was surprised he'd stopped to open the door. I'd fully expected to see a Killian-shaped hole because he left so fast."

Some of the tension eases from my shoulders, and I nod.

Okay. Okay, so this is real now. It's happening. Holy shit.

"Uh-uh, don't get lost in that head of yours, Glory." Cassidy bumps her hip into mine. "I'm going to keep you so distracted tonight that you'll drift right off into blissful sleep."

Cassidy keeps half of her promise. She is a fantastic distraction until she falls asleep, and suddenly, it's just my anxiety and me. I crawl carefully out of her bed and sit down on the floor in front of her tiny little bookcase; my finger trails along the well-worn spines as I imagine both Cassidy and Killian reading them.

Him loving romance novels might be my favorite fact about Killian. He's such a romantic. If he didn't love football so much, I think he'd make a fantastic author. Or maybe I'm just stupid in love with him that I think he shits gold.

Probably a bit of both.

I try to imagine Killian reading these and thinking of me. Since we've been apart, I've done everything I can to avoid him. I grab one at random and lie down on my stomach and begin to read.

HARD FEELINGS

At some point, I do fall asleep because when Cassidy wakes me up, I suck in a startled breath so fast that I start coughing. I groan when I realize I'm in the same position I was in last night, except instead of reading the book, I'm using it as a pillow.

"Do my eyes deceive me? Is Glory voluntarily reading a book? Am I still dreaming?" she teases.

"Ha-ha." I sit up, wincing at how stiff my muscles feel.

Cassidy gives me a hand, pulling me to my feet. I groan at how perky she already is. Cassidy is one of those people who wakes up super alert and ready to go. I swear she's like a reverse vampire. The moment the sun rises, her eyes pop open, all creepily.

She leans down and grabs the book, reading the title. "Ooh, this is a good one."

I grab a half-empty water bottle off her bedside table and grunt.

Cassidy laughs. "I've missed barely coherent Glory. Okay, here's the plan. We'll get some food and coffee for you. Then, I want to show you around. We're meeting the girls from my intramural team to tailgate for lunch, and then the game is at two."

Cassidy and I take scooters to a small café off campus, where everyone behind the counter calls out to her when we go in. I chuckle, happy to see that college hasn't changed my gregarious friend.

We take our coffees and croissant sandwiches to go, and Cassidy begins my tour of the campus. I don't know what I was expecting Stanford to look like, probably something closer to the campuses you see in the northeast. Stanford is something else. It's a beautiful mix of mission and Romanesque architectural styles, and I basically walk around, mouth agape at how beautiful everything is.

For probably the thousandth time since graduation, I have to pinch myself that we're here and this is real. Cassidy and I have been laser-focused on our goals since we were kids, and here we are.

She points out the athletic fields, and I study her carefully when she shows me the soccer fields. Cassidy ended up deciding not to go to tryouts—something that floored me when she told me—but she's determined to double major, the absolute genius that she is, in electrical and computer engineering.

Women in STEM!

Instead, she's opted to play intramural soccer, which provides her the opportunity to still play the game she loves but doesn't take up her entire schedule. I'm excited to meet her friends from her team.

After the tour, which leaves me dutifully impressed, we head back to her dorm to get changed. Since I'm sitting with Stanford, I left the UCLA-branded clothes at home, going instead for a simple straight-leg '90s jeans and a cropped T-shirt with a cute quilted jacket. It's a yellowish khaki, so paired with my jeans, it's UCLA colors but just subtle enough not to get me booed out of the stadium.

Cassidy, on the other hand, is school spirit from top to bottom—in her tight, long-sleeved white shirt with a jersey overtop, black wool leggings, and boots. Her long red hair is pulled into a high ponytail.

I laugh when she tries to take a selfie of the two of us. The angle she needs to get us both in the frame is hilarious until she squats down. True friendship right there.

My nerves start to spike as we head over to the stadium. It feels like there's a swarm of butterflies taking off in my stomach, and I rest my hand against it. Cassidy notices and grabs my hand instead.

"It's going to be fine," she promises.

"He knows I'm coming?"

"I told him when I handed him the journal," she swears.

"It's just weird, like, not a single text or anything," I muse.

"Apparently, their coach is a freak about phones being a distraction before games. It's a total blackout day before and the day of, but he knows."

"Hmm." I let it go as Cassidy yells out to someone named Sarah, and soon, I'm wrapped up in girls, soccer talk, and food.

My anxiety kills my appetite entirely, so I decide to munch on a couple of chips, forgoing the hot dogs and hamburgers everyone else scores from a nearby grill, manned by naked dudes painted in red.

Cassidy sucks down a hot dog in a way that has some of the guys raising their eyebrows, impressed, before tugging me toward the doors when we hear the band start playing. I was surprised she ate a hot dog to begin with, considering what had happened last time at The Varsity in Atlanta, but crazier things have happened. I turn, waving good-bye to her friends, and allow her to lead me through the throng of people.

"We're not sitting with your friends?" I call out over all the noise.

"Couldn't get tickets together," she explains before turning to me. "Sorry, my short friend, we're going to need to climb."

She isn't kidding.

We are at the very, very top. I can't really see much detail, but it does offer a fantastic view of the field and the stands. Outside of the Atlanta United game, I've never been in a filled stadium like this.

The roar of the crowd settles into my bones, and I wonder how the hell Killian is able to play with this many people watching. As much as I'd like to say my games pull crowds like this, it's just not true. Unfortunately, women's sports, especially collegiate sports, just don't bring in the fans quite like a football game.

Do I think it's sexist bullshit? Yep.

"This is insane," I yell to Cassidy, who, thankfully, isn't as wild as the people around us.

HARD FEELINGS

They begin announcing Stanford's team, and I jolt when I hear Killian's name echoing around the stadium, people cheering for him. His photo pops up on the jumbo screen, and I settle my hand over my pounding heart at seeing his face.

He looks like my Killian, except I can see the change our months apart have done to him. His facial hair has grown a lot, hiding the jawline I used to kiss. He just looks ... so different. I can't really place it.

"He's so in his element here, Glory. I wish you could see it more," Cassidy shouts.

I think that must be it. He looks settled, more mature, grown ... not stifled in Galway anymore.

I glance at her to agree and notice a sheen of sweat across her forehead. "Are you too warm?"

Cassidy nods absently and tugs the sleeves of her shirt up her arms. I want to press her because she honestly looks a little green, too, but I hear the whistle blow and focus on the game.

UCLA and Stanford seem to be evenly matched—not that I understand a thing about football, but it's an all-out brawl on the field with neither team succeeding in scoring the entire first half.

I glance at Cassidy again, and her lips have lost nearly all color. "Cassidy, are you feeling okay?"

"Can you get me a water, please?" she whispers, sitting down and handing me a five-dollar bill.

Worried, I hurry, only to curse when I see the long-ass line. It's about ten minutes before I'm able to return to my seat. Cassidy has her head between her legs when I get back, and now, I'm officially concerned.

"Here, take a sip."

I unscrew the top and hold it to her lips. She takes a sip and gags, and my alarm shoots through the roof.

"I'm going to be sick," she announces, jumping up and climbing over me before I'm able to stand.

I grab our stuff and run behind her into the girls' restroom. Luckily, it's relatively empty since the second half has already started. Cassidy smashes into the nearest stall and immediately starts throwing up.

Wincing in sympathy, I wet some paper towels and rest them on her forehead as I hold back the long tail of her ponytail. Finally, when she finishes, she rests her head on her forearm and curses.

"Fucking hot dogs," she groans.

I'm already calling for the Uber. "Cassidy, can you stand? I'll help you, but we need to get out of here. You're too sick."

"I'm sorry, Glory. I'm ruining everything," she cries, and my heart squeezes.

"Stop it. You are not," I argue, helping her stand.

"I am!"

"Cassidy, all I need you to think about right now is not passing out or puking on me for the next ten minutes. That's all we need to worry about, okay?" I yank her up beside me, and I lead us out of the bathroom.

"Are you mad at me?" she asks so pitifully that I turn my head to hide my laugh as we head toward the escalator.

Cassidy is the strongest person I know, but the second she feels ill, she's like this.

"Never, babe. You're my number one," I assure her, standing in front of her on the escalator in case she starts to go down.

We get outside, and I sit her on the curb and check my phone. The car will be here in five minutes. Glancing at Cassidy, who is weaving in place, I pray that I can get her home in time before this really kicks into high gear.

The rest of the night is horrible. Food poisoning wreaks havoc on Cassidy's body, and I don't end up falling asleep until four in the morning. My train leaves at seven, so I have no choice but to leave before connecting with Killian.

My phone is quiet the entire night—something I try my best not to read too much into, but I can't help it.

Cassidy doesn't move when I give her a kiss on the forehead good-bye, and I head to the train station. Fortunately, I'm so beyond exhausted that I sleep most of the way home.

When I come into our room, Marcus and Jenika are chilling, backs against the wall, watching a movie on Jen's laptop.

Marcus whistles sympathetically when he sees me. "Damn, Glory, how hard did you party last night?"

"Ha," I say weakly before collapsing face-first on my bed. "Cassidy got food poisoning. We left the game during the second half; I don't even know who won."

"UCLA!" Jen and Marcus crow in unison.

I simultaneously feel some school pride and disappointment for Killian.

After losses at our high school, our football team would immediately go into tape analysis and basically get read the riot act. I can only imagine how it is at the college level.

Or at least I tell myself this in an effort to explain why he still hasn't talked to me.

HARD FEELINGS

I inhale deeply, smelling my clean sheets, and I wince at how disgusting I am, lying on top of them. I love Cassidy to death, but I swear I can still smell vomit on me.

"I'm going to shower. I hate to ask, but do y'all mind moving this somewhere else? I have got to get some sleep before practice tomorrow morning." I push myself up and grab my shower caddy and robe.

"I need to leave anyway," Marcus confesses, giving Jen a kiss on the cheek.

She glares at me when I make eyes at her. I'm genuinely happy for both of them, but I'm also glad I won't have to deal with cutesy couple things tonight.

When I get back from the shower, Jen is reading with the lights low. I change quickly into my pajamas and crash into bed. My head pounds from a mixture of exhaustion and emotional overload.

I turn toward my wall and close my eyes, breathing deeply and doing some mental gymnastics in an effort to distract my brain. All I want to do is text Killian, but the ball is in his court now.

"How'd it go?" Jen asks quietly when I don't speak for a while.

I shake my head, refusing to turn over because just the question alone has tears springing to my eyes.

Jen curses under her breath. "I'm so sorry, Glory."

I wipe my eyes and blow out a shaky breath. "It is what it is."

"He doesn't deserve you," she defends fiercely, and while I appreciate that, it's just not true.

"Yes, he does," I whisper, and that's what hurts the most right now. He always has, and I fucked things up.

My sleep is dreamless, and for that, I'm thankful. I wake up numb and do my best to hold on to this numbness for the rest of the week. Still nothing from Killian. With every day that passes, that numbness fades, and devastation starts to seep in. I know Jen is worried; she's been carefully watching me.

Anytime I'm not at practice or class, I'm sleeping. I refuse every invitation to go out. I just can't bring myself to put on a smile; it feels foreign on my face. Cassidy has no idea what's going on. She said Killian is dodging her, and whenever she tracks him down, he looks anxious and uncomfortable.

I'd trade anxiety and uncomfortable for this.

In some ways, I'm almost grateful to feel this because at least I know I'm processing in some way, and hopefully, I'll be able to move on. Maybe if I'm able to fully grieve, I won't be thinking about him and what could have been for the rest of my life.

Friday rolls in, and all thoughts of Killian move out of focus because it's game day. Thankfully, the moment I step on the field, the only thing that occupies my mind is my team and winning the fucking game.

The sun sets earlier now as we move further into autumn, but the field is lit up, and there's just something about playing at night. I step onto our field with the rest of my team and wave at the crowd cheering us on. We pull a much smaller crowd than our football team, but the fans are just as loyal, and it never fails to amaze me to see people wearing my jersey number and cheering for me.

It's our last home game of this season, and we're playing University of Southern California, one of our biggest rivals. I haven't started every game, which is fine. I'm a freshman. I don't expect to step out for every game, but Coach has me starting this one, and I can't help but be filled with pride.

Especially knowing my parents will be watching even if it's on TV on the other side of the country. We stretch quickly, and I check my phone one last time, hearting the *good luck* messages from my parents and Cassidy before shoving it down in my bag before Coach sees.

Killian's coach isn't the only one with a no-phone rule on the field.

The game is brutal and low scoring, which is hard enough when you're playing regular time for ninety minutes. Not getting any relief from goals or some sort of satisfaction from the effort you're putting out can take its toll on morale. We rally as hard as we can, but by halftime, we're tied one to one.

We come back energized and ready to end this. The idea that women's soccer isn't as physical as men's is dumb and highlighted by the fact that I smack into the ground hard from a slide tackle. Spitting out dirt, I get to my feet, annoyed at the shitty tackle, and do an internal check that I'm okay.

Giving a thumbs-up, I decide to let the bitch inside loose. Turns out, taking your anger and frustration out on the field is hugely cathartic, so when the final whistle sounds, I'm ready to collapse. We barely edge out a win at two to one, but if the limp handshakes are any indication, neither team cares. We're just happy it's over.

I shower quickly, changing into a hoodie and leggings before blowing off the rest of the team to head back out onto the field. I haven't lain in the middle of the field with my music in ages, and it seems like the perfect idea right now. Mainly since I'll be alone, away from the concerned looks of my friends.

Popping on my headphones, I respond to the texts from my family and Cassidy. I save a photo my mom sent me of Korrie in a little UCLA jersey. I miss my little sister and FaceTime my mom almost as often as Cassidy. It makes me sad that I'm missing so much, but I'll be home for the holidays soon enough.

Most of the lights have turned off, leaving a low amber glow on the field and the stands dark. I drop my bag down and lie full out on my back, pulling

HARD FEELINGS

up my Killian playlist. Hitting play on the song "Coming Back" by James Blake and SZA, I let the lyrics take me away.

I'm not sure how long I stay there before I begin to feel like I'm not alone. Awareness crawls over my skin, leaving goose bumps in its wake and energy coursing through my veins. My body recognizes this change even if it hasn't felt it in months.

I let out a sob and keep my eyes closed, too afraid to open my eyes in case I've truly lost my mind and this is some musically induced hallucination. It's only when I feel lips kiss my temple do I open my eyes and find Killian lying on his back beside me, staring at me. His eyes are bloodshot with circles underneath, hinting that his nights have been as rough as mine. He's trimmed his beard, and I reach a hand out, petting the soft hair along his jaw.

Killian's eyes close at the touch, as if he's savoring it, and my heart squeezes at the naked longing on his face.

"Are you real?" My voice shakes, and I take my headphones off, starved for the sound of his voice.

Killian's eyes open, this time with a wet sheen, and mine burn at the sight. He nods, clearing his throat a few times before finally speaking.

"I've missed you. So much." His voice is gravelly, but it's him. He's speaking to me, and for that, I'll forever be grateful.

"How are you here?" I ask disbelievingly.

"I flew here after my last class," he admits, reaching out to twirl a piece of my hair around his fingers.

"Did you read your journal?" I ask nervously.

He nods. "Our journal now. I came here as soon as I finished."

I sit up. "You just read it?!"

Killian sits up too, turning so his legs encase me on either side, as if he's afraid I'll take off.

"Now, you know how it feels." His lips twitch.

I narrow my eyes. "So, you did it for revenge?"

Killian sighs and grabs me under my arms like a child, cradling me against him. He inhales deeply and exhales loudly as the tension leaves his body. Mine melts into him effortlessly, and I rest my head on his chest under his chin.

"I didn't do it on purpose. I was terrified you were writing to say goodbye. I'd been waiting for you to come to your senses, and when you didn't, I held hope you still cared because you hung on to my most intimate confessions. When you sent it back ..."

"But I came to visit you," I argue.

"You came to Stanford. I'm not the only reason you did that."

It's my turn to sigh. "I should've just called you. I shouldn't have let Cass be the go-between. I was just—"

"Scared?" Killian finishes.

"Yeah." Urgency takes over me; I don't want to waste any more time. "I'm so sorry, Killian. Our breakup had nothing to do with you. It was all me. I was too afraid to go after what I wanted, too afraid of turning into our parents. I let everyone else in my head; it drowned out my own voice."

Killian hugs me tighter to him. "I understand."

Turning in his arms, I hug him fully. "I know you do. I just wish I had talked to you more. Can you forgive me?" I ask, tilting my head back.

Killian leans down, pressing kisses to my forehead, cheeks, and chin before finally capturing my mouth. I sob into the kiss, dumping months of sadness, confusion, and longing into it.

Killian breaks the kiss, nuzzling me. "I think you'll find there's very little I wouldn't do for you. I love you beyond measure, Glory. The hell I've been through these last few months has shown me just how much. I don't want to take another step forward without you by my side. You're my beginning and end."

"I love you so much, Killian," I say simply, and he laughs happily and maybe a bit teasingly as well. I smack his shoulder, laughing. "I'm not as good with words as you are."

"You did just fine. I don't need fancy words, baby. I just need you to love me the best way you know how."

"That I can do," I promise, but I find I need to ask something plainly. "We're back together, right?"

"Yes, baby, you're stuck with me."

We head back to my dorm together; I'm glued to his side, and I wouldn't have it any other way. Jen and Marcus are both there when we arrive, much to their surprise. Marcus jumps up, happy to see another face from home, and I watch them greet each other before Killian introduces himself to Jen.

Watching him interact with my friends, in my dorm, and in my *life* fills me with pure joy. Everything is how it should be. I'm sure this won't be the last time we hit a roadblock—we're still kids—but I know I can say anything to him. Any horrible thought I have of myself, any concerns about our relationship, my hopes and dreams, and I know he's got my back. Not only does he have my back, but he will also do whatever he can to make sure I succeed, that we succeed.

As if sensing I've gone inside my own head again, Killian looks at me, quirking a brow in question when he finds me lurking near the door still. I smile back, letting him know I'm fine, and he unleashes his full Killian smile, dimples and all. I take a mental picture, burning that smile into my brain, and I know that whatever comes our way, even if it's our own bullshit, we'll be fine. We just have to let go and trust the other one to catch us.

Epilogue

I'm sitting at the arrival terminal at Chattanooga Airport, waiting for Cass and Killian to arrive. They're flying in together for the holidays.

Tanner arrived at the airport thirty minutes after me, and dumping his luggage at my feet, he declared he was starving and disappeared. After he took off, I shot him a text to please bring me something to eat. My stomach growls at the thought of food, and I rub it, hoping he hasn't forgotten about me.

I sink lower into my seat, yawning so big that I feel my jaw crack, and I blink my dry eyes in rapid succession. I don't know why I allowed Cass to talk me into taking a red-eye the day finals ended.

To say I'm exhausted is putting it lightly. Finals week in college is another level of stress and exhaustion. I felt prepared, and my coach set me up with great tutors, but that doesn't mean I wasn't up, stressing and chugging caffeine with the best of them.

"Glo Worm, how do you feel about a chicken biscuit and hash browns?" Tanner says from behind me, brandishing a white to-go bag, and I'm embarrassed to say I nearly drool.

"I feel great about it." I snatch the bag out of his hand, and we both dig in, content to be silent until we're both finished.

"How much longer until they're here?" Tanner asks, burping quietly before collecting our trash.

I glance at my phone and stand. "They should be arriving now. Want to head down to their gate?"

"Let's go!" He hops up.

He's trying to keep his cool, but I can tell he's vibrating with excitement. This is the longest the twins have been separated.

I knock my shoulder into Tanner's arm before letting out a tiny squeak. Okay, so Tanner isn't the only one who's extremely excited.

"Are you guys going to run into each other's arms, like at the end of every Hallmark movie ever?" Tanner teases.

"No!" I scoff, only to whip around when I hear my name being shouted.

"Glory!" Killian calls out, standing a head above everyone exiting the plane and looking so beautiful that I end up making myself a liar.

I drop my duffel and take off running as Killian shoves his way through the swarm of holiday travelers to me. We collide with an oof, and he lifts me off my feet. Wrapping my legs around his waist, I stick my nose in his neck and inhale deeply.

"I've missed you," I whisper, smiling when I feel goose bumps rise on his neck.

"I've missed you so much, baby," he echoes and presses kisses along my hairline.

I'm definitely not normally so affectionate in public. I just don't feel comfortable with the vulnerability of it, but even though Killian and I are back together, we haven't seen each other all that much, so seeing him now erases any hesitation.

When Killian came to visit me that first time, he stayed through the weekend, and then it was another month before I saw him again. Even then, it was only a day. He decided to fly home for Thanksgiving, but came to see me first. I ended up having to stay at school because we made it into the playoffs. Spending Thanksgiving without my friends and family was depressing, and even though I had my teammates, it just wasn't the same.

I haven't seen him since then or Cassidy since I came to visit that one weekend. It's been a lot harder than I imagined, figuring out our schedules to see each other in person, but we're both so committed to our weekly FaceTime dates, and we text each other constantly.

Still, when Killian sets me down and I'm yanked into Cassidy's arms, I find myself sniffling back tears.

"You've turned into a watering pot, Glo," Cassidy teases, yanking on my ponytail.

"I haven't seen you in so long." I wipe my eyes before returning to Killian's side, hugging him around the waist.

Tanner loops his arms around Cassidy's shoulders, and we all grin at each other, happy to be reunited. We'll have three weeks together to get caught up on each other's lives before we're all separated again.

"Where's Marcus?" Killian asks as we make our way toward the exit.

HARD FEELINGS

"He's staying in LA. He's meeting Jen's family." I smile softly, thinking of my panicked friend. I helped him pick out flowers for Jen's mom and gave him an easy no-bake pie recipe to bring. I can't wait to hear how *that* went.

We follow behind the twins, and I can see Cassidy gesturing wildly. Only one thing gets her that worked up. Her nemesis, Elias Amir Carmichael III. She never just refers to him as Elias or Eli; it's always his full name with heavy emphasis on *the Third*.

For someone who reads enemies-to-lovers books almost exclusively nowadays, it's funny to me that she doesn't recognize the trope she's living in currently. I saw a photo of him during one of our FaceTime chats, where Cassidy was rage-scrolling on his socials, and, yeah, he ain't bad-looking. If anything, I think how attractive he is sets Cassidy off even more.

I don't point any of this out because, for one thing, if I were to suggest she had not-so-hateful feelings for him, she'd punch me in the boob, but also, I'm perfectly content to listen to her rant about him. Cassidy is hilarious when she's mad.

I'm also one hundred percent shipping them.

"My mom's here," Killian calls out, pointing to the large black SUV sitting by the curb in arrivals.

Elizabeth hops out of the car and rushes to Killian, who greets her with open arms. She's crying happy tears, and it makes my throat close up as I imagine my reunion with my dad. He couldn't afford to come out after making two big trips this year, so I haven't seen him since he dropped me off. I miss him so much.

"Glory!" she calls out, and Killian grips my hoodie, yanking me into the group hug.

Killian and I getting back together went over really well with Elizabeth, further proving that I was living too in my head. Killian told her I'd overheard what she said and how it triggered all kinds of insecurities, which led to our breakup. Did I love that he shared all that with his mom? Uh, no. It was embarrassing. I hated it even more when Elizabeth called me to talk this out with her.

In the end though, hearing her say I wasn't responsible for other people's emotions and the only life I needed to live was my own relieved me of any lingering guilt. She admitted to reacting out of her own issues and that it had nothing to do with me. I'm so happy we're back on good terms. She's been a part of my life as long as her son has been, and we've all lost enough people in our lives; it's time to cherish the relationships that survived that heartache.

She and Sebastian are still not speaking, and I don't blame her. Sebastian has a long way to go to make amends. Him being there and supporting Killian has done a lot to help his relationship with his son, but it's nowhere near enough. My mother being so happy and Korrie being healthy and well cared for have done a lot for me, but there will always be that weirdness.

Speaking of my mom, we've settled into a great friendship. I have employed some strong boundaries to not just protect myself, but to also ensure we have a healthy relationship. They aren't born out of some need to punish her, and for that, I will always be thankful for therapy.

"You both look so grown up!" Elizabeth exclaims, cupping both our cheeks fondly before Tanner and Cassidy bound up to us, receiving the same enthusiastic hello from her.

We all climb in, chatting the entire ride home, and I bite my lip as a smile so huge that it hurts my cheeks spreads across my face.

"What are you smiling about?" Killian asks, looking at me in the rearview mirror.

He's sitting up front with Elizabeth—there's no way his long-ass legs would fit in the back. Tanner's barely do, and his knees are to his chest.

Being the only short person in the vehicle puts me in the middle seat, not that I mind usually.

I'll be working a couple of weeks at the farm, back in the gift shop, like last year. It'll be good to get some cash while I'm away from my part-time job at school. Thankfully, my boss is awesome and is willing to work around my schedule. I know how lucky I am to have that. Still though, balancing everything has been a lot, and I'm so looking forward to relaxing for the next few weeks.

I'll be spending Christmas with my dad, and the day after, Killian and I will drive down to Atlanta to spend a couple of days with our parents and Korrie. I can't wait to see her. She's changed so much since I saw her last. Video chats and constant pictures from my mom just aren't enough. I can't wait to squish her chubby cheeks and breathe in her baby smell.

I never in my wildest dreams would have thought I'd feel this way, coming home. For so long, home to me was Cassidy and my dad. I never felt like that about Galway as a whole, but I'm excited to be back. I'm excited to see my house and sleep in my childhood bed. I can't wait to have breakfast at the diner with all my friends and family. Driving around, listening to music with Cassidy. Refereeing between Tanner and Cassidy. Going on runs with Killian.

Just being with Killian.

All these little things I've come to cherish.

My phone buzzes with excited GIFs from my dad and a picture of Korrie in an elf outfit from my mom, and I clutch it to my heart.

"I'm happy." I grin at Killian.

His face softens, and the gold in his eyes deepens.

I can't wait until we're alone. I've missed the feel of his skin under my fingertips. The taste of his lips, messing his hair up with my hands. I've missed every part of him.

I mouth, *I love you*, to him.

HARD FEELINGS

He smiles that big smile, both of his dimples popping, and taps two fingers over his heart.

I got you.

The End

playlist

Search for "Hard Feelings" by kelsiewrites to listen on Spotify.

"My Enemy" by CHVRCHES, featuring Matt Berninger

"This Is the Last Time" by The National

"Crowded Places" by Banks

"I Hate U" by SZA

"Been Like This" by Doja Cat

"Brutal" by Olivia Rodrigo

"Coming Back" by James Blake, featuring SZA

"Move Me" by Charli XCX

"Spitting Off the Edge of the World" by Yeah Yeah Yeahs, featuring Perfume Genius

"That's Where I Am" by Maggie Rogers

"Heartbreak Anniversary" by Giveon

"Only You" by Cannons

"Fate" by H.E.R.

Acknowledgments

I took a six-year break from writing for a multitude of reasons, but there is one that brought me back to it—therapy. It's something that has changed my life. It unlocked the creativity that was buried under my personal trauma and the collective trauma we've all faced in these last few years. As a result, the first shout-out I need to give is to my therapist. Thank you for helping me get back here. I'm forever grateful.

Glory's situation is fictional, but her feelings in this book are very real. Reconciling who people really are versus what you believe or need them to be is difficult. It can call into question all sorts of things, make you doubt your ability to read people or even understand yourself. I can tell you, now that I'm on the other side, it's worth the work to get to a place where you can confidently implement boundaries and surround yourself with people who respect them.

Finally, I'm lucky to have a fantastic group of women who helped create this book. Thank you to everyone who's touched *Hard Feelings*. Publishing takes a village, and I couldn't have done it without you.

AbOUT The AUThOR

KM Galvin is the author of the Twenty-Something Duet, *Beauty and the Book Boyfriend*, and *Adrift*. She currently lives in Nashville with her pup, Dwight—yes, as in Dwight Schrute! When not writing, you can find KM in the comment section of her favorite authors, begging for early releases, or in the kitchen, trying to re-create something she saw on *The Great British Bake Off*.

Find her on:

TikTok: @authorkmg

Instagram: @authorkmg

Amazon: K.M. Galvin

Goodreads K.M. Galvin

Spotify: kelsiewrites

Made in the USA
Columbia, SC
17 February 2023